A GHOST TOWN ON THE YELLOWSTONE

Other Books by ELLIOT PAUL

LINDEN ON THE SAUGUS BRANCH
THE LAST TIME I SAW PARIS
THE LIFE AND DEATH OF A SPANISH TOWN
THE STARS AND STRIPES FOREVER
CONCERT PITCH
THE GOVERNOR OF MASSACHUSETTS
LAVA ROCK
LOW RUN TIDE
THE AMAZON
IMPERTURBE
IMPROMPTU
INDELIBLE

Homer Evans Murder Mysteries

THE MYSTERIOUS MICKEY FINN
HUGGER-MUGGER IN THE LOUVRE
MAYHEM IN B-FLAT
FRACAS IN THE FOOTHILLS
I'LL HATE MYSELF IN THE MORNING

A GHOST TOWN ON THE YELLOWSTONE

By Elliot Paul

WILDSIDE PRESS

Affectionately Dedicated to

BARBARA MARIE MAYOCK,

My Mother-in-Law

Contents

A GHOST TOWN ON THE
YELLOWSTONE

CHAPTER ONE

The Nearest Railroad Point

TH E town of Trembles, Montana, during the fifteen years it existed, lent much distinction to the Lower Yellowstone Valley and the whole northeastern section of that great state. Trembles is no longer on the map. There are no traces of it left, except in the memory of those who lived there in the early nineteen hundreds. Those who drifted through, on foot, by saddle horse, harness rig or stagecoach, and later by Model-T Ford and bus, en route between the nearest railroad points of Glendive, on the Northern Pacific, and Mondak, on the Great Northern, took little notice of Trembles. In its declining years, when a branch railroad passed a few miles away, no train, not even a handcar, stopped on Cedar Coulee, near which the vanished town was built.

The nearest historical landmark was Johnny O'Brien's old store at Newlon, on Fox Creek. Johnny, who was a spry old-timer before I was old enough to vote, is dead but not forgotten. His establishment, a general store, fell down and blew away just after World War I, so that the sole returning war veteran found nothing left of Newlon, or Trembles. The post-office, of which Old Johnny was postmaster, has long been discontinued, and the handful of ranchers and farmers in that vicinity get their mail at Sidney, the county seat of Richland County.

On the northern horizon may be seen Three Buttes, of

which Audubon made a drawing in 1843. Anyone who thinks he can do better than the great artist and naturalist is welcome to try today. Buttes are not indestructible, exactly, but they change shape very slowly in the course of a few hundred years.

Directly south of where Trembles used to be, the Yellowstone River, as it rushes toward its confluence with the Missouri, splits itself, in sheer exuberance, into many narrow tricky channels to form the group of islands named "The Seven Sisters" by Captain Grant Marsh. Captain Marsh, the foremost skipper of the roaring steamboat days, "grasshoppered" the first steamboat up the Yellowstone from its mouth as far as Miles City just after the close of the Civil War, which sent scores of renegades from both armies into that perilous frontier. The same captain, as an old man, took the last steamboat out of that river.

East of the river lies a stretch of bad lands which, for utter chaos and colorful desolation, match any area on this planet. West of Trembles, where the valley begins to fan out toward the bottom lands of the confluence, foothills start rising from the plain cut by Crane Creek, Fox Creek, Cedar Coulee, Young's Coulee and their unnamed branches. Some of these still flow a few weeks in the year and all of them become raging torrents just after a cloudburst, which almost invariably comes at the wrong season. Their approximate courses are marked by tiny crooked lines on the government topographical survey quadrangle. On nearly all other maps the whole region is blank, except for two quite meaningful words: SIOUX COUNTRY.

According to Joseph Kinsey Howard, in his stirring book, *Montana, High, Wide and Handsome,* when a group of eastern bankers were inveigled out to see that part of Montana and its "prospects," one of the railroad publicity men said, "All this country needs is water."

4

The head banker remarked ruefully: "That's all hell needs, too."

To help give a narrow strip of land on the west bank of the Yellowstone the only advantage it would have over hell was what brought me, and others, into the Lower Yellowstone country in 1907, while the United States Reclamation Service was building the dam and diversion works below Glendive and the canal and laterals that extend along the foothills as far as the Missouri River. There are 640 acres in a square mile. Montana has 146,997 square miles (about eighteen times as many as my home Commonwealth of Massachusetts), therefore, 93,878,080 acres. The Lower Yellowstone project was designed to irrigate, at the most, 70,000 of those, a little more than one-thirteenth of one percent of the state. So it will be seen that those of us who worked for the Reclamation Service on the Lower Yellowstone were trying in a modest way, indeed, to improve the score between hell and Montana. Even that tiny fraction of Montana acreage would have contained my native village of Linden one hundred times.

Trembles, founded in 1907, got its name from a small clump of trees near the mouth of Cedar Coulee. There were few trees to be seen anywhere in that vicinity. The tangle of cottonwoods, alders and underbrush along the river was on a lower level and was not visible from the mesa on which the stage road ran. In the bare foothills languished a few scrub cedars, clinging precariously to crumbling rocks and cut banks. In front of Simard's ranch house, near Newlon, a small grove of tall cottonwoods offered shelter and shade.

The half-dozen trees that marked the site of Trembles were quaking aspens, which are called *trembles* in French. Quite a few of the early settlers of the Lower Yellowstone were French, including the Simards (locally pronounced See-mores) at Newlon. Those early French Catholics, in common with many others elsewhere, if they remembered anything about religion at all, believed that the Cross on which Jesus was crucified was made from the wood of the quaking aspen and that, as a result, all aspens quake perpetually in shame. Be that as it may, the aspens of Trembles shuddered whenever there was enough wind to stir their leaves. The town never experienced what is known back east as a "breeze." Either the wind was high and violent or there was no movement of air whatsoever. In summer the thermometer would have registered one hundred and ten degrees Fahrenheit in the shade, had there been any shade or any thermometer. In winter the temperature seldom dipped lower than fifty below.

That end of the valley, in prehistoric days, was a favorite haunt of an adventurous kind of dinosaur called "tyrannosaurus," which learned to stand on its hind legs and eat meat —that is to say, the flesh of other, less progressive types of dinosaurs. One thing has been eating another in that region ever since. The great herds of buffalo passed through and across the valley, grazing, twice a year, on their north and south migrations. Elk, antelope, white-tail and black-tail deer, beaver, otter and three kinds of bears were plentiful, not to mention wolves, coyotes, gophers and rattlesnakes. The Arickaree Indians were the first human residents and proprietors there. They were driven out, more or less, by the Sioux, after the latter had been chased westward by the Chippewas and forsook canoes for tough little Indian ponies.

While the Sioux were in possession of those fabulous hunting grounds, the first white explorers and travelers arrived. They were Charles Le Raye, an intrepid Frenchman whose gift of description was vague; François Laroque, another adventurer from France, via Canada, who wrote quite lucidly; William Clark (of the Lewis and Clark expedition), and others unknown and unnamed. The explorers were followed

6

by a bunch of the toughest hunters, trappers and desperadoes mankind ever sent westward ho.

Only about thirty miles from Trembles was the field head-quarters of the first trust established on the North American continent that was an absolute law unto itself. John Jacob Astor's men, in the employ of the American Fur Company, maintained their principal trading post, protected by American cavalry and private thugs, where the Yellowstone and the Missouri meet. The post was known first as Fort Floyd, then, in order, Fort Union, Fort William, Fort Mortimer, and lastly Fort Buford, on the edge of the site of which the town of Mondak now stands. This area always claimed, and now claims, the largest number per capita, per square foot, or by any other standard of measurement, of rats, bedbugs and mosquitoes in the world, these rodents and insects being white civilization's substitutes for the buffalo, the beaver and the eagle of bygone days.

After the buffaloes, the fur-bearing animals and most of the better Indians had been cleaned out (not all of them, by any means), the first cattle men moved in and helped themselves to the vast free range, then unsurveyed.

Later, Jim Hill of the Great Northern Railroad had one of history's epic pipe dreams concerning the suitability of northeastern Montana for purposes of dry farming, and the scissorbills started migrating there, building fences when they could get fence posts and wire, and crowding out the cowpunchers and ranchers.

I am not going far into the details of any history I did not witness myself, or hear from men who were there when it happened. Still it is important for the reader to understand that quite a number and assortment of events took place in that desperate scenery, beginning while the world was cooling, and continuing to date. Just lately, after having buried such stalwart characters as "Yellowstone" Kelly, "Lonesome Charley" Reynolds, George Hedderich, Grant Marsh, Johnny O'Brien, George Knickerbocker; Indian warriors and sages like the Gall, Crazy Horse and Sitting Bull, it has produced Leif Erickson, the promising young statesman from the Lower Yellowstone who unseated and rid Congress of Burton K. Wheeler.

Anaconda still owns most of the state of Montana, as his master owned Uncle Tom, but the Lower Yellowstone is holding out. The dust storms of the nineteen twenties blew an enormous portion of the landscape away, but Sidney, the seat of Richland County (a small chunk of old Dawson County), now has a population of twenty-five hundred, and, not more than six miles from the site of Trembles (God rest its memory and help your author to do some justice to it), still flourishes among the sage and sugar beets. In the days of Sitting Bull there were frequently many more Sioux in the neighborhood than there are white men today. Sitting Bull and his Indians starved, as did many of the dry farmers and cattle men. The trappers mostly died suddenly, unless they pleased especially one John Jacob Astor.

Johnny Highpockets, the last resident of Trembles who gave up and went back toward Kansas in 1922, died when he got as far as Omaha, Nebraska. Many other survivors of that stirring American municipal undertaking are alive but are scattered as were the sinners of Sodom, and for various reasons.

In the course of an eventful life (as an observer) I have had many occasions to thank my lucky stars. One of my principal reasons for thankfulness is that, in 1907 and 1908, I lived on the Lower Yellowstone, in and around Trembles and all the way from the roundhouse at Glendive to the only screened building in Mondak, roaming between the bad lands east of the river and the buttes and foothills west. Some of the big

8

cattle-and-sheep outfits were still thriving in eastern Montana; contractors, engineers, Wobblies and bohunks were working on the ditch; and the scissorbills were beginning to come in. I knew and shook the hand of Captain Grant Marsh, listened to his river tales, and lost mildly to him in poker games. I rode on one of the last, if not the last, steamboat he ever piloted and commanded, *The Expansion*. One of my teachers and pals, when I was fifteen years old, was George Knickerbocker, or "Old Knick," an Indian fighter, trapper, and deserter from the old Seventh Cavalry after the Custer fiasco. Knick had been in Reno's command, of which nearly all were saved by the relative good sense of its commander. The name under which Knick enlisted, of course, he prudently never disclosed. But he had a square and noble head which he kept cropped, like a Dutchman, and at the age of seventy-two, when I first knew him, thought nothing of walking thirty miles to Glendive or elsewhere for a beer.

In order to write about the founding of Trembles, which I witnessed, I must go back a few days and remove the scene fifty miles southeast, to the city of Glendive, then and now capital of Dawson County (which was only two and one-half times the size of Massachusetts). Glendive was the nearest settlement to Trembles that might be called a city. There were about 4,000 inhabitants then, including 300 employees of the Northern Pacific Railroad and the transients and drifters who passed through. It was founded mostly by the N.P., just before the last of the Sioux surrendered, because it was a convenient spot for a railroad division point. In an eloquent little pamphlet the N.P. issued for the purpose of inducing citizens to migrate to eastern Montana and thus contribute to the railroad's prosperity and their own experience, it is explained why one railroad division ends at Glendive, and another begins. It seems that between Bismarck, North Dakota, where the N.P. crosses the Missouri River, and Glendive, where the railroad first skirts the Yellowstone, the average grade through the badlands, buttes and prairies is sixty-six feet to the mile. That is tough, for railroad purposes. In fact, those particular miles are among the most rugged and discouraging, for any purpose at all, that have ever been measured. Old Pierre Wibaux was one of the few pioneers who could pit himself against them and live past the Biblical age. Teddy Roosevelt learned enough about the great west in that region to go back east and enter politics, after losing nearly all the cattle on his range in the winter of 1886 and '87. The aristocratic Marquis de Mores, about that time, gave up his packing plant which was to industrialize that part of the west, and decided that it would be less strenuous and more profitable to hunt tigers in far-off India. No one who has seen those bad lands, before the days of automobiles, thermos jugs and national highways, would question the validity of the late Marquis' judgment.

But once a train had reached Glendive from Bismarck, the N.P. points out in its pamphlet, the grade per mile from Glendive to the base of the Rockies is only twenty-six feet to the mile. Therefore, one locomotive can pull from Glendive westward the same load that requires two locomotives to drag it from Bismarck to the Yellowstone. The foregoing is one of the most candid statements in that railroad pamphlet, which I shall quote extensively as a hitherto unrecognized humorous masterpiece of which America should be proud.

Glendive is otherwise described as resting on latitude 47 degrees and 3 minutes north, and longitude 105 degrees and 45 minutes west, which would convey immediately to my seafaring and roaming ancestors that the city would have long hours of daylight in summer and regrettably few in the winter. It is eighty-five or more miles on the river from the N.P. roundhouse to the confluence of the Yellowstone and the Missouri, and eighty-one miles by the old stage road, which today is indifferently paved, and traversed, weather permitting, by an expendable bus.

Very early that morning in June, 1907, I had come up-river on the *Expansion* from the Headgates with a bunch of engineers, foremen and contractors from the government canal then in process of construction eighteen miles downstream. The contractors had made the trip with Captain Marsh in the hope that they could find a few men around town who would go back down-valley with them and work for wages. In those days, and in the circumstances then prevailing, it was easier to persuade men to leave that country than to enter it. The contractors who had made out their estimates and bids in some comfortable office in St. Cloud, Minnesota, or Worcester, Massachusetts, for instance, were taking a heartrending beating.

I had started out from Boston before the high school I had been attending in Malden had finished its term, but the principal promised to send me a diploma, anyway. He sympathized with my desire to see the west and the world. Nothing the teachers had taught me, or that I had seen in New England, had prepared me for Glendive, Montana.

A Catholic priest, Father Brian Congalach, arrived from somewhere east on the No. 3 that morning and was collared soon afterward by the editor of the *Glendive Independent* in order that the priest's first impressions of Glendive might be perpetuated in print. Father Congalach was the first priest to be sent to Glendive, where a church was being built for him at the time. A few phrases from his initial interview are poignant in the extreme.

"I saw quite a few houses built of lumber throughout and a number of these were tastefully adorned with good paint,"

11

Father Congalach said. (His name was pronounced locally "Con-*gay*-lock" with the accent on the "gay.")

His comment about the quality of the paint was one of Father Congalach's first pardonable mistakes. That was the year one of the large mail-order houses was convicted of using the mails to defraud, because of the discrepancy between the house catalogue's poetic description of paint and the stuff subsequently delivered in cans to the customers. Most of the paint Father Congalach was looking at from a distance that morning had been bought by Glendive settlers from that same mail-order house before the authorities had taken punitive action.

In his next paragraph, the earnest young priest made another bad boner. "There were a number of docile pack horses hitched in front of thriving commercial establishments," he remarked. Actually what he had seen were a bunch of broncos tied up in front of some busy saloons. Probably none of those cayuses had been ridden three times. To approach any of them from the right-hand side or get too close behind them was a form of suicide no churchman of his faith could encourage.

Where Father Congalach really let himself go was in describing his first Yellowstone sunset.

"The sunset we looked at," he is quoted by the *Independent* as saying, "appeared a little to the left and just beyond the long symmetrical and useful bridge that spans the Yellowstone River."

How wrong he was about where that sunset was "appearing" was revealed to Father Congalach when, a day or two later, he set out *on foot* toward the principal butte of the region, called "Hungry Joe." This butte had unquestionably stood between him and the sunset, when he was in Glendive admiring his Maker's handiwork at eve. But having walked miles and miles, in the course of which he formed the impression that the butte was miraculously walking westward just as fast as he was, and no faster, he stepped on something soft and heard what he afterward described, in his restrained parochial-school style, as a "startling signal."

He had stepped on a dozing rattlesnake which showed its resentment of the intrusion by biting Father Congalach spitefully on the ankle. The priest, new to the country, was wearing black low shoes with elastic sides, and thin black cotton socks. No rattlesnake on the Lower Yellowstone had had a set-up like that before. Father Congalach made a few "startling" signals of his own. A cowboy moseying along the slope rode to him, hell for leather, tossed him up behind the saddle, and made Doc Mullendore's office in the Hotel Jordan Annex in record time. Doc treated the priest, who by that time was suffering stoically but intensely, with potassium permanganate externally, and Old Crow internally. Father Congalach recovered and throughout long years afterward served God. But his first act when he got out of bed, following the snake-bite incident, was to hustle down to one of Glendive's leading stores called "The Beehive," in the comparative safety of a hired hack, to buy a pair of thick, high-laced leather boots, with reinforced soles and hobnails. From then on, Father Congalach wore thick high boots even in church, and it was a wise precaution. More than once a meandering rattlesnake got into God's house, liked the peace and quiet of the place, and settled down for a good long snooze.

It has been established in recent years, almost too late, that whisky is not good for snake-bite, but no veteran of the Lower Yellowstone would ever believe it. Old-timers used to reach for the whisky whenever they heard a rattler, even before they looked to see where the reptile was. And even granting that whisky may be bad medicine for snake-bite, there is no doubt that the presence of rattlesnakes in any area is a fine thing for the whisky trade. In the year 1907, while there were plenty of ranchers, cowpunchers, river hogs, railroad men, contractors, Wobblies, bohunks and civil engineers around, the daily consumption of whisky per larynx was about as high as has been recorded anywhere in North America.

Father Congalach, once he got acclimated and wised up a bit, did not fall into the error committed by some of the Protestant clergymen who hit Montana years later. He accepted Glendive life, *in toto,* and never tried to reform it, except insofar as it seemed best to recommend caution and moderation to some of his parishioners, individually. He never was quoted by the *Independent* or any of the other local papers as being "against" this or that, and when his bishop made his first visit to Glendive, five years later, Father Congalach met him at the station, wearing chaps, the inevitable high-laced boots, and a stiff-brimmed Stetson hat. It was only because he had a hack waiting, and the station platform was well paved with concrete, that he did not bring an extra pair of safe boots for his superior.

There were some old-timers who looked with misgivings upon any clergymen, of whatever denomination or church, who drifted into Glendive. And there was a little grumbling when lumber, very scarce and expensive all through Dawson County, was wasted on meeting houses or residences for the sky pilots. Father Congalach, however, was welcomed by Glendive in as comradely a way as he accepted the city. One of his first problems involved Phil Twible, the barber who had the second chair at the Bon Ton Tonsorial Parlors. Phil was a good fast barber, in more ways than one, and since beauty parlors with female operators were then confined to the eastern states, Twible was the man most often summoned when any woman in Glendive wanted a shampoo or face massage.

There was a lively competition in social affairs and nuances among the wives and daughters, also mothers and sisters, of the tradesmen and professional men who had come to town to settle permanently and already were prospering. One of the lucky women, Mrs. Perham Cheeley, whose husband was doing well in wood and coal, hay and grain, was troubled with blackheads and read in a Minneapolis paper her husband received intermittently by mail that the right kind of massage would remove the blemishes from her complexion.

Perham, who thought it was setting a bad example in a thriving western city for a merchant to shave himself, patronized the Bon Ton and always waited for Twible's chair. Having been pestered by his wife about massage and blackheads, Perham put the question up to the barber. The latter agreed to call at the Cheeley residence (one of the four built of brick) that evening after supper and massage the face of Mrs. Cheeley. Everything went off well. Mrs. Cheeley—her first name was Utaline—was pleased with the results, and at the next meeting of the ladies' auxiliary of the Modern Woodmen of the World told some of her friends. She was fearful, however, that the other women of her class in town would call Twible and make use of his services, so Mrs. Cheeley said that her husband, Perham, had given her the treatment. This item was relayed by the women and soon all the business men in Glendive were kidding the wood and coal man and asking him to treat them for everything from dandruff to ingrown toenails. Soon Perham Cheeley, in spite of the threats of his wife he called "Yewty," broke down and told the men that Phil Twible had done the trick. Twible was a presentable young man and had such a way with women, young and old, that many husbands did not relish having him pawing their wives, but the women who belonged to the Woodmen's auxiliary (there were six of them in all) overruled their men and one by one were visited, after barbershop hours, by Twible, who massaged and shampooed them to their heart's content.

Everything that happened spread quickly around Glendive. Below the hill on which the Hotel Jordan and the commercial establishments stood, on the east side of the river and about half a mile from the court house, was an enclosure about two acres square, with a high board fence the corner posts of which were adorned with red lanterns which twinkled in the sun by day and glimmered invitingly by night. The wayward men carried the story of Phil Twible's household massages and shampoos to the women the *Independent* described as "inmates" of the lupanars or "hookshops" owned and operated by the renowned Jack (for Jacqueline) Little and Mona Mason. Most of the girls "down the line" decided that what was good enough for the respectable women uptown would be all right for them, too. So when one of them had a hangover, or an attack of melancholia that was one of the principal hazards of her profession, or simply had time on her hands and, being flush, did not feel like working, she would phone up to the Bon Ton to Phil Twible and make an appointment for him to massage her face and launder her hair. For this, Phil asked and got ten dollars, and hack fare each way, which totaled four dollars more. Jack's and Mona's sporting girls made at least two hundred apiece per week, seldom had to buy clothes, and so the fees for Phil's treatments were peanuts to them. Phil got ten dollars a treatment for working on the Woodmen's wives, but no hack ride. In the residential district he had to walk, and carry his tools and towels in a satchel. But no one, male or female, ever walked from uptown to the Glendive red-light district, although a slow walker could have made it from the N.P. station or the bridge in about ten minutes. There was one free-swinging gate in the red-light enclosure, and the customers rode there in closed hacks. The hack never waited. When anybody wanted to ride back up-town, he had Jack or Mona call a livery stable and enjoyed a final round of beer while waiting for the hack-man to show up.

Sadie Bickerstaff, one of the plump and genial hookers in Jack Little's establishment, had a pair of diamond earrings for which she had paid three hundred dollars to a trader off a steamboat at Bismarck. When she was not wearing them, she left them in a little tray on her dresser in her room. One day after a cattle man just off the spring roundup had kept the whole house jumping for the better part of a week, Sadie was in need of a little relaxation. She had Jack, the madam, phone uptown for Phil Twible who arrived at the house that evening and gave her scalp and facial treatment.

In that country, for a man to rob or cheat a hooker was to descend lower in the public esteem than a snake in a wagon track. Phil's conscience began to bother him, although no complaint had been made. So he went to Father Congalach and confessed what he had done.

"Where are the earrings, my son?" the priest asked.

Twible produced them. Both men knew that if Phil returned the jewelry to Sadie himself, his goose would be cooked in Glendive. So the priest imposed on the barber a stiff batch of "Hail Mary's" and, under cover of darkness, set out in a hack for Jack Little's. Neither Sadie nor Jack was vindictive by nature. They accepted the returned stolen goods, no questions asked, and agreed to say no more about the unfortunate matter. Sadie had not suspected Twible, knowing that any number of other men might have pinched the diamonds. Men frequently did things while drunk for which they were remorseful later.

Some weeks afterward, Sadie called for the barber again, and again the three-hundred-dollar earrings were exposed on the tray. There was something about the way they flashed and glittered that tempted Phil beyond his strength, for the second time, and when he got back to his room in the Hotel Jordan the diamonds were again in his pocket.

This time, Phil was too much ashamed to go to Father Congalach, and decided to blow town next day, when the No. 3 went through. But Jacqueline Little was a shrewd and clever woman and she figured what would take place in Twible's weak mind. The first time Sadie's earrings were missing was just after Twible had given her a face massage. Jack and Sadie put two and two together, and, as a matter of precaution, Jack had a talk with her good friend, the chief of police, and suggested that he keep his eye on Twible and the railroad station. So when the barber showed up there, just as No. 3 was coming in, and bought a ticket for Livingston, Chief Kinney was on hand. The chief frisked Twible right then and there and found the earrings in his pocket.

The whole town was disgusted, the men because one of their number would stoop to theft from Sadie, who always treated everybody right, and the women uptown because the same hands that had soaped their scalps and fingered their faces had performed similar services for scarlet women "down the line." Twible was held in the county jail until the next session of the Montana district court in Glendive. He pleaded guilty and was given one year by Judge Price, which was a severe sentence then for any offense short of murder or horse stealing.

In the same issue of the *Independent* with the account of Twible's trial, the editor inserted an item, in the columns on page three headed "Local Events of Interest in the Valley," pointing out that Glendive was growing fast and now afforded an excellent opportunity for an up-and-coming beauty shop.

The wild roses were a week late in blooming that year, so the same editor, following an editorial on that subject, suggested that Glendive had reached the point where an enterprising florist might well prosper.

CHAPTER TWO

The Hazards of Oyster Stew

A BUNCH of us were standing on the N.P. station platform in Glendive that morning in June, after we had come up from the Headgates on the steamboat *Expansion,* when the No. 3 arrived from the east. The ones I knew best were Scotty McVeigh, then a transitman with the Reclamation Service, and one of the best baseball catchers who ever hit that region; Howard Roby, the government warehouse man and forwarding agent, who did errands in Glendive for all the government engineers down the valley; Tom Corkery and Chet Donaldson, both contractors on the ditch; Walter Murray, a wild young draftsman from the south; and Glenn Clawson, a rancher from Tokna and a candidate for Dawson County coroner in the coming election. Clawson was on hand, sober and all spruced up, to meet his daughter Angela, who was coming back from school in Indianapolis to spend the summer on the ranch.

Besides Father Congalach, whose first adventures already have been reported, and Angela Clawson, a popular native of the valley, quite a few strangers got off the train. Some had been riding the cushions, and others the rods, for which the customary fee to the brakeman was then a dollar a division. The "jungle" for bums, known from one end of the United States to the other, had already been established on the river, just above Glendive, and was encouraged rather than molested by such authorities as there were, because some of the tramps could be snagged by the contractors, who fed them heartily at the Nippon Restaurant, plied them with free whisky from a jug, and started them by wagon down the valley, where they would work in the construction camps until they got the wrinkles out of their bellies.

There were two painted women whose names might or might not have been Lou. One was carrying a bird cage. The other wore a feather boa. About six scissorbills, all Scandinavians, got in that morning, too, and were collared by Duff Leiper, a surveyor who made a good living locating claims for settlers and, if possible, selling them private land that lay conveniently near by. Three of the six, a woman and two men, rode away in the locator's rig. Duff Leiper was not dishonest, as locators went those days. He tried to give the smarter ones their money's worth, to avoid unpleasant comebacks, and if a homeseeker looked especially dumb, poor or bedraggled, Duff did the best he could for him, too, and cut his fee to ten dollars, which was not collected on the spot. It was the middle class of homesteaders, in so far as funds or intelligence went, that Leiper considered fair game, and rooked as soundly as the traffic would bear. That was how Duff's conscience worked.

The other descending passengers who attracted my attention made it clear that something unusual was about to happen before they got down the steps to the station platform. Two of them came out together from one Pullman car that had stopped just in front of where I was standing, just in time to come face to face with a third, a big hulking giant in a store suit who was chewing tobacco and had been riding in the car ahead. The pair narrowed their eyes and grunted disgustedly. The big man spat deliberately in the direction of their boots and walked away, into the station restaurant.

21

One of the pair whose boots had almost been spat upon called after the giant in a way that caused Father Congalach to cross himself and cluck reproachfully.

Seeing that the pair were going to follow the big man into the restaurant, I suddenly felt hungry myself and trailed them inside.

Already it was clear to me that the shorter of the pair was the leader. He was five feet six inches tall, with strong hands and broad shoulders. His eyes changed from blue to gray when he stopped smiling. His voice was resonant and his vocabulary rich. But his choice of words indicated at least a high-school education, most likely somewhere in Minnesota. It was not easy to guess about his racial or national origin. He could have been of English, Irish or Dutch parentage, but I thought he had been born in this country.

The big man, whose name, according to the next issue of the Glendive papers, was Baseblud, a Dane, planked himself down defiantly at one of the four round tables covered with linen and set for five. Pearl, the dark-haired N.P. waitress who had an unusually low waistline, approached, and the giant gruffly ordered an oyster stew. Oysters were a novelty in the far west then and were being shipped to Glendive, well-iced, by the keg. Since an oyster stew cost two bits and a full five-course meal could be had for thirty-five cents—a good meal, too—the conclusion to be drawn was that the big Dane was well heeled.

The set-up in the lunch room then was as follows:

The Dane had picked the second table from the end, and was sitting with his back to the counter and facing the door from the platform.

Scotty McVeigh and I were at the counter, on stools, well out of the line of fire, should there be any gunplay. Ruby, the light-haired N.P. waitress whose legs were so long that her waistline was high, was waiting on us. But we all had our eyes on the big man and the two men who had followed him in.

Three of the scissorbills, all men who had escaped the land locator, were at the fourth table, once removed from the Dane's, and were pretending to mind their own business. Notwithstanding their detachment, it was clear that they felt something troublesome was in the air.

Father Congalach, who, having had his first look at Glendive, had come in to refresh himself and meditate, took a stool a little to our right. We had our backs turned to the Dane. Luckily, there was a mirror all along the counter, so we could watch the reflections of the customers without turning around.

Howard Roby, who had been looking under the cars and around the yards for bums he could hire to unload freight cars and load wagons, came in with a look of annoyance on his face. The crop of 'boes was bad that day because the N.P. detective most hated on the division, known as Jay *Pee*miller, had been aboard No. 3 and the brakemen had had to warn the hoboes to make themselves scarce.

I ordered a fried trout with hashed-brown potatoes. Scotty asked for a steak. Back in St. Cloud, Minnesota, he had been troubled with asthma, and in those days it was generally believed in the Middle West that the best cure for asthma was plenty of rare steak and baked potatoes. This theory may have been disproved since then, but I sincerely hope not.

The pair who did not like the big man, and were disliked by him in turn, addressed each other as Heck and Joe. Joe was the leader. Heck was tall and wiry. Anyone in the room could overhear their conversation, and nobody, unless he were deaf, could fail to hear it, not even the three scissorbills who were trying so hard not to get mixed up in anything on their first morning in the country they were to build up and which had been guaranteed by one and all to make them prosperous.

Heck and Joe, the latter leading the way, went over to the table at which the Dane was seated alone.

"Shucks, Joe!" Heck said. "You don't mean to say you're goin' to sit down to the table with a God-damned lousy scab?"

"Why be exclusive?" Joe asked. "This looks like a comfortable place. No drafts . . . good view. . . ." He glanced up as Pearl approached uneasily. "Are these seats taken, miss?" he asked.

Pearl, aware that the next table was empty, shot a glance at it, then changed her mind and answered, "No, gents. Help yourself."

Joe pulled out a chair and sat down, right next to the Dane. Neither Heck nor Joe had seemed to look at the big man or be aware he was there. But Heck still did not like the idea of sitting down at that table.

"Looka here, Joe," Heck said, indicating the free table. "Ain't the view better over this-away?"

"It wouldn't be nice to dirty up that nice clean tablecloth," Joe said. Heck sighed and sat down beside Joe, so that the latter was between him and the Dane. The big man said nothing, only glowered straight ahead and clenched his enormous hairy hands.

"Sinkers and coffee," Joe said to Pearl, and added: "That goes for my friend."

"Draw two in the dark, with *fried*-cakes," Pearl yelled to the cook out back, who appeared just then at the dumbwaiter with the oyster stew and crackers.

"Anything to drink?" Pearl asked the Dane.

The Dane shook his head sullenly and clenched his hands

24

again. His feet were planted square on the floor and he was leaning forward a little, so he could get up quick. Joe, on the other hand, was leaning back, tipping his chair on its back legs invitingly. Heck noticed this and it made him uncomfortable, but his function was not to reason why.

"Did you hear what happened in St. Paul? At the N.P. repair shop?" Joe asked Heck. It was evident that he was talking for the benefit of the Dane and the rest of us.

"You mean that gang of thugs who moved in, when the boilermakers struck?" Heck asked.

"Can you imagine a white man doin' a trick like that?"

"Hell. Them wasn't white men," Heck said. "They must'a been bleached."

Since they had noticed the priest sitting at the counter neither Heck nor Joe had used the name of God in vain. They could get along fine without resorting to profanity.

By this time the Dane's face and neck were a reddish purple. He was spooning up his stew, which was in a bowl four inches deep. Now and then he would throw in a handful of crackers.

The explosion we all were awaiting came so suddenly and in such an unexpected manner that everybody, except Joe, was caught flat-footed. I think Heck was more astonished than the rest of us, but he had the air of being used to surprises from Joe. Had I not been looking directly at Baseblud and his stew, from above and behind him, I might have missed the crux of the situation. I thought I had been watching Joe carefully, too, but in 1907, as always, the hand was quicker than the eye.

How shall I explain without seeming to be indelicate?

The Dane had a big spoon and a lusty appetite, and as the level of the stew declined, the oysters got fewer and fewer. He finally fished up what he mistook for a bivalve

25

until he got it into his mouth and started to swallow. He reached up, frantically, and took the object from his mouth. Originally it had been rolled and crumpled, but as he held it, poised before his distending eyes, it seemed to unfurl. On both sides it was clouded with stew, and was abominably soggy.

With a shriek and a gurgle the big Dane heaved forward, upsetting the table and spraying oyster stew ten feet in front of him. Before he could control his reflexes, Joe had pasted him on the side of the jaw so hard that he bit his tongue. Heck, who once he caught on, got into action quickly, had gone around the table, and when the Dane was jarred his way by Joe's second blow, Heck caught him a haymaker from the other side, which landed on the button. Joe's next wallop sent the big man over backwards where the back of his head hit a metal doormat on which was neatly lettered the initials "N. P." The awful crack, as the Dane's head struck the steel of the doormat, caused Father Congalach to cross himself for the second time since he got off that train.

Whatever else Joe had premeditated, certainly he had never taken account of that doormat. He took one quick look at the Dane's face, gaping upward from the floor, showed dismay if not consternation, tossed a silver dollar on the table, grabbed Heck by the arm and they both beat it out of the station. When last seen they were headed across the yards toward the huge roundhouse which could accommodate, not only forty locomotives, but also a couple of fugitives who wanted to make a quick getaway.

The priest, Roby, Scotty and I were gathered around the Dane, trying to decide whether he already had died, or would last until he could be carried across the way to the near-by Hotel Jordan. The Jordan was where anybody in Glendive was sure to be carried when anything happened to him. Doc Mullendore and Doc Dovee both lived there, and emergency surgical cases were often stretched out on the short end of the commodious mahogany bar.

Howard Roby, accustomed to acting in emergencies, commandeered a baggage truck with iron wheels and handle. We loaded the enormous Dane on it and Roby, with the rest of us trailing along on each side, pushed the baggage truck and its gory load through the dust and across the broad sidewalk to the bar entrance of the hotel. Meanwhile the station agent had been scouring the yards for railroad men willing to carry the injured scab on a stretcher. There were plenty of men around and most of them were not yet organized, but the great majority did not relish helping strike-breakers and the minority unsympathetic with unions did not want to declare themselves.

In the back room of the bar at the Hotel Jordan a lively poker game was in progress. Captain Marsh was sitting in, as usual, and the other players, besides both of the Glendive doctors of medicine, were Chet Donaldson, younger son of one of the biggest contractors on the ditch, a rancher from out near Three Buttes named Alex Wandell, and a printer and editor who had just come to town from Michigan and was planning, if he had good luck, to start a weekly paper down the valley at Sidney. Wallyo Galucci (pronounced Galoochee), the only hunchback in the city, was standing behind Donaldson as mascot. That was Wallyo's profession, and quite a profitable one. Cowpunchers, Indians, Chinks, and nearly all the gamblers were superstitious, and a hunchback behind one's chair was the strongest medicine locally esteemed to bring good luck.

When the poker players saw that an injured man was being lugged into the front room, the two doctors got up and bowed courteously to each other. Each of them hoped the other would take the case, so that the man who showed professional generosity could go on with the game. Roby, who frequently became a sort of master of ceremonies in an emergency, convinced the doctors quickly that both of them would be needed. Grant Marsh, who was a hundred dollars behind at the time, took the interruption graciously and all the players rose and followed the doctors from the back room. Nobody thought of pocketing or counting his cash or his chips. The cards, having been dealt, lay face downward in front of each chair.

Four men had lifted the Dane up on the angle of the bar and some kind soul had folded up a bandanna to put under the injured man's head.

"Turn him over, gents. It's the back of his onion that's hurt," Roby yelled, and obediently the men flopped the limp giant over, then made way for the doctors.

We others stood around, and everyone I looked at seemed interested, but not distressed. Doc Mullendore, the senior and first-comer to Glendive from the east, looked at Doc Bovee, who was a native of Helena and had studied in Montreal. Certain people insisted that both were vets, and they did have a knack with dumb animals. But, actually, both had diplomas as M.D.'s.

Doc Mullendore made a perfunctory examination of the back of the Dane's head, and then felt for a pulse. Doc Bovee got out his stethoscope, but did not find it necessary to use it. The doctors looked at each other again, nodded in agreement, and, with the other poker players, went back to their game, while the rest of us lined up at the bar. It was etiquette then to order mixed drinks when one felt sportive and gay, except on a Saturday or holiday night, but nearly everybody took straight whisky or draught beer, and frequently both, using the beer as a chaser. There was no nonsense about

serving minors, if the minor in question could handle himself and pay for what he ordered. It was the custom, unless
one had entered the bar for a quick one for medicinal purposes, for whoever was buying to order a round for everyone
at the bar, unless the bar was crowded. There was a general
understanding that, when the number of drinkers was three
or less, a silver dollar covered the round. For a larger number, the man buying tossed on a five-dollar gold piece. A
single drink cost one dollar, as did drinks for three. The
fourth round, no matter how many were buying, was always
on the house.

That morning, the house was setting up its second round,
when the officers of the law came in. The body of the Dane
was still lying, face down, covered with an odd piece of
tarpaulin, on the short end of the bar.

The Dawson County sheriff then was Chet Busby, and he
was not very chummy with the city chief of police, Charlie
Kinney, and his force. Busby was a bit officious, and threw
his weight around, and showed such favoritism between
prisoners in his charge that his attitude had caused unfavor-
able comment. Neither the cowpunchers, the men from the
ditch, Captain Marsh and the steamboat men, nor the inmates
of the red-light enclosure were fond of Busby. The editor
of the *Independent* was always gunning for him, and praising
Kinney, however faintly, which meant that the newly arrived
editor of the *Dawson County Review* supported Busby's
every action, even the most inconsistent one, and sniped
merrily at Chief Kinney and his two policemen, Hank New-
mann and Ed Mafrau.

Between them, the officers got the name of the deceased,
but could find out nothing about the identity of the two
fugitives, beyond the fact that one of them had been called
Joe, and that they were of different heights. Those of us

who had been witnesses of the incident in the railroad restaurant and were then in the Jordan bar were under the impression that the dead Dane had been the aggressor, that the unsavory item he found in his stew had got in, accidentally, among the oysters, somewhere in the east, and that the Dane had unjustly blamed the man sitting next to him, forcing the latter to slough him in the jaw. The bump on the railroad doormat had obviously been accidental.

Chief Kinney was perfectly willing to accept that version of the affair and let it drop, but Busby was thick with the railroad officials, not the men, and sought out the three scissorbills who had been in the lunch room when the blows were struck. All three of the scissorbills hated unions and insisted that the Dane had been verbally abused and later set upon because he had defied the agitators in St. Paul and taken a job in the N.P. repair shop when it was offered him.

The investigation got no further, because no one had seen the fugitives since they entered the roundhouse, and a search of the roundhouse proved they were not lurking there.

The consensus around town was that the N.P. ought to put in softer doormats.

CHAPTER THREE

Thirteen on the Stagecoach

ALTHOUGH the coulee crossing and clump of quaking aspens that marked the site of Trembles was nearer Jim Hill's Great Northern on the North Dakota line than Glendive, on the N.P., it was the latter, the seat of old Dawson County, that the people of the valley considered as the gateway to the Lower Yellowstone. Most of the cattle and sheep men, small business men, schoolteachers, and women of easy virtue came in that way. The "back door" at Mondak was favored by the scissorbills.

At that time the country was so thickly settled that old-timers like Ira Bendon of Burns Creek, Johnny O'Brien, or Alex Wandell had begun to complain that Montana was becoming overcrowded. By that they meant that cowboys, riding in the foothills or along the dry creek beds, would sight a ranch house every ten or twenty miles, if they chanced to be facing in the right direction. The few fences that had been put up were near the river, and from there all the way to the Canadian border was still free range.

Along the "ditch," or government canal between Head-gates and the fork of the rivers at Mondak, stood about fifteen contractors' camps, working a total of nine hundred men, including a disdainful bunch of Blackfoot Indians camped between Sidney and Fairview. The Blackfoot braves drove

31

slips for a hardboiled old Scot from Deadwood, James Munn.

When Captain Marsh named the buttes and islands along that section of the river, he tried to make the punishment fit the crime. The boosters for the newly-settled country, following in Jim Hill's wake, chose place names that are gems of wishful thinking. Whoever sees the words Fairview, or Ridgelawn, for instance, on a map, does not conjure into his mind any landscape that resembles the scenery around those towns. The table land was dry and flat, covered with sage brush and occasional clumps of bunch grass. Curlews laid their eggs on the bare spots and jack rabbits lurked in shadows six inches square. A few stray cattle fought the flies and, between times, snatched at the infrequent patches of blue-top or red-top grass. By the middle of June, every stalk of anything the cattle could eat had been dried and cured where it had grown. Faded, scorched and departed was the color known as green. Along the foothills to the north and west, more cattle and a few horses, in small bunches, tried to graze in the blistering sun or seek shade in the treacherous coulees. Within view of the stage road, and all through those plains, wallows worn by the departed buffaloes still were visible, and in or near them bleached buffalo skulls and white bones were lying.

Probably the bad lands east of the river were the most disturbing to view and to contemplate. The Indians called those wild, desolate, incredible volcanic wastes "the hills that face each other." They were tinted ever so faintly, the earth, not the foliage, of which there was none—ancient faded pastels that shimmered in a way that gradually intensified the chalk white, pale indigo, molten silver, brick red, dull ochre and gray. The shapes of those buttes and ravines were not like those of normal hills and dales. Like clouds, the sight of them suggested all kinds of unrelated objects, from brush hooks to catfish heads or grand pianos. Erosion of the sand-stone, streaked with coal the settlers were just beginning to learn to mine and use, had cut and crumbled downward, leaving erratic columns, spirals, obelisks, cones and tunnels. Crazy geologic strata of lava rock or porphyry streaked side-wise, unequally terraced, on all conceivable slants. The hardy Sioux, in their day, could live and travel there, because, no one knows why, occasional springs and even green meadows occur, if anyone can find them. Whoever could not find them died and was eaten by cougars and buzzards.

The morning after the incident of the Dane and the N.P. doormat in Glendive, Scotty McVeigh and I were among the passengers who boarded the stage from the board walk in front of the Hotel Jordan. The hour of departure, for pas-sengers headed down the valley, was seven A.M., rain or shine. Of course, if the No. 3 chanced to be late, the stage waited and both driver and passengers piled into the Jordan bar for a few extra drinks. This worked well because, if the driver got drunker than usual and became reckless on that account, the passengers were better fortified and did not mind the danger so much.

The day was fair. That is to say, the sky was cloudless at that hour of the morning and the sun was damnably hot. The stage horses, although not yet sweating, knew their hides would be damp and gleaming before they had gone a mile past the bridge, so they looked resentfully at the passengers and one another, fidgeted sullenly as prize fighters do before the gong sounds for the opening round, and began thinking of little ways in which they could destroy all hands and the equipment. No. 3 came and went. At first it looked as if there were no one aboard who wanted to go down the valley and Matt Keffeler, the driver, was well pleased for a moment, because he had eleven passengers already, including himself, and was almost pathologically afraid of the number thirteen.

There was a little difficulty in seating arrangements that morning because White Stella, one of Mona Mason's hookers who had decided to try her luck at Mondak, was traveling that day, and Angela Clawson and her father, Glenn, were also booked. Matt decided to put Stella up on the driver's seat, between him and Louis Alcott, a government bookkeeper at La Mesa. Angela sat between Scotty and me, inside the coach, riding backwards. Glenn Clawson was having an embarrassing time of it, since he had been one of Stella's warmest friends for a couple of years and his daughter was not supposed to know that such friendships existed. Of course, Stella would not think of recognizing any of us, while she was outside the enclosure. That was unwritten law and all the hookers observed it. They spoke to no one uptown who did not speak first to them, and then they did not reply unless they knew quite well the man who offered the greeting.

When the ten paying customers were in their places, three aloft, four on the back seat, facing forward, and the three of us on the front seat facing backwards, and Matt was just about to mount to his own seat, he saw, hurrying toward the stage from the depot three Chinks, one tall and two short. The tall one was Ah Fong, No. 1 Boy at the Perham Cheeleys' and who was tacitly acknowledged by both whites and Orientals as the boss Chinaman of the Glendive area.

When Ah Fong told Matt that the two small Chinks were going to Sidney to act as cook and flunky, respectively, at a contractor's camp near there, the stage driver turned green. It would not be hard to fit the two tiny men into the commodious coach, and everyone knew that the more tightly packed the passengers were, the less they would be jounced, banged and jostled as the horses went over the rough road on a dead run. But eleven plus two makes thirteen, whatever the nationality of the individuals might be.

All the men, in the coach and standing around the hotel platform, joshed Matt about his fears and he tried to pass them off lightly. But, watching him closely, I was astonished to see that he was really afraid. His inherent dread of the unlucky number was stronger than his nerve, which, God knows, was plenty strong. No timid man drove four or six half-broken horses of the kind the stage company provided.

Finally Ah Fong paid his countrymen's fares and the two small Chinks were seated, their baggage, in exotically painted tea cases and colored cloth, was tossed onto the roof of the coach and tied securely, and we started out, a full twenty minutes late. I think that only the fact that one passenger, an engineer named Babb, was getting off at the Headgates, a mere eighteen miles down-valley, decided Matt Keffeler in favor of taking on the Orientals. The first change of horses would occur at Burns Creek, just above the Headgates, and Babb would be met by his stable boss with a saddle horse there.

We hit the Glendive bridge, which Father Congalach had described as "long, symmetrical and useful," on a trot. The priest had not then been close enough to that structure to notice that the iron work was unpainted and rusty, and that the floor boards were well-worn and broken through in places.

Matt had two mean small mares in the lead, and a team of high-rumped raw-boned geldings at the wheel. The rattling of the iron work on the bridge frightened the off leader and the near one stuck her foot through a hole and tripped, recovering just in time to avoid being run over by the gaunt gelding behind her. It was customary to cross that bridge rather slowly, but Matt could do nothing now except try to keep the broncs between the traces and the stage on the planks. Had I not been sitting beside Angela Clawson, who, having been raised on a ranch, was carrying on a pleasant conversation as if nothing unusual were happening, I might have been more nervous than I was. The two Chinese, dressed in cheap black cloth and slippers, native style, and wearing queues, stared this way and that with beady eyes, like fowl in a crate.

We hit the dirt on the west side of the bridge. There the road skirted the side hill, rough and dusty. Across the river were bad lands and, although the dry creeks and coulees through which we dipped and scrambled had almost no water in them, but only treacherous stones, the Yellowstone was running high, wide, and muddy. The nearer we got to Burns Creek, the faster Matt drove those four ill-matched horses, who now were covered with lather and whose distended nostrils were red. Matt plied his blacksnake whip impartially, sometimes to dislodge horse flies, at others to punctuate the stories he was telling Stella. Matt always carried with him a handy jug of red-eye, so Stella, Matt and Louis, aloft, had a drink whenever the going was smooth enough.

We had to stop twice that morning, between Glendive and Burns Creek, once to drop off a case of canned milk for a cattle rancher back in the foothills of the south fork, and again when one of the big geldings picked up a stone in his shoe. On that occasion Scotty, who was a first-rate horseman from birth, got out with Clawson to hold the leaders while Matt pried the stone loose.

While the stage was stopped and some of the passengers were circulating around it, Stella said little or nothing. But while it had been moving she had explained to the driver and Louis Alcott why she was making the move from Glendive to Mondak.

"After two years in Mona's joint, a girl gets to be too Godblasted much of a lady. She can't let loose, even when she's drunk," Stella said.

Her point of view was understandable. The two principal madams in the Glendive stockade were both smart women and fine troupers, but not at all alike. Jack Little, short, squat and stocky, had a hoarse whisky baritone voice. She wore black silk stockings and a short, stiff ballet skirt that left quite an area of flesh tones uncovered, and was the "hail-fellow well-met" type. Mona Mason, on the other hand, had been a Southern society belle before, as she put it, she "got on to herse'f." Jack, in a tough land, wanted her cat-house to be the toughest spot, and attended to the bouncing herself, if anybody got unruly enough to warrant being thrown out. Jack's theory was that "men don't shoot women unless they love 'em." Mona was a soft-spoken, polite and languorous woman, who seemed to have no bones, and never raised her voice. She thought that, since Montana was doing so well by her, she should bring some Southern grace and hospitality into Montana, and she did. She could not get many Southern sporting girls, that far away from home, and the few she got from Dixie could not stand the Montana climate. So she trained the Middle-Western hookers who drifted west from Chicago, Omaha, Kansas City and St. Paul not to shout or drink beer from bottles, and no matter how many times they had to leave the dance hall or the parlor in the course of a night, they were required to put their corsets back on and hook them properly before they appeared again.

Cowboys, punctilious by nature, seldom failed to take off their hats when they entered Mona's parlor, and Mona never forgot to give them gracious permission to wear them in the dance hall, if it made them more at ease. In fact, many a cow-puncher on the Lower Yellowstone went to Mona when he had a difficult or sentimental letter to write to a girl back home, or somewhere far away, and Mona's choice of words was so apt and tender that many a respectable romance was expedited.

Jack and Mona were firm friends, and each one benefited by the tactics of the other. Plenty of men, after a carouse at Jack's, where practically anything went, found it restful to breeze over to Mona's and improve their manners for a while. Conversely, after a few hours in the atmosphere of organdies and magnolias, Mona's clients had the urge to join the roughnecks at Jack's, where a lusty din was *de rigueur*.

Angela Clawson, who knew much more about life, theoretically, than her father thought she did, bore no resentment whatever toward Stella, who did so much to make the region safer for respectable girls. And Stella frankly admired the rancher's daughter, who could go east to school and come back home without being a prude or a snob. It was purely on account of the men's strict notions that Stella and Angela did not speak to each other.

When the stage pulled up in front of the Burns Creek store and corral, Engineer Babb's stable boss was standing by with a saddle horse, all right, but Johnny Highpockets, a lanky and rather pathetic-looking scissorbill, was on hand to take Babb's place. Matt, the driver, was not aware of this at first, since he had followed the sweating horses to the stable and had to help subdue a couple of the broncs he was to drive from Burns Creek to Tokna, where the next relay was waiting. The horses we picked up at Burns Creek were too wild to be trusted in town. One broke his halter rope, kicked the watering trough to pieces, and tried to crush the stable boss against the corral fence, while another walked gently up to Matt and, according to the latter's statement, spat plumb in his eye, then snickered.

I think that Matt Keffeler would have refused to carry

Johnny Highpockets and continue down-valley with his jinx of thirteen aboard, had it not been contrary to the customs of the country to leave a man stranded on a sagebrush flat forty miles from where he wanted to go. Besides, Johnny was the helpless type who pottered around at something completely futile from dawn until dark, and men disliked to refuse him anything. He had been working for Donaldson, a contractor at the Headgates, to get enough money together to buy himself an outfit of working clothes and file on a claim.

"Hell, Matt," said Louis Alcott, "nothin's goin' to go haywire between here and La Mesa, where I get off."

La Mesa was twelve miles farther down the valley, and no unusual hazards lay on the road, when the weather was dry. It was then about ten-thirty in the morning, and the weather was dry, indeed. We all had some beer at Bendon's store, and it was good and cold, but before we had gone a mile we were thirsty again.

The stage reached La Mesa without further mishap, except that in crossing the wide stony channel of Beef Slough, a lead horse stumbled and fell down. The bronc was jerked to his feet by his partner, who lunged wildly in the other direction just in time. The engineers' camp at La Mesa consisted of six olive-green government buildings with board walks between them, a large stable, corral and woodpile, and all around the fenced area a fire strip had been plowed, a dozen furrows wide. There Matt nearly gave up, for when Louis Alcott got off, in no state to keep books that hot afternoon, old George Knickerbocker, known as Old Knick, who had been crumb boss of the camp since its establishment, wanted to ride down to Mondak to see about some flower seeds. That he would also enjoy one of his tri-annual periodic drunks was understood, as a matter of course.

By that time, not even the harsh brand of whisky in

Matt's jug would cheer the driver. When he noticed that a phalanx of dull gray-blue clouds was gathering on the western horizon he stopped talking, even to Stella, and doggedly awaited the worst.

"Heck, Matt, you only got six miles to go to Tokna, across a flat so damn level you could use it for croquet," Ed Wilson, the La Mesa stable boss, said.

"Want to take my place?" Matt asked.

Ed shook his head and grunted, "Unh-unh."

"How many get off at Tokna?" Clawson asked, enjoying Matt's panic.

"You do," Matt said. "You're almost home."

"Me, and Angela, if she can pry herself loose from them two young engineers," Glenn said. "Anybody else?"

Lew Kiichlii, a Finn ranch hand who worked for Dunlap, woke up and mumbled that he got off at Tokna, too.

"That makes three, Matt," Glenn said. "You know you ain't never goin' to find three passengers at once in Tokna. Have you ever before?"

Tokna, on Dunlap Creek, was shaded by a grove of tall cottonwoods. As we neared it, the sun was still shining and the shadows of the leaves dappled the creek and the bare area in front of the postoffice and the company corral. Less than a mile up the creek was another grove of trees and the spacious ranch house, stable and corral of Annius Gregory, whose cattle ranged from there north and west over about five thousand square miles. Of course, this range was shared by the McKenzie outfit at Three Buttes, Alex Wandell, and a dozen other cattle men between the Yellowstone and the Missouri.

This was the first place along the stage road that looked permanent and prosperous. To me, fresh from the east, it

40

was the shade that made the difference, and the sight of running water, even though it was only four inches deep and left green and white stains of alkali along the stones.

In the old days, Tokna, an Indian word meaning "Reliable" or "Nearly always there" (weaker than "tok-tokna," meaning "invariably there"), had been the scene of violent incidents with which Old Knick, who joined us at La Mesa, was familiar.

Knick, from choice, had climbed up on the driver's seat with Stella and Matt, knowing that the latter would be sure to have a jug of whisky, and had refreshed himself as soon as he was safely out of sight of the La Mesa buildings. The government engineers, that is to say, the top ones in authority, had ruled that no alcoholic beverages, not even beer, could be brought into camp, and imposed the same rule on the contractors and sub-contractors along the ditch. That meant that whisky or beer intended for anyone in the reclamation service or working on the canal had to be cached by whoever delivered it, somewhere outside the camps, to be retrieved under cover of darkness and consumed discreetly and surreptitiously. As a matter of fact, Old Knick, knowing that a few drinks were likely to make him as loco as a Brule Sioux, never drank while on duty, and, as a consequence of his habitual restraint, his occasional binges were violent indeed.

Tokna looked peaceable and quiet enough, as our stage splashed through the creek, and the three passengers got ready to leave us. But when Matt pulled up his four horses (considerably less wild than they were when he had hitched them up at Burns Creek), in front of the postoffice to unload the mail sacks, he (and all of us) saw standing there another group of three, namely: Old Annius Gregory, his daughter Letty, and her fiancé, Bat Horner, the champion liar of the county. We all let out a roar of laughter, and Stella whooped with joy at the sight of Matt's face when he realized that he still had thirteen passengers. For sound effects, the cottonwoods rustled in an angry puff of wind, and distant thunder rumbled somewhere up the creek.

It was then one o'clock in the afternoon, and there was no beer at Tokna.

CHAPTER FOUR

The Founding of Trembles

THE four cayuses we took on at Tokna were the meanest of the lot. They all were small and tough and had enough in them of the Indian strain that enabled them not only to rear, strike, kick, bite and sideswipe, buck, throw themselves and break wind at will, but also to think and plan. From the way they looked the outfit over, it was clear to any student of horse physiognomy that they had been conspiring all morning in their stalls. As if by prearrangement, they allowed themselves to be led into their places and hooked up without any hostile demonstration. The little mare in the lead, on the near side, was a pinto of at least four clashing colors—gray, sorrel, white and buckskin. She had a bald face with one blue eye. The other was brown, with flecks of red. Her nose was humped and stubborn, her underlip long and petulant. Someone, while laid up in the bunkhouse with a broken arm, had named her Crocus, because that early spring flower had been used by the Sioux to poison their enemies.

Matt had had dealings with Crocus once or twice before. She was not unbroken, like most of the other broncs in the stable, but was ten years old, and so smart that she could turn the lever at the watering tub, when she got loose from the stable at night, flood the corral and empty the storage tank. This she did only when the well was getting low.

For years afterward, Matt swore that, while he was hitching

43

the other horses that day, Crocus, looking over her shoulder, counted the passengers, and nickered softly to herself. From Tokna to Sidney, where the last relay of horses would be taken on, was a drive of about twenty miles. The stage road had slowly edged away from the river, so that at Tokna it was at least six miles away. For the most part, the road was flat, very dusty, and the crossings at Sears Creek, Crane Creek, Fox Creek and Cedar Coulee were normally not difficult ones.

Scotty and I were quartered then at Newlon, but since we would pass through there fairly late in the afternoon, too late to do much work that day, we had agreed to dump off our stuff at the small surveyors' camp and go on to Sidney, for supper at the Valley Hotel, where we could get buckets of warm water, fresh flannel shirts, and spend the evening with the most lively and hospitable hostess in the lower valley, Mrs. Baron, the wife of one of the grocers and general storekeepers there. Although Sidney was then a small town, already there were two factions among the women who lived there and the social life was brisk in the extreme. The prudent element rallied around Mrs. Thavanot, whose star boarder was the Rev. Theo Oates. The gay set was led and animated by the charming Mrs. Baron, for whom, in Glendive, Scotty and I had bought a keg of oysters, and had agreed not to tell the sad story about the Dane until the midnight feast was over.

We still were sitting on the front seat, inside, riding backwards, and between us, to take the warm and fragrant place vacated by Angela Clawson, was the bashful and rangy Letty Gregory. Johnny Highpockets and a stranger named Bert Lacey were at my right. Letty's father, Bat Horner, and the two silent Chinks were among those who sat opposite. Nowhere along the line, although it must have seemed to them as if they had ridden half-way back to China, did the Orientals try to get off the stage. Ah Fong had told them to stay where they were until Matt, the driver, indicated that they had reached Sidney.

Everybody was glad to see Bat, who had been eight years or more in the country. He was a short, wall-eyed little man, then in his thirties, with an enormous pair of bat ears that stuck out from his small and close-cropped head. He and Letty Gregory, who loved him dearly, made a touching couple when side by side, or face to face. Letty was the tallest woman in Dawson County. She was a thin, plain, quiet girl between six and seven feet high, and about five years older than Bat. Bat admitted freely that, in order to kiss her, he had to stand on a stump or a soap box.

"Shucks! I have to stand on the platter to kick a duck," he often said.

Bat and Letty had been engaged seven years, and finally got married in 1910, after he had saved enough money to build a house of their own and buy some land that had water on it. Old Man Gregory, whose language, even in the presence of ladies he knew, was more expressive than elegant, repeatedly had offered to set them up in style, but Bat insisted on standing on his own feet and Letty never questioned his judgment. She never questioned anybody's judgment.

Riding in a stagecoach was never dull when Bat was present. First of all, he noticed that a couple of the buttons were missing from the leather cushion underneath him.

"Matt!" he hollered up to the demoralized driver, "ain't Sheriff Busby been a'ridin' down here lately?"

"I wish he was here right now, to get his neck broke with the rest of us," Matt said.

"How'd you know the sheriff had been ridin'?" asked

Johnny Highpockets, who was a natural-born straight man, and sincerely anxious for any kind of knowledge.

"Ain't you never seen that pair o' false teeth the sheriff carries with him?" Bat asked.

"He don't wear no false teeth. I seen him uncap a bottle of beer with his teeth, a while back," Johnny said.

"He don't wear 'em in his mouth. He wears 'em down below, so's he can bite the buttons off of cushions," Bat said, and Johnny's jaw sagged a minute while he thought it over.

Once Bat got started on Johnny Highpockets, we all sat back and relaxed, all except the Chinks, who could understand nothing, so we thought.

"I hear you're goin' to file on a claim," Bat said.

"That's what I aim to do," admitted Johnny, touching his pants pockets to be sure the money was still there.

"Where'bouts?" asked Bat.

"West of Newlon, somewhere," Johnny said.

"Under the ditch?"

"No. That costs too much," said Johnny. "Soon's the government gets water there, I hear they'll soak a man for it."

"Ever tried dry farmin'?" asked Bat.

"They say a man can grow a good crop o' grain. There's rain enough, they say. A feller read me from a book the railroad had printed. Twenty-five to fifty bushels to the acre, without no irrigation, it said."

A clap of thunder and zigzag lightning to the west just then caused Johnny to smile and nod.

"See what I mean?" Johnny said, very pleased.

Old Annius Gregory glanced westward and said: "Them clouds are blue. We'll get some hail, instead of rain."

"Don't hail melt, and turn to water?" Bat asked.

"Not till after it's cut down all the grain," Annius said.

46

"Hey, Matt!" yelled Bat to the driver, over a rumble of thunder. "Got any hail bonnets for them broncs?"

"Can't kill them broncs with bullets, let alone hail," Annius answered. Matt, trying to figure if he could make Newlon before the storm broke, said nothing, but plied his whip.

We were almost to Crane Creek then, which meant nothing at all in the way of shelter. The hail storm struck. All the horsemen hopped out as Matt, with difficulty, pulled the four broncs to a stop on the flat. Scotty, Annius, Bat and the driver started unhitching the four horses. The first hail stones were no bigger than marbles and, while they hurt and stung a little, they were not dangerous, except for their stimulating effect on the horses. Johnny Highpockets and I, not knowing what to do, exactly, watched the others. Letty, the stranger and the Chinks sat in the coach, then the stranger got out and insisted on helping Stella from her perch and establishing her comfortably inside. Letty looked at the hooker pleasantly, nodded and smiled.

Matt decided, as the hail stones increased to the size of hazelnuts, to tie three of the horses together, so they could shelter each other, after a fashion, and not get far away. The fourth, little Crocus, settled her fate promptly for herself. She walked over to the stagecoach, on the lee side, dragging the 110-pound Bat Horner at the end of the halter rope, stuck her head underneath to see how things were, got down on her knees and wriggled to a place of shelter.

"Good," Matt said. "Tie her fast to the hind wheel, Bat. Then if these others break their ropes and run away, we can mount her and catch 'em."

"Who's goin' to mount Crocus?" Bat asked. "Not me. I'm engaged."

With a startling thudding volley the hail stones came down, angled sharply by the wind, as big as hen's eggs, and Johnny

47

Highpockets, although his arms were over his head as he rushed for the stage, was felled and had to be dragged in by Scotty and Annius, both of whom were nearly knocked senseless in the process. Old Knick, whooping and shrieking defiantly, stuck his bullet head under the seat and was pelted about the body so severely that he was black, blue and lame for a month. In the coach were huddled the terrified but silent Chinese, who were picked up bodily by Stella, to make room. She sat them on her lap, one on each plump knee, where they remained, without changing expressions. Letty, who had the sharpest bones I ever encountered, was sitting on mine. Somehow, twelve of us jammed ourselves in, out of reach of the murderous hail.

It seemed a long time, and a noisy, confused time, with all of us sweating and stuffed in together, hail and Old Knick's boots drumming on the roof, and no sounds from the mare, Crocus, who was under the floor boards. Then the quality of the sound changed; there was a sharp clap of thunder that Bat swore hit the end of the wagon tongue; the steady drubbing diminished in dynamics and volume, stopped altogether; the sun came out mockingly from between the departing clouds; and a darn fool meadow lark sang as blithely as if nothing had happened.

As best we could, we all piled out of the coach and looked around. Within sight the sagebrush flat was covered with egg-sized hail stones very cold and slowly melting. There was no sign at first of the three missing stage horses, except their broken halters and ropes.

"The damn critters have broke loose from each other," Matt said.

Crocus, as if hearing the comment, wormed her way out from under the stagecoach, stood up, with no attempt to pull back on the rope that hitched her to the off-hind wheel, and sighed. Not only was the pinto mare unhurt. She was practically dry.

Matt was looking fearfully at Crocus, knowing it was up to him to try and ride her and round up the missing horses. The driver was pale green. He was no bronco buster, and never had been. He could drive anything that had legs, but up on top of a horse he felt conspicuous and awkward. Bat, who was a good rider, let him suffer a while, then went over to Letty and shook her hand solemnly.

"So long, Letty. You been a good fian*cee*. When you git that there melodeon, play it now and then for me," he said.

"Bat Horner," Letty said, blushing, "you ain't a goin' to try and ride that she-devil!"

"Matt, here's, got two wives back east, so they say. We can't let him get killed," said Bat.

"Ten to five that mare'll massacre any man who tries to ride 'er," said Old Gregory, producing a drawstring leather purse and showing gold and silver inside it.

"I'll take you up on that," Bert Lacey said.

"Can a sportin' girl get in?" asked Stella, who had just accepted another drink from the jug.

Bets were laid, in amounts that made Johnny Highpockets' eyes bulge.

"What if he don't get killed all the way?" he asked, cagily.

"Deader'n a mackerel, or all bets is off," Old Gregory insisted.

"For God's sake, don't say a thing like that," Matt implored. "We've had that there jinx with us ever sence we left Glendive. Thirteen! Bat! I won't let you risk it. The company'd be liable."

Throughout the discussion meadow larks sang and Crocus, her lower lip quivering but otherwise motionless, stood with her head level, so the halter rope sagged.

Trying to appear calm, Bat edged around behind the stage and unfastened the halter rope from the off-hind wheel. Very cagily he approached, inch by inch, the left side of the pinto, murmuring:

"Now be nice, you cranky little bitch."

Scotty was shaking his head. When he made up his mind about anything, he was very positive. "No man can ride her, bareback. If he had a saddle, maybe, but not bareback," he said.

"He won't have no stirrups to get his foot caught in," Annius said.

The pinto stood perfectly still. Bat put his hand on her scrawny, discolored mane, stroked her humped nose. She did not even blink. He rubbed her back and she almost smiled.

"Heck!" Bat said. "This mare ain't mean."

"Bat. I forbid you," Matt said, taking a step forward.

The moment Matt moved, the pinto laid back her ears and planted a shining Neverslip shoe between the third and fourth buttons of his leather vest. He sat down gasping and rolled out of the way.

"Easy, girl," Bat said, and the pinto smiled again.

Bat rubbed her again and got on. She stood quietly. He nudged her with his knees and she started forward, but not in the direction Bat was trying to guide her. No matter what he did or said, she single-footed steadily back toward Tokna, until Bat had to slide off. He tried to hold the halter rope and would have succeeded had Crocus not stood up on her hind legs, quick as a cougar, and struck out with both front feet. One hoof grazed each of Bat's shoulders and before Crocus could strike again, the little man no longer was there.

Crocus did not chase him. She merely held her head to one side, so the rope would not trip her, and sidled around the stagecoach and our group, at a safe distance on the side toward the foothills. Just then we saw, coming up from the distant bed of Fox Creek, the missing horses, and riding behind them, just to one side, a small dark cowboy on a lovely sorrel horse with flowing mane.

"That's Mexican Joe," Matt said.

Crocus saw Mexican Joe and the three other horses as soon as we did, and stepped away faster toward the foothills. By the time the Mexican had roped the other horses, one by one, and brought them up so they could be re-haltered and hitched, Crocus was out of sight. The Mexican bronco buster set out after her on the fleet sorrel. As fast as his horse was, it took him quite a while to catch Crocus and rope her, and a longer time to lead her back to her place. Matt thanked Joe, who grinned and said, "That's nothing, Don Mateo," then rode back toward Newlon on a trot.

By that time, it was six o'clock in the afternoon and a storm was gathering up Fox Creek and Cedar Coulee and moving toward the stage road slowly.

"That ain't hail. That's rain, and plenty," Old Gregory said.

"If you ask me, it looks like a young cloudburst," Bat said.

"God damn me, if I don't wish I'd stayed back east and gone to jail," Matt growled, as we started up again, to beat the storm into Sidney, which was thirteen miles away.

"How far are we from Sidney?" Bat called up to Matt.

"Them damn engineers never measure anything right," Matt answered, but everybody knew, or was promptly reminded, that we had thirteen miles to go.

At Johnny O'Brien's store and postoffice at Newlon, we stopped only two or three minutes, only long enough to dump and grab the mail sack at the surveyors' camp. The rain started to fall, and before we got across Fox Creek it was coming down in bucketfuls and the creek began to rise.

While for weeks it had been a trickle of water not twelve feet wide, and six inches deep between stones, it now had spread to fifty feet and was over a foot deep, rushing and churning so impetuously that small round pebbles were racing along the bottom.

Old Annius yelled up at Matt again, this time in earnest.

"Think we'll make it across Cedar Coulee?" he asked.

"No," Matt said, succinctly, and lambasted the broncs with his blacksnake. He could hardly see them through the rain.

"I never seen a wetter whore," Stella confided to Knick as she wrung water from her skirt.

She hardly finished speaking before the storm passed over toward the Yellowstone and where we were the sun shone again and another fool meadow lark rose, singing and warbling.

After the rain the smell of sage was fresh and almost overpowering, mixed as it was with Letty's eau de Cologne, the spicy, exotic aroma of the Chinese, and the men's whisky, bay rum, tobacco, and sweat. The ensemble was set off with a strong dash of horse fragrance. Matt and the others who could see forward sighted the clump of quaking aspens a few miles ahead, their damp leaves shimmering in the slanting sunlight, their shadows supernaturally long. They stood on the south bank of the coulee, so that we would pass them just before plunging down into the torrent the cloudburst had poured into the rocky silted channel that an hour before had been perfectly dry. Cedar Coulee started in a crevice between foothills, fifteen miles west of the stage road, and at the crossing ran between two steep cut banks, not more than ten feet high, one hundred feet apart. The bottom of the channel was covered with smooth stones, patches of silt washed from the hills, small rocks and sizeable loose boulders that had been dislodged and rolled down at a time when the watershed had been drenched suddenly before. This happened at intervals of ten or twelve years, unless some poor devil was counting on it.

Matt, in spite of his fears and his whisky, was alert and competent, now. He could only guess how deep the rushing waters would prove to be, whether the weight of the stage and its thirteen passengers and the pull of the four cayuses would prevent the coach from being overturned or washed downstream, whether the horses would bog down in the soft silt, or be disabled by the large rocks that were churning and tumbling along. There were floating snags, and others that were stuck for the moment.

Perhaps what decided Matt to try the crossing, full tilt, was the attitude of little Crocus. She was running so fast that her belly seemed to skim the mud. Both her front legs and hind legs were stretching and reaching as far as they would go. The pinto mare had no intention of stopping for a mere flood, when six miles ahead was food, drink, a dim stable and sizeable corral. As usual, the other three horses took their cue from Crocus. When the raging coulee, alive with bile-colored foaming water, snags, rocks, drowned gophers and a dead steer or two, was a quarter of a mile away, Matt realized that he could not slow up the horses if he wanted to. Crocus, for one, had the bit firmly between her teeth, and one of the lines under her determined stubby tail. She must have figured that, when the stage lurched down from the level of the flat into the coulee, it would tip over, to the sorrow of its human load and destruction of its freight, and that, somehow, she would be able to make the other bank and get on to Sidney. If not, she could swim almost indefinitely or climb up on the overturned stage.

The passengers, all aware that a crisis was approaching, reacted in characteristic ways. The Chinese sat, as before, stoically. Johnny Highpockets was white beneath his tan. Bert Lacey was not happy at all, but when Scotty, who kept his head in emergencies, began to loosen the tarp on his side, so that if the stage capsized we would have a better chance of getting out, Lacey performed a similar service on the opposite side. Bat Horner was leaning forward, sitting on the edge of the seat.

"Johnny," he said to Highpockets, "if you got too much money, better throw it out. It might weigh you down."

The Mormon carpenter who was headed for a camp below Sidney, and who had taken no part in the conversation and the proceedings, having dozed intermittently all the way from Glendive, now was wide-awake, but was not clear enough in his mind to appreciate the danger.

Aloft, beside Matt, who was busy trying to get the line clear of Crocus's tail, Stella was grinning almost with satisfaction. She had wanted a change from the quiet and decorum of Mona Mason's place, and was getting it. Old Knick was growling happily, like a bear in the spring, having no intention of dying until he had got to Mondak and spent every dollar he had.

I was nervous and afraid, but, as always, was watching the others.

I was conscious of the stage suddenly slipping downward, from under me, and my Stetson hat being jammed down to my eyes by an impact from overhead. Then of ice-cold waters churning and rushing along, just over the hubs, of the bumping of rocks against the wheels, of complicated changes in the sounds and a slackening of the speed and momentum. But the stage was upright and was moving along.

"We'll make it," Scotty said, turning to me and smiling, his light blue eyes looking paler because of his tenseness and tan.

Old Man Gregory reached for his drawstring purse, to

place a bet, but no one took him up. Bat was whistling, but no one could hear the tune, not even Bat.

Above the roaring and din I heard the crack of Matt's blacksnake whip and his piercing yell.

"Crocus! You crummy little bastard! Get in there, sweetheart!"

Crack! Crack!

We were past midstream now, and still moving, but slowly, and it seemed to me the whole rig was sliding downstream.

The Orientals tried to hold their heelless slippers up out of the wet.

Bang! A heavy boulder struck the near-hind wheel. The stage careened, recovered, inched onward. Then I felt the floorboards rise, my chin hit my chest, and we were lurching upward on the bank.

A second later we were on level ground and rolling at top speed again. Old Gregory put away his purse and everybody suddenly looked foolish, and smiled, again excepting the Chinese who simply put their feet back on the floorboards. Aloft Knick yelled; Stella cackled. Bat turned to Highpockets.

"Montana weather," he said. "You'll sure enjoy it."

"It's always exceptional," said Scotty.

Then there was a crunch, a sag, a spill to the left, and the stage, with little slackening of the speed until we hit the ground, turned over on its side, was dragged a few yards by the frantic, kicking broncos and we were piled up, one over another, with the Mormon carpenter, Old Gregory, Scotty and Bat Horner on the bottom.

The first thing I saw clearly was Knick, lying like an old suit of clothes, face down, five yards away, on the flat, with Stella, her petticoats over her head, on top of him, and Matt

Keffeler, lines still in his left hand and feet in the air. They had been thrown clear of the stage and the rest of us.

Bert Lacey was able to climb out, on the upper side, and we passed him Letty, then the Chinese, who were unhurt. The Mormon carpenter tried to climb clear, and discovered that one of his ankles was out of commission. Scotty got out next, and hurried to help Matt, who had risen to his feet and was trying to quiet the horses, all of which had gone berserk but could not kick or lunge themselves clear of the tangled harness. We helped Old Gregory get out. I felt myself all over, and except for a badly bruised elbow, I seemed to be intact. The jug of whisky had rolled three yards past Knick, who, as I reached his side and disentangled Stella, began to grunt and then swear under his breath.

The hooker was dazed but conscious, and one of her arms hung limp. Since Bat, Old Gregory, Scotty and Matt were struggling with the horses and harness, I tried to help the injured. I cut away the sleeve of Stella's jacket and waist. Her arm was swelling fast, but as near as I could tell, it was broken above the elbow. The elbow seemed sound and the bones of the forearm. Both her wrists were badly sprained.

She sat up, then we helped her to rise, Old Knick and I, and sat her down with her back to the good hind wheel of the stage, from which the horses, by that time, had been unhooked and disentangled. The big boulder that had hit the near-hind wheel had weakened it, so that at the moment everyone had been rejoicing and our journey's end seemed near, it had collapsed and tipped the rig clean over.

The tool box of the Mormon carpenter, the luggage the Chinese had packed in ornamental tea boxes and colored cloth, bedrolls, the keg of oysters, all the stuff that had been tied on top of the coach was scattered, but, for the most part, undamaged. Bert Lacey had brought a big tent and a small one, and various articles with which he had planned to set up a saloon farther down the valley. He surveyed the landscape, saw the inviting clump of quaking aspens on the far side of the coulee, the torrent of which had already subsided considerably, tipped back his hat and scratched his head.

"Why wouldn't that be a good place for a town?" he asked.

"As good as any," Old Man Gregory said.

Bat Horner began selling Johnny Highpockets on the idea that the land south of the coulee and west of the quaking aspens was fine for dry farming. Bat explained to Johnny that, as soon as the government started work on that section of the ditch, he could get a job with a contractor and still live on his claim and prove up.

Since her arm had not yet started hurting badly, Stella had a few ideas of her own. She liked Lacey, and if he was going to settle there, and found a town, she could camp farther up the coulee, just off the government land, and have a hookshop of her own. Newlon was not far away, and neither was Sidney. There were ranches, employing cowhands in the foothills farther west, and men from outside the valley would be working on the ditch.

It was Mexican Joe, riding to our rescue for the second time that day, who suggested the name of Trembles.

CHAPTER FIVE

The Founding of Trembles (Continued)

BEFORE dark that evening, the flood in Cedar Coulee had passed and a man could wade across without getting wet up to the top of his boots. Three two-horse rigs were driven to the wrecked stage from Johnny O'Brien's and Simard's ranches at Newlon, and another from the surveyors' camp. Still another came up from Ball's livery barn in Sidney. Six men on saddle horses, besides Mexican Joe, put in an appearance within the hour.

O'Brien was agreeable to the idea of a new settlement at Trembles, so were Annius Gregory and the Simards. So many new people were coming into the region that a few more near at hand would do no harm, and would bring in trade. Doc Morrill from Sidney rode up with Bill Ball, examined Stella's arm and the Mormon carpenter's ankle and in each instance confirmed my amateur diagnosis. The doctor set the break in Stella's arm, wrapped it in splints and gave her a sling of black silk to take the weight off it. He could not be sure whether any bones were broken in the Mormon's ankle, but bandaged it and gave him some pills to ease the pain, since good Mormons did not drink whisky.

One of the Simard boys agreed to drive Stella, Knick, the Gregorys and Bat Horner to Mondak, and before they started out it was agreed between Bert Lacey and Stella that she would come back as soon as her arm was sound and he would put up a couple of tents for her up the coulee. Meanwhile she would stay with Big Emma Tubbs, who ran the hook-shop in Mondak for which Stella had been bound.

Everyone was puzzled to find Old Man Gregory, his daughter and her fiancé riding on the stage, since he had several rigs and innumerable horses of his own. Annius explained that he had ordered a melodeon for Letty, from Monkey Ward in Chicago, and also a new Studebaker (in those days a first-class all-purpose wagon). He needed some new harness and intended to buy a couple of horses in North Dakota, drive them from Mondak back to Tokna, and then sell them at a fancy price to the government. This made the best of sense, especially the quick turn-over to Uncle Sam of the kind of horses that would be for sale on the Dakota border in that season, considering the demand.

Already Bert Lacey was thinking how nice it would be if he could keep the Chinese cook and flunky and set up an eating-house beside his saloon. But he knew that if Ah Fong in Glendive had promised the pair to James Munn, the contractor, the boss Chinaman would keep his word to the letter. Bert confided his problem to Johnny O'Brien, who offered a solution. Johnny assumed that any pair of traveling Chinese would have pipes, a set-up and a supply of opium in their luggage. Knowing that Munn was a fiery old Scot who had little patience with foreigners' devious ways, Johnny believed that if he had his friend, Mert Honey, a deputy sheriff, take the Orientals into custody and search their belongings, Munn would lose interest in them before they were released. Mert, the deputy, was among those who had ridden up from Sidney in the rescue party, and quickly agreed. So the Chinese and their possessions were driven back to Newlon and Munn, when he arrived on the scene, reacted as expected, gave his timekeeper hell for trying to hire heathen in the first place, and drove away, disgusted, in his spick-and-span. buckboard.

Bert's smaller tent, 8 by 12, was set up in the shelter of the quaking aspens as twilight deepened, about ten o'clock that evening, and the larger one was stowed. away to be erected as soon as Bert could get a load of lumber for a floor and bar. With a stump of blue crayon, Bert started figuring on a piece of broken board that had drifted down the coulee in the flood and was dry enough now for anything. He had about three hundred dollars in cash, and seven hundred more in a Glendive bank. That would have been enough to set him up in a flourishing saloon on the main street of an already established lower-valley town. He had had Sidney in mind. But to found a town of his own, with a saloon, restaurant, hookshop and all, would strain his resources. He wanted to order things, right and left, with the future (at least six weeks away) in mind. Bert was a promoter, as well as an understander of Chinks, hookers, old-timers, scissorbills, surveyors and the rest of mankind.

Seeing that Old Johnny O'Brien was watching him quizzically, Bert looked up from his wishful arithmetic.

"What's the matter? Rockefeller's disease?" Old Johnny asked. "Rockefeller's disease," paradoxically, in that country, meant a shortage of cash.

"I only figured on just one saloon," Bert said, ruefully.

"Go as far you like. Annius and me'll back you," Johnny said. Annius Gregory had long before departed for Mondak. Probably, by that time, he was already there, against the Yellowstone bar. But the old-timers who had prospered in that country backed each other up, and spoke for one another, when occasion arose. No one ever knew how much money O'Brien had, but everyone believed it was plenty.

I cannot say what went through Bert Lacey's mind. He was a stranger in the land, without acquaintances, or large assets. He had saved his thousand dollars, working hard in a clothing store in St. Paul. He had heard talk about Montana, read the classic railroad pamphlet, made the trip, and there he was, sitting on a bedroll beneath some quaking aspen trees. A man of authority and prestige in the country had just said: "Go as far as you like."

Bert smiled and said, "That's friendly of you, Mr. O'Brien." He and Johnny made a trip to the engineers' camp, phoned Captain Marsh and ordered lumber, whisky, beer, ice, simple furniture, dishes, and an Edison phonograph with plenty of records by Ada Jones and Billy Murray. There were many other items: a Monkey Ward catalogue, bandannas, towels (large and small), glasses, a couple of wall clocks, windows, with frames and weights, kegs of nails, small tools, two-man saws, big mirrors, canned milk, coffee, several tarpaulins, slickers, mackinaw coats and buffalo robes. It was understood that Bert was to stick to the liquor and entertainment business, and not compete with Johnny's general store, and that the postoffice address of whoever settled in Trembles would be Newlon, Montana, to boost O'Brien's postoffice into a class with Sidney's, if possible.

Johnny did not like the hotel business, and detested running a livery stable. There were dozens of sidelines he had had to dabble in, for the convenience of his far-flung customers from the foothills. He was more than willing and anxious to turn some of them over to Lacey or anyone who would settle near the clump of quaking aspens on Cedar Coulee.

While Scotty and I were standing around, I was introduced to Joe Simard, one of the innumerable Simard brothers. Joe was a wonderful fiddler, and by that I do not mean violinist. He did not know how to hold a bow or to finger properly, but as far as dance music went, he could play circles around any man who had hit the Yellowstone country. To distinguish him from Mexican Joe, who also was a remarkable natural musician, Joe Simard was known as "French Joe."

French Joe had heard that Old Man Gregory was going to Mondak to pick up a melodeon at the Great Northern freight house there and bring it up the valley to Tokna. He also had heard that Clawson's older daughter, Angela, had come back to her father's ranch to spend the summer vacation. Either one of those items would have been enough to stir up French Joe and Mexican Joe and start them organizing a dance.

On the stage that day, when Letty Gregory had said she was afraid she could never learn to play the organ her father had bought, I had offered to teach her. Thus Lacey had learned that I liked music and could play a little. Bert relayed the information to the musical Mexican and Frenchman, who were excited about the prospect of an addition to their two-man band. Then, as always, any chance to play was all I needed to set aside other desires and responsibilities, and the three of us soon were talking music so fast that we prac-tically could hear it.

Without consulting the Gregorys, who were to be our hosts and entertain the whole countryside as well, we fixed the date of the dance a week from the coming Saturday. Joe Simard promised to intercept the Gregorys and Bat Horner, when they drove up the valley in their new Studebaker with the melodeon. French Joe urged Scotty and me, who still planned to go to Sidney for a midnight feast at Mrs. Baron's, to get in touch with the wife of the editor of the *Sidney Herald* and have the dance announced in "Notes from the Lower Valley" in the next issue. Back east, such procedure would have been a bit high-handed, but not on the lower Yellowstone.

As soon as Joe Simard had ridden out of earshot, Bert Lacey took me aside, filled with fine enthusiasm.

The Founding of Trembles (Continued)

"We got to have a piano at Trembles. That's more up to date than a melodeon," he said.

I am sure that Bert had fogotten completely that Trembles then consisted of one 8 by 12 tent. Already, in Bert's mind, his new town was rivaling Sidney, Tokna, Fairview and Ridgelawn.

"There aren't any pianos for sale in Glendive," I told him.

"Glendive, hell! St. Paul! We'll have it shipped by express. Never mind the expense! When my big tent's up we'll use it for a dance hall every Saturday night, if you'll play. I'll put up a bigger dance hall, built of lumber, afterward," said Bert.

Bert did not talk like an hysteric or an *exalté*. His plan was sound. Time, which had moved so slowly through that valley —carrying with it the march of the dinosaurs, the migrations of buffaloes, Indians, trappers, roundups—was accelerating its beat, getting into tune with restless, prodigal, hopeful, wasteful, destructive, tolerant America.

CHAPTER SIX

Courtship by Mail

JOHNNY HIGHPOCKETS (christened Johannes Peder Heipagets) shared the 8 by 12 tent with Bert Lacey that night. The air was cool. The leaves of the aspens were still. Moonlight intensified the contrast between the slate-blue of the sage and the buff and mottled dun of grass clumps in between. The flood of silver submerged the bad lands across the Yellowstone and silvered strata of white, so that crags stood out in darker relief and tones of the spectrum were blended.

There was something incomparable and unforgettable about the lower Yellowstone moonlight; a quality of timelessness; night life enveloped in silence which was broken only by the whine of the coyote that started on earth and ascended, a thin geyser of sound. When the voice of the prowler reached its apex, it broke into clusters of barking, never loud, but diversified. Then moonlit silence. Much was taking place, nocturnally, on that seemingly deserted plain. The curlews were asleep and the meadow larks were nesting on the ground. Jack rabbits were in their burrows, gophers in their holes which they shared with owls and bull-snakes. The rattlers rested on flat warm stones, until the night air cooled them, and they found the sand and clay more hospitable.

On the slopes and in the coulees the cattle—steers, cows and calves—were browsing or dozing. Forgotten were the hail

6 4

stones that had pelted them and raised welts which they switched with their tails. Gone was the rain, and almost gone the fragrant smell of rain and the odors it stirs in the old Montana sod, the sage; the mulch; the clay; the lingering stench of a creature that has died; the heavy, smoky tang where a fire has been; wild roses amid the rocks, wide open at night; larkspur, wort, and the mildly pungent loco weed. Owls and night hawks with muffled wings flew low. Buzzards roosted on dead trees that had been struck by lightning. No dinosaurs, but only their bones in the hidden ledges. No buffalo, but only their wallows and bleached skulls. No Arickarees, no Crows, no Sioux, but only a few Blackfoot, the last to surrender, camped a few miles below Sidney, to drive slips on the government ditch. At Fort Peck, one hundred miles north, beyond the foothills, a few Gros Ventres.

Deer in the thickets by the river? Yes. A few. Antelopes in the draws and depressions? Quite a number. Mountain sheep and cougars in the bad lands? Naturally. Wolves? Busy. Coyotes? Plenty. Toads? Cold as the air. Frogs? Croaking and piping at the waterholes. Grouse, prairie chickens, sage hens, cedarbirds, woodpeckers, finches and doves? Present, but neither seen nor heard. Night, like a river, is deeper when more narrowly confined between the banks of dusk and dawn. Over all, the prodigal moonlight.

In eastern Montana, then, the sparse human life had not disassociated itself from the plants and animals, birds and reptiles, calms, storms and seasons. Man and nature were coexistent and interdependent, heterogeneous, unified.

The men and women who had been spilled from the stagecoach that day were scattered now, singly, in pairs and in groups. White Stella, with her arm in a sling, Matt and Old Knick were in Big Emma's hookshop at Mondak, and with four or five other revelers were singing, off-key, a topical song

of which anybody was welcome to improvise a verse if he or
she were able. The chorus, in *drei-viertel* time, went like this:

> *They* say *that us* Mormon *boys* ain't *got no* style,
> *But* style *all the* while,
> Style *all the* while.
> *They* say *that us* Mormon *boys* ain't *got no* style,
> *But* style *all the* while,
> *All the* while.

Matt, when his turn came, rose to the occasion. He felt,
then, full of food and whisky, like a very lucky man.

> (*Solo*)   *They say that us stage drivers ain't got no style,*
> (*In ragged*   *Style all the while,*
> *unison*)   *Style all the while.*

> (*Solo*)   *Give us* red-*eye and* beer *an' our* bel*lies do* bile,
> (*In more*   *Style all the while,*
> *ragged*   *All the while.*
> *unison*)

Stella, in her shrill soprano, gave out:

>   *Who sez that us sportin' girls ain't got no style?*
> (*Solo*)   *But style all the while,*
> (*Whisky*   *Style all the while.*
> *chorus*)   *If our left arm gets busted, we're decent a while,*
> (*Solo*)   *Style all the while*
> (*Chorus*)   *All t-h-e w-h-iiiii-le.*

In her stall in Ball's barn at Sidney, little Crocus dozed
fitfully, and between times meditated on a banner day's mischief and chewed on the boards of her feed-box.

The Mormon carpenter (Nephi Pratt) was in a tent with
matched board walls at Lzicar's camp, on the ditch. He was
groaning and killing bedbugs with a tack hammer, intending to sue the Bendon Transportation Company on account

of his ankle, and to send ten percent of the proceeds to the church in Salt Lake.

Scotty and I were at Mrs. Baron's, in Sydney, eating oysters baked on the half shell, with a rasher of bacon and garnished with chopped green onion tops. Mr. and Mrs. Baron, Zoe, the regular telephone operator from Mondak who was on vacation, Charley Tufts, an inspector on the ditch who had been an assistant professor at Yale, Doc Morrill, and Annie Rongfto, waitress at Mrs. Ball's Valley Hotel, were present. After supper, Mrs. Baron, who had studied elocution in Milwaukee, read a few selections from the N.P. pamphlet on the lower Yellowstone, as we sat in a half-circle before a small open fire.

"For purity of air and salubrity the country is not surpassed anywhere in the United States. Malarial and kindred diseases are wholly unknown, or if brought into the country by some unfortunate victim of swamps and fever-breeding districts vanish almost at once. The pure air and absence of dampness and fogs bring relief. . ."

There she hesitated because her husband was suffering from consumption and she was extraordinarily fond of him. For the printed words "relief to weak and diseased lungs" she substituted "relief to weak characters from temptation."

At the moment, although he was unaware of it, Scotty was developing a case of typhoid fever, which laid up three out of four of our surveying party that summer. I chanced to be the lucky fourth, and also escaped the epidemic of smallpox that struck the following winter.

Doc Morrill called our attention to an advertisement in the *Glendive Independent:*

"Don't pay alimony to be divorced from your appendix. There will be no occasion for it if you keep your bowels regular with Dr. DeWitt's Early Risers."

A Ghost Town on the Yellowstone

The two Orientals were sleeping in Johnny O'Brien's stable loft at Newlon, and since it is so hard to know what one Chinese is thinking about when he is awake, no one would attempt to guess what two of them were dreaming about when asleep.

Tall Letty Gregory was lying catty-cornered across a short bed in the Yellowstone Hotel in Mondak, while, downstairs in the back room, her father and Bat Horner were engaged in a game of solo. Men from Tokna did not ride all the way to a railroad town to waste the hours in sleep. They could snooze most of the winter, at home.

Dawn came early in June. Bert Lacey got up, put his pants and boots back on, and went to the coulee to wash. There was enough water for that, although it was muddy and slightly alkaline. He tried to drink it, but it was no go. He saw Mexican Joe, on his sorrel, loping down the road from Newlon, leading a pair of extra saddle horses. One was a big rangy gray. The other was a mule, whose ears flopped rhythmically.

With difficulty, Bert and the Mexican woke up Johnny Highpockets, who sat up, rubbed his eyes, and slowly remembered where he was and what had happened. Johnny put on his pants and boots and, without bothering to wash, got aboard the mule. Bert mounted the gray, which sensed at once that he had never been on a horse before and started off at a brisk trot, its roughest gait. Bert grabbed the saddle horn and tried to ease the bumping, managing to keep hold of the lines at the same time. The sorrel, never willing to let another horse get ahead of it, lit out on the dead run and Mexican Joe, in morning exuberance, grabbed off his broad-brimmed hat and slapped the sorrel's sides with it. While the sorrel raced into the lead, the gray broke into a gallop, which, although it was perilously swift for Bert, was easier on his legs and privates. Johnny's mule paid no attention, but moved along in a steady single-foot gait that, in the course of a day, could eat up many miles.

At Simard's ranch they all had breakfast of ham and eggs (about six each), bread, butter, fried-over potatoes and canned beans, with dried apple pie for dessert, and mugs of coffee with canned milk and sugar. French Joe, two of his brothers, Alf and Treff, and a couple of ranch hands joined the group. The conversation centered around Highpockets, much to the latter's embarrassment. Before the meal had got fairly started, Johnny O'Brien and Charley Tufts came in. Tufts, although he had an inspector's job with the government, intended to stay in the country and go into the sheep business. "The Professor," as he was called, to his chagrin, spent as much of his time as he could, early in the morning and after work at night, with the ranchers and old-timers, more eager to learn what they had to teach him than any of his former pupils had been to absorb Latin, Greek, philosophy or the history of religion at Yale.

Somebody had left uncalled-for in the Newlon postoffice several numbers of a monthly periodical printed in Chicago and entitled *Heart and Hand*. The format was not unlike that of the Monkey Ward catalogue, except in thickness, and Johnny O'Brien had inter-leafed the pages from *Heart and Hand* into the mail-order catalogue known familiarly as "The Sheepherder's Bible."

"Highpockets," O'Brien began, "I understand you're fixin' to do some dry farming around here."

"I'm going to work for Mr. Lacey, while I prove up on a claim," Highpockets said, as much to get himself accustomed to his change of plan as to enlighten the old-timer.

"But later on, you're goin' to raise grain?" O'Brien asked.

"Oats and wheat," Highpockets said.

"No alfalfa?" O'Brien asked.

"They say that needs irrigation," said Highpockets, regretfully.

O'Brien snorted indignantly.

"Them easterners," he said, "with the assurance bred o' profound ig'orance, and the presumption which is ever ready to assert without knowledge, decry the Yellowstone country—claim it's a arid region, where rain never falls and snow is scarcely ever melted."

Highpockets, always confused by long words, or too many words of any length, frowned and tried to catch up with the flow of O'Brien's eloquence.

"Did yesterday's hail cut down the crops?" Highpockets asked.

"To some extent. Not more than forty percent. But that storm was meant for Dakota," said O'Brien. "We never have hail around here, unless it hits us by mistake. The warm current from Japan, which causes Oregon and Washington to be drenched, prevents hail and blizzards from entering the Yellowstone. Yesterday, it must 'a got diverted by a passel o' seals. That won't happen again. Will it, boys?"

The boys shook their heads sagely, in the negative.

"Irrespective of the weather," O'Brien said, "a man can't do dry farming alone. Both easterners and westerners agree on that."

"You mean I'll have to hire help?" asked Highpockets. "I only aim to farm a hundred and sixty acres."

"I didn't say nothin' about hirin' help. You can get what help you need for nothin', and have company besides," said O'Brien. "All you have to do is get married."

"I don't know no women around here. They're scarce, and all spoke for," Highpockets said.

"Heck! These women around here ain't no good," said O'Brien. "They're just a bunch of goldbricks. They educate their feet and their behinds and let their heads go to hell. If you stick a pin in 'em, they don't even say 'ouch.' "

He appealed to the "boys" again, and they all nodded gravely, meanwhile destroying fantastic quantities of eggs, meat, potatoes and bread, washed down with coffee and "canned cow."

"The women I knew back in Iowa didn't like me worth a darn," admitted Highpockets. "I don't talk much, always was broke, and can't dance."

"So much the better. When a feller dances, he sweats, an' when he sweats he stinks," said O'Brien.

"I sweat somethin' fierce," said Highpockets, ruefully.

"Eat some rock salt on a hot day. That helps," said French Joe. "That is, if it don't turn your stomach."

"Old Knick tells me that if a man chews sagebrush, it cools him off, inside," suggested Charley Tufts.

"That's what the damn-fool Sioux used to do," O'Brien said, and added, grudgingly: "It works, too."

Tufts nodded. He was avid for Indian lore and wisdom. He was a tall, lean, thoughtful man, with humorous gray eyes which blinked behind rimmed spectacles, a high forehead and lantern jaw that wagged sideways when he chewed. His hands were long, his wrists knobby. He held his elbows wide, like those of a trap drummer. One of the least competent of the division engineers, under whom Tufts had worked for a time, had picked up, on a trip back east, an item from Tufts' past career and had taken delight in retailing it throughout the valley. Until then, no one had known that Tufts had taught dead languages and philosophy in an eastern college.

It seemed that Professor Tufts had been well liked by faculty and students, although he had had no close friends. One day, after years of teaching subjects no younger men

71

seemed to care about, Tufts had excused himself from the classroom, in the midst of an inept recitation by a football star, and no one at Yale, until Engineer Bromfield strayed into New Haven from Montana, had heard from Tufts again. He had shown up at Glendive in 1905, when the reclamation work was just starting, had asked for a job, and been taken on as a rodman, which required no civil service rating. When the first civil-service examination for inspectors of earthwork and concrete was held, Tufts had passed with practically one hundred per cent, was placed at the head of the list, and soon was assigned as concrete inspector on the canal, under Fritz Bromfield. Because Tufts knew so much more about everything but women than his superior did, the latter soon asked that Charley be transferred. Charley went to work farther down the valley, under Engineer Hays, from Maine, who was not the jealous type and liked having a first-class intelligence around.

What happened to Tufts between his exit from the classroom at Yale and his appearance in Glendive, he never mentioned. But he was neither frustrated nor unhappy. He knew what he wanted—namely, a sheep ranch—and was on the way toward getting it. Of all the men who were in the valley when I was, Tufts had the most profound grasp of its history, its wonders and its significance, and this knowledge he improved every hour of every day. For me, his presence and his willingness to accept me turned out to be a remarkable piece of good fortune. He implanted in me an awareness of the past, as well as of the continuous present; of civilizations that had risen, declined and passed away, and the heritage they had left for those who were receptive. To find Charley Tufts and Johnny Highpockets in the same neighborhood offered a striking illustration of the wide possible variations in mental capacity. Of the two, the dunce and the sage, it was hard to say which was the more kindly, worthy or accommodating.

Tufts was going into the wool business and Highpockets was to be a "scientific agriculturalist" (as Jim Hill of the Great Northern insisted on describing dry farmers, under protest from many distinguished scientists). O'Brien at the breakfast table at Simards' that morning included them both in his harangue in favor of matrimony.

"Listen here," O'Brien said, opening what appeared from the outside to be the current Monkey Ward catalogue. He turned the leaves, mumbling, "Em. Marriage department. . . . Here it is," he said, at last. "Wives for westerners . . . sheepmen, farmers. . . . Dry farmers. Here's a whole page of dry farmer's specials, at $32.15. That's the fare from Chicago."

Highpockets, as O'Brien had guessed correctly, could not read, but only sign his name. The scissorbill, amazed, gaped over O'Brien's shoulder as the latter continued:

"Edna B., blue eyes, brown hair, light complexion, age twenty-five. Hear what Edna writes:

"'I was raised on a farm, love flowers and forget-me-not embroidery. Am affectionate, never quarrel, can cook, bake and do light housekeeping. I never went to a doctor in my life, only two or three times to be vaccinated, which was required in order to stay in school.

"'Would like to exchange letters and pictures with some man about forty who is serious and patriotic, object matrimony. If he drinks, please state extent. I like the smell of tobacco, and sashay, and wear becoming clothes.

"'Travel no obstacle if fare is paid. Young men under twenty-five need not apply, as they are fresh and selfish, and know nothing about what a girl's heart is.'"

Highpockets' eyes were bulging. He was smacking his lips. "I like the sound o' that one," he said. "Edna B. She's for me."

"Fine," O'Brien said, and all the boys nodded approval. "Now let's see what the Professor draws. . . . Mmmmm." He turned a page of the concealed *Heart and Hand*. "Wives for . . . pee . . . plumbers, prospectors . . . professors. Wives for professors. Here's one named Lossie. Lossie Schermerhorn. I'll read what it says:

> " 'I am small but "Oh, you kid!" Love clothes and shopping but am not extravagant or loud. The man I marry must know a lot and be masterful, as I have not had much education in school and am inclined to be willful if a man lets me get away with it. Then I lose respect for him and cease to be true. By that, I mean nothing wrong. Only going out with other men to see if I can respect them more than those who give in when I get mad.
>
> " 'I can work but prefer to save my strength and looks for my husband. Of course, cooking meals for two, sweeping, dusting, etc., are not really work but only pleasure if two people are in love with each other.
>
> " 'I will send a picture but do not take very good pictures, being a brunette. I weigh 100 pounds avoirdupois, with dark-brown eyes and need no corsets.
>
> " 'I like men who laugh once in a while and don't squeeze money till the eagle screams. We only live once. Yes, no?' "

Highpockets, now quite eager and excited, said promptly: "Me, I like the first one better."

"Fine," said O'Brien. "We'll write 'er and she's yourn."

"I got to build me a cabin first," Highpockets protested.

"Nonsense! The correspondence and all may take time. We'll get a letter off to Monkey Ward on the upstage today. Got a picture on you?"

Highpockets shook his head, but that did not stop O'Brien. Treff Simard sketched remarkably well, so the old-timer induced him to make a drawing of the bewildered scissor-

74

bill. Treff got a piece of notepaper and a pencil and in a few minutes had a sketch of Highpockets that was good, if slightly flattering. Seeing that in the sketch he was wearing a necktie, Highpockets quickly felt his throat, and frowned, again.

"I'll have to git me a tie that's all tied, and hooks in the back," he said.

"How about it, Professor? Will you write a letter for Highpockets?" O'Brien asked Tufts.

Charley grinned and his eyes gleamed.

"Tell her to hold her hosses till I get enough pay from Bert, here, for a one-way ticket from Chicago," Highpockets said. "And that cabin oughtta be built."

"Not at all," said Alf Simard, expansively. "Edna can sleep here, till you're ready to carry her over the sill."

"Not on your tintype," O'Brien said. "Nobody knows how many there are of you Simard boys, and one's worse with the women than the other. . . . Only Joe. He's crazy about his fiddle, and a damn sight better off."

"I'll lend Johnny a tent, soon's I get enough lumber to put up a few solid buildings," Bert Lacey said.

"Ain't them buildings up yet?" demanded Old Johnny, crustily.

Bert was in a hurry to get to work on his new town, but had to wait while Charley Tufts wrote a letter to be mailed that afternoon. It was addressed to Edna B., care of *Heart and Hand,* but Johnny Highpockets believed it was going to Monkey Ward, and drew out his signature.

The body of the letter read as follows:

"I, John P. Highpockets, the undersigned, am a hard-working scientific farmer located just outside the growing town of Trembles, Montana, on the Lower Yellowstone.

"I have read your letter, Edna, and assure you that, while I am only twenty-eight at present, I am not unmindful of the

7 5

yearnings a girl's heart develops if she is not otherwise occupied.

"Instead of a photograph, which looks distant and cold, I am sending a sketch of myself by the cowboy artist of the valley, Treff Simard.

"When you send your picture, please have it taken with a hat on, and, if possible, send me a pair of your old shoes, well-worn, as I have a friend, a Professor, who is an expert in scarpology.

"For references, I can give you the Hon. John O'Brien, postmaster of Newlon, Montana, and Bert Lacey, Esq., who may be addressed also at Newlon.

> " 'My love bird, loosed in eastern skies
> I prithee hasten west
> Let nothing earthly slow your flight
> To our scientific nest.'
> Sincerely,
> (Signed)   John P. Highpockets."

After Highpockets had signed the letter, Tufts read it to him. A troubled look passed over the scissorbill's honest face.

"You didn't say nothin' about drinking," he said.

"Ah, no," said the Professor. " 'If he drinks, please state extent.' That's what Edna asked."

Up to this moment, Charley Tufts, who would hurt nobody's feelings, had thought the whole thing was a harmless joke, but he saw, as he looked more closely at Highpockets, that, although no one else in the room was taking the matter seriously, the scissorbill was pathetically in earnest. He reread the letter, decided that it could do no harm, and, taking up the pen again, affixed the following:

"P.S. I drink some, but less than the average per capita in Dawson County."

Then, on his own, the Professor added, in order not to lure a well-meaning young woman to the valley under false pretenses:

"I have practically no money at present, but good health, good habits and industry are capital enough for any young man to start with in this country."

The phrase about the health, habits and industry Charley had cribbed from the N.P. pamphlet he had heard Mrs. Baron read the evening before.

CHAPTER SEVEN

A Day on Which No Notes Were Made

WHEN the surveying party of four members, consisting
of Frank Banks, chief of party; Scotty McVeigh, instrument
man; Elliot Paul, rodman; and Lem, for Lemeniah Gabel,
teamster and stake artist, had to disband temporarily because
all the members except me went down with typhoid, I was
given a job as "cost-keeper" up on Division Two, between La
Mesa and a point upstream from Beef Slough. I was quartered
temporarily in the government camp at La Mesa, and, since
I had to cover between twenty and thirty miles along the
ditch, on horseback, each day, I was assigned two four-footed
animals, both of which were listed on the government books
as "horses, saddle." These were selected by Ed Wilson, the
La Mesa stable boss, of whom I was to see a great deal in the
course of the ensuing years, on that and other construction
jobs.

Ed Wilson was a man who seemed to me to have schooled
himself to be mean, and I never was convinced that he was not
playing a part. With only two exceptions, everyone in the
valley disliked Ed, and he gave them all sufficient reason.
Charley Tufts and I both had a sneaking suspicion that, at
bottom, Ed was not mean and stingy, but soft and rather wistful. His eyes were blue—there was a distinct preponderance
in that country, then, of blue-eyed people—his cheekbones
were high, like an Indian's. His habit of grinding his teeth

together, as he chewed tobacco or snuff, had developed his face muscles abnormally. There were lines of worry in his forehead and crow's feet around his eyes, but the worry was not on his own account. He was well paid and, according to Johnny O'Brien, had every dollar that ever had been handed to him cached in tobacco sacks and tin cans in the hay. Ed seemed to worry about the U. S. Treasury most of all, as did many of the high-ranking civil engineers who were quite naïve about public affairs. Ed would gouge the last two bits out of a settler, a bum or a ranch hand for any little thing they had to buy at the La Mesa stable, and it required prac- tically an Act of Congress to persuade him to lend a horse to any young man who wanted to ride a few miles in order to call on a girl. In all these minor economies he had the back- ing and encouragement of the project engineer, Frank E. Weymouth of Maine, and, I must add in all honesty, of the construction engineer, second in rank, my older brother Charles.

In selecting two saddle horses for me to ride along the ditch, Ed Wilson had to take into account a number of con- siderations. He knew that I was a brother of the construction engineer, and that Charles would resent any favoritism to- ward me on that account. Also Ed liked me as much, or disliked me rather less, than he did most of the engineering crew. Ed never prayed or wrestled with demons or angels, but he thought laboriously about something all the time he was awake. His own interests came first, those of the distant and amorphous "government" seemed to be second. There was room for almost no more.

"I got a fine little pinto mare I just bought down the valley, and a nice bay gelding named Jim," he said to me at break- fast, the morning I was to start out. "Now Jim's got one bad habit. He'll go along all right, most all the time, but when

7 9

he sees a tumbleweed or a shadow, or hears a snake or a piece o' paper blowin', he jumps sidewise."

Already he had left more than one rider sitting down in the dust and the cactus, but having done so, Jim would not run away. He would stand still until the rider was ready to re-mount.

"I'll watch him," I said, sincerely. Fortunately, my reflexes were swift and sure.

Ed did not mention the name of the pinto mare, but when he showed her to me, and cautioned me to speak kindly to her and be extra careful when I went into her stall, I asked:

"Wasn't that mare one of the stage horses?"

"Yes," said Wilson, brightening. "She's smart. She's harness broke, too."

"Come, Crocus, you crummy little bastard. Get over, little sweetheart," I said to the mare, and she stepped obediently to the right side of her stall. I noticed that Crocus was one of the few inmates of the La Mesa stable who had a stall all to herself.

"You know her?" Wilson asked, surprised.

"We've met before," I said.

"Maybe you'd like to ride Jim the first day out," said Wilson, relenting. If I got killed, there might be a comeback on him.

I knew that his suggestion about Jim, who had only one bad habit, was a challenge, and was determined not to weaken. If I didn't ride Crocus that day, I would have to take her out the next day, after she had had twenty-four hours more to think and plan in her stall, eating hay and oats the while.

"I'll take Crocus," I said.

I unhitched the halter rope, took off the halter, and slipped the bridle over her ears. I did not put the bit in her mouth, because I wanted to water her before we started out. I led her to the trough in the corral yard and let her drink, then coaxed her to take the bit. She resisted playfully a while, then let me adjust the bridle.

"Dear little old woman from hell," I murmured, cajolingly.

Ed was watching from the corner of his eye, pretending to be otherwise occupied. Crocus stood still when I put on the blanket and lifted the saddle on her back, but before I could pull up the cinch, she had taken a deep breath and swelled several inches. I waited until she had to exhale, then tightened up the cinch and fastened the buckle. I took both lines in my left hand, turned the left stirrup, grasped the saddle horn with my right hand, and swung my leg over. Luckily I caught the right stirrup. She turned her head around, to look at me with her pale blue eye. I nudged her with both knees, oh, very gently, and we started away. Ed Wilson, astonished, opened the corral gate and we passed through. To strike the section of ditch on the downstream end of Division Two, I hit out across the sagebrush flat straight east. At that point, the camp was four or five miles above the canal.

Since Crocus was to take me fifteen miles up the ditch, and the same distance back, I started her out on a walk, to let her warm up slowly. It was seven-thirty in the morning and the whistle blew in the contractors' camps at eight o'clock. A jack rabbit hopped out from a clump of sagebrush almost under Crocus's feet. She stiffened, and snorted, and jumped a little, playfully. Nothing more.

"This is going too well," I said to myself. "She doesn't want to throw me so close to the camp."

The sun was strong, but the ground had not yet absorbed its heat. After walking her a couple of miles, I nudged her and she started single-footing smoothly. For any horse, that is the ideal gait if he or she is sure-footed enough and does not trip. I had pencils and a notebook in the pockets of my flannel shirt, and tied to the back of the saddle, in the pocket of my slicker, the government instructions and regulations about cost-keeping.

The first sub-contractor I visited that morning I shall call B. F. Shoat, because men as meek and unlucky as he was live to be a hundred, and still may be struggling against fate. No one ever called him by his first name, or initials. He was always B. F. Shoat. He had watery gray eyes, most likely from wearing an old short-brimmed felt hat in a country where everybody, to save his eyes, wore a broad brim or a visor. One arm was shorter than the other, and slightly lame. It was said all through the valley, and in Glendive, that B. F. Shoat was so hard up that he fed his men one day and his horses the next, and with that reputation, when labor was scarce and the demand was high and varied, drifters picked up in Glendive by the agents of the various contractors went first to the camps where the grub was not so vile and the horses not so discouraged.

B. F. Shoat had contracted with Donaldson and Company, earthwork contractor in Divisions One and Two, to dig a short section of the ditch opposite La Mesa at a lower figure than Donaldson was getting from the government. Shoat was under bond to Donaldson, who, in turn, had given surety to the United States that the work would be performed according to specifications.

Everything happened to B. F. Shoat, except good luck. When I reached the rim of the sidehill cut on which Shoat's fresnoes were just starting work, about fifteen minutes late, as always, I hesitated, not knowing just what Crocus, who had behaved like a multi-colored drab angel all the way across the flat, would do. The descent was steep. The slope was of slippery clay on top and sandy near the bottom. I saw B. F.

Shoat, whom I had never met, standing indecisively in the bottom of what was to be the canal when it was finished.

Crocus, sensing that I wanted to get down to where he was, stepped cautiously on the clay, sat down on her haunches and slid until we reached the sand, then somehow got on all fours again, her front legs stiff, her hind legs jack-knifed forward. In gaining the bottom, a few feet from B. F. Shoat, we dislodged a few cubic yards of sand that sifted down. As I dismounted, to introduce myself, Crocus jumped four feet to one side, snorting, eyes bulging. She was looking at the sand we had brought down with us, as was B. F. Shoat. I saw that it was alive with insects shaped like one of the signs of the zodiac, about an inch long and almost transparent.

"Now ain't that funny. I never seen none of them before," said B. F. Shoat, reaching down to pick up one of the insects and examine it. The insect flipped its wicked little tail over and stung him on the palm of his hand. He dropped it, blinded with pain, and turned pale. It was a scorpion.

Now no one, before or since, had ever encountered scorpions, as far as I can ascertain, within hundreds of miles of the Lower Yellowstone. They belong in hot southern countries.

I saw that B. F. Shoat was really sick, and helped him to his tent, where he slept, kept soiled, dog-eared books, a few tins of Copenhagen snuff, sacks of Durham, work gloves, and other inexpensive articles he re-sold to his men at cost. He was his own timekeeper, not being able to afford another.

His hand had swelled, his breath was coming short, his eyes were glazed. I yelled for his stable boss, a dull, unresourceful man named Horigan, who had been fired by Donaldson because a horse had kicked him in the shoulder and broken his collarbone.

I was no naturalist, or doctor, either. I was not sure, but

something told me that the insect that had bitten Shoat was a scorpion. I tried to remember whether scorpion bites were fatal or how serious they were, and to guess what could be done to relieve a man who had been bitten. Shoat was then on the verge of collapse, as much from uncertainty as from pain. Either one would have been enough to disable me. My head roaring and heart pounding, I took out my jack-knife, sterilized the point of the sharpest blade in the flame of a match, got Horigan to help hold Shoat's arm steady—of course, it was his good arm—and made an incision, above and below the bite. The patient bled like a stuck pig, so then I put on a tourniquet, made from a bandanna and the closed jack-knife.

There was no medicine in Shoat's camp except horse liniment and salve. I never thought faster. Rattlesnake poison, I had been told, was slightly acid. Perhaps scorpion virus resembled it. What could I find around that barren camp that was alkaline? Cement had lime in it, I thought. By that time, half the men in camp, who should have been working, had gathered around, but nobody had any suggestions. I sent for a handful of cement, and stuck it into the cuts I had made, in powdered form. Then I asked the cook to bring me some baking soda and made a supersaturated solution of that for Shoat to drink, a glass every half-hour. The foreman helped me get Shoat onto his bunk, and in a short time, the pain eased up a little, and I took off the tourniquet slowly. The nearest doctor was in Glendive, thirty miles away, and the nearest phone in Donaldson's camp, ten miles away. So, instead of digging up misleading figures for the boys in Washington that morning, I spent the hours sitting on an empty dynamite box at the side of Shoat's bunk, administering black coffee and soda water, by turns. At noon he sat up, weakly.

His hand and arm were swollen, sore and painful to the touch, but both of us were sure he was going to live.

He thanked me feebly as I rode away, along the line where the stakes indicated the canal was to be, in the hope of making Prentice's camp for the noon meal. My new note-book was still empty.

Noel Prentice, also a sub-contractor under Donaldson, but an agreeable and relatively prosperous one, was a good host and a fine fellow. He was small and alert, with dark hair well-combed and plastered down with vaseline. His cook put out the best grub along the ditch and even had screens on his kitchen tent, although the mess tent was too big and rangy to be protected from the flies. Other cooks, including Shoat's and Donaldson's, put currants in the cake and bread they made during fly-time, in order that the inevitable black specks might not disconcert the 'boes and the Bohunks. That the presence of flies in all the cooking, coupled with the commodious open latrines, had much to do with the preva-lence of typhoid in the valley that summer is more than likely. Those are matters one does not like to dwell upon while exposed, perforce, to such conditions, but only long afterward, in some spot where sanitation is ideal. I did notice, however, that nobody, including the most rigorous and strict of the engineers, made a move to do anything about sanita-tion, except in the engineers' camps. On what theory it was considered that the health of laborers at $2.00 a day, and scarce, is less valuable to a community or a government than those of rodmen and cost-keepers at $60 a month, engineers at $2,400 a year, or Secretaries of the Interior, at $15,000 a year, I never ascertained, but I thought a lot about it. I am still thinking about it, and the answers are disturbing, now as then.

In that season, typhoid was hitting the camps pretty hard.

Anne Prentice, Noel's daughter, risked it. She was dainty, coquettish, pardonably vain, spoiled, unusually particular about her clothes. Her skin was pale, her voice low and seductive. She made no pretensions to learning or abstract culture. That is precisely the type of girl who can spend a summer in a typhoid-ridden camp, among the roughest and crudest of men, have a good time each day and improve her health while others are dying. Anne would rather suffer from cactus spines than change her dainty slippers for boots, although she wore well-polished riding boots while on a horse.

One of the differences between Noel Prentice and Chet Donaldson, superintendent of Donaldson's camp and son of C. L. Donaldson, came out when one of the men working for them got typhoid. Donaldson would fire the sick man, roust him out of the bunkhouse, with violence if possible, and start him walking toward Glendive, up the thirty-mile dusty stage road. A contractor, Donaldson figured, could not afford to let sick men take up bunks that should be filled with men who could work, and no contractor could be expected to feed or house a man after he had been fired. Noel Prentice did not go so far as to believe that he was under obligation to feed, house or care for a bum who had contracted typhoid while in his employ, but he let the sick men hang around until there were enough of them to fill a wagon, and then provided the team, wagon and driver at his own expense to take them as far as Glendive, just east of the bridge.

The Glendive officials, particularly Chet Busby, the county sheriff, grumbled and swore because so many men with typhoid and little else were being dumped there. The county pest-house was full. There was little room in the jail. Even a relatively kind-hearted man like Chief of Police Kinney saw no other alternative than to round up the sick and dying hoboes and Bohunks and chase them out of town, if they could ride the bumpers or walk.

I was hurt, shocked and angry, to the point where my well-wishers felt obliged to keep urging me to take it easy, and reminding me that a kid just out of an eastern high school had a hell of a lot to learn. The best of men, most of them, pointed out that nature was cruel, that grasses fought and struggled on the lawn, that fishes swallowed other fishes, that when the boss elk of a herd got beyond a certain point, a younger one gored and kicked him out of the bunch he had ruled, that frogs dry up and shrivel when the water holes go dry, that wolves eat calves in winter, that spiders trap flies in summer, that shooting stars, once dim, do not light up again. How all this checked up with men being free and equal—all men, mind you—and each of them being entitled to life, liberty and the pursuit of happiness, I could not figure out.

When I got to Prentice's camp that day, I found Noel Prentice in his well-stocked commissary, where on the shelves were ranged snuff, cigars and tobacco, pipes, a few tailor-made cigarettes for the luxury trade, stout boots, raw-hide laces, blankets, corduroy coats, pants and caps, overalls, gloves, playing cards, candy, nearly everything a man needed in camp. Throughout the Prentice camp, the contrast with B. F. Shoat's layout was equally striking. The mess-tent was large and white, the can was concealed by a high board fence, the stables were neat and clean, the stock well-fed and glossy.

Prentice, his superintendent, time-keeper, chief mechanic and his daughter, Anne, ate in a smaller tent the other side of the kitchen from the mess-tent, and I was asked to join them. I had met Anne and enjoyed her company at several of the dances, to which she had been escorted in each instance by a different young man. I liked her immediately because she reacted so surely toward music. In the small mess-tent, the table was covered with oilcloth, the dishes were of a better grade of tin, and the table talk was of a more restrained order than that of the main mess-tent, in which the men, stampeding into the place as soon as the flunky started banging the iron triangle, grabbed first for their tin saucers, slapped a piece of pie on them, and dumped a helping of pudding on top of the pie, before they started yelling for the rough stuff.

The cattlemen of the valley and the foothills, whenever a critter looked ailing, slaughtered it and sold it to the contractors for beef or lamb, even though it might be horse, contraband elk, or a decrepit old sheep which had been gnawed in part by coyotes. There were no inspections, no regulations, no holds barred. The government purchasing agents could be a bit more fussy, so the ranchers had to go to extra pains to hoodwink them.

That day, at Prentice's private table, we had a meat slum, with flour gravy and spuds, macaroni and cheese (known in the mess-tents as "roughlocks"), canned tomatoes stewed in water, canned-apricot pie, and, of course, the inevitable bitter coffee with sugar and canned cow. After the meal, Anne took me to her private tent, in the shade of a cottonwood and safely removed from the men's bunkhouses, to ask about a few moot points in the game of auction bridge, and serve me iced lemonade. I had dried, watered and fed Crocus myself, and tied her in a shady, quiet stall, having removed her bridle, saddle and blanket at the risk of never getting them on her again.

By the time I had told Anne what I knew about auction bidding and play, it was so far along in the afternoon that I had just time to ride fast to Donaldson's camp, and back to La Mesa along the stage road. I was in no particular hurry to get back to camp on account of the supper served in the La

Mesa mess-house. I could do better than that by staying where
I was, at the Prentice camp, and afterward enjoying a game
of cards. But Scotty McVeigh was burning up with typhoid
in the smaller of the two bunkhouses at La Mesa and I was
his unofficial nurse. All I could do was bring him broth and
feed it to him with a spoon, bathe him as best I could, and sit
on him when he got too active in his delirium. He was un-
believably patient and unexigent, suffering stoically while he
was himself, and struggling against fate like an unmusical
Beethoven when the fever crazed his brain. Doc Morrill
from Sidney came up to see Scotty and the other patients on
Division Two about twice a week, and left instructions and
medicine. On Saturday evenings, when I had to be down-
valley to play for the dance at Trembles, Old Knick rallied
round, and took care of Scotty and Banks. Lem, the teamster,
had been removed to his brother's ranch on Deer Creek.

I lit out on Crocus from the Prentice camp up the canal to
Donaldson's Camp No. 1. I dreaded this call, because of all
the men I had met out west I disliked Chet Donaldson most.
There was no direct reason. He was nearly twice my age. We
had exchanged less than fifty words. But his eyes had a sullen,
bestial light, his mouth drooped at the corners in a way that
indicated inherent cruelty and lust for vengeance on the weak
because he had, somehow, been slighted or his insatiable ego
had been undernourished.

When I approached the section of the ditch on which
Donaldson's earthwork gang was working, Chet, his Stetson
tipped far down on one side of his handsome red head, was
standing, arms akimbo, near an orange-peel bucket that was
puffing, whirling, rising high toward the boom, then descending open, clawing and holding the dirt, clamping tight, then
wheeling toward the fill and dumping it there. Crocus began
to stiffen and tremble. There was no reason she should not.

89

She had never been close to anything like that before, and, to be honest, the way the thing snorted, reared, plunked down, up again, and whirled away, with escaping snorts of steam, whirring of the hoist drum and cable, and shouts of the signal man, my own nerves were tingling. My imagination has always been lively enough to react to the terrific in-computable forces displayed by powerful machines, which tear into earth and rock, toss heavy loads around like ping-pong balls, and root like prehistoric monsters.

"Easy there, old girl," I said, and relaxed the pressure of my knees.

Crocus stopped, and was about to turn tail, but I kept her head facing the hoist. I dismounted, stroked her neck, and led her around toward the corral, giving the orange-peel and its crew a wide berth. Having hitched her in a shady place, I walked over to where Chet was standing. He was facing me, arms still akimbo, his face distorted in a derisive grin that had no mirth in it.

"What's the matter? Lose your nerve?" he asked.

"The horse was scared," I said.

"Horse, hell! You're still white around the gills yourself," he said. "If you need any underdrawers, we got 'em in the commissary."

I don't know what got into me. Just the sight of Chet made me mad, and when he talked it was worse.

"Like to ride her yourself?" I asked, my voice thin and pitched too high.

"If it's worth while," he said. The crew and some of the skinners had overheard and were listening, now.

I was nervous, all right, but somewhere in the back of my head something was functioning. I remembered how sweetly that mare had behaved all day, and it seemed to me that an outburst of her alter-ego was just about due. Chet Donaldson was a big heavy man, and Crocus was small. To him, it looked like a cinch.

"One hundred dollars says I can ride her up here and hold her here while the bucket is dumped twice," Chet said.

"Make it sixty," I said. I had only ten dollars on me, but that would not matter. Sixty was my month's pay.

"I'll get my spurs," he said.

I had seen his spurs in Glendive. They were long and sharp, of a type no one should be allowed to wear.

"Unh-unh," I said. "You don't ride my horse with those spurs of yours. Take mine."

"All right," he said. I took off my spurs, which were blunt and short. He fastened them on, and we walked, side by side, to the corral where Crocus was hitched. I stood back, well back, and Chet started to untie her. Crocus stood as quiet as a statue, so quiet that anyone less sure of himself than Chet would have been forewarned. He led her away from the corral fence a few steps, took both lines in his left hand, put his left foot in the stirrup and started to swing over. Crocus, quicker than a cat, hopped four feet away when Chet was in mid-air and when he came down, plunk on the ground, with, luckily, his left foot clear, she reared up on her hind legs and came down, front legs stiff. Had he not rolled away fast, she would have nailed him then and there.

A few yells and jeers from the crew caused the blood to suffuse Chet's already red face. He got up, lines still in his hand, his teeth clamped tight together.

"Want to call it off?" I asked.

"Not so's you'd notice it," he said.

"Let me hold her while you get on," I suggested.

That made him madder than ever.

Crocus was standing quietly again. The second time she let him get on, but before he could find the right stirrup, she

91

brushed his leg against the corral fence, nearly breaking his knee. He hit her over the head with the back of his quirt, not quite stunning her, but his left hand, still clutching the lines, was pulling leather frantically. She started away, in the direction opposite to the one in which he wanted to go, and when she got up speed, threw herself as neatly as Ty Cobb ever slid into a base.

That finished the performance. Both the stable boss and I sat on her head while Chet got his left leg out from under. She got up, shrugging philosophically and shaking her head. I led her back to the corral fence and tied her again.

Chet glowered, walked a few steps with a double limp, and said:

"Want to make it double or nothing that you can't ride her up there, yourself."

If Crocus had not been listening, I would not have dared take him up, but she turned her head and looked at me from the pale blue eye. I had a hunch, that was all. I thought she knew that she could do him more damage by showing him up, so I went over, unhitched her, and got on.

"While the bucket's dumped twice," he muttered.

I nodded and headed Crocus for the ditch. She scrambled up the fill and took me over almost under the bucket. The hoist whirred, the bucket spun aloft, poised itself, came down, plunk. Crocus flicked at a horsefly with her tail, paying no more attention than she would have to a passage from Scripture. We stayed there until the bucket was dumped, whirled back to the cut, lifted, dropped, filled and dumped again.

"All right, kid," Chet said, with the best grace he could, and counted out one hundred and twenty dollars in gold. It was the largest amount of money I had ever handled, on my own.

92

The whistle blew, on the steam shovel, farther along the ditch. Work was over for the day. I dismounted.

"Have a drink?" Chet said.

"Thanks," I said, and we walked down to his office, in a tarboard shack. I hitched Crocus outside. I knew that the end was not yet, that Chet Donaldson would never lose a grudge, but I had grown so fond of Crocus that nothing else mattered. I was trying to think what a man could do for a horse, and the things that came to my mind were pitifully few. But I made up my mind, then and there, to buy her, somehow.

Inside the shack, Chet poured out a very stiff drink of whisky, and as he handed it to me, said the most insulting thing he could think of, off-hand.

"You won't tell the big brother I got you drunk," he said.

"I'm not drunk," I said, and held my breath as I swallowed the fiery red-eye. To stop myself from gagging and heaving, I repeated to myself a verse Charley Tufts had read me.

> "Vice is a monster of so frightful mien,
> As to be hated needs but to be seen."

Chet's attention was diverted by the sight of his time-keeper, Tom Bone, who was approaching the shack next door, which was called the office, with five or six 'boes in tow who had come down the road from Glendive. Tom was taking their names. Chet, without further regard for me, sauntered out to look the new men over. I wiped my eyes, while his back was turned, then followed. Tom was talking with one of the men about to be listed on the payroll, a fellow about five feet six inches tall, with strong hands and broad shoulders, the sight of whom caused me to start in surprise.

"Fidlio G. Sharpe," the man said to Bone, and spelled out his first and last names. He was the fugitive who had sat next

to the late big Dane in the N.P. restaurant, a few weeks before, at which time he had been addressed as "Joe."

After Fidlio G. Sharpe had finished with the time-keeper,
he turned around to give the camp the once-over, in his self-
possessed way. In doing so, he caught sight of me, and his
eyes changed from blue to gray.

I pretended to pay no attention, and went over to unhitch
Crocus. Chet Donaldson was busy, bothering the time-keeper
and sizing up the other 'boes. Fidlio, his bedroll over his
shoulder, edged over to me.

"Have we met before, kid?" he asked, trying not to show
his nervousness.

I looked him in the eye and said evenly:

"Unh-*unh!* Not that I can remember."

He looked at me closely again and I smiled. "But you look
like a guy with good ideas . . . about diet, for instance," I
added, *sotto voce.*

Fidlio relaxed.

"Any of those other guys around, who might have seen me
before?" he asked.

I shook my head in the negative. "Scotty McVeigh, who
was with me, is sick with typhoid fever. Roby, the government warehouse man, is in Glendive. So's the priest. Nobody
around here's seen those three scissorbills," I said.

"What's your name? Mine's Sharpe," he said. He did not
offer to shake hands then, not wishing to have it appear that
we knew each other too well.

"Paul," I said. "Elliot Paul. I work for the reclamation
service . . . with the engineers."

"A goldbrick," he said, dryly. "Why not?"

"Good luck," I said, and, getting on Crocus, was about
to ride away.

"Any suggestions?" he asked, under his breath.

"That red-head superintendent's a prince. . . . You know how to spell?" I said.

He nodded. "I've heard tell of him," he said.

"The Prentice camp's better, five miles down the ditch," I said, "if you don't like it here."

Again he nodded. "I'll try it here a while," he said, "but much obliged."

He smiled, his eyes quite blue again. I made a gesture of farewell but not good-bye, and started back for La Mesa. I had been on the verge of asking news of Heck, his side-kick, but restrained myself in time. I knew I should see more of Fidlio G. Sharpe, alias "Joe," and that he would tell me as much as he thought best, and no more.

My notebook was still empty when I got back to camp.

CHAPTER EIGHT

A Rancher and His Daughter

As SOON as Bert Lacey had been informed that the piano he had ordered from St. Paul was in Mondak, he drove over into North Dakota to fetch it. From Zoe's telephone office he phoned me at La Mesa that the first big dance at Trembles would be held on Saturday night.

It was not easy then for any of us to get away early enough on Saturdays to spend an evening far from camp. We were supposed to stay on the ditch until the contractors quit at five o'clock. Then we had to drive or ride from five to fifteen miles back to camp, wash ourselves from a bucket and basin, put on the kind of clothes we had taken off, only fresh from the laundry, and start out for a thirty-mile ride. Since the more respectable people went to bed before midnight, our choice of company usually was automatically restricted to the livelier sort.

Somehow, I always managed to find means of transportation. I was not convinced that my presence along the canal was so vital to the best interests of the country that a few hours, more or less, made any difference to the government. They made a great deal of difference to me. I had no intention of being cooped up in camp when I could be enlarging my experience and outlook elsewhere. I felt that I owed it to myself to see as much of western life and get acquainted with as many different people as possible, and that rules and regulations, there and everywhere, should be interpreted according to one's individual needs and temperament.

So that Saturday I arranged to be near the stage road, below La Mesa, when the stage came along, just before noon. I knew that if I turned Crocus loose, so near the stable, she would find her way to the camp gate. Old Knick had agreed, grudgingly, to be on the lookout for her and put her away, out of sight. Old Knick and Crocus were a pair to see together. The pinto mare would lay back her ears, nip at him, kick without ever hitting him, and respond to his muttered curses and threats by wriggling the skin on her flanks and shoulders, balking, jerking at the lines and, whenever he was on her back, by stumbling every four or five yards and stopping abruptly to knock flies off her belly with her hind feet.

I rode to Tokna on the stage, sitting up beside Matt and watching the way he drove the four wild horses. When we reached Dunlap Creek, I got off and walked up the creek to the Gregory ranch, where, whenever I could get there, I gave Letty a "lesson" on the melodeon. She always had cocoa and sandwiches on hand. It was astonishing that a woman as thin as Letty could have drunk eight or ten cups of cocoa every day for nearly forty years without taking on weight.

It was certain that Old Annius, Letty and Bat Horner would be starting down the valley for the dance, in mid-afternoon. I knew they would be glad to take me along. How I should get back, in time for work Monday morning, was a problem to be considered later.

My success at teaching has always been variable. If a pupil was apt, we got along fine, whether the subject was music or anything else I happened to know about.

There was no question of any extra-curricular studies in connection with Letty Gregory. She was more than twice my age, and pathologically shy. All the affection she had stored up in a bleak life on the ranch was centered on Bat Horner. Her father was crazy about music. Before Letty was at the melodeon ten minutes, dutifully trying to play a few five-finger exercises, Annius would come in, impatiently, coax her gruffly to get off the stool, and ask me to play "The Campbells Are Coming," "Moneymusk," "Endearing Young Charms," and similar melodies of long ago, from the north of England or Ireland.

Between lessons, Letty would practice faithfully, as I indicated, from the "Methods" that had been thrown in with the melodeon. In all the hours she struggled with those music books and the instrument, she did not learn to pump with her feet while playing notes with her fingers. Instead, she had to pump the bellows full, then play until the air was exhausted. Her feet were so big that she used only the front half of them on the pedals. Her arms and fingers were so long that she had to sit well back from the keyboard, and lean forward in order to read the notes. Mexican Joe, in one-sixth of the time, could have learned to play practically anything, forward or backwards.

And still, I remember to this day the long room in which, by a window shaded by cottonwoods and admitting their pungent aroma, I seemed to lose myself at that small melodeon, playing better than I knew how, because of Old Gregory's rapture. He, tough, hard-working old rancher that he was, having been cut off from cultural pursuits since boyhood, was filled with awe and wonder. He sat down as long as he could, then stood up. His foot tapped in time, or his head swayed this way and that. His eyes gleamed. His breath came short. He tiptoed, so as not to interfere. He tried to be nonexistent, so I would forget to stop. He, who had given orders and taken none, as far back as he could remember, meekly asked permission to call in some of the boys, took them away from their work, and winked at them, as they were standing around the room, hats in hand, as proudly as if he were playing himself.

"Now, Letty," he would say, reproachfully, "why the Sam Hill can't you do that?"

"I dunno, Pa," she would say, regretfully, and look at the music books and the instrument as if they were hostile devices from an outside world she knew but dimly.

Letty had never formed the habit of reading. The sewing she did was plain. She cooked passably, in huge quantities, swept and dusted the roomy old ranch house, and through the long evenings, since Bat Horner had come into the country, she sat in dim lamplight with him, on the sofa, holding his hand in hers. She had spent all her years on that same ranch; hot summers and bitter winters. She had suffered when the cattle, in an unlucky year, would stand in the snow, their backs to the wind, and slowly die, when the hay was gone. The ranch hands, indoors, did not fluster her much. She had got used to having a crowd of men in the dining room, at meal hours, but out of doors she was almost as shy and help-less with them as with strangers. None of them, until Bat had happened along, had tried to get close to her, notwith-standing that she was the only woman within miles.

Annius Gregory had reached the point where he could en-joy his work, having money and stock, a commodious ranch house, a devoted daughter for company, and almost as much hired help as he required. He had not prayed since boyhood, but he had worried a lot about Letty, and little Bat Horner, with his huge ears and ready wit, was the answer to Old Greg-ory's hopes. The ranch, the bank accounts, the land and the stock would go to Letty, when Annius died, and by that time he hoped that Bat would have a place of his own, and assets which could be joined with the family fortune.

Of course, the ranch was only two miles from the stage road, so it had never been considered a lonely or isolated one. Back near Three Buttes and north toward Canada, the ranchers and their women did not get the news every day, and see rigs drive back and forth six or eight times a week. And Letty, a second-generation ranch woman, had been conditioned to that relentless routine from birth.

It was strange that when Bat and Letty sat together, he found little to say, and she practically nothing at all. When he was in the company of men, he kept up a continual chatter, always piquant and amusing. Letty had a deterrent effect on his conversation. And when Old Man Gregory was with them, he and Bat carried on as if Letty were absent, except that now and then they would say things to make her blush and squirm.

In many ways, Bat was the ideal mate for Letty Gregory. He did not try to adjust her to the increasing complications of valley society too fast. Within five years after they were engaged, Letty enjoyed going to dances and dancing with the men who asked her. She got used to Glendive, a little— the Jordan Hotel, the Bee Hive, and the Opera House.

Any kind of theatrical or vaudeville performance transported her. For Letty, to be able to sit quietly in a darkened hall, with Bat on one side and her father on the other, and see performers nurture hope, abide by faith, overcome disappointment, and find refuge in each other's arms, never ceased to be soul-satisfying and wonderful. In the theatre, she could suffer and worry, knowing all the time that the end would be right. That belief in happy endings did not spoil her appreciation and pleasure, and of all the members of an audience, Letty would be most deathly uneasy while the villain was getting in his dirty work.

She knew that in former years there had been bad men

and desperadoes in Tokna. Never had the city or eastern type of villain penetrated that far. Those sinister men were soft and slick. She knew that if she had been stalked by one of them, she would have fallen, first crack out of the box. The defenselessness of stage heroines she understood better than anyone. It was terribly true that women were frail, and needed strong, right-thinking men to guide them.

No wonder the best artists in the heyday of the theatre loved to play those western towns. The list of Thespians whose posters still may be seen at Virginia City, Helena and Butte contains the cream of the artistic and theatrical world, in an epoch when dramatic art was riding high. None of them ever saw the town of Tokna, or the face of that tall awkward girl in their audience, but plenty of the near-great and quite-good hit Glendive, and they must have felt Letty's intensity. Old Man Gregory, while he reacted to old-fashioned music, did not let himself go while seeing a play. He felt that in real life, all the dramas would have ended a few minutes after the first act started. The hero or the girl's father would recognize the heavy by his makeup and clothes, and would do away with him without formalities. And as for mortgages, with red seals and ribbons around them, he would have torn them in bits, the way he did subpoenas, if they inconvenienced him.

Once in a while, after several melodeon lessons, Letty would loosen up a bit with me, and talk about a show we had both seen at Glendive, or one she had seen before I came into the country. The memory that caused her to shiver and tremble, bite her fingers and turn pale, was that of a performance by a traveling pioneer hypnotist named Peden. Letty identified that man's extraordinary powers with the malevolent force displayed by stage villains. At tense moments, and especially when Peden had called for volunteers from the audience in

Glendive, Letty had almost had hysterics. Her teeth clacked and chattered, she gripped the arms of her menfolks so hard she left bruises. In spite of herself, she had felt her body rising, rigid, from the seat, and a pull toward the stage like that of an undertow or river current.

"I'll kiss a pig, if both the old man and me didn't have to hold her down," Bat told me.

Peden, she assured me, not only hypnotized his own wife and himself, but rabbits, chickens and pigeons. Chet Busby, the sheriff, who boasted that no man could make him do what he didn't want to do, got down on his knees, and bucked like a bronco, in front of a hallful of people, and swore afterwards that he'd done nothing of the kind.

The Rufus Rastus Minstrels affected Letty, who had never seen a live Negro, and mistook the white troupers in their burnt cork for the genuine African article, to such a point that she would giggle and squirm at the mention of them.

The behavior of the characters in the one-reel silent pictures, first displayed in Glendive in 1907, confirmed all Letty's suspicions about life outside her valley. She laughed until her thin sides ached, grabbed for Bat and Annius, gurgled and gasped at the comedies, but thanked her stars on the way home that she never had found herself where folks cut up that way.

Being between six and seven feet tall, Letty got more of a kick than anyone in the valley out of the "original historic Mrs. General Tom Thumb and her escort of European midgets." But when I stood near Letty, on a Fourth of July, and was thrilled until my head started ringing by the spectacle of a Gros Ventre War Dance, staged by a bunch of Indians from the Fort Peck reservation, Letty was bored and unmoved. Symbolism, for her, did not exist.

At the time I was trying to teach Letty to play the melodeon, her father had stock worth nearly a quarter of a million dollars. Nevertheless, they lived in a house that was solid, but crude, inconvenient and drafty. The upstairs rooms were never heated, and downstairs only the huge kitchen range and broad open fireplaces could be used to fight the cold. There were no means of fighting the heat.

Letty Gregory was the only "girl" I met who had been born and raised on a ranch in eastern Montana and wanted to stay there. A few of the other ranch girls did stay in the country, by accident, because they met young men, poor, irresponsible but attractive, got into emotional and sometimes physical difficulties, and had to revise their dreams to fit the facts.

CHAPTER NINE

Dancing with High Boots On

WHEN I caught sight of Trembles, after an absence up the valley of about a month, I realized that Bert Lacey was not only a dreamer but an organizer and builder. The groups of tents and newly finished or unfinished buildings, nestling just south of the feathery quaking aspens, already gave an impression of permanence and expansion.

Bert had three tents in his group. The largest was for temporary use as a dance hall, the middle one housed his saloon, and the third, 8 by 12, was for Bert and Highpockets to sleep in. Highpockets did most of the sleeping, but he worked hard, under Bert's direction, twelve hours or more a day, and folded right after supper. The contractors along the canal, according to a new law passed in Washington, could only work their men eight hours a day, six days a week. Both the bosses and the workers resented the restriction heartily. But ranchers, farmers and municipal promoters could work as long as they liked, and their help as long as they could stand it. In a sense, Bert was a slave-driver, not because he was ungenerous or inconsiderate. He himself had such a supply of energy, and such impatience with the limitations of time and human striving, that men who tried to keep up with him collapsed, one by one.

East of the stage road, near the south bank of the coulee, about fifty feet from Bert's group of tents, he had put up a building with new lumber, throughout, and painted a sign (at Charley Tufts' suggestion): CATHAY CAFÉ. Captain Marsh had brought down on the *Expansion*, among many other articles, barrels of crockery dishes, cooking utensils, oil-cloth and an eight-burner kitchen range with two ovens. There the two Chinks, who now were called Ah Cook and Ah Flunk, toiled practically all the time, as fatalistically as a couple of screech owls. A few days after they had gained confidence in Bert Lacey, they had slowly let it be known that they understood quite a bit of English and could communicate in pidgin talk themselves. Ah Cook's cuisine was up to the mark, and Ah Flunk's service in the dining room was deft and assiduous. There were two tables for ladies, and those had checkered cloths.

A log stable and spacious corral were far enough along for use and their proprietor, Lucian Gibbs, who had been working in Bismarck and wanted to go in business for himself, had put up a sign reading: RAG TIME LIVERY BARN.

Half a mile or more up the coulee, Stella and another hooker Big Emma Tubbs had lent her until she could get a brace of new ones from the Twin Cities were installed in two tents, and a stout log house was half built. Bert had sent Stella plenty of ice, and sawdust to keep it in, what beer she needed, blankets, quilts, sheets and towels, and a couple of suitable chromos for the walls, entitled "L'Allegro" and "Il Penseroso." According to the prevailing mood of Stella's joint, one of those was invariably turned to the wall.

Uprights for a blacksmith shop had been set, just east off the stage road, and the blacksmith, Shunk Cundiff, had obtained the exclusive agency of the Glendive Steam Laundry, so that packages of wash already were being accepted and delivered by means of the daily stage.

As soon as Bert had time to put up another building like

105

the one that housed the Cathay Café, he had arranged to sublet a corner of it, and a bedroom, to a widow who had written him from Deadwood and who wanted to install a lending library and do plain and fancy sewing. Her name was Lela Weckerling. She had a little girl, aged ten, named Helen. No one had seen Mrs. Weckerling, but already the local wags were speculating about her and planned to wear clean shirts and neckties the day she put in an appearance.

In a tent near the blacksmith shop, on the west side of the road, Lambert McGlynn, a very tall and lanky barber, was carrying on with a wooden non-adjustable chair on a low platform, until he could save money enough for a board shack and a real barber chair. McGlynn had enormously big feet, even longer than Letty Gregory's. He had a way of standing, implements in hand, flat-footed and immobile from the slim waist down, his back concave, his arms gesticulating, and his tongue following the contours of the work he was doing with shaving brush or scissors.

Two scissorbills, brothers named Villerup, had bought 160 acres apiece, straddling the coulee, between Stella's "Little Casino" and the stage road crossing. They were building a log cabin on contiguous corners of their land.

The more people who gathered in Trembles, and the more complicated the pattern of life there became, the more confused and vaguely worried was Johnny Highpockets. His correspondence with Edna B., conducted with the aid of Charley Tufts, Johnny O'Brien, and the Simard boys, had reached the point where the date was set for her to meet him in Glendive. It was only a few weeks distant, at the time of the first Trembles dance, and whenever Highpockets had a minute to think, we would see him standing, mouth slightly open, forehead creased with perplexity, wondering what he was getting into and how it all had happened. Nearly always he would touch his pants pockets, where he kept his gold and silver coins, and a faint vacant smile would illumine his candid countenance. He had money, and was earning more. His claim, on the sage-covered slope to the west, and in sight of Lacey's growing saloon, had been filed upon, in proper order, so they told him. One hundred and sixty acres were his, to all intents and purposes, if he could fence them, put them under cultivation, build a house, and live on them five years. All his new friends and well-wishers assured him that he could fulfill the government requirements, and if nothing would grow, or a drouth lasted two or three years, he could always get a job with Bert.

"See that there peg?" Bert said, pointing up to a peg on the hatrack in his saloon.

"That there one to the left?" asked Highpockets, who liked to be explicit.

"That's yourn," said Bert. "Any time you get hard up—which you won't—hang that doggoned old louse-cage of yours up there, and you're workin'. Now quit worryin'. It's bad for the town to have you standin' around lookin' as if you'd been sent for and couldn't come."

Highpockets nodded, smiled wanly, and tried to reassure himself.

"Now this woman, Edna B. What if she don't like me?" Highpockets asked.

"Then I'll put her to work in the hotel," said Bert. "An' if she don't like you, then Charley Tufts'll have to marry her. He's jointly responsible."

Charley, who had overheard, was increasingly troubled, too, about the Edna B. affair. It was one of his cardinal principles not to interfere with anybody else's fate. Edna had sent a photograph, and Charley kept it with him, most of the time, to study her face. According to his request contained in the

107

first letter he had sent in Highpockets' behalf, Edna had been photographed with a hat on, and the hat bothered Charley as much as her rather wistful face. The photograph was a cheap one, awkwardly posed and inexpertly taken by the kind of city professional of that period who tried to make all his female subjects turn out to look like either Fritzi Scheff, Minnie Maddern Fiske or Mrs. Leslie Carter.

It was clear that Edna was not the aggressive, self-reliant type, but rather the clinging vine. There was a certain disturbing dignity in the set of her shoulders, as emphasized by her puff-sleeved jacket. From Charley's sensitive viewpoint, nothing about her seemed exactly right, and nothing very wrong, except the many signs of her capacity for suffering. A dozen times he had been on the point of trying to call the whole thing off, and in each instance was talked out of his qualms by Bert Lacey and Johnny O'Brien.

The slant of Edna's hat was in her favor. It was a straw hat with a ribbon and a touch of grapes that would have been pert, had not Edna's rather grave face appeared below it. The fact that she wore it tilted slightly to one side was supposed to indicate that she was amiable, kind and generous. Charley had tried to make it clear, in the last two letters that had been sent to her, that Highpockets was a diamond in the rough, without much schooling, that his plans for a homestead were in their early stages, and that he had little money. Edna did not seem to be much interested in book-learning, creature comforts or the size of her prospective husband's purse. What she wanted, apparently, was a man to whom she could be useful and who would be kind to her.

"What does that mean?" Charley asked me, to be able to think aloud and try to straighten out the matter in his mind. Without waiting for an answer, he continued:

"It means that she has been a misfit, somehow, and that the

people around her have not been particularly kind. She must have had an unfortunate affair."

Edna had complied with what must have seemed to her a strange request, and had sent out one of her old shoes. It was small and neat, but well worn. It had a moderately high heel and instep. The heel was worn down quite noticeably on the outside and a little toward the back.

That meant, according to Charley (and Professor Gross of Leipzig) that Edna was dreamy and imaginative, with a longing for romance and adventure.

With increased foreboding, Charley had looked out across that sagebrush flat, and then at Highpockets, who was baiting a simple rat trap altogether wrong.

"Charley," Bert Lacey said, "you give me a pain in the neck. Any girl with a grain of sense will take to one or the other of you."

Not only Bert, but practically all the men in the vicinity had insisted that Charley would have to take on Edna, if she passed up Highpockets. I think even Highpockets was vaguely counting on that. The thing had got on Charley's mind to such a degree that he had talked it over with Milly Baron, our wise and willing social arbiter. She had mischievously made the same suggestion on which the men were unanimous. She adored making matches and Charley, then thirty-eight, was a challenge to any match-maker. If ever a man was a natural-born bachelor, theoretically, practically and by reasoned preference, Charley Tufts was. Mrs. Baron (I never called her Milly) did not overlook the tender way in which Charley handled that old shoe. She had offered to take in Edna, as her house guest, if the girl wanted a little time in which to make up her mind, and it was evident that all Mrs. Baron's tact and persuasiveness would be directed in Charley's behalf, and not for Highpockets.

109

Another facet of the trying situation was troubling Charley. Edna B. (the B. was for Bispham) already was known and referred to throughout the valley as "The Monkey Ward wife." That nickname would stick, no matter how many years Edna stayed. Would it not bruise her tender feelings? As far as Highpockets was concerned, it was a mark of distinction. Most of the young men back where he came from got married because they had to, and the fact that he and Edna had negotiated at a distance seemed unquestionably respectable to him.

"You can't back out now, after raising a woman's hopes so high," Mrs. Baron said to Charley, who admitted there was logic in that point of view.

Anyhow, the $32.15 had been sent for Edna's railroad fare. As a matter of fact, Charley, without Highpockets' knowledge, had made out the money order for an even $50, in case she should want a few bottles of pop or a paper-covered Laura Jean Libbey to read en route.

That first Saturday evening I was too busy on my own account to bother much about Charley's predicament. The piano was a big ungainly upright, heavy and durable, the tone was fair and the action easy. But in getting it out of the freight car, in and out of the warehouse in Mondak, and hauling it thirty-odd miles by wagon over the stage road, it had been jarred sadly out of tune. That would never do, to start our series of Saturday night dances with an out-of-tune piano.

I had never tuned a piano, and neither tuning fork nor tuning key had come with the instrument. So I detached the Trembles blacksmith, Shunk Cundiff, from the crowd that packed the bar, and explained my problem. Shunk was a resourceful iron worker, drunk or sober. He lighted up his forge, fanned it with the bellows, and heated the head of a tack hammer white hot. While it was soft and pliable, he

110

stuck it over one of the short square metal posts that held the top of the piano strings, withdrew the hammer head and let it cool. He had greased the little post, so the hot metal would not stick. He fitted the hammer head back on its handle, and I had a tuning implement. So before it was time for the dance to start, I had evened up the pitch of the strings. Mexican Joe and French Joe watched the whole process with avid interest. The little Mexican bronco buster had brought his diatonic accordion with twelve bases; an ocarina, or sweet-potato whistle; a guitar with double bass strings; a set of hard-wood blocks; a harmonica; and a fiddle. French Joe had his fiddle, with an extra bow and strings, and a Jew's harp. Lam McGlynn, the new barber, had played the drums in his youth, but had none with him, so Shunk Cundiff had made for his use a small drum from a big lard pail and a jack rabbit's skin. French Joe, who was practically a sculptor—all the Simard boys were talented, one way or another—had whittled out a pair of drum sticks from Indian medicine spoons. With the home-made drum, the wood blocks, a triangle and a pair of cocoanut shells, McGlynn was able to furnish percussion that just about balanced the band.

I had already played with the Mexican and Joe Simard, at the homecoming dance for Angela Clawson, at Tokna, so we understood one another. But that time I had to play a melodeon, which is not emphatic, like a piano. McGlynn had learned drumming from a teacher, and played according to rote, more or less, without imagination, but with coaching he would do. Most of his drum parts I had to write out for him. The other boys were inspired, magnificent musicians. It was a cinch to follow them, and impossible to lose them. Neither of them knew what printed notes meant, nor had need of that knowledge. French Joe was the leader.

"Six-eight, in G," he would say, before we started a strange piece, if that described the rhythm and the key. Then he would tap two measures with his big hob-nailed boot, and bear down on the strings. Mexican Joe hit the chord on his guitar and I on the piano. The first time through, we chorded and listened to the man who knew the tune. After that, we let ourselves go. After Joe Simard had done a few variations, he would chord and I would take the tune for a couple of rides, and then, as I was finishing my last chorus, I would look over at the pint-sized Mexican, who now must be playing and grinning at the left of the Throne of God, and never repeating himself. I do not know which of those musicians I admired the more, or which of them was more surprised that a teen-aged kid from Massachusetts could play in their style. I never regretted that being at the piano kept me from dancing. I was crazy about what I was doing. I never got tired, although we played from ten o'clock at night until breakfast time Sunday morning. Outside the tent, we could hear the roar and diapason of the boys at the bar, the clinking, laughing, yelling, and occasional shooting, which did not mean bloodshed, very often, but only that some cowpuncher was having a better time than he could stand, and had to let off steam.

That first Saturday night in Trembles, when Lam Mc-Glynn made his initial appearance with the band, we found that he had a physical peculiarity that handicapped him as a musician. Without his being aware of it, a few drinks made him hard of hearing. The more whisky he had, the deafer he got, and, since he played mostly from notes I had scribbled, his performance after midnight grew more independent of ours with each dance tune. Lam, as I have suggested, was not a very good drummer, but he was dutiful, and played every note. If he had a few left over, when the rest of us had finished, he thumped them out, anyway. His work as a barber was somewhat like his musical efforts. He was steady, reliable, and not very skillful. In those days, back east, it was unwritten law that if a barber cut a customer while shaving him, no charge was made for the shave. McGlynn tried to enforce this, in the beginning of his stay at Trembles, but the customers would not permit him to ruin himself.

I noticed, while we were playing that first evening, that Charley Tufts hung around the band and watched the drummer rather wistfully, and later, when Lam got to the point where he wanted to lie down and rest for a few hours, I asked Charley to take over. Tufts did not look like a musician, but he habitually held his elbows widespread, and that made it easy for him to play the snare drum. After a few pieces, Charley did a better job without notes than Lam did with them. And always, after that, Tufts, who took no pride in his immense scholarship and humanity, was as pleased as a schoolboy when anyone remarked how well he played the drums. Men of scope are like that. They all have what the French call *"un violon d'Ingres."*

In Bert Lacey's little 8-by-12 sleeping tent, and in the "private dining room" of the Cathay Café were the babies and very young children who had been brought along by their parents or guardians. They slept there, side by side, in rows and windrows, and many is the time I saw Shunk Cundiff or Ah Flunk or Ah Cook glance in, and cover one or two of them up while the dance was at its height and the bar was roaring.

Because Bert was so fond of those quaking aspen trees, it was unwritten law that broncs should not be hitched to them and that men who felt impelled to fire off their six-shooters should not stand under them and shoot up through their tender leaves. Anything else, within reason, a man could do on those Saturday nights.

A Ghost Town on the Yellowstone

Lucian Gibbs, of the Rag Time Livery Barn, had a couple of hacks and put on an extra driver, so any men who wanted to could go up the coulee and say howdy to Stella and stocky little Fern, who was as dark as Stella was white. I think she was Syrian or Greek. Stella never had a bouncer in her place at Trembles. Men who got noisy were shushed by the others, in extreme cases by means of what were called "nutcrackers," that is to say, full bottles of beer. The drunks were stretched out between clumps of sagebrush, and their faces were carefully shaded with their hats from the moonlight, if any. It was the general belief that men who slept with the moon shining full on their faces got loco, especially if their mouths were open and the moonlight got down as far as their gullets.

The Saturday nights at Trembles did much to reassure me that men are capable of self-government. There were three times as many dancers that evening as could function comfortably in Bert's big tent, so the men took turns. At the dances on the Lower Yellowstone, it was the women who mattered. They danced continually, with all comers, and were outnumbered ten to one. Therefore, if a few men strayed away for a while, nobody was likely to miss them.

All told, there were more than a hundred people, not counting the sleeping children, at Trembles that night, and more than twenty of them were women. Frank Crowe, builder of the Boulder Dam years later, then a young government inspector, and Bob Sass, whose sister Crowe married, came over from Munn's camp. Clarence Dean Olney, in later years City Engineer of Cincinnati, danced frequently with Zuleika Donaldson, Chet's red-headed sister. Many of the others never came into the public eye, outside the valley, but were more prominent at the dance that night.

The women in a pioneer community had to have a special kind of tact. Ranchers' daughters like Letty Gregory, who

114

had had little social experience, were protected by their pathological shyness, and, if they were as homely and rangy as Letty, by their looks. The Clawson girls were both good-looking, of contrasting types. They had known a number of the cowpunchers since they were children, had said frankly ever since they were big enough to dance that they would never marry a man who would keep them on a ranch, and favored the young engineers. Angela was grave, low-voiced and freckled. Gypsy, the younger, was blonde, with violet eyes, and as willful as a bird.

Little Jennette Simard, who had so many brothers, was tiny and graceful, and extremely French in her manner. Being the darling of a large jolly French family, Jennette had never been lonely. Frail and ephemeral as she looked, she could ride almost as well as Mexican Joe, and more than once had won local races, at Sidney, astride the spirited Simard stallion, a fleet sorrel named Napoleon.

Anne Prentice, comparatively new to the country, and having none of Zuleika's understanding of a man's feelings, was the kind of a flirt that one would have expected to find in a more highly organized and restrained society. All through her girlhood she had read the society pages of Sunday newspapers, and identified herself with heiresses and famous men's daughters who had dozens of suitors from which to choose. Anne was not in the least affected. She merely acted naturally in an environment that called for special precautions on the part of a young woman. Therefore, trouble and tragedy were always in the air around her, while she was in the Lower Yellowstone.

When love struck a man on the desolate flats and coulees of eastern Montana, it struck hard. Men, lonely and isolated from feminine contacts, for the most part, went loco if a woman got under their skin. The stricken males moved in a daze, lost weight and appetite, changed color, and, at the stage where sound sleep departed from them, would babble and rave to anyone who would listen sympathetically. Most of the women who inspired these crises of anguish and folly realized that they were representing, not only themselves, but all womankind, real and legendary, and tried to let the sufferers down as easily as they could. The part such a woman had to play was difficult. Nearly always, rivals were men enough to be aware that they had much in common, in losing their wits about the same woman, and tried to be decent to one another. The best of them tried terribly hard, and now and then succeeded. But, unfortunately, to quote a phrase from the editor-typesetter of the *Sidney Herald*, sometimes "jealousy overthrew self-mastery" and lamentable incidents occurred.

The young man who drove Anne Prentice to the dance that night, in a hired rig, stands out in my mind because he was the first "southerner" I got intimately acquainted with. There had been no descendants of the rebels in Linden, Massachusetts. Walt Murray was from Virginia and spoke the western central Virginia brogue that is mistakenly called an "accent." I was fascinated by what Walt could do with words that were familiar, when considered separately, but in their pronunciation and arrangement became hauntingly musical and gently expressive. Also, Walt's manners were perfect, in their quaint *genre*, bringing to life, for me, the illustrations I had seen of gentlemen in wigs and knee breeches, bowing before ladies like Dolly Madison and Theodosia Burr. I understood immediately that Walt's manner of speech and his gracious behavior, when he was sober, attracted Anne Prentice in subtle ways she herself understood but dimly. Besides being articulate, soft of speech and courtly to a degree which set him apart from all other men, young or old, in the valley, Walt had other qualities that held out the promise that he would succeed, if he ever got through sowing his wild oats. The way his mind worked, when he was attending to the affairs of the project, was a direct contradiction of his indolent movements and inconsequential talk in mixed or female company.

Walt had all the gentlemanly vices of his breed, including that of improvidence. He was hot-tempered and reckless, and at the same time limp from early dissipation, so that when he got himself into trouble, someone else had to get him out. He was sentimental about home and mother, the lost cause of the Confederacy, and particularly voluble in expressing the things he had been taught to believe about Negroes, who in his mind ranged from anthropoid apes with violent hydrophobia to harmless childish mimics who learned long words a little more readily than parrots did, and who were unsurpassed as servants, mammies and cooks. From the day I met Walt until we said good-bye I never believed that a word he said was founded on fact or reality, but I was sure that he believed that he was spreading wisdom and truth. How anyone with such a muddled head could be so good at his complicated work puzzled me then, as now.

Scotty McVeigh and I had been responsible for introducing Walt to Anne Prentice, and we had so many occasions on which to reproach ourselves for that careless act that neither of us could count them. We had arranged one evening to ride over to the Prentice camp from La Mesa, to play auction with Anne and Zuleika Donaldson. There was no telephone in the Prentice camp, the only contractor who had been permitted to install one on the government line being Donaldson, because of his geographical position on the ditch and importance as the contractor responsible for all the work on two divisions. Zuleika had been ill that day and phoned me at La Mesa, asking me to find a substitute, so that the four-some we had planned would not be spoiled. I thought of Walt. He borrowed a horse, and rode with Scotty and me, and Anne was well pleased at the substitution in our game of a presentable young man for a strikingly handsome young woman, who was not Anne's type at all.

Scotty and I were partners, and I never remember having played a more confusing game. Walt could not deal without spilling cards all over the floor. He could not remember what suit was trumps. Anne seemed to be doing everything possible to demoralize him further. After Scotty and I rode back to camp, Walt stayed for hours. He was never quite himself again.

As soon as Anne saw that Walt believed himself to be perfectly serious, she was as kind and gentle as she could be, within the limits of her nature. She made it clear, however, that before any man could talk marriage to her, he must have or make enough money to support her in the style to which her doting father had accustomed her. Walt, always unstable, was thrown into a pitiable state. Hitherto he had got drunk and had spent his month's pay whenever he had the chance, had suffered headache, nausea and mild remorse, and got himself straightened out in a few days, during which he was especially careful and conscientious with his work. Now that drinking and spending was a form of acute self-destruction, and carried with it a feeling of despair and un-worthiness, he drank harder and borrowed from everybody he knew, to hide his financial debacles from Anne. Everything he did, outside of office hours, during which he acted and felt like an automaton, involved a moral conflict, and if ever a man was unequipped by nature, heredity, experience and environment for moral tussles of any kind, that man was Walt. Reality, for him, became identified in his mind with alcoholic nightmares and hangovers. The more remote Anne seemed to be, the surer Walt became that he must marry her or die in the gutter. I do not know how Anne felt about that, but all the rest of us agreed with him. He was a dead duck, if he could not pull himself together, and the chances of that seemed to me about on a par with mine for being President. Walt was so persuasive that he even got into my brother Charles for a couple of hundred dollars, and the men who managed that, in the course of Charles' lifetime, could be counted on the toes of a sloth.

On the night of the first dance in Trembles, the Prentice-Murray affair was heightened and complicated by the entry into the field of Chet Donaldson. Chet, making cynical and adroit use of his sister, Zuleika, kept the ever-punctilious Walt dancing with Zuleika as often as possible, while Chet took over Anne. Immediately, Chet, in his domineering way, assumed that he was the king pin, and that Walt did not matter. Walt, crazy with jealousy and inflated with southern resentment and fury, played into Chet's hands, and behaved so badly that Anne got cross with him. I am sure that Anne did not know she was dealing with a passionate, undisciplined, hysterical boy on the one hand, and a ruthless killer on the other, who thought he was destined to rule whatever he saw and wanted, and was more powerful than God.

Noel Prentice saw the danger without delay, and was caught in the middle. Having committed himself to carry out a sub-contract, under bond to Donaldson, Prentice could easily be ruined, if things went wrong. Chet had many ways of making them go wrong, if he took it into his head to use them.

I was not worried about Chet, and not much about Anne. Walt was my problem. I wished heartily that Scotty was not laid up with typhoid, and that I was not confined to the piano.

119

I toyed with the idea of warning Anne that if she did not stop flirting with Chet, and encouraging him, someone would be killed. Donaldson always carried a six-shooter in a holster on the right hand side of his belt, and I had heard that he spent hours, by himself, in the coulees, shooting at tin cans or egg shells.

Ed Wilson had told me, right after the time Chet had tried to ride Crocus, that Donaldson had attempted to buy the mare, and only had failed because it was impossible to sell government property without having it first condemned or certified useless by a special board of appraisers. The red tape involved would have blocked the sale during Crocus's remaining lifetime. Chet, of course, wanted to break her spirit (at the age of ten) or beat her to death.

As the night wore on, and I got more and more involved in the music, Walt began to feel his drinks, which he never held conspicuously well. His eyes were glazed; he slumped as he leaned on the bar. Once or twice, his foot slipped while he was dancing. His face and neck had changed color, to an angry purple with his office pallor underneath. Meanwhile, Chet became a little louder, more debonair, more confident. Everything seemed to be going his way, and every minute he held Anne tightly in his arms, dancing two-steps, schottisches and quadrilles, his quick infatuation was inflamed. He knew he could not simply waylay her, overpower her and take her. The country was lawless, but all the cattle men and their help had rigid ideas about rape. Chet assumed, as a matter of course, that he would have to marry Anne, to get her. It had not then occurred to him that she might refuse. From the way Anne acted, I could not blame Chet much for that. Anne was deeply annoyed with Walt, interpreting his immature behavior as lack of stamina (in which she had some justice) and indifference about pleasing her, in which she was as wrong as a woman could be.

About two o'clock in the morning, it appeared to me, as I watched the reflections move in my mirror at the piano, that Walt Murray seemed to have got a firmer grip on himself. He did not stumble when he danced. Walt was wearing a blue serge coat, a light flannel shirt and a black four-in-hand tie, low patent-leather shoes and black silk socks. He was dancing, then, with big Mrs. Wandell, a voluble and genial woman of forty who weighed two hundred pounds and was as light on her feet as Maude Adams or Jimmy Cagney. At his partner's insistence, Walt had relaxed his southern scruples to the point of unbuttoning all the buttons but one of his double-breasted jacket. Result? The bottom of it flared as he swung Mrs. Wandell just behind me and something hard and fairly heavy in his lower left-hand coat pocket hit me in the back and caused me to miss a beat in the bass.

"God!" I said to Charley Tufts, alarmed. "Walt's got a gun in his pocket."

Tufts frowned disgustedly. "Now what bloody fool would lend him one?"

"Luke Landry," I said. Luke was another trouble-maker, like Chet Donaldson, only not so well fixed and with less reason to be careful. Luke was a concrete foreman in Donaldson's camp, and hated Chet bitterly, as most of Chet's subordinates did. I had seen Walt and Landry in conversation outside the dance tent, and had noticed that they walked away, together, into the shade of the quaking aspen trees. I knew that nothing would please Landry as much as to see someone shoot Chet, preferably in the belly, where it would make him suffer most.

As soon as the band finished playing the quadrille we were on—the music was "The Arkansas Traveler"—Charley and I made a bee-line for Bert Lacey and impressed him with the importance of our errand. Bat Horner, who could always be counted on to think of something, was also taken into our confidence. If Scotty had been there, he would have gone straight to Walt, made him go outside, and would have taken the revolver away.

"Quit worryin', boys," Bat said. "I got it figured out."

He did not explain his plan, but went over to Walt and invited him to have a drink with us, at one of the café tables. The bar was too crowded for any kind of maneuvers. On the table was a small kerosene lamp, burning low. As Walt, Charley and I sat down and Bert went back to the bar, where Highpockets and one of the Villerup brothers were helping with the rough work, Bat took the lamp away to fill it up with kerosene. Ah Flunk was flying around the room, waiting on everybody at once, but he could not quite keep up with everything.

I noticed that when Bat came back with the lamp, he set it down near Walt and, by means of restrained grimaces, made it clear to me that I should edge my chair well away from it, and keep out of whatever might occur.

In a moment, after Bat had had time to seat himself on the opposite side of the table, between Charley Tufts and me, the lamp flared up, with a puff like a small explosion, and started flaming, inside the chimney. Walt, nearest it, made a grab for it with his right hand, and had lifted it only a few inches, intending to carry it outside, when it flared again and burned his hand so badly that he dropped it on the floor. Bat promptly extinguished it by smothering the fire with sugar from a large sugar bowl, then stamping it out with his hob-nailed boots. Meanwhile, Ah Cook emerged from the kitchen, almost too promptly, with some olive oil and flour. Doc Morrill, who was at the bar, got his bag from a room in which children and babies were asleep and bandaged Walt's hand. The pain was not terrible, but it sobered him up considerably. Soon the Doc had Walt's right arm in a sling, and Horner was triumphant. So was I, for just about a minute. Then I remembered that Walt was left-handed, and noticed that the gun was in his left-hand pocket. He could draw it about as easily as before.

Bat, I learned afterward, had slipped a little gunpowder inside the lamp chimney before he had lighted it. Hence the flaring combustion and mild explosions. Ranch hands and carpenters frequently experimented with lamps and powder, in the long winter evenings when the range was snow-bound, and knew just how lamps would behave. If only he had placed the lamp on Walt's other side, all might have been well.

At the table we had chosen, Charley Tufts, Bat Horner, Walt and I were sitting. Ah Flunk had brought a new lamp, and Highpockets another round of drinks. The other two Samaritans and I were horrified when Walt stood up, pale and resolute, his right arm in a sling, and said, with meticulous politeness:

"If you'all'll be kind enough to excuse me, ah'll pay ma respects. . . ." He glanced toward the corner table where Noel Prentice, Anne, Chet Donaldson, Zuleika, and Mr. and Mrs. Baron were sitting. Before we could object, Walt had started in their direction, painfully dignified and icily calm. He did not even stagger.

"Cripes!" Tufts said, as Walt got out of earshot. "The burns have cleared his head, just enough to make him more foolish than he was."

We all were plenty worried. We watched Walt's steady progress, as did Bert Lacey and many of the more prudent barflies and visitors.

We saw Donaldson's eyes light up, balefully, as Walt approached. Noel Prentice spilled his coffee and a few drops trickled on Mrs. Baron's skirt. She was so apprehensive that she did not even notice them. Walt approached, addressing Mrs. Baron, as the senior lady.

"Do you mind if I join you'all, Mrs. Ba'on?" Walt asked, formally, then turned to Zuleika and Anne. "Or you, Miss Zuleika? . . . Or you, Miss Anne?" he added.

All of them murmured, "Certainly not," or words to that effect. There was no extra chair, so Walt took one from a near-by table and brought it over, using his uninjured left hand. Chet was sitting on the edge of his chair, trying to look unconcerned, and eager for trouble. To me, the tenseness of the situation was heightened because so few of the men in the room seemed to find it otherwise than amusing.

Anne was sitting between Mr. Baron and Chet. To my astonishment, when Walt got back with the chair in his hand, and seemed about to wedge it in between Chet and the girl, Chet smiled disarmingly, with utter confidence, and moved his own chair away, so Walt would have room for his and would have the place at Anne's left.

From the corner of my eye I saw Landry standing at an angle of the bar, watching every move with satisfaction. After all, it would be hard even for a sentimental southern boy like Walt to miss completely a large man sitting not a foot away from him.

Walt placed his chair, flecked a little dust from the seat with his silk handkerchief, and sat down, gravely, about six inches too far to the left. As his blue-serge trousers seat hit the floor, jarring the near-by lamps, Chet let out a guffaw, and a split second later, the whole café shook with laughter. Walt did not try to rise, but sat where he was, his face vacant, as if someone had dealt him a solar-plexus blow. Someone had, but his name was John Barleycorn.

If most of the others were relieved, Anne was more annoyed. She had not wanted Walt to make an exhibition of himself, but only to annoy Chet, who was becoming too possessive. Chet, beaming with satisfaction, and Bert Lacey lifted Walt by the shoulders, lugged him into one of the rooms reserved for sleeping children, and stretched him out on the floor. Walt could make no resistance, and was asleep before they had turned around.

With a heart relatively light, I rushed back to the dance hall and resumed my place at the piano. I was not at all satisfied, however, with the turn events had taken. Chet Donaldson was now in possession of the field, and could not restrain himself from swaggering fatuously. Anne turned all her smiles on him.

Bat Horner, curious to know whether I had been right about who gave Walt the gun, kept his eye on Luke Landry and soon saw him slip into the kids' dormitory. Presumably he got his six-shooter back.

We played more square dances than any other kind, but the two-steps were very popular and occasionally someone called for a waltz, or a schottische. The band was warming up "Under the Bamboo Tree," in brisk two-four time, Donaldson was two-stepping gaily with Anne, and I was trying to reconcile myself to seeing him start off with her, just after breakfast, in Walt's hired rig, when Tom Bone, Donaldson's time-keeper who had stayed back in camp to keep an eye on things, appeared at the flap of the big dance tent, streaked with sweat and dust and showing other signs of a long hard ride in the saddle. Tom went straight across the crowded floor, not waiting for the end of the two-step, and braced Chet who, pouting and glowering like a stubborn child, let go of Anne and followed Bone out into the open air.

Not thirty seconds later, the news sped around Trembles.

125

"A riot at Donaldson's camp."

The two Joes, Charley Tufts and I kept on playing and nearly everyone continued dancing or drinking, but Chet Donaldson, leaving Zuleika with Noel Prentice, appropriated Walt's hired rig, the fastest available, and started pell-mell up the valley.

A few minutes after Donaldson had got out of sight, Luke Landry, having rounded up the other able-bodied men who worked for Donaldson, started off on a big clumsy saddle horse, with two wagon loads following. No one seemed to know any details about the trouble. But Mert Honey, the deputy sheriff from Sidney, started riding north at full gallop.

Walt Murray was still dead to the world at nine o'clock the next morning, so Anne rode back to camp with her father, in a petulant frame of mind.

CHAPTER TEN

A Prosperous Contractor's Camp

WHAT happened at Donaldson's camp in the course of that starry summer night and ensuing hot Sabbath morning was told me, separately, by Fidlio G. Sharpe, who took a more active part than he had intended; Tom Bone, the old time-keeper, a periodic drunkard, who gave me a batch of figures now and then so that my cost sheets in quadruplicate would not arrive in Washington without a mild sprinkling of facts; and two of the Bohunks I already had got acquainted with. One was an Austrian, a hard-rock foreman named Leopold Schrems. The other, a huge tall Herzegovinian named Milo Bilek.

World solidarity between wage earners, an ideal much talked about by socialists, anarchists and anti-capitalists generally, around the turn of the century, was far from being a reality, either in crowded industrial cities (now much more overcrowded) or among the migratory workers of the west. Fidlio G. Sharpe, under still another name, had attended the first convention of the Industrial Workers of the World two years before he hit eastern Montana, and had heard for the first time the Wobbly "Preamble" that begins:

"June, 1905
"The working class and the employing class have nothing in common. There can be no peace so long as hunger and want are found among millions of working people and the few,

127

who make up the employing class, have all the good things of life.

"Between these two classes a struggle must go on until the workers of the world organize as a class, take possession of the earth and the machinery of production and abolish the wage system.

"We find that the centering of management of industries into fewer and fewer hands makes the trade unions unable to cope with the ever-growing power of the employing class. The trade unions foster a state of affairs which allows one set of workers to be pitted against another set of workers in the same industry, thereby helping defeat one another in wage wars. Moreover, the trade unions aid the employing class to mislead the workers into the belief that the workers have interest in common with their employers.

"These conditions can be changed and the interest of the working class upheld only by an organization formed in such a way that all its members in any one industry, or in all industries if necessary, cease work whenever a strike or lockout is on in any department thereof, thus making an injury to one an injury to all.

"Instead of the conservative motto, 'A fair day's wage for a fair day's work,' we must inscribe on our banner the revolutionary watchword, 'Abolition of the wage system.' The army of production must be organized, not only for the every-day struggle with capitalists, but to carry on production when capitalism shall have been overthrown."

In a construction camp nearly half a day's journey, at top speed, from the nearest law enforcement officer, who, incidentally, did not care a tinker's damn what happened in said camp, the economic status of the individuals had a considerable range. The contractor, if he was ruthless and smart, could make a small fortune, personally, and keep most of it. Taxes were not high, and fell upon real property owners who were residents of the country. The elder Donaldson, for instance, paid taxes on his residence in St. Cloud, commercial buildings he owned for investment, and land. There was no income tax, profits tax or sales tax. Donaldson and Company, a corporation, made a net profit in eastern Montana of between $20,000 and $100,000 a season (from spring until late fall) according to the astuteness and luck of Donaldson, senior, and the estimators and construction men he hired. The company paid $130 a year in taxes to Dawson County, about as much as Alex Wandell, the rancher, paid. Chet, the superintendent of construction, was marked down in the time book at $400 a month, or $4,800 a year. Besides this he got a slice of the profits amounting to from $5,000 to $15,000 more. That was big money in 1907.

The employees who worked under Chet were paid, roughly: master mechanic, $300 a month; head rigger, $200 a month; foremen (of which there were three), about $160 a month; stationary engineers, $5.00 a day, or $140 a month; carpenters, $4.50 a day, or $126 a month; sub-foremen, $4.00 a day, or $112 a month; skinners and muckers (white or American) $2.25 a day or $63 a month; Bohunks, $2.00 a day, or $56 a month.

So Chet Donaldson "earned" on an average, $1,250 a month, and had the large resources of his father's good credit behind him. Milo Bilek drew $56 a month, if he worked hard every week-day, and, of this, seventy-five cents a day, or $22.50 a month, was deducted for "subsistence," that is, meals and a bunk, which was taken out in full, no matter how many meals he missed. In addition, he spent $5.00 a month at the contractor's commissary for work gloves, clothes, sweets and tobacco. That left him about $28.50 to cache in his sock or send back to Herzegovina.

A Mormon carpenter like Nephi Pratt, who would get

129

$4.50 a day, pay $22.50 for subsistence, spend $3.00 in the commissary, would have roughly $90 a month to send home and $10.00 to send the Mormon church. Were he a gentile, like Bruce Skinner, he would have $100 a month clear. So the difference between $100 monthly, over and above subsistence, and $28.50, represented the difference in economic brackets between the skilled carpenter or mechanic and the unskilled foreigner or American bum. Spiritually, culturally or intellectually, the differences were much harder to evaluate, since a Bohunk hard-rock foreman like Leo Schrems had had a fair education in Austria, had served as a trusted noncom in the army of his Emperor, preferred Brahms to Billy Murray, read German, a little English and a smattering of French, and had traveled in several countries. Nephi Pratt, on the other hand, could count up to twenty if he were not hurried, and had believed, when his Mormon bishop had told him so, that the bishop would meet Nephi on the seventh star he lived on, after his death on earth. Nephi would have been indignant, indeed, if anyone had told him to his face that Joseph Smith had not been able to translate into English by means of transparent magic stones (Urim and Thummim), the text written by God in "Ancient Egyptian" on the golden plates of the original Book of Mormon.

The boss Bohunk, Leo Schrems, on the other hand, believed only that dead men rose up never, and that rivers eventually got to sea. Leo would have smiled tolerantly if anyone had told him of the Mormon lore. The lusty mountaineer, Milo Bilek, believed in God, and also that if he spat over his left shoulder when he saw the new moon, his mountain sweetheart back home would be true to him, if she was not tempted too strongly.

Very few of the migratory workers who built the first railroads, canals, dams and roads that were essential to the growth and development of these states were married. Very few of the hoboes, "natives" or "white men," whatever a man chose to call them, had any formal ties or loyalties whatsoever. If they had had families, for the most part they had lost track of them, and the great majority were glad of it. So were the families, no doubt. Those who were sure about their birthplace and remembered anything about it, looked upon it and whoever had stayed there with scorn. Their frequent contacts with governments—local, municipal, county, state or federal—had been such that they wished anyone well who could kill or maim the agents of "law and order" or who attempted in ways, large or small, to overthrow any constituted authority. Their country, consisting of neighbors, strangers and officials, had done nothing but kick them around and they owed it absolutely nothing except revenge for their indignities, from their point of view.

Their attitude was not comforting to fans of the *status quo,* but that is the way the men felt, the sixty or seventy percent of the migratory workers who described themselves as "Americans."

They worked as long as they could stand it, then an irresistible impulse would come over them to drop what they were doing, go to the "office" and ask for their time. Then they would start up the long dusty road, toward Glendive or Mondak. Usually they had about six weeks' pay in their pockets, a sum approximating thirty-five dollars.

They had no feeling of responsibility, duty, continuity, ambition, competition or inferiority. They all enjoyed their food, the whisky, and a riotous night. They would spend all their money the first evening and then unload a few cars of cement, steel or freight before they rode the chilly box cars to Bismarck. In Bismarck there was more temporary work for them, if they wanted it. The Twin Cities would be their next stop.

And no sooner would they hit Minneapolis or St. Paul than they would go broke again, separate, and think of nothing, individually or in pairs, but going somewhere else.

Pure bums were neither philosophers nor idealists, except in the small incidental or accidental percentage that bank cashiers, for instance, are philosophers or idealists. They listened to what other men, preachers, politicians or theorists had to say, with a detached attitude. Their comment was summed up in their song about "Pie in the Sky."

Of the one hundred men who worked in Donaldson's camp, at any given time, at least thirty of them would be thoroughgoing bums, who could be waylaid, lured down the valley and be counted on to work a maximum of about six weeks. Donaldson, one of the more high-handed of the contractors, was said to keep three gangs busy, one coming in, one on the job and a third, having quit, walking out.

Very few of Donaldson's employees above the rank of hobo were married, or ever expected to be. The muckers were drifters, the skinners were farm hands, displaced. One in four of the mechanics, stationary engineers, carpenters or foremen had wives, in distant places, and provided for them. Something in the nature of the various occupations got into the souls and fibers of the skilled workers and made them similar to other men of their trade, in certain respects, and different from men of other trades. With a little practice, almost any time-keeper or foreman, not to say sociologist or psychologist, could guess the trades of strangers who rode in, dusty, on a wagon, and see that Abe Johnson was a carpenter, Nick Ford was a rigger or a hoisting engineer, while Tim Buttleman was a foreman, and a slave-driver, at that. Abe, the carpenter, was thrifty, reticent, mystic and eccentric; Nick, the rigger, was a gambler, ladies' man, a wit and a likeable fool; and Tim was a man to keep away from, distrust, and fear.

The carpenters who had wives mailed them most of their pay, wrote letters regularly, sent their children to public school, somewhere out of Montana, and expected, some day, to be boss carpenters or even builders in some new town. They were either trade unionists, or stubbornly anti-union. Their work, in a construction camp, was to build, set up and remove collapsible wooden forms into which concrete was poured and tamped to harden. Also they put up, took down and repaired the shacks, made rough tables and benches for the mess-tent, handles for broken scrapers, bunks for the bunk-houses, stone boats, platforms and shelves. They moved, worked and thought slowly. They were cautious and opinionated. Each one was jealous of all the others and did his utmost to make the boss carpenter look silly. Abe Johnson, the boss carpenter at Donaldson's camp, was like the other carpenters, only a little more so. He carried a card from some Iowa local of the carpenter's union, A.F. of L. In a government camp on the Lower Yellowstone that meant nothing at all. Men, of whatever trade, took what they could get and quit if they did not like it. Anybody could be fired by a foreman any time, without notice. The foreman did not even have to think of a pretext. If he fired too many men at inconvenient times, the superintendent canned him.

Nick Ford, Donaldson's master mechanic, was one of the few married men who was continually distraught on that account. His wife was back in Erie, Pennsylvania. She was very handsome, gay and extravagant. When they were together they fought all the time, stopping long enough between bouts for reconciliations that were quite as violent, in reverse. After they had been together a few weeks, and both were exhausted, Nick would light out for some construction job, the farther away from Wanda, the better. He was a minor genius at his work. With only the crude facilities of a blacksmith shop Nick was able to keep the orange-peel bucket, clam-shell bucket, pile-driver, two derricks, and two steam shovels running, although the local bituminous coal, shipped from the lower valley, was not of the best grade and the stationary engineers who drifted into eastern Montana, intending to stay a few weeks only, were not the most skillful and cared less about what happened to Donaldson's machines than Chet cared about their health or happiness.

Each time Nick saw his wife, or heard from her, she told him she was still faithful, but hinted strongly that she might not always remain so. He told her and wrote her, invariably, that he did not care a hoot what else she did, but if she let another man touch her he would massacre them both.

"A working stiff's got no business marryin' a pretty wife," Nick said to Fidlio G. Sharpe and me. He had just received a letter and, as usual, it upset him. The only thing that upset him more was not receiving a letter.

"Mark her up, so the ruling class won't want her," said Fidlio. "That's what the Indians up in northern California used to do. There was a huskier tribe in Oregon that used to pop down and steal the good-looking squaws. So the braves tattooed all the women."

"Wanda's so handsome that I haven't got the heart to spoil her face," Nick said.

"Get behind her, on the edge of a crowded platform, an' push her under a train. No one can prove it's not an accident," Fidlio said.

"The Sioux used to press out the juice of the spring crocus, for poison," I said.

Fidlio looked intensely interested, in his quick, bird-like way.

134

"On the level?" he asked.

"That's what Old Knick says," I told him.

He looked at me sharply, forgetting Nick and his troubles with Wanda.

"What's this I hear about you findin' scorpions, a batch of live ones, on Shoat's section of the ditch?" he asked.

"There's a big nest of 'em in a sand pocket on the side hill," I said.

"All you damn Wobblies think about is sabotage," said Nick. "You're lucky not to have hearts."

"Better join. Then you'll lose yours, and be of some use to your class," Fidlio said.

"Bugger my class! It's got me into more trouble than anything else," said Nick.

CHAPTER ELEVEN

Mixed Causes and Effects

THERE are many who questioned in 1907 and who still are not convinced that "the working class and the employing class have nothing in common." However, in a contractor's camp under government direction in the Lower Yellowstone forty years ago, the Wobblies' view of the situation had much to sustain it. Migratory workers were necessary, if the dam was to be built and the canal and laterals dug. Anybody who had the strength or weapons could kick them around, at will. There was no police or government protection, no obligation on the part of the contractors to do anything for them. The contractor's profits depended on his ability to get as much out of them as they could give, for the least possible return. Had not the workers themselves been split up into factions, they could have taken over the countryside, as the Sioux, John Jacob Astor's trappers, and the cattle barons before them had done.

Days were long in the summer season. Before seven in the morning, the air was fairly cool, and after six in the evening. The working hours were all in the dazzling heavy heat of the day, from eight A.M. until noon, an hour for the mid-day meal, then from one P.M. until five. The law restricted the length of the working day to eight hours, and overtime was permitted only when an emergency existed. The workers, practically without exception, would have liked to work three or four hours overtime, and on Sundays. In that way they could pile up enough for a binge or a journey in a shorter time. Unless they were lucky enough to have a rich inner life, there was nothing to enlighten or amuse them in camp.

The diet, in a contractor's camp, was badly out of balance and designed principally to discourage men from going too often to the can, on the bosses' time. Common laborers who got the trots in a hot spell were fired. Stationary engineers or other skilled workers might be permitted to lay off a day or two, in their bunks. Breakfast was at seven o'clock, and consisted of oatmeal with condensed milk, fried sow belly or yesterday's stew meat with left-over potatoes, fried in lard, and coffee made in huge metal cans from which the grounds were seldom dumped. At noon there was stew made of meat the butchers could not dispose of elsewhere, boiled spuds with their unwashed skins on, stewed canned tomatoes of the cheaper brands, macaroni and cheese baked in large shallow tins, or watered canned corn. For dessert there was pie made from dried or canned fruit, rice, tapioca or bread pudding, or stewed prunes. The evening meal was like the noon meal, without pie, and with boiled beans instead of macaroni or corn.

Very few men read much in those camps. Out of doors, there were flies, bugs and dust. In the tents and bunk-houses the light was always bad. A few Mormons pored over the Book of Mormon or church tracts. A handful of men read back copies of their home-town newspaper. For the great majority, reading was confined to the Montgomery Ward catalogue.

Card playing was done mostly in the stables, because in the bunk-houses the noise and light kept other men awake. About one-tenth of the men gambled everything they had, losing to the lucky or more skillful ones. There was not much cheating, or many complaints about cheating, because if a man were caught at it, he was beaten up and thrown out of camp without first aid.

On week-days, most of the men turned in early and slept more or less soundly until the first whistle blew in the morning. If they were lousy, as they usually were, they would turn their flannel shirts inside out just as they lay down, and try to get to sleep before the lice could get inside again. But the dreary stretch of hours from five P.M. on Saturday afternoon until Monday morning dragged miserably. The government insisted on one day's rest in seven, but, even in case of its own employees, made no provision to entertain them or transport them where they might find recreation. Men who enjoyed themselves too much on Sunday could not work as well on Monday.

Those who had money rode from the camps to Glendive or Mondak, and later, to Trembles, closer at hand. The others had to sweat it out, with fraying tempers. Riot and bloodshed were weekly occurrences and some of the most patient, self-conscious and quiet of the men became the most violent when they went berserk.

There was something in the air at Donaldson's camp on the Saturday of which I write. Little things started going wrong, and set off bigger things. A less self-sufficient and more sensitive superintendent than Chet Donaldson would have sensed trouble in the offing. Luke Landry, the concrete foreman, did. So did Tim Buttleman, who was new on the job and had two gangs, with slips and fresnoes, working on the fill.

First thing in the morning, Donaldson told Landry to take the forms off a section of flume across Beef Slough.

"Olney [the division engineer] said to leave 'em on till he got here," Landry said.

"Is Olney running this job, or am I?" Donaldson asked.

"I ain't," said Landry, and sent for Abe Johnson, the boss carpenter. Before Johnson got there, Donaldson rode away, to throw his weight somewhere else.

"The brass nuts sez to take off the forms," Landry said.

Abe, the slow-thinking Swede, frowned and grunted. "We're not supposed to take off the forms until the engineer is here," Abe said.

"That's what I told the fat-head," Landry said.

Abe got his crew together with some difficulty. Knowing that the forms were due to come off just after noon, he had scattered his carpenters and helpers on several odd jobs around the camp. When finally they got the forms loose from the section of flume in question, Landry turned purple and swore. Under Donaldson's instructions, he had cheated on the mixture, and the concrete along two pillars and the outside wall of the flume was honeycombed.

Clarence Dean Olney came riding down the canal bank and into Beef Slough.

"Good morning," he said to Landry.

Landry continued chewing tobacco and grunted. He hated all engineers, especially polite ones, but he wanted Donaldson to get the works.

"Who told you to take off those forms?" Olney asked.

"The boss," Landry said.

"Without an inspector on hand?"

"That's what he said," continued Landry.

Olney rode over to the warehouse, where Donaldson's buckskin horse was standing. Donaldson, the warehouse man and Fidlio G. Sharpe were inside. Olney dismounted and went in. He was a small, dapper man from New England, very strict and conscientious.

"Did you tell Landry to take off those forms from the

flume?" Olney asked, without preliminary, going up to Donaldson, who towered a foot above his head.

"I knew you'd be along in time," Chet said. "I phoned La Mesa, and they said you'd started."

"I got here in time, all right," Olney said.

"You wouldn't make me take out good concrete . . ." Donaldson said, cowed because his father would be furious, and blame him.

"Good or bad," Olney said. "In this case, it happens to be bad. You told Landry to patch it up, and put the forms back on. Try one more trick like that, and I'll report you to the Federal District Attorney. That's fraud."

Donaldson, sweating and getting redder, was almost bursting with rage and humiliation but he could not talk back. Olney turned without another word and left him standing there. The engineer rode over to the fill, where Tim Buttleman was standing. Tim had not met Olney before, but he noticed that his shirt was clean, that his nails were well-cared-for, and that his riding boots were nicely polished.

"Hey, dude," said Buttleman, making a gesture with his thumb. "Come over here."

Olney paid no attention. He was looking for the fill stakes the surveying party had set the afternoon before. Most of them had been knocked out of place and kicked away. A skinner drove a slip over one that was still standing, flattening it.

"Are you the foreman?" Olney asked Buttleman.

"What do I look like?" asked Buttleman.

"That I prefer not to say," said Olney, dismounting. He stood near his horse and in a minute Chet Donaldson came riding up the fill. As usual, Olney wasted no words.

"We put in fill stakes here yesterday afternoon. Look at 'em," Olney said.

Chet glowered at Buttleman.

"Can't you keep your God-damn skinners off those stakes?" Chet asked.

Olney, without glancing at either of them again, rode away, toward Prentice's camp, but seeing Zuleika standing in the flap of her tent, he swerved from the canal and stood, Stetson in hand, talking with her a moment.

"Shall I see you at the dance tonight?" she asked.

Olney had not intended to go, but he answered, "If you're going, I wouldn't like to miss it."

"I wouldn't like to have you miss it," Zuleika said.

Chet, watching them from the canal bank two hundred yards distant, swore and gritted his teeth. He hated seeing men he disliked being attentive to his sister. And she usually seemed to prefer the men he disliked most.

Chet could not swallow the idea that Olney, or anybody else, was incorruptible. He must have a weakness, somewhere, and a price. And that went for Charles H. Paul, the construction engineer, who was as fussy as Olney, and for Frank E. Weymouth, the project engineer, who gave those other damned Puritans a free hand. Chet could understand his own motives and actions, in cheating the government whenever he could, in ways large or small. But what did Charles H. Paul and Clarence Dean Olney get for themselves by squeezing the blood out of a contractor who had made an injudicious bid, or who was inexperienced in that kind of country, as who was not?

At noon that day, things got worse. The stable boss rode over from the stage road with a big sack of mail. Chet, who liked to mix into everything, took the sack away from Tom Bone, unlocked the padlock, opened it, and dumped the contents on the floor of the office, behind the counter. Men, having finished the noon meal in about fifteen minutes, crowded in and around the tar-paper shack. Some of them were expecting letters or newspapers; the majority just liked standing around and watching something happen.

Among the letters dumped out by Donaldson on the floor were many—many more than usual—with foreign stamps and addressed in strange, none too legible handwriting. All these Donaldson weeded out and threw contemptuously into a corner. "White men" were served before "Bohunks."

Tom Bone, the old time-keeper, had noticed how many Bohunks had showed up at the mail hour that Saturday. While Donaldson was calling out names and distributing letters and papers to the "white men," Bone started to retrieve the Bohunks' letters.

"Let the sons of bitches wait," Donaldson said.

"O.K.," said Tom Bone, disgusted.

The Bohunks, and especially the intelligent Austrian hard-rock foreman, Leo Schrems, heard and understood all this. The general run of hoboes baffled them, because the same types did not exist in Europe. The Bohunks, most of whom were peasants, vineyard workers, hostlers, or unskilled workers in century-old established villages or cities, thought the American bums were uncouth, savage, ignorant—members of the criminal element who had drifted outside their sphere. There were thugs in Europe, but they did not work. The police knew them all by name and kept track of them. In eastern Montana there seemed, to the Bohunks, to be no responsible authority at all. In this observation, as in many others, the Bohunks were not far from right.

When, finally, Donaldson, after a series of studiedly exasperating delays, told Tom Bone to pass out the Bohunks' mail, nearly all the Austrians, Herzegovinians, Montenegrins, and Bosnians received letters that seemed to be disturbing.

Their American bosses and fellow workers watched them with a mixture of scorn, hatred, resentment and suspicion.

Leo Schrems called Milo Bilek to his side. Although Milo spoke the Herzegovinian highland dialect almost exclusively, the huge mountaineer understood a few words of German. With Milo as interpreter, Schrems tried to make a little speech, to quiet the feelings of the others. Chet Donaldson horned in, rudely.

"Say what you have to say in English," Chet said. "What's going on here, anyway?"

Fidlio G. Sharpe stepped into the group. "Austria's making war on Herzegovina and Bosnia," he said.

"Thank you," said Schrems, courteously.

"Who gives a damn about that?" Donaldson asked.

"All of them do," said Fidlio. "Leo, here, and a dozen more of 'em come from Austria, and some of the others come from the little countries that are being attacked."

"How come you know so God-damn much about Austria?" Donaldson demanded of Fidlio.

"I read and listen," Fidlio said. "And some of what I read and hear, I savvy."

The bums who were gathering around heard this and grinned.

"Well, tell these friends of yours that if they want to cut each other up, it's all right with me, but there'll be no fighting inside the limits of this camp," Donaldson said.

"I understand. We are not responsible for what our governments do, and do not wish to fight," said Schrems.

"Yellow, eh?" said Donaldson.

Schrems, with some pride, made a gesture toward the huge mountain men.

"There are no better fighters in the world than these," he said.

"All right. Let 'em fight, but not in this camp," said Donaldson.

"Agreed," Schrems said.

The whistle blew, and everyone started back toward the ditch.

Chet Donaldson, caring less than nothing about foreign affairs, was disturbed about Fidlio. Maybe, Chet thought, I ought to give him a better job, and get on the right side of him. Chet could not fire him, because he knew too much.

The telephone rang. Chet answered it.

"Olney speaking," said a crisp New England voice at the other end of the line.

"This is Chet Donaldson," Donaldson said. "What can I do for you, Mr. Olney?"

"I thought you'd like to know that the La Mesa switchboard is working again now. It's been out of order since yesterday afternoon," Olney said, and hung up.

Thirty seconds later Chet remembered that he had told Olney, that morning, that he had phoned La Mesa and been informed that Olney was on his way up the ditch. Chet's face and neck got flame-colored and he swore under his breath. Chet had seldom put in a more trying day, and it was by no means over.

The arrangement about week-ends between Chet Donaldson and Luke Landry, who was next in rank in the camp, was that one of them would stay on the job every other week-end. It was Landry's turn to be off. Chet knew that he ought to stick around, but he could not bear to miss the dance at Trembles. He had heard it was a lively spot, and wanted to look it over. So he hunted up Abe Johnson, the stodgy, good-natured boss carpenter, and, to Abe's dismay, put him in charge of the camp. He also sent for Tim Buttleman and Tom Bone, and told them to help Abe keep an eye on things and to carry out Abe's orders. Then, before the whistle blew, Chet rode around until he found Fidlio G. Sharpe, who was in the warehouse fitting some new pickhandles into old picks.

"Hey, reader!" Chet began.

Fidlio looked up and stopped work, but said nothing.

"You look like a smart guy," Chet said.

"There's lots I don't know . . . yet," said Fidlio, matter-of-factly.

"How'd you like a job as foreman? Beginning Monday?" asked Chet.

Fidlio shook his head in the negative. "Unh-*unh*. I'm a workin' stiff," he said. "It takes a bastard like Buttleman to be a foreman."

Buttleman, just then, was beating a balky horse with a heavy metal chain.

"Suit yourself," Chet said. "Don't say I didn't give you a chance."

"Much obliged," Fidlio said, and went on fitting pickhandles.

The whistle blew.

Out on the fill, Buttleman stopped beating the horse, by force of habit. As he walked away, the horse fell over. Donaldson rode up.

"What's the idea?" he asked Buttleman. "Do you think horses grow on trees?"

"That one might have, for all the sense he's got," said Buttleman.

The horse got up, sweating, bruised with welts, and trembling. Buttleman walked over, just in time for a rock, thrown from somewhere out of sight beyond the fill, to hit him on the elbow and knock him flat. The horse reared up and tried to trample him, but was too weak, and fell over again.

"My arm's broke," said Buttleman. "Who threw that rock?"

145

"Somebody who don't like you," said Donaldson. "That's an act of God. The firm's not liable."

Chet rode away, got dressed in his best and flashiest, and with his sister, Zuleika, rode over to Prentice's camp, where Noel Prentice was waiting for them with his two-seated rig. Walt Murray had already started down the valley with Anne Prentice.

Right after the evening meal, Fidlio walked over to the stage road and followed it a short distance, then retrieved from a clump of sagebrush a jug of whisky, wrapped in a gunny sack. This he had ordered from Matt Keffeler, the stage driver, several days before. Fidlio did not drink the whisky, but took it back into camp and cached it in the warehouse. It was three days until payday, the first of August. Tom Bone was busy day and night, checking and transferring the notations in his time book to the payroll. He could not refuse whisky, and one drink sent him up like a kite. It was part of Fidlio's plan of sabotage to get Tom drunk, so he would ball up the figures, and send the whole camp into confusion. Fidlio had found in Donaldson's camp only ten men who had I.W.W. cards, and most of them were not paid up. The dues were fifteen cents a month, but somehow the bums seldom got around to paying them. Fidlio had talked to about a dozen other workers who had never belonged to the Wobblies, and had signed up most of them for membership in his amorphous "mixed local." So of the hundred men in Donaldson's camp, Fidlio already had a following of twenty-two, who were not averse to concerted action.

Buttleman, with his arm in crude splints and a sling, was going from one end of the camp to the other, sounding out the "white men" on the idea of running the Bohunks out of camp.

When this was reported to Fidlio, he sought out the hoboes

most sympathetic to his own ideas, and repeated to them for the hundredth time that the I.W.W. drew no class, sex or national lines. A working stiff who spoke Austrian or Greek or Montenegrin was as much a fellow worker, and member of the proletariat, as a native American.

By ten o'clock, when on ordinary nights most of the lamps had been blown out, all the bunk-houses, shacks and tents were still alight, and Fidlio was sure there would be a fight.

The Bohunks were about forty in number: twelve from central Austria, six each from Bosnia, Herzegovina and Montenegro; and the remaining ten including Spaniards from Asturia, one Greek, two Polacks who had worked in the lumber woods, and three lonesome and melancholy Latvians, technically Russians, who suffered most from the heat and had picked up or developed independently a dialect of English that sounded unlike human speech. They all were quartered in a board bunk-house with dirt floor and tar-paper roof. Four tin wash basins and empty soap boxes were provided, and a special Bohunks' latrine at some distance, consisting of an unpeeled log on two uprights, to distinguish it from the "white men's" latrine which had a peeled log and an old Monkey Ward catalogue chained to one of the uprights.

The Austrians, whose government was embarking on piracy, felt sad and ashamed, and were treated with touching consideration by the mountaineers, whose hearts were as big and sentimental as their bodies were huge and durable.

The Asturians, brave men then as ever, knew how to sympathize with fellow Europeans who were being persecuted by the minions of the Hapsburgs, having suffered under Alfonso XII and left their beloved Spain on that account. Years later, when I was in Spain, how I loved and remembered those first Asturian *dynamiteros* I had known on the Yellowstone and understood so imperfectly.

147

By and large, from one end of the sixty-foot board shack to the other, and all along the double tiers of rough bunks infested by bedbugs and gray-backs, there was a great deal of understanding within the walls and it went no farther. Outside of Fidlio, Charley Tufts and a handful of other informed men, no one in the Yellowstone country, least of all the editors of the weekly papers in Glendive, Sidney and Mondak, knew Fact No. 1 about European politics or sociology.

In the Bohunks' bunk-house were three medium-sized kerosene lamps, two provided by the company and one that had been bought and installed near the middle by Leo Schrems and his best friend, also a former sergeant in the army of the Austrian emperor (whom they both wished heartily in hell), Lazlo Richter. It was Lazlo who owned a zither and played it inexpertly and nostalgically from time to time, and who read paper-covered books like *Das Kapital* now and then, of an evening, when he was not too homesick or tired. Lazlo, according to Leo, neither agreed nor disagreed with Karl Marx. In the course of three years' reading, Lazlo had not got to the point where he understood where Marx was heading or what Karl planned to do when he got there.

What Lazlo intended to do was simple enough. He intended to work for $2.00 a day, unless he could get higher wages, until he had enough money to buy a small inn near the center of his native village. Then he was going to marry an up-to-date young Austrian girl who was not afraid of hotel work, and be content and happy if his enterprise netted him the equivalent of fifty cents a day, plus bed with young wife, and the kind of board they could cook and wash down with native wine.

Two bunk-houses similar in construction to the one occupied by the Bohunks were filled with "white men." When,

148

at ten-thirty, Fidlio saw that neither of them was dark, that several of the men had been drinking, and that Buttleman, with his broken arm, was buzzing back and forth between them, he checked with the Wobblies he could count on. What they told him caused him to go straight to the office, where Tom Bone was struggling with the time books, tired, shaky and sober.

"Tom! You'd better start riding down the valley as hard as you can, to get Donaldson back here," Fidlio said.

"Nothing's happened yet, has it?" asked Tom. But he was worried. Tom was not unintelligent, and had managed thus far—he was forty-five—to hold down his jobs in spite of his periodic binges. There are some men who tend to like their fellow creatures and wish them well, and others who find it natural to loathe them. Tom was one of the latter. He hated everybody, most of all himself. His views were reactionary and violent. He agreed that the working classes were exploited, and wished they could have been driven with whips, in chains. A man who got rich, in Tom's opinion, was smarter than one who stayed poor, and entitled not only to the good things of life, but unquestioning protection on the part of police and military, politician and priest. He adored Mark Hanna, Chauncey Depew and Old Joe Cannon as politicians, and thought Rockefeller and Morgan were one hundred percent right in grinding every cent from the poor or getting huge sums by trickery from the not-quite-so-rich. He thought Sam Gompers, considered by Fidlio a reactionary sot, was an enemy of society and progress and should be hanged. Tom liked to read about strikes that failed and workers that were starved or massacred. He admired city landlords who threw tenants out into blizzards, and their sticks and rags on top of them. Any damn fool, according to Tom, could see that force and money were what counted.

Tom decided to pass the buck to Abe Johnson, the stolid middle-aged Swede, who was, technically, the ranking boss now left in camp. He and Fidlio went over to Abe's tent. Abe had put up a private tent for himself, because he could not stand the dirt and bugs in the bunk-houses. He had a folding chair, had built himself a table, and had installed springs in his bunk. He had a wash stand, a mirror, writing materials, soap for toilet and laundry purposes, a galvanized wash tub, a washboard, and several unfinished pairs of snowshoes and skis he was making, to sell the ranchers and tradespeople in the valley before he went east to spend the winter with his wife and two children.

As soon as Abe heard that Tim Buttleman was fomenting trouble between the hoboes and foreigners, Abe decided that it was his duty to seek out the dirt foreman and protest. Abe was not young or athletic, but he could not be buffaloed.

Fidlio, admiring the Swede's guts, if not his judgment, sent word post-haste to the Wobblies in the two "white men's" bunk-houses to see that the boss carpenter did not get hurt. Three of them waylaid Buttleman, when he was on his way from one bunk-house to another, knocked him senseless with what they described as a "piss elm club," and rushed him down toward the river. There they gagged him and trussed him up between stout clumps of sagebrush and an old dead tree.

When Abe Johnson, his face and hands washed, his hair combed carefully, to add to his natural dignity, walked over to the nearest bunk-house where Buttleman might be and, hearing a din within, entered, a few of the Wobblies were near the entrance.

"Has anybody seen the dirt foreman?" Abe asked.

A bum roared and pounded for quiet and relayed the question. Nobody had.

"Excuse me. Thank you," Abe said, meticulously polite, and went to the other "white men's" bunk-house. There the same thing happened. No Buttleman.

Abe went to the Bohunks' bunk-house and entered. Most of the Bohunks were gathered around Lazlo Richter and his zither, and were singing, not loudly, but quite harmoniously, a Balkan mountain song about Dania a star, and Dania a young woman, who were equally inaccessible to the singers.

The Bohunks were as polite as Abe, and after exchanges of heel clicking and bows, assured the boss carpenter that no one had seen Buttleman recently. Milo Bilek spat quickly behind him, which indicated that the longer he went without seeing Buttleman the better he would be pleased.

It looked to Abe as if Buttleman had blown camp, and left Abe stranded, and Fidlio, now in possession of the facts about where Buttleman actually was, did all he could to foster this conclusion. Abe, not wishing to be made the scapegoat, ordered Tom Bone to ride down the valley.

Some of the "white men" who were not Wobblies decided to rush the Bohunks and run them out of camp, on their own, but when they started out to do so, Fidlio and one of his lieutenants stood on each side of the exit, just outside, with pickhandles. The bums got confused and fought among themselves, then went to bed. Two other Wobblies performed the same function at the other "white men's" bunk-house, with the same results.

All around, the curlews slept, at a respectful distance from the camp, jack rabbits lurked in their burrows, snakes changed from cold stones to warmer dust, and in the great dome of inscrutable heaven, myriads of stars looked down.

Meanwhile, the Bohunks stopped singing, but they stayed

inside their bunk-house, and Leo Schrems talked earnestly to them. They were not on the Yellowstone to win friends and influence people, but to make money enough on which to live happily back home. They were men of dignity, who would defend themselves if attacked, and as Leo said this, the Asturian *dynamiteros* took the precaution of attaching some fuse and caps to short sticks of nitro-glycerin soaked into sawdust. But the Bohunks were not attacked, and when the mêlée died down in front of the other bunk-houses, the Bohunks doused their lamps and tried to go to sleep. As a matter of fact, nearly all of them did.

Lazlo, Leo and Milo kept watch, because they were too disturbed and restless to lie down.

It was five o'clock in the morning before Milo smelled smoke and saw that the far end of the Bohunks' bunk-house was afire. He and the two Austrian ex-sergeants roused all hands, but the lumber was dry, there were only a few buckets, and not much water handy, so by the time the forty Bohunks got their blankets and possessions safely out on the flat, half the building was aflame. Luckily there was no wind, but somehow a piece of flaming tar-paper got on the roof of the warehouse and the warehouse and its contents had gone up in smoke and were smouldering when Chet Donaldson, having accumulated more bluster with each of the thirty miles he had ridden, came dashing into camp on a spent saddle horse that had carried him from Tokna, and, seeing the smoking ruins and the Bohunks huddled on the flat, charged into them, roaring:

"You lousy Bohunk bastards. You sons of bitches!"

Milo picked up a pickhandle and started roaring after Donaldson.

"He called my countrymen bastards! I split him in two," Milo bellowed, and Lazlo, to restrain Milo and prevent his getting into trouble, picked up another pickhandle and tried to intercept Milo. Both having been expert at quarter staves since boyhood, they began cracking and sideswiping and Donaldson, drawing the six-shooter we had all been afraid he would use on Walt Murray, aimed at the huge mountaineer, missed, and shot Lazlo, player of zithers, stone dead.

By that time, Mert Honey, the deputy sheriff from Sidney, rode in, and took charge. An hour later the Bohunks, having collected their pay, started down the valley, sadly, bedrolls under their arms, having arranged to have the body of the Austrian turned over to his friend Leo when the authorities had finished with the inquest.

The inquest took less than five minutes and the coroner's verdict was that Donaldson had shot the unnamed Austrian in self-defense.

When found, Tim Buttleman was in such bad shape, with an infected arm, and delirious with fever and sunstroke, that Donaldson had him rushed to Glendive in a rig and into the small hospital there. Promptly he was forgotten until he showed up next spring at another camp.

CHAPTER TWELVE

The Tongues of Men and Angels

HAVING just passed through a winter so cold that railroad rails buckled and snapped in two, a spring that delayed the wild roses ten days, several cloudbursts in the wrong places at inconvenient times, a hail storm that cut down half-grown crops, and a fierce epidemic of typhoid, the ranchers, cow-punchers, townsfolk, tradesmen, farmers and construction workers in the Lower Yellowstone were treated to some really hot weather in July and August.

As soon as the members of our surveying party were on their feet again, thinner, sallow, and slightly weak in the knees, I was relieved from my ignoble job as cost-keeper and sent down to the government camp near Newlon, and so handy to Trembles that I could walk there, in a pinch.

I had got around the government red tape and had come into possession of Crocus. It had not taken me long to learn what the defunct Sioux and others had learned before me, that in dealing with a distant government of laws and men, it was not practicable to sail straight into the wind. Considerable tacking was necessary to reach any objective.

There was nothing illegal about exchanging animals, if the government agent, from his point of view, got the better of the deal in behalf of Uncle Sam. I bought from a rancher a pinto mare, with assorted colors approximating those of Crocus. This mare was short and squat, had been ridden four times, and was only six years old, according to her teeth. I borrowed Ed Wilson's iron, clapped a government brand on the little stranger, and one evening switched her for Crocus. She seemed quite content.

No one knowing Ed Wilson would suspect that he was soft-hearted enough to bother with such a sentimental transaction, but a change had taken place in Ed's bleak, bitter life. One day when he was fresh from Lam McGlynn's barber shop, I had introduced him to Josefa Dotsen, a young woman of Norwegian extraction who, with three of her brothers, had bought a section of land near the river, opposite the Newlon government camp. The Dotsens' cabin was two miles east of our surveyors' camp. Josefa had a high-school education, was tall and strong enough to be strict, and had agreed to act as school teacher in Trembles, beginning in the fall.

Josefa had been looking hopefully for a "serious" man who wanted a capable wife and might get along with her taciturn brothers. With her glasses on, in the simple, practical clothes she made for herself or bought at the stores, she seemed rather forbidding. But somehow, she and Ed Wilson recognized symptoms in each other of loneliness. I saw my chance to get on the good side of Ed. The Dotsens were very poor, in cash money, and too proud and upstanding to ask for credit in the stores. I told Miss Dotsen that if Ed would let me exchange the other pinto for Crocus, informally, I would board Crocus at the Dotsens' new barn, paying a generous rate in advance, each month, and that when I left the country, the mare would be hers.

My friend Scotty had recovered from the fever, so I never lacked companionship. Charley Tufts was near at hand to lend me the benefit of his philosophy and erudition, and Crocus was available for me to ride after working hours, and before, in case I felt my boyhood urge returning to get up before sunrise and commune with the birds.

The woods consisted of cottonwoods and alders. In the place of Linden meadows were sagebrush flats. The Montana hills had been shaved bare by a retreating glacier, and most of the birds were strange to me. But when the Yellowstone was low enough to ford, I often rode as far into the mysterious bad lands as I dared, and tried to expand my capacity for sheer wonder in order to get used to them. By that time, Crocus and I understood each other well enough so that I could loosen the cinch at the water's edge and she would swim, with me on her back, if she got out of her depth in the current.

It has always seemed to me that a man cannot fully appreciate the pleasure he takes in the company of others if, between times, he does not relish being alone. Only I am not sure that in the presence of certain of the dumb animals, one is alone. One gets along better with dogs, cats and horses if one does not try to transform their various qualities and attributes into human traits, but is content to understand them in their own fashion. One talks to them, because obviously they understand what one says, in any language. They respond, in turn, and if our brains are more complicated, voluminous or active than theirs, the attempts of animals to communicate with us give us many prime chances to use them.

The whole countryside at that time was keyed up, in anticipation of Edna Bispham's arrival, to the extent that the rival social factions in Sidney, headed by Mrs. Baron and Mrs. Thavanot, respectively, were sparring for position. The livelier set hoped to involve the Monkey Ward wife in dances, midnight suppers and hay-rides; the other to win the future Mrs. Highpockets into the fold of the Methodist church.

156

Since the anti-saloon crowd had no more chance of drying up Dawson County than the geysers in Yellowstone Park, its members were conniving with politicians and real-estate men to split off a chunk of that spacious old county, and form a new one in which the fear of God and booze would be stronger, in proportion to its size and population.

The reforming element had picked a candidate for Dawson County sheriff to oppose the unpopular but liberal Chet Busby, and had a lawyer who wore a come-to-Jesus collar and string tie to run against Judge Price.

One evening late in July, Johnny Highpockets, having hauled many barrels of water from the river and put in the rest of the day cutting prickly pear fibers with which to clear his water of mud, had eaten his supper in five minutes flat, and gone straight home. His cabin now had a floor and four uprights. With a tarpaulin for a roof, it was all right to sleep in. Johnny had his boots unlaced and his britches unbuttoned when he heard discreet hoofbeats outside and a male voice, deep and rich, say, "Ahem!"

Johnny jumped a foot, and ripped his britches along the center seam. Holding them up as best he could, he stumbled to the doorframe.

His caller was the Rev. Theo Oates, of Sidney, mounted on a broad-backed work horse belonging to the Thavanots.

"Good evening, Brother Highpockets. God bless you," the Rev. Oates began.

Highpockets, in his dismay and astonishment, mumbled something that sounded like "Glub!" Then he begged his visitor to excuse him while he changed his pants.

"Not at all necessary, Brother," the preacher said. Then he took a closer look and added: "Pray do, if you'd feel easier. I'll stay out here and enjoy the sunset."

"That won't be due for an hour or two yet," Highpockets

said, apologetically. "The days ain't hardly started gettin' shorter."

"God takes His Own good time, His wonders to perform," the preacher said.

"He sure as hell does," agreed Highpockets.

To be pleasant and establish an easy camaraderie, Rev. Oates decided to be facetious.

"When your bride-to-be becomes Mrs. Highpockets, she'll have mending to do, it seems," he said.

"She sure as hell will," said Johnny, again unconscious of having used the right words to the wrong person.

"You speak of hell often," said the preacher, as Johnny emerged from the shelter. "Are you taking steps to avoid that awful place?"

"Wherever a man goes from Montana won't seem too bad," Johnny said.

"I understand that the future Mrs. Highpockets is arriving shortly from mmmm . . . errrr . . . Chicago," the preacher said.

Johnny looked worried, as always when he was reminded of that fact. The number of days was beginning to get near the range where he could count them on his fingers. As a matter of fact, Johnny could count and figure quite accurately on his fingers. He was not swift, but fairly accurate.

"That's right, mister," Highpockets agreed.

"Any plans for the ceremony?" asked the Rev. Oates.

All arrangements, Johnny told him, were in the hands of Bert Lacey, his employer, and Professor Tufts. Try as he might, the Rev. Oates could not penetrate that simple defense. Johnny knew, dimly, that the preacher disapproved of saloons, and, consequently, had cast aspersions on Bert, his benefactor. Johnny was not anti-religious. He had never given his immortal soul a passing thought, except very briefly, while the stagecoach was tipping over that day in early June. But no man, no matter what kind of collar he wore, could slander Bert Lacey, or try to put him out of business. Johnny was easy to influence and sway, in many respects, but not when his loyalties were touched. He was relieved to see Charley Tufts approaching.

"Good evening, sir," said Charley to the Rev. Oates, in his best Yale manner.

"Ah! Professor Tufts, I presume," the preacher said.

"Professor *emeritus*," Tufts said.

"We call him Tufts for short," said Johnny.

Both the educated men smiled, and nodded, in a friendly way.

"I was asking Mr. Highpockets if he had made arrangements for his wedding ceremony," said the preacher.

"Just what I rode over to see you about," said Charley, and both Johnny and the preacher showed surprise.

"You mean. . . ? You mean that you wish me to officiate?" asked the Rev. Oates.

"Hadn't we better check with Bert on that?" asked Johnny, fearfully.

"I've already consulted with Mr. Lacey," Charley said.

"Indeed," said the Rev. Oates, sensing possible complications. Then he added, affably:

"You are a scholar, I understand, Professor Tufts. How splendid! We must have some good talks."

"*Adonoi uevovrechchoh! Anachnu nedabare!*" said Charley, in excellent Hebrew.

The Rev. Oates beamed and extended his hand.

"Imagine being privileged to speak in the language used by Our Saviour Himself," he said, quite wistfully.

Sweat broke out on Johnny's forehead.

Charley was on the point of reminding the preacher that

159

Jesus of Nazareth probably did not speak Hebrew, but a dialect, most likely, of Aramaic common to nomad carpenters and sheepherders in the Holy Land two thousand years back. He refrained from doing so.

"If Our Lord should return to earth, as promised, you would be able to converse with Him," the Rev. Oates continued, still ecstatic.

"According to George Bernard Shaw, all the angels in Heaven have been obliged to switch to English, since angels from English-speaking lands are such inept linguists. In that case, you, yourself, would be able to talk with the Lord, directly," Charley said.

"I have a smattering of Latin," the preacher said.

"Do I have to get married in some Bohunk language?" Johnny asked, alarmed.

"All you have to do is say 'I do' when I nudge you," Charley said.

Bert Lacey, having had weeks in which to elaborate on his plans for his new town, and having seen his saloon and dance hall succeed beyond even his expectations, was beginning to think in terms of months and years, instead of days and weeks. With his sense of showmanship, Bert had arranged that Mrs. Weckerling, the Deadwood seamstress, should arrive from Mondak on the same day Edna B. was delivered f.o.b. Glendive by Monkey Ward.

Bert's plans for the joint reception of the town's first ladies were revealed to the Rev. Theo Oates by Charley Tufts in a most tactful way. Naturally, the Professor did not disclose everything, in detail. Lacey had been worrying considerably about the fight to split the county, in order to give Sidney a county seat and the church crowd a majority in the new county votes. If Bert built up Trembles as a gay open town, only to have its best features snuffed out in a few short years, he was building on sand. On the other hand, if the gay minority in the new county had only to slip over Cedar Coulee in order to relax, Bert would be ideally situated.

Bert proposed to offer the Sidney boosters, through the Rev. Theo Oates, the political support of the voters from Cedar Coulee south and westward, and let the new county go dry, if they would agree that the southern boundary of the proposed new county would be fixed somewhere north of Trembles and its grove of quaking aspens.

So Charley Tufts offered the Sidney Methodist Church the Highpockets wedding ceremony, with Parson Oates presiding. This was to be free and open to all, and if an overflow crowd showed up, the vows were to be taken on the church porch, so that those who were seated within and the others who stood without, could witness the affair. Babies born in Trembles or southward were to be baptized in Sidney, Trembles couples would be married there, and the Rev. Oates would get the lower Dawson County funerals.

It was further understood and agreed that there were to be no churches in Trembles, and that any of its inhabitants so minded would attend services in Sidney.

Everybody won, and nobody lost. The Rev. Theo Oates convinced Mrs. Thavanot, and the civic leaders of Sidney, that the arrangements were beneficial and sound. The local politicians who wanted a county of their own in the lower end of the valley would be assured of their goal. Cedar Coulee would be an ideal boundary line, between the sheep and the goats.

That was how matters stood on the eve of the day when Johnny and his entourage started out for Glendive, to meet the N.P. morning train.

CHAPTER THIRTEEN

Old Knick and the Monkey Ward Wife

DURING the last few days before Highpockets' bride was to arrive, all able-bodied men around Trembles and Newlon pitched in, whenever they had spare time, to help Johnny finish his cabin. Logs and lumber, hogsheads of water, staple kitchen supplies, and other necessary objects and articles were hauled along the south side of the canyon. Since the soil was hard-packed, dry, and held down by the roots of the sage and tough bunch grass, a road from Trembles to Highpockets' claim came into being incidentally as wagon wheels, stone boats and horses coursed back and forth. The claim had not been fenced, but some of the posts were in place.

Johnny's friends had consulted one another about wedding presents, and those selected were eminently practical. Bert Lacey, never hesitant about straining his credit, was making the most princely gift, which would not have been within Johnny's means for years to come. Although the services of the only available well-digging outfit, run by Old Buck Mavity of Fairview, were badly needed in Trembles proper, Bert sent Mavity up to Highpockets' place, and the veteran water wizard, after an incredible amount of prospecting over the ground, with willow wands and other occult devices, had chosen the spot, and struck water at eighty feet, which, considering that Johnny's land was on the slope toward the foothills, was not bad.

Old Knick and the Monkey Ward Wife

The famous railroad pamphlet, and the "encouraging words" spread far and wide by Jim Hill, assured prospective settlers that the Yellowstone country was bubbling with sweet springs and that wells could be dug overnight.

The well itself was less than half of Bert's present to Edna B. He had sent to Montgomery Ward for four "Clipper" windmills, complete with twelve-foot wheels, fifty-foot towers, springs, quadrants, pumping jacks, anti-freezing and sanitary double stock waterer, and two horsepower "Always Ready" gasoline engines with drop-forged steel crank shafts and "everlasting" machine-cut gears. One mill and one engine were for Highpockets. When it is remembered that Bert Lacey came into the country in June with $1,000 and in July committed himself to an outlay of $500 to assure his servant, Highpockets, of water on his claim, one can form an inadequate idea of Bert's generosity.

The moment Old Knick, at La Mesa, heard that Highpockets was going to have a windmill, the old Indian fighter and ex-cavalryman got itching feet. Old Knick was as complex a character as I have encountered in years of wandering. Knick, in his day, had potted quite a number of Indians. On the other hand, he had lived in harmony with various bands of Rees, Crows, Blackfoot and Sioux, with russet female company. Most probably he had quite a few half-breed offspring on various reservations. He would curse Sitting Bull, deride any statements about the Medicine Man's nobility, and in the next breath tell of instances of Indian courage and wisdom.

Knick read nothing but seed catalogues, and had no ear for music. He could say, on hearing a whine in the night, whether it was uttered by a wolf or coyote, male or female, far or near. But, according to his own statement, he could not tell whether somebody was squeezing a bob-cat's tail in a door jamb or playing a record on the phonograph. Although Knick at seventy-two could perform feats of strength and energy, he was so lazy that, according to the champion liar, Bat Horner, the old man would stand for hours with a match head against a wagon wheel, waiting for the team to start so he would not have to scratch the match himself.

From the first days in 1905, when the preliminary surveyors and reclamation service officials came into the Yellowstone to start work on the irrigation project (to the disgust of old-timers), Old Knick was employed, off and on, in some capacity. Knick made the trip upriver in the *Expansion* with Captain Marsh in order to report to the government men whether or not it was still navigable. The engineers learned more from Knick than they did from the famous steamboat captain. Grant Marsh had seen the country largely from the deck of a steamboat, or the back room of some hotel.

George Knickerbocker had roamed the bad lands, flats and foothills, dodging Indians and trapping beaver and otter, so that he knew every foot of the lower valley and the country between the Yellowstone and the Missouri, as far up as Fort Benton, and as far down as Bismarck.

In 1907, Knick was crumb boss at La Mesa. A crumb boss in a construction or engineers' camp filled kerosene lamps, cleaned the chimneys, lugged wood and kept fires going in cold weather, removed the grass from between cracks in board walks, lent a hand when there were oats to be stacked or hay to be unloaded, walked the fire strip now and then, when the grass got extra dry, and notified the stable boss when stray horses or cattle wormed their way into or out of the barbed wire enclosure.

As imperfectly as Knick reacted to a concord of sweet sounds or fine sentiments expressed poetically, his sense of color was as keen as Audubon's. No one ever found out where or how Knick had been raised, but the year Sitting Bull surrendered, Knick went to work as roustabout at Fort Buford. He was a deserter from the army, but he took that chance and was fairly safe in doing so, since hot debate as to the conduct of Major Reno at the battle of the Little Big Horn had raged in army circles, in Congress and the press ever since Custer's defeat, and no one in authority wanted too many eyewitnesses to be brought to light. Old Knick— of course, in the Fort Buford days he was not so old—was always a favorite with certain of the officers' and engineers' wives.

At Fort Buford, several of the officers' wives had tried to beautify the desolate spot with flower gardens, and in every instance had failed, lamentably. Knick finally broke down, and started planting goldenglow, lupines, what he called try-tonies, tiger lilies, and whatever flowering plants for which the seeds and bulbs were brought him by the river captains. Knick carried the water in buckets from the Missouri River, running the risk of stray arrows or bullets from the Sioux encamped near by. Whatever Knick planted grew, and he had to look extra fierce and scornful in order to hide his tenderness for each blossom, shoot and vine. That somewhere he had learned gardening from a master was evident, and also that he had inherited and developed an eye for color that enabled him to buy thread in town to match women's clothes, without carrying samples.

At La Mesa, Knick was not encouraged to beautify the camp because the engineers felt that there was so much talk around the valley of government waste and extravagance that settlers and politicians might murmur if high spots of garden colors enlivened the drab La Mesa plain. So Knick threw up his government job and hiked to Trembles, stopping at Newlon to buy a few small tools on the way. There was beer and whisky at Newlon, but Knick did not touch a drop. Instead, he walked up the slope to Highpockets' place and those in town who looked toward the horizon saw his grim, stocky figure outlined against the evening sky.

Old Knick could not have been thinking about the old days, or he would not have exposed himself that way. He was looking across the sagebrush flats, the tents, cabins, board shacks and water barrels, beyond the tricky convolutions of the Yellowstone, a little less muddy in low water season, to the twisted buttes and bad lands. At that hour of the evening, the faded tints of sandstone and disintegrating granite, of coal and chalk-white alkali, were blending and deepening: overtones and vagaries of the spectrum, nuances versus brilliance, desolation into mystery, the slow nightly death of the dinosaur gods. And if the distant rumble of a heavy wagon stirred echoes of thundering hooves; if shadow shapes streaming from sage took fleeting forms of bison; it is for such purposes that vistas seen and sounds heard are stored in the memory, submerged, but not lost.

In the cabin on the claim, or out, Highpockets disliked no one, disdained no one. He was an unspoken apology with patched pants. Knick, on the contrary, had much to complain about. The plows were overturning good grass, destroying roots and all. Barbed-wire fences cut forests of space into kindling. Knick had as much personal regard for Highpockets as for gawky curlew chicks whose necks he had wrung, now and then, for the passing tactile pleasure. Knick feuded with curlews because their shapes were stringy and their cries were maudlin. Meadow larks irritated him because their songs were sweet, when everything was going wrong. Meanwhile he spaded and prepared a flower garden for the Monkey Ward wife.

166

Old Knick and the Monkey Ward Wife

In the Highpockets cabin, now nearly complete, but un-furnished, Johnny slept in one corner, farthest from the door, on well-worn quilts and blankets. Knick, always with a final contemptuous look at the excess properties, stretched out on the board floor, with his boots for a pillow.

The day finally came when Johnny, in company with Char-ley Tufts and Mrs. Baron, had to dress himself in store clothes (another wedding present technically for Edna, from the Smith's Clothing House in Sidney) and start for Glendive in a two-seated rig loaned for the purpose by the Rag Time Livery Barn. The inhabitants of Trembles—there was a size-able bunch of them then—watched him depart, and a couple of cow hands shot off their six-shooters. When the welcom-ing trio drove through Newlon, they were saluted by the O'Briens, the innumerable Simard brothers and *petite* Jen-nette, Josefa Dotsen and her three rangy, taciturn brothers, and what were left of the surveyors and engineers, number-ing four, from the government camp. Scotty and I had con-trived to get to Glendive, he because of the need for a check-up on account of recent typhoid, and I because, luck-ily, one of the consulting engineers I shall call Stackpole was due for an inspection of the project.

So on the morning that the struggling No. 3, with two locomotives, brought Edna from the east, Scotty and I were waiting on the N.P. platform.

Howard Roby was busier than usual around the railroad yards that morning, since the early freight from St. Paul had dropped off the box car and gondola filled with windmills, furniture and materials ordered by Bert Lacey. Bert had hoped that the stuff would arrive ahead of Edna, so that when she first saw her new cabin it would be ready for occu-pancy. The N.P. had disposed otherwise. The cars, with their

167

contents, were on a side track, and were to be unloaded that morning.

Highpockets was wearing a store suit, of serviceable navy blue, shoes that pinched and squeaked, a white cotton shirt with soft collar, and a bow tie that would stay level only during earthquakes. Charley Tufts had on a new flannel shirt of pale blue-gray, a Stetson with a stiff brim—in contrast to that of Highpockets', which flopped—high-laced boots and riding breeches of a conservative cut. He was so nervous that he had complained that a cat which had walked through his room at the Hotel Jordan had been stamping her feet. Mrs. Baron looked as pleased as if Mrs. Thavanot, of Sidney, and Mrs. Perham Cheeley, of Glendive, had just carried out a successful suicide pact.

The No. 3 was late that morning. Roby and a few railroad men, with the aid of an old switching engine and crew, were attempting to detach the two cars of stuff billed to Bert Lacey and shunt them onto the government spur, so that the contents could be loaded into wagons. There was a gondola loaded with drums of kerosene in the way, so the switching engine, guided by professional and amateur signalers, clunked into it. The couplings caught, but the engineer started away too abruptly. The back of the gondola, which had been wobbly to start with, gave way and a kerosene drum dropped to the track. The engineer stopped, threw the engine into reverse, backed too far, and ran over the drum of kerosene. A spark from some other engine set the oil afire. Before anybody could do anything much, a gust of wind fanned the flames. The box car in which Highpockets' furniture, "Always Ready" engine for the well, and other essentials were waiting, caught fire. Three or four men ran this way and that for crowbars. The switching engine puffed and snorted forward, spilling more drums of oil.

When the smoke had cleared away, the box car and High-pockets' furniture and equipment were either burned or ruined. The gondola containing the four fifty-foot metal towers was intact.

Finally No. 3 steamed into sight, slowed down and came to a stop alongside the platform.

My teeth were chattering.

Assorted passengers descended, to the number of six, including Engineer Stackpole who, temporarily, had slipped my mind. Then appeared at the head of the steps of the car nearest us a pale young woman in a blue-gray tailor-made suit that caught up the identical tones of Charley Tufts' new shirt. The garments might have been made from the same bolt of cloth. Edna B. was nervous, but strangely self-possessed, timid as a bird. As she stepped down, an inch or two of her slender ankles were revealed. Her foot was neat and shapely. She was smoothly corseted. Her coat was long, with square shoulders and severe lapels, and it hit her just at the level where, presumably, were her knees. The skirt, box-pleated, went down to the top of her ankles.

Edna's hat was of darker blue felt, with a fifteen-inch brim, a sort of inverted cloth basin about four inches high, wound with ribbon on the bias, set off by a perforated metal buckle and two feathers, dyed deep blue and wishing to be gay. Her face and pale hands were those of the photograph. Her eyes were dark blue and wistful, her forehead clear, her mouth very sensitive around the corners. She knew she was to be met at the train and was first aware of Charley's blue shirt that exactly matched her suit. So, taking a deep breath, Edna smiled at him.

A moment later, Mrs. Baron stepped up and introduced herself, then Highpockets, who was quaking like an aspen.

169

Edna glanced again at Tufts, taken aback, then turned to face Johnny.

"You're Mr. Highpockets?" she asked.

"I sure as hell am, ma'am," Johnny said.

"This is Professor Tufts," said Mrs. Baron.

"Oh," said Edna, and looked up at Charley again. "Our . . . that is . . . your shirt is just like my suit," she stammered.

"A coincidence," said Charley, who looked older than he had the day before. "We'll do everything to make you comfortable. . . . I'll put on another shirt," he added, without his usual self-possession.

"Please don't. You mustn't take the trouble," Edna said.

Howard Roby interrupted, hat in hand, to tell Highpockets that his stuff had all been burned. Highpockets heard what Roby said, but he was in such a state that he could not make sense out of it, just then.

Meanwhile, Mr. Stackpole had halted on the edge of the group, near me. I was about to apologize for not having greeted him sooner when he nodded amiably and took me aside.

"That young woman who just arrived. I was given to understand, by an official of the railroad, that she was being sent, by a mail-order house called Montgomery Ward, to marry a settler out here," he said, and I saw that his curiosity had been aroused.

"Yes, sir," I said. "In a manner of speaking."

"On the train I attempted to engage her in conversation," said the big engineer. The sartorial perfection of his attire was already attracting considerable attention, since Edna and her entourage were moving slowly away, toward the Jordan.

"Conversation is quite obviously not one of her foremost accomplishments," Mr. Stackpole added.

170

"She's getting married, tonight, down the valley," I said.

"Ah. Excellent. To the intelligent-looking chap in Gobelin blue?" he asked.

"No. The other one," I said.

"Preposterous!" said Mr. Stackpole, emphatically.

CHAPTER FOURTEEN

Developments after a Shooting Case
Is "Closed"

T H E coroner of Dawson County and nearly all the inhabitants and transients, after the neat report to the effect that Lazlo Richter, described simply as "an Austrian laborer," had died from a shot fired "in self-defense" by Chester E. Donaldson, assumed that the incident had ended. So did the thirty-nine sad and resentful Bohunks who started, two and two, down the valley, that hot Sunday morning. They knew they had no chance for justice, or even explanation.

Chet Donaldson swaggered and blustered around his camp, phoning his agent in Glendive for more men, and trying to get the burned bunk-house and warehouse replaced. But Anne Prentice was occupying the major share of his thoughts. Lots of women had fallen for Chet, his debonair ways and handsome features. He had not lost his head about one for years, and he knew, this time, that he was out of his depth. He had to have Anne, and to get her he must marry her. Chet felt no remorse for having shot a Bohunk. Before the smoke had cleared from his six-shooter, however, he had begun to worry about how Anne would take the news. So he dressed himself with care, slicked up his red hair with Ed. Pinaud's hair tonic, and presented himself at the Prentice camp.

172

Developments after a Shooting Case Is "Closed"

It was the hottest hour of the day, and one of the hottest days of the summer. Chet found Noel Prentice sitting morosely in his office shack, checking payroll figures with the time-keeper. Noel was employing about eighty men, all told, just then, and half of them were Bohunks. The other half, encouraged by the fact that the foreigners had been "run out" of Donaldson's camp, were muttering in groups and there had been some talk of a similar move to rid the "Americans" of unfair competition.

Like men of his type, today glibly classified as paranoiacs, Chet was able, on occasion, to act contrite, sympathetic and humble.

"I feel like hell about what happened," Chet said. "I suppose you heard."

"Yes. I heard," said Noel.

"If I hadn't stepped in when I did, there'd have been a lot of bloodshed," Chet said.

"Men who carry guns end up by shooting somebody," said Noel.

"I've got a tough bunch over there," Chet said.

Prentice made no further comment.

"Is Miss Anne at home?" Chet asked.

"She's still asleep," Noel said. He did not suggest that Chet sit down and wait.

"I'll take a ride over to B. F. Shoat's camp, and stop in on my way back," Chet said.

Noel said nothing at all.

Meanwhile, at Trembles, Walt Murray was experiencing a few of the worst hours of his life, thus far. He had awakened at noon with a smarting, bandaged right hand, a splitting headache that kept white lights shooting under his eyelids, a taste in his mouth that made him think of camels, and a blank in his memory. When he could sit up, he saw through a crack in the door, ajar, Ah Flunk with a dustpan and broom. Slowly, bit by bit, he was able to place himself. He tried to rise, finally succeeded, and balanced himself, by means of his left hand, in the frame of the doorway. There was no sound of music, but quite a few men were at the bar. They saw him in the mirror and let out a roar. Bat Horner was among them. He went over to Walt and said, "Good afternoon."

"What day is it?" Walt asked.

Bat led him to a table, ordered black coffee, made Walt drink two big mugs of it, took him outside to the water barrel and helped him soak his head. Then Bat told him a little of what had happened. Before he got fairly started, Walt's face became almost maniacal with apprehension. He slapped his left pocket.

"The gun you had's gone," Bat said, laconically.

"Where's Anne?"

"Back in camp," Bat said.

"Who took her there?" asked Walt.

"Her old man," Bat said.

"Why didn't somebody wake me? What happened to my hand? And what about my rig?"

"Christ couldn't have waked you. Besides, Donaldson borrowed your rig," Bat said.

"I've got to see Anne," Walt said, and staggered across to the Rag Time Livery Barn. There Lucian Gibbs apologized for letting his rig go, without asking him, and offered Walt another. As soon as Lucian could get the substitute rig hitched up, Walt climbed in and started south along the stage road. With each mile, his memories grew clearer. He recalled how Anne had looked at Chet, and Chet's possessive, overbearing way with her.

174

Developments after a Shooting Case Is "Closed"

Chet was riding along the ditch between Prentice's camp and the shabby layout of B. F. Shoat.

A plan was forming vaguely in Chet's inflamed mind. The profits Chet had hoped to make at his camp were threatening to become losses, instead. If he could ruin Shoat, so that the Donaldson firm would not have to pay him for his summer's work, and, by helping Prentice, put Noel under obligations to him, Chet could make a better showing, financially, and bolster up his chances with Anne. The construction season was relatively short in eastern Montana. Contractors could not move dirt economically until after the frost was well out of the ground, in March or April, and they had to close up camp when winter came. That might be around November first, or as late as January first.

When Donaldson got as far as Shoat's camp he rode toward the office. Shoat had only thirty men, of whom ten were Bohunks. As Chet rode over the crest, he saw B. F. Shoat and a few men playing horseshoes in the shade of the stable tent. There were no wooden buildings in that camp, except the tar-paper shack called the office, where B. F. Shoat slept, and a timber-lined cave on one of the side hills, used for storing powder.

As Chet rode nearer, he saw that the contractor was playing with a bunch of Bohunks. Most of the "white men" were asleep in their bunks. Chet was still wearing his gun, but he did not relish going nearer any foreigners who had heavy iron horseshoes at hand. So he yelled at B. F. Shoat:

"Come up here, Shoat. I want to look over your ditch."

B. F. Shoat got up, and walked reluctantly to the canal bank. He was far behind schedule with his section of the ditch, having run into the most troublesome kind of rock ledges, protruding only a few inches above the level where the canal bottom was to be. That meant that he had to blast them, carefully, from the top, and when he blew out the rock below the level of the bottom he had to fill in again, to preserve the shape of the canal. Not only that, his plant and equipment were old, held together with hay-wire, his "white men" were sullen and rebellious because the food was so bad, his horses ready to drop, and only the Bohunks, whom he treated with consideration within the limits of his means, were ready to stand by him.

"You oughtta be ashamed, associatin' with those Bohunks. Can't you find white men to play with?" Chet began.

"We are all God's critters," said B. F. Shoat, who was deeply pious.

"How in hell do you expect to get this canal dug in time? The summer's more than half gone, and you're not a quarter through," Chet said.

"Maybe we'll have a late fall," B. F. Shoat said.

"Maybe you think you'll get an extension of time," said Chet. "But you won't. Not one day."

"Your father's a reasonable man," B. F. Shoat said.

"My father isn't running this job. He's left it up to me."

"I'll do the best I can," Shoat said, humbly.

While Anne, as lovely in sleep as awake, was peacefully unconscious in her tent, Fidlio G. Sharpe, back in Donaldson's camp, was carrying on a campaign of his own.

The Wobblies had comparatively few slogans and principles, but the few they had were easy to state and to understand. If one granted that the working class and the employing class had nothing in common, and that a struggle must go on until the workers owned and controlled the means of production, thus ending the wage system, the other premises were not difficult to accept. Foremost among them was the watchword:

176

"An injury to one is an injury to all."

Fidlio, as he indoctrinated small groups of Donaldson's "white" workers, reasoned as follows:

1. In a war between the working class and employers, more is accomplished by striking at powerful and ruthless employers than weak and amiable ones.

2. A foreign worker is one of the workers of the world, with the same standing and entitled to the same protection as one who happened to be a citizen of the United States.

3. If a worker is shot dead in cold blood, and the law of the land has no agents to enforce it, the dead man's fellow workers should step in, and revenge him.

4. The most effective weapon the workers had was sabotage.

"We'll make such a mess of this job that hoboes will write songs about it," he said to his fellow Wobblies.

Fidlio did not waste a moment getting started. The notes in the time-books had been scribbled by Tom Bone and nobody else understood them or could unravel them. On those notes depended the monthly payroll, the preparation of which had barely been started by Bone. If his records of the hours each employee had worked during July were lost, each and every man on the job could claim full time for the month, and if enough of them stood up for their rights, Donaldson would have to come through, or the government would step in.

On this question of the government's relationship with the contractors on the ditch, Fidlio had had long talks with me. He had not told me why he wanted to know, or what he planned to do. But I was glad to give him what information I could.

The subject of the engineers' responsibility for conditions and conduct in a contractor's camp was a troublesome one just then. The engineers in charge of the Lower Yellowstone project made it a practice never to interfere in a contractor's affairs unless the government stood to lose money. The government had no labor policy, except that of dog eat dog, and the unwritten law that "reds," who then were called "socialists" or "anarchists," were dangerous. Gompers' A. F. of L., then as now, abhorred the idea of class war, or class antagonism, distrusted and expelled "radicals," kept one craft engaged in pettifogging disputes with another, and played ball with the big employers. Political activity was taboo, both with the A. F. of L. and the I. W. W.

The I. W. W., which nourished the idea of industrial unionism in its infancy, as against the old-fashioned and ineffectual craft union theory, would have nothing to do with politics or politicians. The Wobblies believed that political activity was futile.

I had a talk with my brother, Charles. My conscience was troubling me. I loved, respected and admired my older brother, and the level head he had, so utterly different from mine. Ordinarily I would have cut off my fingers rather than bring tales to him of what I saw on the project, good or bad. I wanted to form my own opinion about what I saw. Particularly, I did not want any of my friends or acquaintances to think that I was an informer. But when I felt sure there was going to be a bloody battle, with the "white" hoboes as aggressors and the Bohunks as victims, I thought he ought to know.

"Boss," I said. (That was his nickname at La Mesa.) "There's going to be a riot at Prentice's camp."

"What makes you think so?" he asked.

"The 'white men' there, after what happened at Donaldson's camp, want to run the Bohunks out of the country. The same thing's getting started in some of the other camps." I mentioned a few by name.

We talked until past midnight, one of the longest talks we ever had. Slowly he was impressed by the accumulation of stray bits of information I gave him.

"You like the Bohunks, don't you?" he asked.

"Yes," I said.

"Better than most of the 'white men'?"

"That's because I can't understand all the Bohunks say," I explained.

Charles looked surprised, but he considered carefully what I had said. He thought everything over, carefully, and never made snap judgments.

"If you could understand all the languages, you'd like one as well as the other?" Charles asked.

"Probably," I admitted.

"We can't like everybody. We have a few good friends. You seem to make friends with people much easier than I do. We dislike a few people so much that it bothers us to see them, or hear about them. Most of the men and women you'll meet come in between. They're fine, if you don't get too close to them, and if you do, you'll be disappointed and confused. That's why civilized men have developed codes of manners. That's the only way to keep others at the distance you prefer. If you're cordial with everybody, then everybody's on your neck all the time. If you're snobbish, nobody likes you," he said. Then he added: "If you hate too many people, you'll wear yourself out."

"I don't care so much whether I like other people as whether they like me," I said.

Charles shook his head and gave up. "Since you were a foot high," he said, "I've never been able to figure you out."

"If you ever do, tell me," I said, sincerely.

Before I left, to ride down the valley in time for work next

179

morning, Charles went back to the subject of the impending riots.

"If I go to Glendive, and speak to the sheriff . . ." he began.

I was horrified, and interrupted frantically:

"For God's sake, Boss, don't do that!"

He was amazed by my earnestness and positiveness.

"Why not?" he asked. "Isn't the sheriff responsible?"

"He'll deputize all the wrong men. They'll be worse than Vigilantes," I said.

Charles looked at me closely, and sadly.

"Why in hell do men have to fight with one another?" he asked. "And what can we do about it?"

I did not try to answer either question.

I finally got the information that, if a contractor did not pay his men, the men, singly or severally, could take action against him that would tie up his plant. Since a tie-up menaced the interests of the government, the engineers would have to step in and, if the contractor still failed to meet his payroll, the government could call upon the bondsmen to make good.

Contractors were paid by the special fiscal agents of the Reclamation Service according to estimates of work accomplished—that is, so many cubic yards of excavation, so many linear feet of piles driven, so many yards of concrete laid, etc. But from each monthly payment, the United States "held back" ten percent, as a safeguard against a contractor's failing to finish the job. In July, 1907, for instance, Donaldson had completed about one-third of the work on his contract for Division Two. If his contract amounted roughly to $1,000,-000, he would have received $300,000 and the government would have "held back" $33,333.33. If a contractor defaulted on his contract and his bondsmen had to make good, the contractor would be permanently out of business, and bankrupt besides.

The above information I relayed to Fidlio G. Sharpe. He already had struck a telling blow at Donaldson. That Sunday noon, before the body of Lazlo Richter had been buried unceremoniously, Fidlio began passing out whisky to Tom Bone. After the second drink, Fidlio left the jug where Tom could reach it. In half an hour, the old time-keeper was roaring. The figures and notes he tried to keep in lines and columns jumped, hopped and scrambled. He started to light his pipe and tossed the burning match into a box of carbon paper, which caught fire.

The little blaze in the time-keeper's shack was not serious, but the Wobblies, who had been forewarned that something might happen, in pulling the drunken Tom to safety and extinguishing the flames, managed to get possession of the time-book and deliver it to Fidlio.

Fidlio promptly loaded the drunken Tom Bone into a rig bound for Glendive.

As soon as Chet Donaldson got back to his camp after a most unsatisfactory interview with Anne Prentice, he rode over to the time-keeper's shack, which was dark, to find out why Tom Bone was not working on the payroll. He found the shack empty, a few charred papers on the floor, and no Tom. Roaring, Chet rushed into the bunk-house where the crumb boss slept and jerked him out of his bunk.

"Where's the time-keeper?" Chet asked.

"He got pie-eyed and left camp," the crumb boss said.

"How? On foot?" Chet asked. The 'boes, aroused from their sleep, began to twitch, scratch and growl.

"Pipe down!" one of them yelled.

A chorus of jeers and catcalls started raggedly, then grew. Someone who recognized Chet yelled:

"Look out, mates. It's Deadwood Dick!"

Chet, insane with rage, reached for his gun and someone threw a cold lantern, which hit a post near his head and shattered, spilling kerosene. He heard the noise of heavy boots being banged on the bunk boards, more growls and yells, and beat it out of the door. His camp was out of hand. The payroll was not ready. Chet retreated ignominiously to the damaged office shack, and sat down, trying to get himself together. The departed Bohunks had been paid off. That left sixty of the "white men" to be taken care of, on the morrow. Chet could not face the ordeal of struggling with the accounts. He could think of no one capable of doing the job for him except Fidlio G. Sharpe. Old Abe Johnson was too slow. Landry could barely write his name. He had fired the warehouse man for letting the warehouse burn up. So Chet decided to give up a trip to town and have his agent ride down from Glendive with the emergency funds. Then he collared the night watchman and sent him for the crumb boss. Chet did not have the nerve to go into that bunk-house again.

The crumb boss, at Chet's instructions, went to Fidlio's bunk and roused him. Fidlio was not asleep, but he pretended to be.

"The boss wants you," the crumb boss said.

"What for?" asked Fidlio.

"Search me," the crumb boss said.

Fidlio got up, washed, combed his hair, and dressed, taking his time. When he got to the time-keeper's shack, Chet was pawing at the drawers, shelves and pigeonholes, and papers were scattered all over the floor.

"Hello," Fidlio said.

Chet started nervously, wheeled and straightened, then became friendly and obsequious.

"I want you to do me a favor, Sharpe," he said.

182

"What favor?" Fidlio asked, non-committally.

"Bone, the bastard, 's got drunk and blown the camp. You've got to help me with the payroll," said Chet.

"I'm no pencil stiff," Fidlio said. He was weighing the pros and cons. If the workers were eventually to take over production, some of them would have to learn about management. Fidlio hoped that while he was fussing with the payroll, which he would pad just as far as the traffic would bear, he might get a look at the books that showed the profits. He wanted badly to know, for his own sake and for the cause, what the profits were on a job where men got $2.00 a day.

"You won't let me down?" asked Chet, as if he and Fidlio were old college roommates or childhood playmates.

"I'll give it a whirl," said Fidlio. "Where's your time-book?"

Chet bit his lips, but he had to come clean.

"I can't find it," he said.

CHAPTER FIFTEEN

For Better or For Worse

GRANT MARSH, captain of the stern-wheeler *Expansion*, started down-river from Glendive, the morning the Monkey Ward wife was due, a full three hours before the N.P. train got in from the east. The captain had a cargo of cement billed to the Headgates, and a large number of passengers who wanted to go farther down the valley.

The Yellowstone was losing its volume, velocity and depth, following the high-water season in June. Still there were few difficulties of navigation for a seasoned expert like Marsh, who had spent his life on America's great rivers and conquered them, one by one. Captain Marsh had learned to steer from Mark Twain, helped save Grant at Shiloh by transporting Union troops by water, and had brought the remains of the 7th Cavalry out of the Yellowstone after Custer's debacle on the Little Big Horn.

On most of his voyages that made history, Captain Marsh had preferred to dispense with the services of a pilot. Pilots were notoriously exigent and none of them knew the rivers as well as he did. Also their fees were high, and while Grant Marsh did not weep or moan when he lost a cold thousand at cards, he was extra careful with the company's money—any company he worked for. In this instance, however, in order to please the Glendive county officials, he had taken on a relative of the sheriff's, as pilot, and let him steer when the going was easy.

Throughout his life, Marsh was known far and wide as a fair and amiable man, when not aroused, but as the years went by, he followed the usual Shakespearean pattern, modified by his outdoor life and iron constitution. He talked a lot about the old times and famous voyages, told stories about what had happened on board the steamboats and ashore, and did not like being interrupted. Nearly everyone in Glendive, in authority or out, admired the old man and gave him all the leeway. But in 1905 or 1906, a young editor came to Glendive from the Middle West (referred to as "the east," like the front end of a Masonic Hall). The newcomer, in order to keep up lively quarrels and antagonisms between his weekly and the other eastern Montana sheets, took a new and progressive stand. Editorially, and in his so-called "news columns," he pooh-poohed all talk about the good old days and stalwart pioneers.

"Glendive has a past, of course," the new editor wrote. "The past has buried itself, and so much the better. Let us look at our valley, as it is now, and will be in the future. The watchword is progress. The old-timers would have us believe that the countryside has gone to the dogs. Actually Glendive is growing by leaps and bounds, bringing itself up-to-date. Most of the improvements are proposed and carried out by the newcomers, with modern ideas, in spite of the inertia of the dwindling band of has-beens who fought Montana's acquisition of statehood, and practically everything that has taken place since."

This editor was always gunning for Captain Grant Marsh, because Marsh was the most renowned of the pioneers. The editor did not overlook Lewis and Clark, or Audubon, the publicity-loving Custer who lost all his men, the old Indian

185

chiefs, the outlaws, or the notorious Vigilante leader, "Flopping Bill." But Marsh was at hand and the others were gone. So Marsh was usually described in that particular weekly newspaper as "The Ancient Mariner." Not everybody had read Coleridge's classic, but the readers sensed that the title was disparaging.

No celebrities from the outside passed through Glendive without meeting and paying their respects to Captain Marsh, if possible, and, in each instance, the new progressive editor got no first-hand information as to what was said or done. When General Arthur MacArthur, the father of the general now governing Japan, stopped between trains at Glendive, with the victorious Japanese General Kuroro and his staff, in the course of an officially chaperoned tour of the United States and the Jamestown Exposition, all the visitors gathered in the Hotel Jordan to shake hands with Grant Marsh and listen, through an interpreter, to his account of the record-breaking trip (financially) from Fort Benton to St. Louis in the *Luella* with $1,250,000 in gold dust aboard. The Captain also told of the walking race he had lost to the Brule Sioux, Fast Walker, in the course of which the latter walked right over the horizon and left Marsh miles behind. What pleased the Japanese the most, according to Charlie Kinney, the chief of police, was Marsh's tale about how a bunch of Sioux Indians, under Sitting Bull, chopped several cords of cottonwood logs (relatively worthless as fuel for steamboats), stacked them on the bank of the Missouri where Marsh and his steamboat were to pass, and by means of a vegetable dye the squaws cooked up from native bark, stained the ends of the logs on the river side to resemble cedar. The Indians figured, correctly, that if the white captain believed the wood was cedar, he would make fast to the bank. Having taken all that trouble, the Sioux psychologists felt sure Marsh would then decide that he might as well take on the cottonwood in case of emergency. That is what Marsh actually did. The old man liked telling stories in which he came out on the short end, as well as reciting his triumphs.

When the rig I was driving for Worthington T. Stackpole reached the Headgates, the last of the cement was being unloaded from the *Expansion*. As soon as the consulting engineer learned that Captain Marsh was going down-river as far as Elm's Ferry, near Sidney and Trembles, to my great delight, Mr. Stackpole asked if we could not drive the rig on board, ride down on the steamboat and be put ashore in time for the Montgomery Ward wedding. Mr. Stackpole could not seem to get Edna Bispham off his mind, particularly the fact that she seemed to be marrying the wrong man. The engineer was paid a large fee, daily, for investigating the problem of navigation, with reference to the government dam, and could think of no better way to get a consensus in the valley than attending such an important social function and taking an informal poll.

Captain Marsh was pleased to have a distinguished guest and, in order to devote his time to Mr. Stackpole, turned the wheel over to the licensed pilot, who was thick with all the county politicians.

Just before we shoved off from the Headgates landing, we saw pass along the stage road the rig from Trembles containing the bridal party. Mrs. Baron was sitting in the front seat with Highpockets, who was driving. In the back seat, Charley Tufts and Edna B. were in earnest conversation. Very little of what Charley said escaped the ear of Mrs. Baron and afterward she summarized for my benefit the gist of what she had heard.

I think before Edna met Charley Tufts on the Glendive railroad platform she had been entirely on her own. From that moment she depended upon Charley for guidance. In the course of their first ride down the valley together, Charley pointed out the landmarks among the foothills and the wondrous bad lands. From him Edna learned about the tyrannosaurus and flaming volcanoes, the ice caps that, receding, had shaved the plains clean, the buffaloes, gentler aspects of the fur trade and the Indians, the great roundups, the sheep-shearings, and the birds. He showed her the cheery meadow larks which had so little judgment; the gawky curlews which had to have an enormous amount, in order to survive. He did not mention bears, mountain lions, bob-cats or snakes, until a lithe blue racer crossed the road, ahead of the trotting horses. Then Charley explained that in the Yellowstone country there was only one kind of poisonous snake, and that he, unfortunate creature, was equipped to give warning of his presence, and did so. Charley was eloquently apologetic for snakes which had developed poison sacs and venom. Edna had never realized how difficult and hazardous life had been for snakes. She had never known that they cannot hear very well, or see very far, and that their only defense is camouflage or flight.

Edna was vibrant with sympathy for the male and female snakes who started out, each spring, to find mates, and could not be content with just any kind of wandering snake, but had to find the right one, that was marked and patterned and tinted exactly as the male or female of the species in question had to be.

In the beginning, no snakes were poisonous and those that had become so, and were becoming more so, were changing because of conditions over which they had no control, Charley told her.

Charley did not talk about the struggles that had taken place, the bloodshed, holdups, injustices, nor stress the fact that all former sets of inhabitants of the valley had been superseded and had passed into oblivion. He raised no doubts in her mind about dry farming, or irrigation, or whether Glendive would ever be comparable with Chicago or St. Paul. Where Edna had come from, she had now and then picked flowers, but she did not know their names and habits. Charley identified the various native plants and blossoms, as they revealed themselves along the roadside: the berries, cactus, sage and grass.

To prepare as tactfully as he could for the nickname, "the Monkey Ward wife," the Professor explained in what great esteem that mail-order house was held throughout the western country.

"Everybody out here joshes everybody else. You mustn't mind," he said.

She did not say so, in so many words, but made it quite clear with her candid blue eyes that, as long as he was near, she would not feel hurt by anything.

We realized, when we saw them from the deck of the *Expansion,* that they would get to Sidney before we did, but the steamboat made excellent progress downstream until we were approaching the group of islands called "The Seven Sisters."

Mr. Stackpole and Grant Marsh had been talking and drinking all afternoon.

"I shall find it hard to report that the Yellowstone is not navigable, after having enjoyed this voyage and your hospitality," Mr. Stackpole was saying.

"It's that damn N.P. railroad that wants to bottle up the river," said Captain Marsh. Then a look of pain and distress passed over his face. He got up without a word and ran for the wheel. There, he shoved the political pilot aside and tried his utmost to miss the channel into which the *Expansion* was headed. It was too late. We heard and felt the scraping of

189

the bottom on a sand bar. The old steamboat rose slightly at the bow.

The pilot, who was drunk and dismayed, turned on Captain Marsh.

"If you'd let a man steer who knows how, you old buzzard," he said.

The aged Captain did not argue. He shoved the pilot over to the rail, picked him up bodily, and heaved him overboard. There was less than three feet of water and the pilot, dripping and cursing, had to wade ashore, from island to island. Marsh would not let him come aboard again.

The Captain assured us that he would have the *Expansion* afloat again within an hour, but it was quicker for us to have our rig and horses put ashore and drive the short distance to Trembles, and thence to Sidney.

"See you at the wedding," the Captain said, from the head of the gangplank. And he kept his word.

While Edna, the Monkey Ward wife, was riding northward *down* the valley, Mrs. Weckerling and her little daughter, Helen, were riding southward *up* the valley toward Sidney. So everyone who chanced to be along or near the stage road had a look at one or the other of them. They met in Mrs. Baron's house, arriving within five minutes of each other.

To the bride's dismay, she had been separated from Charley Tufts and Highpockets immediately they reached the town in which the wedding was to take place. She had seen the cabin on the claim, as the rig had passed by, two miles distant, and seemed to be increasingly uneasy as she neared their destination.

Just as Mrs. Weckerling was shown in, Edna was saying that she must have a word with the Professor. Mrs. Baron had taken the suggestion lightly, since Edna had been talking continually with Charley Tufts during the hours they had spent driving down from Glendive. The entrance of Mrs. Weckerling turned the focus of attention from Edna to her. She had been driven up from Mondak by the tall, sway-backed Lam McGlynn. The barber had been selected for the honor, because he was the man who stated more often and more positively than anyone else that he did not propose to get himself entangled with a woman, whether she was handsome or as homely as a rail fence.

The widow from Deadwood must have been about forty, but was very well preserved. She considered gravely, and hesitated before accepting a glass of whisky to refresh her after the long dusty drive, but once she had it in her hand, she tossed it down with noteworthy address. Mrs. Weckerling was a trim brunette, with olive skin and heavy, well-matched eyebrows. Her hair was dressed high, and very neatly. She wore kid gloves and thin lisle stockings. Her hat was decorative, but not extreme. The little daughter, Helen, was a solemn child with tense, quiet manners and eyes as big as bantam's eggs.

"It tastes of grain," Mrs. Weckerling said, appreciatively, as she swallowed her snifter.

The little girl turned her deep eyes upward, without moving her limbs.

"Helen, dear child, doesn't like to have me drink, do you, darling?" Mrs. Weckerling said.

"No, Mama," the girl said, convincingly.

"Her dear father, and four of his brothers, went that way," Mrs. Weckerling explained.

Edna was standing uneasily in her petticoats and stocking feet, having removed the blue suit and her shoes. Her figure did not escape the eyes of Mrs. Baron and the widow. It was lithe, strong and firm. The fewer clothes Edna wore, the better she looked, but the more ill at ease.

191

"Stop fretting," Mrs. Baron said, kindly.

"Shall I have a chance to speak with Mr. Tufts, after I'm dressed?" Edna asked. Already she had agreed to a white wedding gown her hostess had found in the variegated stock of Baron's store.

Mrs. Baron turned to Mrs. Weckerling, an amused glint in her eye.

"Miss Bispham has taken a fancy to the best man," she said.

"There's safety in numbers," said Mrs. Weckerling, and Edna blushed, but had to give up her talk with Charley. It seemed to worry her no end.

When the bride was escorted to the church, there were at least two hundred and fifty of the valley folks waiting, a hundred inside and the rest in the open air. Edna did not know, and no one told her, that her wedding was helping to cement an agreement which constituted a happy *modus vivendi* between the church people and the rounders and would be instrumental in splitting a large chunk off one corner of vast Dawson County which would become a dry oasis in a sea of intemperance.

Meanwhile, Charley Tufts had been having a difficult time with the groom. The moment Edna had been whisked out of sight by Mrs. Baron, Highpockets began to show consternation.

"Charley," Johnny said. "There's somethin' a'botherin' me somethin' fierce."

"What is it, Johnny?" Tufts asked.

"I ain't never been married before."

"No more have I," said Tufts.

"I mean to say, I ain't never slept with no woman," Highpockets said.

"Few men can say as much to an innocent bride. I'm proud of you, Johnny," said Tufts.

192

"Heck. It wasn't my fault," Johnny said, hastily, more upset than before.

Highpockets looked at Tufts, miserably.

"I never was in such a hole, Charley," he continued. "It would'a been bad enough, if she and me were goin' to git up there to the cabin in the dark. You know as well as I do, Charley, that the dog-gone dance'll last till breakfast time, maybe ten-'leven in the forenoon. Everybody'll be watchin' and grinnin'. God can strike me dead, Charley, but I'll make a awful fizzle of things. I should'a thought o' this, before we got Edna way out here. What'll she think o' me, Charley? And who can blame her?"

Charley was most reassuring. The possibilities were not such that he cared to dwell on them, but he did the best he could to help his friend.

"You won't have any trouble. She'll be tired and nervous, too. Just forget your troubles, for a while, and go right off to sleep," Charley said.

Highpockets was more aghast than ever. "How can we haul off an' undress, right there in that little ol' cabin, in broad daylight?" he asked.

"Go out, and give her a chance to get undressed and into bed," said Charley.

"There ain't but one bed," Johnny said. He sighed, sweating like a sieve.

"For two bits, I'd get myself drunker'n a goat," Highpockets said.

"That's vulgar," said Charley. "You mustn't touch a drop, till it's all over."

"I keep wonderin' and figurin' how in Sam Hill I got into this jackpot," Johnny said.

It was in that mood that Highpockets, having been induced to put on his black suit, was led to the Methodist church.

193

CHAPTER SIXTEEN

A Friend of the Family

◆

AT THE dance that night, the women sat on benches around three sides of Bert's new "opera house." One end was occupied by a platform stage, 12 by 14, with dressing rooms on either side, and provisions for installation, later, of a stage curtain which also could be used as a magic lantern or motion-picture screen. For days before the opening, Nephi Pratt and Bat Horner had scraped and planed from the new pine boards all traces of pitch that had oozed out. Bert wanted to be sure that none of the women ruined their dresses on Highpockets' gala night.

By the time the banquet was over, about 11:30 P.M., everything was ready at the hall. The band was comfortably installed on the stage, and I turned the piano at such an angle that I could watch the dancers without using a mirror. On Lam's new bass drum, Treff Simard had lettered neatly:

TREMBLES RAGTIME BAND

For Edna, now actually a bride before God and man, a straight-backed chair with arms had been brought up from Sidney. Naturally, there was no seating arrangement for High-pockets who, like the other men, stood in and around the doorway, or waited in the bar and café.

Today, that array of women would look incongruous, be-cause of the wide variety of their costumes. Some were beauti-

194

ful and stylish, others in old-fashioned clothes they had brought from the east and middle west, the farmers' wives and daughters in crude home-made dresses and sensible shoes. Conspicuous among them were Anne Prentice, Zuleika Donaldson, Josefa Dotsen, the Clawson girls, tall Letty Gregory, Mrs. Baron, and the petite Jennette Simard, who looked frail and fairylike and was indefatigable. Some of the women from the foothills wore shawls. The working girls, Zoe Speaslis and Annie Rongfto, had an exotic appeal of their own. Many of the church women, including Mrs. Thavanot, although they did not dance or approve of dancing, made concessions that evening and sat in the dance hall, drinking pop and iced lemonade.

Right after the wedding ceremony, I had turned Mr. Stackpole over to Captain Marsh for the evening, and by the time the dance was under way, they had organized a poker game in Bert's original 8 by 12 tent. I ducked the reception at Baron's store, but was waylaid by the Prentice party, including Anne and her group of men who were crazy about her. It did not take me a moment to see that Walt Murray and Chet Donaldson would not be likely to destroy each other that night, because Anne was putting both of them on the rack by her almost immodest advances toward Scotty McVeigh. Scotty, who liked her well enough, but was a friend of Walt's and did not relish hurting his feelings, behaved as best he could, and his restraint seemed to provoke Anne to further extremes.

The southern boy, stunned and grieved by the new threat to his happiness, sulked and pouted on the outskirts of the group. Chet Donaldson, aware that he must change his tactics, developed a sudden liking for Scotty and showed him every consideration. It may be that Chet had already made plans to ask Scotty to work for him, or possibly he got the

idea that night. Chet was hard hit by the sabotage and shortage of men in his camp, where everything was going wrong.
He realized that he needed reliable foremen and assistants.
So, as soon as possible, in a magnanimous manner, he took
Scotty aside and offered to double the pay he was getting from
the government if he would act as assistant superintendent
for Donaldson and Company.

"We're planning a complete reorganization," Chet said.

Scotty, a very canny Scot, detested Donaldson and did not
warm up to the proposition.

"Couldn't do it, Chet," Scotty said. "At the end of the
season, I'd be out of a job for the winter."

"I'll keep you on all winter, in the office in St. Cloud,"
Chet said.

"Let me think it over," said Scotty, but his manner made
it clear that he had no intention of accepting.

"Why not be frank?" Chet asked. "You got something on
your mind that's holding you back. What is it?"

"You want me to tell you?" Scotty asked.

"Come out with it," Chet urged. "I'll answer your ob-
jections."

"I've heard, from more than one source, that Donaldson
and Company's going broke," said Scotty.

Donaldson flew into a rage, the more violent because of
his former restraint.

"Who said that? Let's talk with him, face to face," Chet
roared.

"You know I can't tell you that," Scotty said.

"You could if you were a friend of mine," Donaldson said,
his red eyes glowing with rancor. He had done everything
possible to keep up the impression that he was making money
and his firm was prospering.

"I'm everybody's friend," said Scotty. "But I read the St. Cloud paper."

Chet's face sagged and he glowered. His father, pressed hard on account of Chet's lagging contract, had just sold his thoroughbred harness stock, a stable of twelve horses that everybody in St. Cloud knew had been the apple of Old Man Donaldson's eye.

"Don't think I mentioned that sale to anybody," Scotty said.

"It wouldn't be good for you, if you did," Chet said.

Scotty shrugged and walked away, and from that time on responded to Anne's flirtation, so that everybody noticed what was happening between them. Walt spent the rest of the night at the bar, drinking soddenly. Chet got into the poker game with Grant Marsh, Worthington T. Stackpole, Noel Prentice, Annius Gregory and Perce Gardner, who was just about to open Trembles' No. 2 saloon. In trying to force his luck, Chet lost all he had with him and had to appeal to Bert Lacey for a stake to continue playing and lose more.

About two in the morning, Lela Weckerling, who had been seated near Edna during the several dances from which she had asked to be "excused," rose gravely and said that she was developing a headache and thought she should lie down for a while. Edna and Mrs. Baron nodded assent, the band started up, and little Helen, who was making a beeline for her mother, was waylaid and swung into a parade for a reel by Old Man Mavity, who was spryer than a colt, and twice as high.

I did not notice particularly when Mrs. Weckerling came up on the stage, but when she touched a door that, unhinged, was resting against the door frame of one of the "dressing rooms" and I saw and dimly heard the door fall down and she did not seem to notice, I thought it was a little strange.

The dressing rooms were not in use that night, although each had a lantern in it, suspended from a hook in the ceiling. In the now doorless one chosen by Mrs. Weckerling, there was a carpenter's bench Bat Horner had neglected to remove and two empty horseshoe kegs that served as stools or chairs. The other members of the band were facing out front, so I was the only spectator. The sightly brunette widow from Deadwood unbuttoned her dress, stepped out of it, and carefully laid it across the carpenter's high bench. Then, in underwaist and petticoats, she sat on a keg, crossed her legs, removed one shoe, then the other. By the time she was erect again, moving in a stiff-legged fashion like a somnambulist, looking for a nonexistent mirror, I realized that she had had too much to drink and undoubtedly was under the false impression that she was at home.

Later, I found that Bat Horner, who was playing practical jokes when he was not spinning yarns or doing carpenter work, had spiked the ladies' punch bowl.

As soon as little Helen came around my way, I beckoned her to my side, but Old Buck Mavity came, glanced into the dressing room and let out a roar. Mrs. Weckerling then was down to her corsets. Of course, she was completely covered, except a modest area of neck and throat, and a space between her corsets and the top of her black silk hose. Helen looked up at Old Mavity so piteously that he turned and left the stage, and did not even tell the others what he had seen. The little girl went into the dressing room and somehow persuaded her mother to put her clothes back on. Having got that far, however, Lela folded and tried to stretch out on the carpenter's bench. I made reassuring motions to Helen, sought out Mrs. Baron and she, by means of aromatic spirits of ammonia and smelling salts, revived Mrs. Weckerling to the point where she could be led through the stage entrance and safely to her room in the Cathay Café building.

The little girl, sad, but resigned, did not return to the dance, the first she had ever attended. Bert Lacey tried to persuade her, and guaranteed that her mother would be well guarded by Ah Cook and Ah Flunk.

"I shouldn't have left her by herself," Helen said, self-reproachfully.

A little later I saw Charley Tufts dancing with Edna, and they continued out the main door. I turned the piano over to Mexican Joe, my star pupil, for a while, knowing nothing pleased him better, and sat with Mrs. Baron.

There was a woman no young man would be likely to forget, through the years. There were no bounds to friendship, except the obvious physical ones. She told me, that night, why she preferred not to dance.

"My husband's ill, you know," she said and looked at me frankly. "It disturbs me to be whirled around, held tight, and feel men's arms around me. I'm sure you understand."

All the others called her Milly, but I stuck to "Mrs. Baron." Years later I read *Cakes and Ale*, which I hold to be Somerset Maugham's masterpiece, and whenever he mentioned his heroine, "Rosie," I thought of Mrs. Baron. Although Mrs. Baron was sophisticated and coolly self-possessed, she also had the artlessness and lack of guile that Rosie had, and a similar stature. To paraphrase Maugham, she was "all gold, her face and her hair" and yet she gave a "silvery effect." She also belonged to a generation "that did not fear a certain opulence of line." She taught me that, like the Merry Wives of Windsor, American wives of that epoch "could be merry and be honest, too."

When I read Balzac's *Lily of the Valley*, the opening scene where the adolescent boy throws himself upon a lovely woman's bosom, impelled by some irresistible desire, I understood that, too, and kicked myself for having failed to do so. I must beg the reader's indulgence, having been, at the time I knew Mrs. Baron, only sixteen years of age. But love of all descriptions surcharged the air in the lower valley of the Yellowstone. I wish nothing finer for that cataclysmic and neglected region than its retention of that quality that set the hearts of men, and boys, into tailspins, as if Cupid, in that ancient Sioux country, had chucked his bows and arrows and learned to use a tomahawk.

While I was enjoying the proximity, the wisdom and the fragrance of Mrs. Baron, Charley Tufts was deep in conversation with Edna, in the shade of the quaking aspen trees. Edna, as soon as she was clear of the dance hall and the batteries of curious eyes that followed her wherever she went, clutched Charley's arm and started sobbing, softly.

"Naturally, you're nervous," Charley said.

"I told them I had to see you before I was wed," said Edna. "I kept saying it, over and over again, and no one paid attention. They talked about my dress. When I got to the church it was too late."

"You wanted to tell me about something? About yourself?" Charlie asked.

Edna nodded, and hung her head. She was miserable, all right, evidently not thinking so much about herself as her husband.

"Shall I tell you what's the matter?" Charley asked. "It's easier for me to say it."

"You know?" Edna asked, incredulous and abashed.

"I think so," said Charley.

"And you like me just the same?"

"Better," said Charley. "We all make mistakes."

"It wasn't my fault . . . I don't think . . . Not much," Edna said.

"I'm sure it wasn't," said Charley. "We get confused, at such times."

"You, too?" she asked, in astonishment.

"Everybody does," Charley said.

"Not Johnny," Edna said, sadly. "He's told me already that I must forgive him if he makes an awful mess."

"Is that all he said?"

"That's all. Just that," said Edna.

"Fine. Fine," said Charley. "You see, the usual situation's reversed. Instead of the bride being all fussed and afraid, it's the groom. You'll have to be considerate and patient."

"He may not want me, after I tell him. I don't mind, for myself. I want to be fair to him," Edna said.

Charley carefully avoided pursuing that phase of the situation. "You mustn't tell him anything," Charley said.

"You mean, he won't know the difference?" Edna asked.

"Of course he won't," said Charley.

Edna hesitated.

"If you tell me not to tell him . . ." she began.

"I do tell you not to," said Charley.

"You know I'll do anything you say," Edna said, and dried her tears.

"I'm the friend of the family," Charley said, and led her back to the dance hall.

CHAPTER SEVENTEEN

Preceding the Baptism of Frost

◈

THE heat of summer converted the lower valley into a vast oven, parching the grazing lands and dry farms, clamped under the relentless sky. The fragrance and stenches were all of the mature summer season, ranging from the slumbering sage and hay that had been cured while growing and was standing where it had grown to the pungent stink from the carcass of a dead animal. Sights, sounds and odors played a vernal symphony in subdued vibrant tones, sizzling, scorching and simmering. It was not uncommon to see three separate thunderstorms following various small creek beds in the foothills, and if one of them passed over, or near by, there was a steamy intensification of the sensory stimuli for a moment, then all was hot and arid again.

The Yellowstone was reduced to puny, ineffectual dimensions. All the thoughts of the inhabitants, settlers, transients and drifters were faded and discolored by the temperature and accumulative strain of doggedly combating it. One inhaled the heat, and exhaled it, hotter. The faces and hands of the men exposed to the sun became leathery and almost inexpressive. Their movements were slower and more methodical. Their words, when they escaped, were often barbed. Even a cloudburst or a hail storm would have afforded a respite, but those were withheld.

Then, in September, when the harvest work was nearing

its end, nature ushered in, imperceptibly, a period during
which the valley justified the words of the poet who had com-
posed the railroad pamphlet. "For purity and salubrity of
air" the Yellowstone country was, for the time being, "not
surpassed anywhere in the United States." Most of the grain
had been gathered. Long sections of the canal had been dug.
The homesteaders who had arrived in the spring now had
acquired a few months of experience and had gained "knowledge of the peculiar methods and means by which nature
made compensation for what they had been accustomed to
regard as necessities."

One of the first symptoms of a change of season was the
wider space between flies, around the cook shacks, mess-houses
and squatters' kitchens. There were flies, but they were not so
noisy and there were not as many of them. The skinners did
not look so drugged and sleepy, or the horses so weak and
wet as they trod the ellipses and circles, moving dirt from
where it was to where the government specifications indicated
that it should be.

The men who had time to spare took out hunting licenses,
at the rate of $1, and the game birds, fat and plump from
having eaten ripe berries, the seeds of the grasses, and what
they could glean from the stubble on the dry farms, graced
more frequently the tables in ranches, town houses and hotels.
That year there were grouse, prairie chickens, sage hens, fool
hens, a few partridges, pheasants, and brant, and even an
occasional wild swan. On the pools of the Missouri and Yellowstone a few of the early ducks settled down, and the luckiest
hunters got a shot or two at Canadian geese, snow white
from the Arctic, their flesh faintly flavored with sarvis berries and juniper.

The song birds beloved of Audubon—larks, bluebirds,
thrushes, orioles, woodpeckers, finches and cedarbirds—were

protected. The curlews were not mentioned in any of the law books. Those gawky cousins of the plover and stone plover had laid their mottled eggs in the open, diverted enemies while the young ones were hatched and learning to get along, and were leaving, in groups, for less rigorous lands.

The color of the sky changed from the mushroom blue of scorching porcelain to a clearer azure tone. The days were slightly shorter. Sick men got well, and well men ate like wolves. The stores in Glendive and Sidney, and along the long stage road, at the intersections with creeks and coulees, did brisker business after farmers had sold their hay and grain.

Once in a while, not often, it came over me that a short year before, as Labor Day was approaching, I had been dreading incarceration in the Malden High School for my senior year, and that, as I had sat on the porch of 63 Beach Street, Linden, I had wondered what was going to become of me. As the Saugus Branch trains had come in, bringing commuters from Boston, I had watched them straggle up the street and scatter to their respective homes for supper. If the first man worked in the rope walk at Charlestown, I felt sure that I was not going to work in a rope walk. Most certainly I was not going to be a doctor or a lawyer. There was no money for the college education, medical or law school, and the bleak years to follow. Manufacturing shoes or steel required capital. With capital, why should anyone want to manufacture articles? It would be better merely to spend the capital.

After a spring and summer on the Yellowstone I no longer speculated about what I should do, or worried about the money to do it with. I had not made any conscious decisions, but I knew that I should never live in a town like Linden, or be cooped up anywhere at all, for long. Trembles, Montana, was as different from a New England suburban village as any community could be, and still remain on the planet. I knew that I should not stay forever in Montana. The sensible way of life seemed to me to be a wandering existence, with frequent changes of scene. I had no impulse to take root anywhere, although I was glad that so many other people wanted a community to call their own. Otherwise there would not be strange towns and cities to visit and enjoy. What had depressed me about the "jobs" or "occupations" the Linden folks had was their permanence. In Montana, I felt that I could do almost anything the others did. In a pinch I could work in a store or a bank, or in the harvest fields, or a construction camp. After six or eight weeks, if I got restless, I could change my job, or blow.

I had a remarkable chance to learn about the fundamentals of hydraulic engineering, and I grasped them quickly. There was nothing difficult about learning to use the surveying instruments, keep the necessary notes and records, or compute quantities of earthwork or concrete from a set of plans. I even found time to teach myself trigonometry, a subject which had not been included in my high-school course.

From my point of view, what was important had to do with independence. I felt as if, in any populated place, I could earn enough to eat, drink, sleep, amuse myself and get acquainted with the people. The serious-minded, industrious men I had met impressed me, but I did not feel at ease with them. Those who enjoyed life, casually, whatever their social standing, admitted me to their fraternity. Having suffered continuous embarrassment from lack of funds all through my childhood and school days, I took the keenest pleasure in tossing silver dollars or twenty-dollar gold pieces on counters, treating my companions, and keeping in brisk circulation what money I got. In Linden, Massachusetts, there had been plenty of people who were poor. Some were worthy, the more lovable of them, unworthy. In eastern Montana, men were frequently broke, but that was not poverty. There was no poverty. The lousiest and laziest of the bums was rich on payday, and for two or three days afterward. The most prosperous rancher or merchant might have a bad year, or a stroke of tough luck, and find himself working for a pittance for a while. He could soon get on his feet again. America was like that, then.

The town of Trembles was now well established, and could face its first winter without fear of privation or loneliness. Its four "Clipper" windmills, fifty feet high, now were complete with engines and accessories, and marked roughly the boundaries of the town. Their wheels spun in unison, sometimes briskly, again frantically. The pumps clanked. The wells were low, but not dry. One on the slope near the foothills to the west stood on Highpockets' claim. The second was east of the stage road, not far from the corral behind the new hotel and the Cathay Café. The third was north, and farther east, used in common by the residents of the "east side." The fourth was near the entrance of the town, on the "west side," and provided water for the settlers in that area. North and south, the center of town extended two miles. East and west, it covered the slopes and flats all the way from the foothills to the Yellowstone, a distance of about six miles. In area, it was twelve times as large as Linden, Massachusetts. Its population swelled each day, not explosively, like a bonanza town of a gold rush, but slowly and spasmodically as tradesmen and farmers came in. Stella's "Little Casino" had expanded. Stella now functioned mostly in the capacity of landlady. Besides the little dark girl, Fern, there were two others: Dora, who had hair down to her knees, like one of the Sutherland sisters; and a tall, rangy woman who called herself Alfy, and formerly had played first base on a ladies' baseball team.

A half-mile nearer the stage road, the Villerup brothers had lived most of the summer in their cabin without furniture, having loaned what they had to Highpockets. Early in September, Highpockets' shipment arrived, and he returned the bed, table, stove and chairs, while Edna took the borrowed bedclothes back to Josefa Dotsen, with thanks.

Between the stage road and the Yellowstone lived a farmer named Fred Fude, with an anemic, furtive wife named Flo, and a niece thirteen years old, Tena Hastey. Bert Lacey had not liked the looks of Fude, and had not wanted him to settle in Trembles, but Mrs. Fude was so weak and discouraged that Bert did not have the heart to turn them down.

On the flat between Highpockets' cabin and the stage road, Bert had had the brush removed and had laid out a baseball diamond. Small grandstands made of used boards had been put up along the first and third base lines. There was a high backstop, and the deep outfield was near enough the Little Casino so the girls could watch the games and still preserve their segregation.

The third-base bleachers were two hundred yards from the barber shop, cobbler's godown, and the Rag Time Livery Barn, all of which stood along the west side of the stage road. From the coulee southward, the buildings were: the cobbler's lean-to and barber shop, where Steve Galucci and Lam McGlynn lived; the livery barn and corral, occupied by Lucian Gibbs. A one-story bungalow and stable had been put up by Doc Cherry, the veterinarian. Then came the Westside Saloon, owned and operated by Perce Gardner, from New York City. Wherever Perce traveled, a bit of true New York went with him.

The drug store, which had been built by the Simards,

as an investment, had been rented to a small, alert Scandinavian medical student named Kurt Mook, who was so fair that he was practically an albino.

Half a mile west of the road was the cabin of Peer Arndt, a house painter, who lived there with his sisters, Mayme and Etta, fifteen and seventeen years old, respectively.

The Trembles school was to be housed temporarily in Bert's opera house, and Josefa Dotsen was already sure of four pupils, all girls: Tena Hastey, Helen Weckerling, and Mayme and Etta Arndt. Josefa was glad there would be no boys, until she had had a chance to get used to teaching.

On the east side of the road, starting again at the coulee and clump of quaking aspens, stood the Trembles Opera House, the Cathay Café and Clark Hotel. Next came Hi and Henry's Harness Shop; Shunk Cundiff's blacksmith shop; the Eastside Saloon, run by Willy Lederer from Williston; a two-story house, put up by Johnny O'Brien for an investment, rented to Buck Mavity, the well-digger. Mavity had moved to Trembles from Fairview, causing much jealous comment, and brought with him his racy old mother-in-law, Mamie Rhorer, and his wife, Addie, who was as meek as her mother was forceful.

Opposite the drug store was the meat market, the proprietor of which was a hard-working old Alsatian named Hans Sauerbier, who had pale eyes set deep in hollow sockets, enormous hands and feet, long arms and short legs, and spoke with an accent like Weber and Fields tied together. No matter how hard Hans worked, on dance nights he would sit on an empty box near the piano, and whenever there was a lull, ask us to play *"Strassburg, Ach Strassburg, du bist ein' schoene Stadt."* Hans would listen, rapt and helpless, tears streaming down his lined, weatherbeaten cheeks. The world knows that my piano playing is nothing miraculous, but I have had some listeners who could give the best of Paderewski's cards and spades.

West of the road, between the main buildings of Trembles and the river, was a claim of 160 acres, fenced and with a few acres under cultivation. This belonged to a Kansas farmer named Cever Seale, and his wife, Rachel.

"Neither one nor th' other of 'em 'sworth a damn for anything but work," Bert Lacey said.

The single men ate regularly at the Cathay Café and spent most of their evenings in the saloons. Bert had cordially welcomed his two competitors, from New York and Williston, respectively. They arrived just in time to save his own place from being overcrowded. Perce Gardner's place was a refuge for those who liked *bon ton* and quiet. The Eastside Saloon was patronized by farmers who wanted to worry about crops while they drank.

No one slept in the Opera House, except in cases of emergency. Bert had a room and an office in the Clark Hotel. The two Chinks, the stable boss, and the new bartender lived in the Cathay Café.

Mrs. Weckerling and little Helen, Annie Rongfto, the chambermaid and waitress who had quit the Valley Hotel in Sidney in order to serve Worthington T. Stackpole now and then, and Howard Wise, who had quit Donaldson's camp in order to act as hotel clerk and manager, slept in the hotel and took their meals in the café.

So the residents of Trembles, which that spring had not existed, now numbered thirty-nine, of whom twenty-four were men and fifteen women and girls.

In the Glendive newspapers, items began to appear frequently that read like this:

A Ghost Town on the Yellowstone

"Bert Lacey, genial hotel, restaurant and saloon-keeper, of Trembles on Cedar Coulee, is in Glendive for a load of supplies."

One week, early in September, the east bank of the Yellowstone, near the Glendive bridge, was lined with people about nine o'clock each morning, to watch two elephants from a traveling circus stand in the shallows and spray each other joyously from their trunks. The school hours were shifted, so the children could see the frolic, and everyone, including the elephants, had a marvelous time. Bert Lacey met the proprietor of the show in the bar at the Jordan and offered him special inducements if he would move the circus through the lower valley and give Saturday and Sunday performances on the baseball field at Trembles. As usual, when he set his heart on anything, Bert closed the deal.

Just about that time, the first motor vehicle to be owned and operated by a resident of the valley was shipped in by Frank Banks, a civil engineer who now is in charge of construction work on the All-American Canal in southern California. Banks was an enthusiastic pioneer motorist, but after he had had a few embarrassing experiences on account of the fact that the Montana livestock stampeded and ran for their lives whenever he passed near them, he took his practice runs early in the morning, before rigs were likely to be on the road near the dangerous barbed wire fences.

Banks started southward from Trembles. Because the leading circus wagon was in a slight declivity when he approached, at twenty miles an hour, Frank did not see it in time. That wagon contained the two circus lions, one male and one female. It was drawn by four horses which bolted for their lives when the chugging motor bike, raising a formidable cloud of dust, rushed toward them. The wagon driver, who had been dozing and was caught unawares, did his best to get

210

his team under control. Frank, always considerate, swerved off the road, and bumped over the sagebrush until his machine tipped over on him. The terrified horses missed the wire fence, but in doing so tilted the wagon and the lions' cage at a perilous angle, and smashed the side into a solid corner fence post. The smashed wagon righted itself and kept going, but the lions leaped out and instantly were lost to sight in a cloud of dust.

Worthington T. Stackpole was spending that night in the Clark Hotel at Trembles. He had taken a strong liking to the town and its people, and enjoyed especially his long talks with Charley Swift and Howard Wise, the hotel clerk. Also his expansive nature had responded to the warm admiration Annie Rongfto, the chambermaid and waitress, developed for him. Since both of them were by nature discreet, and the hotel was usually quite busy and active in the late evenings, Mr. Stackpole made a practice of leaving his door unbolted, in order that he and Annie might chat in whispers in the early mornings.

The two lions streaked northward along the road and when the dust thinned and they found themselves among buildings, they both loped into the first dim opening they saw. That chanced to be the front door of the Clark Hotel. Wise, who had a room off the hallway near the door, was a sound sleeper. He said afterward that he heard a faint sound of paws running over the floor outside, but he assumed that a couple of stray dogs had got in and would go out again when it pleased them.

The male lion, in the lead, dashed up the wooden stairs and along a narrow corridor, facing which, at the end, was Mr. Stackpole's door. The lion stood up on his hind legs and let his front paws rest against the panels. Inside the bedroom, Stackpole, in his elegant silk pajamas, was wide-awake. Hearing the slight scratch on his door, he smiled happily and tip-toed across the floor to open it. He saw, teetering before him, not Annie Rongfto, his impulsive Montana sweetheart, but the underside of a full-grown king of the beasts that smelled stronger than U. S. Indian Affairs. Too startled to be frightened on the instant, the big engineer bellowed, "Down, sir, dammit," and slammed the door.

Annie, in a near-by room, heard Mr. Stackpole's hearty voice and what seemed to be a commotion in the corridor. She decided it would be more discreet to postpone the two-some they had planned, so she went back to bed for a twenty-minute snooze. Meanwhile the he-lion slunk downstairs and out the front door again, just in time to avoid astonishing Lela Weckerling, who, wrapped in a toweled bathrobe, with her hair in braids, was on her way to the washroom for a morning bath. Bert had not been able to install modern plumbing, but provided on the second floor of the Clark Hotel a small room with zinc-lined floor, a large rubber bath mat, kerosene stove and washboiler filled with water, and an enameled bathtub set on griffin's legs.

Having modestly pulled down the window shade, and locked the door behind her, Mrs. Weckerling slipped off her robe and hung it on a hook. She looked at her limbs and well-rounded curves, smoothed with satisfaction her clear olive skin, glanced in the wall mirror to detect gray hairs and, finding none, she smiled, then took a dipper of warm water from the boiler and was about to pour it in the tub. At that moment she saw Queenie, the lioness, who was cowering in the tub. Queenie snarled and recoiled, coming up on her haunches.

Mrs. Weckerling sank noiselessly down to the floor in a dead faint.

The lioness was one of the tamest wild animals in the

circus. She calmed herself, got out of the tub cautiously, sniffed the inanimate form of the naked woman, then went over to a corner and sat down to think things over. How many times Lela revived, saw the beast staring at her and swooned again, she was unable, afterward, to remember.

Lam McGlynn, coming down the corridor for his morning wash, tried the bathroom door and found it locked. He paced up and down the hallway a few times, then tried the door again. Little Helen, who always was somewhere near by when her mother was out of her sight, appeared at the head of the stairway and told Lam who was bathing.

"I didn't hear any water splashing," Lam said.

The little girl went over to the bathroom door, listened, then peeped through the keyhole. She saw and heard nothing but a sound like a lot of cats purring. Puzzled, she tapped on the door. There was no answer. Alarmed, she knocked, louder and louder. No response.

Lam, intending only to gain admittance for the child, pushed hard on the door. The lock gave way, and the lioness darted out, dodged little Helen who was screaming, and dashed down the stairs, just in time to knock Bert Lacey, who was on his way up to see what was wrong, bum over bandbox.

Inside the bathroom, Lela regained consciousness just in time to realize that Lam McGlynn, in his shirtsleeves, was sprawled over her, with a mad grimace on his face. She fainted again, and Lam, completely rattled, picked her up, bare as an egg, and rushed up and down the hallway with her draped across his shoulder, trying to find a room in which to deposit her.

Finally, Annie opened her door, gasped, and said:

"Mr. McGlynn! This is a respectable house!"

213

Lam, weak from shock, shoved his way in, unceremoniously, dumped Lela on the bed, and took flight.

"What's going on here?" Bert asked.

Little Helen dashed across the hall with her mother's bathrobe.

About that time, the circus wagons drove up the street, and the lion tamer rounded up his two fugitives.

Engineer Stackpole descended to the café for his breakfast, beaming. When Bert showed up, having cleared up the incidents in his mind, as best he could, Mr. Stackpole remarked:

"Mr. Lacey! You have here a unique establishment. Never banal. By no means dull. I envy you, sir."

CHAPTER EIGHTEEN

Handfuls after the Harvest Man

IN THE states east of the Dakotas, at the beginning of the century, a community the size that Trembles had reached in its fourth month of existence would contain families related to one another by ties of blood and common experience, and people who had gone to school together. The bond between the citizens of Bert Lacey's young town was quite as strong as those, but of a different nature.

Men and women who settled in Trembles all had a healthy urge to free themselves from irksome interference and restraint and to better their condition. By interference, I mean governmental, social, economic and conventional. To use a watchword of the dreaded I. W. W., in Trembles "an injury to one" was, indeed, "an injury to all."

Bert Lacey was government, unquestionably. The Dawson County officials, seated fifty miles away, were government, to a lesser degree. When the control became as remote as the corrupt state "government" of Montana, and the inept bureaucrats in Washington, it was looked upon with suspicion and disdain. Not that the folks in Trembles were naturally unpatriotic. Those of German, Scandinavian and Danish extraction had a deep nostalgic feeling for their homelands, but they were also grateful to the United States for having received them and given them a chance to vanquish poverty and build a future for their children.

215

The prevailing force in Trembles was hope, hope that amounted to a surreligious fervor. One of the most fervent optimists in Trembles was the school teacher, Josefa Dotsen. At first shunned and ridiculed because of her meticulously correct speech, her resolute eyebrows and pince-nez, her severe mannish clothes and disconcerting directness, Josefa grew in the esteem of her townsmen. While she cooked and kept house for her three hard-working brothers, and accepted the courtship of the dour Ed Wilson of La Mesa, Josefa sent east for up-to-date school books and studied them hard. She had not been trained as a teacher, but she was determined that the children placed in her charge should not be short-changed in education.

The four girls, Josefa's pupils that first autumn—the solemn Helen Weckerling, the house painter's sisters, Mayme and Etta Arndt, and Fred Fude's niece, Tena Hastey—responded to Josefa's solicitude, in their separate ways. Helen was helpful and conscientious. The Arndt sisters, irrepressible tomboys, played baseball and even football with the men, but in school, out of deference to Josefa, they were quiet if not still. Little Helen learned whatever was assigned her the way she cleaned off her plate at meal times. The Arndt girls had quick, restless minds, and now and then got ahead of Josefa's explanations. Tena Hastey was the problem. She would have been prettier than any of her classmates if she were not so listless and pale. She looked half-starved, but would not eat. Most of the time, when the others in the class were paying attention either to the teacher or something that was going on outside, Tena would sit in a kind of troubled reverie and would start, guiltily, if anyone spoke to her. Her eyes were downcast, her clothes crudely made and unbecoming. However loosely they hung, they could not conceal the unusual voluptuousness of her body.

216

Handfuls after the Harvest Man

The teacher knew it was useless to discuss matters with Tena's aunt, the slatternly, almost toothless Flo Fude. The aunt was frightened out of her wits whenever Fred, her husband, came in sight, and lived in a timorous stupor when he was away. No one ever caught Fred beating her, or heard screams or sobs in their cabin. It was ominously silent. For days and nights on end the Fudes would not speak, except at meal times, when Fred would snarl, "Pass this, or that."

In every way, Josefa tried to win Tena's confidence and find out what was the matter. In each approach, she failed.

Then, one September evening, just as twilight was deepening, Bert Lacey and the others at the bar, now called "The Central," saw Mrs. Fude come rushing out of her cabin, her hair awry, her shawl clutched tightly around her.

For a moment, the drinkers were not alarmed by Flo's behavior. She always acted half-crazy. But when she started walking faster and faster and then broke into an awkward run, they were troubled. She was not running toward the main part of town, but zigzagging across the flat, stumbling over tumbleweeds and uprooted sagebrush. Shunk Cundiff took after her, and she started running faster. The blacksmith easily overtook her. A few seconds afterward, Lam McGlynn and Bert caught up with them. Mrs. Fude was unable to say a word, only moaned and muttered. When the men suggested taking her back to the cabin, she broke away and started running again.

"Plumb loco," said Lam McGlynn.

Bert and Shunk took a graver view of the matter.

"Let's go down to the shack and see what's going on," Bert said.

"The damn scissorbill's got a loaded shotgun on nails, up over the door," said Lam, the prudent member.

Nevertheless, the men started toward the Fude cabin while the distracted Flo ran straight into Cever Seale's new barbed-wire fence without seeing it. The recoil threw her flat on her back, and she lay there, uninjured, but incapable of further exertion.

The cabin door was open and what the men saw caused them to rush in, three abreast, and overpower Fude before he could get hold of his gun. Fude, a powerful brute, was handicapped because his pants and drawers were down around his ankles. Tena lay, dishevelled, on the bed, trying to cover herself.

Shunk Cundiff was boiling. Bert was white with fury. Lam McGlynn was sullen and disgusted. Fude, roaring and defiant, was straining at the rope with which they were tying him up.

"Shut up, you bastard," said Shunk and let Fude have his elbow, full force, in the face. Fude tried to bite, and they gagged him with a dirty rag.

"Send for Mrs. Weckerling," Shunk suggested to Bert, nodding his head toward the girl on the bed. Bert shook his head, regretfully.

"She's having one of her . . . headaches," Bert said.

Bert turned to Lam McGlynn. "Take Fude's horse and ride up for Edna," he said. Lam started away.

Bert and Shunk Cundiff looked each other straight in the eye. This was a crisis in the early history of Trembles, the first major crime.

"We ought to string him up, right now," Shunk said.

Fude growled, choked and started struggling again, until Shunk subdued him with a kitchen chair.

"Go easy, Shunk," Bert said. "We got to be lawful. I'll send for Mert Honey."

"Mert's out hunting somewhere," Shunk said.

"Then we'll have to take Fude and the girl both to Glendive."

Charley Tufts came riding up to the doorway, and quickly sized up the situation. He blamed himself, bitterly.

"I might have known," he said. "It's been as plain as day, now that I look back on the way they've all been acting."

Charley went over to the bed and touched the girl's forehead.

"Never mind, Tena," he said. "No one's going to hurt you. You'll have to tell the sheriff what happened."

She began to cry, softly and listlessly.

"I should'a told the teacher," she said.

Bert thumbed uneasily toward the bar and the rest of the town.

"We'd better keep this between ourselves . . . till we get him to jail. Some of the boys might take it into their heads he ain't worth feedin'," said Bert.

Charley rode back to the livery stable and arranged for a rig, then he told the crowd that Fude had gone out of his head, and that the girl was sick. When the rig drove up to the door, just after Edna Highpockets arrived on the scene, Fude, trussed up like a goose, was loaded into the back seat. Bert got in beside him. Charley, Edna, and Tena sat up front, with Charley driving.

"We got to catch Flo, for a witness," Bert said.

"She's lyin' over by Seale's new fence," Shunk said. So they drove over that way. They had to tie up Flo before she could be persuaded to go along.

Charley drove all that night, and they got into Glendive in the morning. Chet Busby, the sheriff, listened to the girl's story, without showing much emotion. Flo would say nothing. She was too badly frightened and demoralized.

Meanwhile Edna, having sat beside Charley through the long night hours, was aware of a tingling inner happiness. She was sorry for the girl, and shocked by the behavior of

Fude, but all that was secondary. Her eyes were shining, and when she spoke, her voice was breathless. Anyone could see how she felt about being with Charley, and Charley was vaguely disturbed. He knew that their situation was intensifying itself, and could think of nothing to do about it. Highpockets was blissfully content. Edna worked hard and faithfully, took the best of care of her husband, and their farm was shaping up well.

The other residents of the lower valley did not know what had happened in the Fude cabin until days later, when the Glendive weeklies contained the story of Fude's arrest and escape. Sheriff Busby had taken Fude to the jail, after the initial questioning, and the next morning the jailer put Fude on the water-hauling detail. Fude and another man lugged a barrel over to the tank, near the fence, and Fred kept right on going.

When informed of the jail-break, the Dawson County sheriff shrugged his shoulders and posted a few notices, offering a reward of twenty-five dollars for Fude's capture, dead or alive.

White Stella, when she got the news, flew into a tantrum, and, with the help of Lacey, put up two hundred dollars of her own money to swell the reward.

"By God," Stella said. "If it's only worth twenty-five bucks to catch a son of a bitch who's raped his own niece, just a kid, with his poor wife lookin' on, how in hell can we expect any God-damn Christ-forsaken morality around here?"

Shunk Cundiff kicked himself for weeks, because he had not followed his instincts and knocked off Fude while he had the chance.

"There's such a thing as bein' too bloody lawful," he said.

Most probably, Sheriff Busby's decision as to the amount of the reward did not reflect so much his indifference about

220

incest and rape as his disgust at a bunch of men who would lug an offender of Fude's type fifty miles from the scene of the crime in order to bother the county officials. The Vigilante tradition was not far back in valley history, and its code still struck a responsive chord in the hearts of violent men.

The business men of Trembles, aided by the Simards, the O'Briens and Annius Gregory, made up a purse, and we held, also, a benefit dance, to raise a fund so Bert could buy back the Fude lot and bank the money for Flo and Tena. Mrs. Baron convinced everyone that the girl would be better off away from her aunt, and somewhere far enough from the valley so the story of what had befallen her would not rise up to make her miserable. Zuleika Donaldson, who was going east for the winter, offered to take Tena with her and give her a part-time job, so she could go to school. Flo, to whom nothing mattered much, became a fixture at the Clark Hotel, where she scrubbed and cleaned, and slowly recovered a modicum of self-confidence.

The new owner of the former Fude cabin and dry farm was a half-breed Sioux called Petekillemquick, whose wife, a Brule Sioux, worked the land assiduously while Pete watched gravely, seated on his doorstep, and smoked Indian tobacco weed in a gaily-ornamented pipe.

Thinking of Petekillemquick reminds me of the bunch of Blackfoot who worked on the ditch for James Munn. Their names were all too difficult for Tooda Peckham, the time-keeper, to list on the payroll, so Tooda and I thought up some appropriate ones borrowed from various soft drinks then in vogue. The Blackfoot braves learned to recognize their new names and, in some instances, grew quite fond of them. Old "Nut Sundae," for instance, learned to scratch his new name with a stick in the dust. Munn, the sturdy old Scot, would not permit the Indian squaws actually to drive the slips, so the braves had to do that. The moment the whistle blew, however, the braves would drop the lines they were holding, right where they stood, and the squaws would take the horses to the corral, unharness them, water them and feed them. In the morning, the squaws harnessed the horses and drove them to the ditch, handing over the lines to their men on the dot of eight o'clock.

The Indians insisted on being paid every evening, right after work, and because the contractors were so short of skinners, Munn humored the redskins to that extent. They would go immediately to the commissary and buy whatever took their fancy, mostly cheap candy bars, so the money got back into Munn's till within a couple of hours. It would have been simpler for the contractor merely to give the Indians the goods and debit their accounts, but the Blackfoot warriors were strong for formality, and would not agree to that.

The Indians ate roast dog, and liked it. Also, the squaws made a quite wonderful sausage from chopped deer meat, lean and fat, flavored with a native herb that smelled like thyme, but was slightly different. It had purple flowers in the early summer, and some of the Asturian *dynamiteros* made a delicious clear liqueur from them, by adding alcohol, sugar and cream. The keg in which this was made was turned end over end, every twenty-four hours for about ten days, before it cleared, and was strained. Getting the alcohol was not too difficult, but the cream was another matter. They had to walk miles to the Dotsen ranch, where Josefa had introduced a milk cow, one of the rarest creatures to be found in the cattle country.

Josefa churned her own butter and marked the pats with a little decorative seal from Norway. I remember that it depicted a sinister, gargoyle-like little imp called Loki.

When the new dentist set up shop in Trembles, over near

the drug store, quite a few of the cowpunchers and roustabouts, who had been putting off having aching teeth yanked, rode in, and always took five or six drinks of straight whisky before submitting to the operation. Old Hans Sauerbier, across the street in his meat market, would watch the dentist's clients enter Doc Vargus' office. Applied dentistry seemed to exercise some kind of baleful influence over the German. Almost nothing else would distract him from his work. When he was not selling meat, or cutting and preparing it for display, Hans was sweeping out the shop, chasing flies, or scouring and scrubbing his blocks and counters. But the moment anyone showed up at the dentist's, Hans would drop whatever he was doing and watch the proceedings through the window. Doc Vargus' window did not have any shades for quite a while, and when the shades finally were delivered, Doc did not have the heart to shut off Hans' view. No one objected.

Joe Jeffries, a cowpuncher from Three Buttes, came in one afternoon with a face swollen on one side to the size of a melon. Doc, according to a notion then prevailing that abscessed teeth should not be pulled until the abscess was reduced, begged Joe to wait a while, but Joe was in such pain, and had suffered so long, that he drew his six-shooter and threatened to shoot up the office if the doc delayed the extraction. Doc called for volunteers to hold Joe down, and did the best he could, but it was a messy, bloody affair. Joe was so strong that he tossed his friends around like sacks of potatoes. He bawled and bellowed like a bull. Mamie Rhorer's pet pig, Apple, that wandered around the main street when he was not following Mamie, was so affected by the uproar that he went into hiding and did not show up again in Trembles for three or four days.

That performance drew Hans all the way across the street.

The old German stood in the dentist's doorway, jaw sagging, eyes bulging, trembling in every limb, straining this way and that, as if he were both the patient and the doctor. When finally the ordeal was over, and Joe, bleeding like a shoat, staggered into Perce Gardner's Westside Saloon to drown the pain in hooch, Hans stumbled back to his butcher shop in a trance. For an hour, he talked to himself in horrified *Plattdeutsch*, holding his own jaws in his enormous capable hands.

In the middle of that night, Doc Vargus heard somebody run into his bedroom, gurgling and gasping out words in a language Doc did not understand. As soon as Doc could wake up, light the lamp, and pull himself together, he saw Old Hans, like a short, misshapen John the Baptist, staring and bleeding at the mouth. Hans had three teeth on a platter.

"Speak English, Hans. You know you can," the dentist begged.

Hans tried to switch, and partly succeeded. In his incredible dialect he insisted that he had dreamed that he was pulling out his own teeth, with his fingers. When he woke up, three front teeth were missing. Hans found them in the bed, and rushed over for help.

"I can't put 'em back," Doc said, examining the exhibits and looking into Hans' open mouth to count the holes. "Lucky you didn't swallow none of 'em."

For a week after the teeth-pulling dream, Hans was afraid to go to sleep again, for fear of yanking the other teeth out of his mouth. When he got to the point that he was perishing from fatigue, Bat Horner had the brilliant idea that Hans should sleep with mittens on. The old German tried that, tying the mittens securely around his wrists. Thus protected from himself, he slept soundly, and mastered his obsession.

Lam McGlynn, who slept at the Clark Hotel for a while,

had as much trouble getting his rest as Old Hans did. Ever since the morning he had seen Lela, naked, had held her in his arms and inhaled the perfume of her hair, Lam could not keep his mind on his work, or take refuge in oblivion at night. In spite of himself, when he was trying hardest not to think about her, he remembered the texture of her olive skin. Barbers develop a tactile sense to an extraordinary degree, sometimes, and can distinguish between customers merely by the feel of their cheeks.

The customers at the barber shop realized that Lam was preoccupied, and it did not add to their peace of mind. On dance nights he did worse and worse with the drums. One Saturday night he got the wrong piece of music (Lam was the only member of the band who could not play without notes) and started off in schottische time, a slow four-four, while the rest of us were playing "Bill Bailey" in a brisk two-four. As a joke, we all dropped out, and Lam, his eyes fixed adoringly on Lela, who was unconscious of the fact, played a long drum solo while the dancers two-stepped, grimaced and roared.

Wherever he went, of course, Lam was kidded unmercifully.

"Hell, Lam! Her bathrobe was hangin' right up there in plain sight. Why didn't you grab it, and cover her up?"

"I got rattled," Lam insisted. "I didn't know what I was doing."

The first evening that Lam suggested to Mrs. Weckerling that they go for a walk along the coulee, in the moonlight, one of the cowboys caught Apple, hid in a clump of sagebrush, and turned the pig loose just after Lam and Lela passed by, on their way back to town. Lela, always nervous out of doors at night, screamed and clutched Lam so tightly that she almost strangled him. Before they got out of the clinch, they were engaged.

Poor little Helen made a painful scene with her mother later that night.

"Oh, Ma. Please don't get married again," she said.

"You're too young to understand that your mother, in a manner of speaking, was compromised. Mr. McGlynn is a gentleman. We must do what is proper and right," Lela said.

"Don't do it, Ma. We got into more trouble doing right than any other way," the child wailed.

Over Helen's protest, the date was set for the wedding, the following June. Lela had a fondness for June weddings, and believed in moderately long engagements, she said.

Lam, the grave and solemn one, became gay and expansive. Sometimes in the evening he would walk up to Highpockets' place and ask Edna for some of the late-blooming flowers from her garden. These he would shape into a bouquet, bind with a ribbon, and present to Lela. Soon Mrs. Weckerling, reassured by the town's approval and sympathy, responded to Lam's attentions and, discreetly, gave more play to her affectionate nature. She had hoped to find a man who was higher in the scale than a barber but, in Trembles, considerations like that seemed to make little difference.

Helen did not relax or relent. "He'll change, Ma. He'll act just like Pa did, after you and him got married. Remember?" the little girl said, when McGlynn was not present.

Old Buck Mavity grinned, as he overheard that.

"That kid's got quite a memory, to recollect what happened as far back as that," Buck said.

CHAPTER NINETEEN

The Accomplished Female Friend

ONE day early in September, Fidlio G. Sharpe telephoned me from up the valley, asking me if I would buy a sack of English walnuts and send them to him by stage. He was now at B. F. Shoat's camp, where the work was progressing as never before. It chanced that Mr. Stackpole was going up to the Headgates and wanted me along; so I turned the level and transit over to the former teamster, Lem Gabel, who in the past few months had become proficient at reading, writing and arithmetic, and could stake out ditches as well as anyone. That was the way with our grade party. When Frank Banks, the chief, got sick, he moved Scotty McVeigh up a notch. When Scotty went down with typhoid, I got a chance at the instruments. Now it was Lem's turn. We all were making progress, then. Since that time, Banks has become a well-known engineer, Scotty has handled big jobs as superintendent of construction, and Lem had been county clerk, successful rancher until his land blew away, and now is a trusted earthwork inspector on the All-American Canal. Furthermore, they all read my books as fast they appear. We have seen one another infrequently, in the course of forty years, but never have felt out of touch. Should we all chance to meet, tonight, we would go on from where we left off previously, with no need for adjustment.

Why Fidlio had taken a sudden fancy to walnuts, when

he believed in austerity for labor leaders and had a mild scorn for gourmets, was not clear until I brought him the walnuts. It seemed that there was an I. W. W. convention about to meet in Chicago and he and Heck, the man who had arrived with him in Glendive, were planning to bum their way back east in time to attend. I had not seen Heck, or heard about him, all summer, for what turned out to be an understandable reason. Heck had run afoul of the anti-Wobbly authorities in Bozeman, where he had organized a bunch of harvest hands and taught them not to work for less than $6 the twelve-hour day. In short, he was in jail.

The ingenious Fidlio had access at Shoat's camp not only to the scorpion bed, which he had carefully removed to a sand bank in one of the foothills some distance from the ditch, but also to the powder and dynamite supply. As he chatted with me, he carefully pried apart a number of the walnuts, stuffed some of them with dynamite, others with fuse and percussion caps, and a few with short matches. These he sent to a fellow worker in Bozeman, who took them to Heck on visiting day. Heck blew out one wall of the jail, without injuring himself or anyone, escaped, and joined the delegation from Montana to the Wobbly convention.

One would have thought that Fidlio, having put Chet Donaldson in a hole that looked like ruin, added dozens of new members to his organization, and learned a lot about working conditions for migratory laborers on the Yellowstone, as a basis for his report to the executive committee in Chicago, would have been content with his summer's activities. Actually, he was a little depressed that evening. The scab he had removed in Glendive had been preying, not on the Workers of the World, but on a local of the A.F. of L., an organization of craft unionists more concerned with jurisdictional fights than the fate of the prisoners of starvation.

"Why should I have horned in? I might have got in trouble and neglected my work," he said.

Besides, he was slightly mixed up concerning another phase of his ideology. Because B. F. Shoat was poor and was being kicked around, Fidlio had helped him, if not saved him.

"A man shouldn't be soft-hearted," Fidlio said. "An employer's a foe, gol darn it. I couldn't have done more for Shoat and Prentice if I was Sam Gompers himself."

"That all comes out of Donaldson," I reminded him.

He brightened a little. "Maybe the foes who are thoroughgoing skunks should be dealt with first," he grudgingly admitted. "That may be sound policy. I'll have to ask the central committee about that."

I never saw Fidlio after that, but I heard, on reliable authority, that he died of pneumonia in the course of the Lawrence textile strike in 1912, in my home commonwealth. On his gravestone, some Wobbly carved a wooden shoe.* In the days when the C.I.O. was going strong, and the outlook for labor looked temporarily hopeful, I thought of Fidlio and saluted his memory, regretting that he had not seen the fruits of his pioneer work for industrial organization and his fervor for a workers' brotherhood. Time marches, off and on. If hell exists, and there is any pie down there, Fidlio will have access to the bakery.

In October of 1907, the air was clear and cool above the Yellowstone. The sky was cobalt blue, and the brown and yellow leaves of the cottonwoods along the river would have

---

* The word "sabotage" is derived from *sabot*, which is French for "wooden shoe." At the time of the first industrial revolution in France, a worker tossed his wooden shoe into a machine and since then similar acts intended to slow up work and thus exert pressure on employers have been classed as "sabotage." Among the Industrial Workers of the World, sabotage was their principal weapon in the war between the classes. Meetings of I.W.W. locals were called to order by presiding officers who used symbolic wooden shoes as gavels.

warmed the heart of Vincent Van Gogh, who, unluckily, was not present.

One evening, just after dark, a rig drove into Trembles, a covered buggy with black top and shining yellow spokes. It stopped near the quaking aspen grove, by the side of the road. The horses were weary.

A few men noticed the strange rig standing there, but no one paid any particular attention for a while. Finally Kurt Mook, the young druggist, heard the horses shaking their heads and harness and pawing the ground impatiently. He approached the rig, peered inside, and saw that a man dressed somberly in a dark suit and stiff collar was sitting motionless in the driver's seat. The lines had slipped from his hand.

Kurt spoke. The man neither answered nor moved.

Kurt went closer, and touched the stranger's hand. It was cold.

Excitement quickly spread. Doc Cherry, the vet, was summoned, also Doc Vargus, the dentist, and, of course, Bert Lacey. There were no signs of violence on the corpse, and no indications that he had suffered convulsions or pain. His pockets contained no identifying marks whatsoever. No liverymen in Glendive or Mondak, or anywhere in between, could identify the buggy or the horses.

For Bert Lacey, a new and startling problem had arisen. Trembles had acquired its first dead man. The nearest undertaker was in Glendive, and Bert knew too well how fed up the Glendive officials were with having trouble from the lower valley towns dumped on their shoulders. Bert decided to take care of the corpse himself. He had it iced, after Doc Morrill from Sidney had assured one and all that the stranger had died "from natural causes."

"His heart stopped and he quit breathing," Doc said. "That's the way most of us go."

230

News items about the dead man and the rig were printed in the *Sidney Herald,* the Glendive papers, and the *Mondak News.* Not a ripple of information resulted, and no one claimed the body. The Glendive coroner was sent for, held one of history's shortest inquests, and dropped the matter.

There were no county, state, unwritten or other kind of laws forbidding well-intentioned folks from burying a corpse on the flats or in the foothills, but Bert Lacey was not the man to do things halfway. The pilgrim whose earthly journey had ended in Trembles must have a proper funeral, and be laid to rest in a suitable graveyard, Bert insisted. So Bert donated an acre of land, across the coulee from the quaking aspen trees, had it cleared of brush, staked out lots and pathways, and a grave was dug by the cobbler, Steve Galucci. Treff Simard, the artist and sculptor, chiseled out a soft granite slab, and this was what he carved on it:

HERE LIES

J O H N   D O E

Who He Is, We Don't Know,

Only God, Who Made It Happen So

? to October 5, 1907

The Rev. Theo Oates, who delivered the funeral oration in the presence of about one hundred men and a dozen hardy women, on a Saturday afternoon, said, in part:

"Ye all were strangers in the land of Egypt.

"For each, there is a time to be born, a time to wander, and a time to die. To our brother, who drove into our midst and passed on to the higher land, we owe this last tribute. We are glad that God found us worthy of receiving the body of one of His children, at the moment when He took to His bosom the soul. We are grieved that we had no opportunity to know our brother better, or to ease his last moments.

"What is our debt to this stranger, we who also have been strangers? He who lies here before us will be the first to ascend directly from Trembles, Montana, to the throne of the Most High. And God will look down in His infinite mercy. He is looking down right now. And He will bless this growing community, and all who are in and of the community, and who, in turn, will enter that greater community, where neither moth nor rust do corrupt, and a place is prepared for one and all. And one and all of you may then seek out this man, and learn of him what now, in God's infinite wisdom, is withheld from our knowledge."

Howard Wise, now Bert's right-hand man, was here, there and everywhere, while the obsequies were being arranged and the ceremonies were carried out. He had no more expectation of interviewing the departed stranger in the sky than of striking a rock in the foothills and causing to gush forth a miraculous stream of 100-proof bourbon, but he entered into the spirit of whatever he undertook. Shunk Cundiff, Lam McGlynn, Bert Lacey and Charley Tufts were the pallbearers. The floral tributes came from Old Knick's garden, where hardy autumnal plants were still in bloom.

When the mourners were gathered at the graveside and the first thuds of earth resounded on the coffin, Lela Weckerling, weeping sympathetically, was seen to change expression, show consternation, and hurry away. Lam McGlynn already had returned to the barber shop to get ready for the Saturday trade.

A moment later, several of the men and women noticed that a live stranger was approaching. The stage had just arrived and departed.

The newcomer was conspicuously dressed, with a wing collar, checked suit and spats. He wore a flowing tie, had a ruddy complexion not acquired in the open. His hair was black and plastered down with vaseline. His black mustaches were waxed. He walked to the edge of the grave, looked down, and respectfully removed his derby hat and held it over his left breast, uttering a sonorous "Amen" after a brief silent prayer.

"This is Trembles, I believe," he said to Bert Lacey.

"Yes, mister. I'm Bert Lacey," said Bert, extending his hand.

"My name is Alanson La Rue! Is there a Mrs. Weckerling here?" the newcomer said.

"She was just overcome, and went back to the hotel," Bert said. "Are you a friend of hers?"

The man struck an attitude, beamed, and recited, in a trained voice that confirmed the impression that he was an actor:

> *"Will not a beauteous landscape bright*
> *Or music's soothing sound*
> *Console the heart, afford delight*
> *And throw sweet peace around?*
>
> *"They may! But never comfort lend*
> *Like an Accomplished Female Friend."*

Just then Bert caught sight of little Helen, standing with the school teacher. They were hand in hand.

"There's Mrs. Weckerling's little girl," Bert said.

The actor's surprise was eloquent, but professionally controlled.

"Indeed! Her little girl, you say? A daughter, may I presume?" La Rue asked.

Lacey was irked by his patronizing tone. "Look, stranger," Bert said, quite brusquely, "if you want to use fancy words,

I'll go get Professor Tufts. He can talk the spats off any dude who wears 'em."

La Rue, unruffled, glanced down at his spats with a critical eye and said:

"Will you present me to the child?"

"How long since you seen Mrs. Weckerling?" Bert demanded. "She's well liked around here, mister, and has plenty of friends."

"Excellent. Excellent. Lela was always one who made friends," La Rue said as they walked over to where Helen was standing.

"This is Helen," Bert said. Josefa Dotsen, not liking the looks of the flashy stranger, raised her eyebrows and patted Helen's shoulder.

"Helen! A name that caused the rise and fall of kingdoms. How old are you, Helen?" La Rue asked.

"I'll be eleven in March, sir," Helen said.

The actor shook his head and sighed. *"Tempus fugit,"* he remarked. Then added, "I would a word with your good mother."

"You know my mother?" Helen asked, uneasily.

The newcomer hastened to reassure her. "Your dear mother and I, many times and oft, have sat on the same trunk, on lonely platforms," La Rue said. "She was a very passable Viola in her day, and a shapely Rosalind."

"My mother is resting," Helen said.

"Was she friendly with the deceased?" La Rue asked.

"No. He came in dead," Helen answered, somewhat confused. With misgivings, the girl escorted La Rue to the door of her mother's room, which Helen shared.

"Mama!" Helen said, after tapping lightly on the door. "There's a gentleman to see you."

"Open, I prithee, Lela. It is Alanson who, like Lazarus of old, has returned from the dead," La Rue said.

The door opened and Lela, in her black dress, stood face to face with the man. For a moment neither of them spoke, then he said:

"Surely it would be proper to invite me in, my dear."

Lela, at her wit's end, motioned La Rue to enter and asked Helen to go out and play for a while. Stubbornly the little girl shook her head.

"Please, Ma," Helen pleaded.

"It is best," her mother said, firmly. Desolate, the child obeyed.

As soon as Lela and La Rue were alone, the actor said:

"You seem to be hesitant in welcoming your lawfully wedded husband, my dear." With that he took from a pocket nearest his heart a document in pasteboard covers on which a scroll of orange blossoms had been traced in gilt, long, long ago. "I carry the certificate . . . here," he said, touching his breast with a flourish.

Lela sat on the bed and began to cry, softly.

"I thought you were dead," she sobbed.

"There, there. Don't cry. What can't be cured must be endured. Your error was an understandable one," said La Rue, suavely.

"But what shall I do? I'm engaged to an honorable man," she said.

"That is easily rectified," he said.

"You deserted me," she said.

"I absented myself, 'tis true," he said. "Those were days when actors' souls were sorely tried. I wanted fame and fortune, to lay at your feet."

He glanced down with a grimace of appreciation at Lela's

shapely feet, which she withdrew under her skirt with
alacrity.

"Those slender white feet," he mused, pursuing the subject. "Praise heaven they still are intact. My own vicissitudes
have brought me corns, if not bunions. Perhaps a little warm
soda water would restore them. Is that obtainable in this incredible place?"

There was only one man in the community to whom anyone could turn when in a predicament like Lela's. Alanson
La Rue had no desire to be cruel to Lam McGlynn. The
drama of the situation appealed to his actor's mind and he
felt deeply sympathetic. However, he was in straits, at liberty,
and needed a long rest. He had no intention of stepping aside,
in the near future. La Rue was glad that a man of the world,
like Charley Tufts, was at hand. Tactfully, La Rue did not
stress the fact that Lela had committed bigamy, with innocent intent, and that he, La Rue, was the only one who
possessed tangible evidence to that effect.

"Appeal to Mr. McGlynn, in behalf of the child," La Rue
urged. "No scandal should blight her life."

Alone with Lela, Charley tried to find out what her wishes
were, and soon understood that they were none too clear. She
had been madly in love with La Rue, as a young woman, and
his romantic fascination was reasserting itself.

When the barber shop closed that first evening, Charley
took McGlynn aside and tried to explain the dilemma. Lam
took it very hard. It was as if he had been struck with a pole-
axe in the middle of his forehead. He could not, in all justice,
feel bitterly toward Lela. Actually, he loved her more des-
perately than ever.

"You mustn't make it hard for her," Charley said, and
Lam disconsolately agreed.

"I'll have to leave town," Lam said.

"Stay and face it like a man," Charley urged. "Who knows? La Rue may get the wanderlust again."

"You think there's a chance?" asked McGlynn, with pathetic eagerness.

"It's better not to run away. A man can't escape from himself, no matter where he goes," said Charley.

"You quit that doggoned college, didn't you?" asked Lam.

"There was no woman in the case," Charley said.

"The boys'll ride me, something fierce," said Lam. "And suppose I forget myself, when I see 'em together, and cut somebody's throat?"

"Lela wants you to stay," said Charley.

"Did she say that?"

Charley swallowed hard. "In effect," he replied. "You see, Lam, her peace of mind depends on how you act. She can't chase away her lawfully wedded husband. She married the second one with the best intentions in the world. She loved you, and accepted your proposal, innocently and sincerely. Try to think about her," said Charley.

"If you can tell me how not to think about her, then I'll say you're the smartest educated man I ever knew," said Lam.

Charley blushed and bit his lip. Was he being fair to Lam, or was he not? He could advise him to move on, leave his newly established trade, his shack and equipment, and the good friends he had made who would stand by him during his lifetime. But Charley had acquired an affection and regard for Trembles, and what it signified. He saw that Lam was hurt to such a degree that, if he went away, he would go to his downfall.

"Lam," he said, finally, "may I tell you something, just between us two?"

"Go ahead," Lam said. "At least, I can keep my trap shut. That's something I can do."

"Suppose I should give you my word that it's possible to love a woman without possessing her, to see her, day in and day out, with another man, and stay around, because it's best for all concerned? Could you take my word for that, without mentioning names?" Charley asked.

Lam extended his hand.

"Thanks, Professor," he said. "I'm not smart, but I get what you mean. Let's go in and have a drink. I'll stay."

CHAPTER TWENTY

Temptation in Cornflower Blue

ALANSON LA RUE had caught the interest and imagination of everyone in Trembles before he had been there a week. He had replenished his wardrobe in the Sidney stores and through Montgomery Ward, and Lela had mended, turned and refurbished the clothes that had arrived in his large theatrical trunk, after she had redeemed it by mail from a pawn shop in St. Paul. He awoke, habitually, about nine o'clock in the morning. As soon as he tapped with his cane on the floor, Lela, who had been busy at least two hours, would tiptoe back into their bedroom and raise the shades. Then she would bring him a steaming cup of coffee from Ah Cook's kitchen. If she spilled a drop into the saucer she would apologize and wipe it off before he had a chance to chide her. If the coffee were not quite hot enough, he would send it back, but he was always meticulously polite about it. The formality and elegance of his language, while not as sound as that of Mr. Stackpole, whom La Rue admired, was impressive to his neighbors in Trembles.

"The deep of night has crept upon our talk," La Rue would say to the men at the bar, before he bade them good night. If he felt an urge to go out to the elaborate new backhouse, he would sigh and quote from *Julius Caesar*, in which he had played not Julius, but Trebonius.

" 'And nature must obey necessity,' " he would say. "Fur-

thermore, gentlemen, necessity must conform with nature
. . . Anon!"

He never simply left a room. He made an exit.

With each dinner and supper, to which he referred as
lunch and dinner, La Rue drank a glass or two of wine—champagne, in fact. Ah Flunk had learned just how to cool it.
La Rue made it a practice to promenade up the main and
only street, after each evening meal. He still wore spats, a
sizeable glass stickpin, and carried his gold-headed cane. At
Perce Gardner's shipshape Westside Saloon, La Rue would
take a liqueur, sometimes an elaborate *pousse-café* in five
colors, and farmers would peer through the windows to watch
Perce mix it and La Rue drink it.

After her first flurry of dismay, Lela had settled down to
a steady routine of sewing and waiting on her husband. She
actually trembled at the frown which occasionally furrowed
his brow. La Rue never let any kind of slip on Lela's part
go unremarked.

"I hope, my dear, that it won't be necessary to speak about
this again," he would say, when he found one of his shirt
buttons sewed too tightly against the fabric. La Rue liked
them to hang on a longer thread, so there would be a little
play. He could not reconcile himself to canned milk; so little
Helen brought a small pail of cream from the school house,
where Miss Dotsen delivered it. Once, when somehow a
mouse slipped into the cream, and the tender-hearted child
rescued it with difficulty, Helen did not mention it to her
step-father. She never relaxed an inch in her hostility to him
and disapproval of her mother's acceptance of him.

"Why strain harsh discords and unpleasing sharps?" La
Rue would ask the child. He never scolded her or did anything directly to annoy her.

240

"I beg your pardon, Mr. La Rue," she would say, and purse her lips tight, looking down at the floor.

"Not many young ladies can boast of a step-father who is a step backward, not forward," he reminded her.

Although he did no work whatsoever, La Rue did not appear to be conspicuously idle. He took so much trouble with the minute details of his daily life that he was fully occupied.

In spite of their natural hostility at first, nearly all the men soon began to admire and like the suave actor. They admitted freely that if they could make a woman step around the way he did, they would get hitched right away.

"Gentlemen," he would say, "our land will be reduced to a mere matriarchy if some of us do not assert ourselves."

No man ever brightened more perceptibly at the sight of a pretty woman than Alanson La Rue. On one occasion when Baron and Schneider in Sidney had a display of women's silk stockings in shapely dummy legs in their window, La Rue rode all the way down there, three days running, to walk up and down, frankly admiring them. The sight of Edna High-pockets, passing in a rig, would cause La Rue to burn his manicured fingers with a match. He was never far away when the four girls emerged from the school house in the afternoon. He liked to watch their legs, as they passed along the street, and made no bones about admitting it.

An event which daily attested to La Rue's courage occurred each morning about ten-thirty, when La Rue entered Lam's barber shop and was shaved.

I do not think La Rue intended to be cruel, and I am sure that Lam did not relish displaying his insane jealousy. Lam, by that time, wore a carefully laundered white coat while at work. Whenever I could, I watched the performance.

"Good morning," La Rue would say.

Lam would try to be equally polite, but could never manage more than a grunt. Many times, in stropping the razor he was to use on the actor's smooth pink cheeks, Lam got so flustered that he cut a good strap clean in two.

La Rue, seating himself histrionically in the adjustable chair, would pretend not to notice. As for me, I would feel goose pimples all over. But I understood, as did everyone else in Trembles, that it was part of Lam's self-discipline to give La Rue a perfect shave, without as much as nicking a pimple, day after day. La Rue almost never had any cause for complaint. Once in a while Lam tipped the chair back a trifle farther than La Rue liked to have it.

"Would you mind . . . A little higher, if you please," La Rue would say.

Lam, biting his lip and turning livid, would readjust the chair. Sometimes, before he started on the area around La Rue's jugular vein, Lam would turn away and stare at the wall without seeing it, to master himself. But both men knew they had entered a grim contest, and neither would be a quitter.

The completely subdued Lela seldom made a request of any kind to her lord and master, but one night, after Lam had quite badly cut Old Buck Mavity, who had followed La Rue in the chair, Lela protested, meekly. La Rue had undressed ever so carefully, got into bed beside her, and was about to take her in his arms, a nightly formality he never neglected or slighted. Lela murmured:

"Darling."

"Love of my wayward youth," he whispered, in her shapely ear.

"Would you do something for me?" she asked softly.

"You know, my dear, that you have but to name it," he replied, incautiously. Just about that time each night he was almost divine in his tenderness.

She hesitated, then took the plunge.

"Darling, couldn't you shave yourself, or go to Sidney?"

"Madam," La Rue said, sternly, "this is not the moment when I relish discovering stray thoughts in your mind about a former rival. Compose yourself, I prithee."

No more was ever said, in the privacy of their bedroom or elsewhere, concerning McGlynn, and the next morning, on the dot of ten-thirty, La Rue appeared at the barber shop and, after Lam had brushed him off meticulously, handed the barber a two-bit piece in addition to what La Rue called "the customary honorarium."

There was no scramble, after the accident to Mavity, among the regulars in Trembles to take their turn in Lam's chair just after he had finished with La Rue. That spot was reserved for unwary transients and outsiders.

The clear cool weather lasted through November that year, with the moon so bright that we could read the weekly newspapers in its light. Just before Thanksgiving, the Governor of Montana issued a proclamation, the final words of which were as follows:

"In all that makes for the broader and higher life in Montana, the year has been one of progression."

A few days before Thanksgiving, when we all were awaiting the arrival of a wagonload of live turkeys from the Dakota side, we saw La Rue emerge safely from the barber shop. He was in unusually good spirits that morning, and decided to take a "constitutional." Swinging his cane and humming blithely the tune of "It's a Good World After All," the actor started up the stage road toward Newlon, and when he was nearing Fox Creek he saw a rig approaching, and noticed that the off horse had picked up a stone and was limping badly. The driver, Chris Lentz, a Mennonite from the small colony that had settled up Fox Creek, halted the horse. Seated beside Old Chris was his daughter Cora, dressed in ill-fitting homespun. Her oval face had the beauty of a classic virgin who would develop into a more classic madonna. She had a corona of thick chestnut braids, soft dark eyes, a wistful small mouth, perfect nose and an aura of saintliness.

La Rue, lifting his fawn-colored derby gallantly, bowed to Cora, who for the first time had been brought by her father and fiancé, Eli Hauser, into town to do some necessary shopping.

"Good day, miss, and to you, sirs," La Rue said.

"*Grüss Gott*," muttered the two men, nervously. Cora, who had never spoken with a strange man outside her sect, was too embarrassed to do anything but widen her expressive eyes and turn quickly away.

"I am forced to admit, with the poet," La Rue continued, "that there's too much beauty on this earth for lonely men to bear."

There was a strained silence. None of the occupants of the rig knew what La Rue's words meant, but it was clear that his intent was to pay Cora a compliment. That, to the Mennonites, would not have been permissible even for a neighbor of their faith. La Rue caught on that they did not understand English, and, by means of skillful pantomime, indicated that he, as well as the horse, had gone lame. Very uneasily, they refrained from protesting when he got into the wagon, sitting on the back end, with his legs dangling from the tail-board.

It was thus that they made their entrance into Trembles, and Cora, who had heard but not understood a constant stream of tributes, was in such a state that she wished she had stayed in the colony, and not ventured into the perilous world. She tried not to steal an occasional glance at the hand-

244

some stranger, who was dressed as she imagined Solomon in all his glory might have appeared, and had an aplomb that seemed to carry its own authority.

Meanwhile, the wagon bringing the live turkeys Bert had ordered from Mondak had broken down just south of Sidney and Old Hans Sauerbier, the butcher, who was riding with the driver, was herding them along the road on foot, keeping them in order with a long alder rod. As the strange procession neared Trembles, everyone turned out to watch and cheer Old Hans, who was beaming happily, since he seldom held the limelight. The turkeys had come from North Dakota farms and dealers all the way back to Minot, and from points as far north as the Canadian border.

Immediately, arrangements were made to raffle off some of the birds and La Rue was selected to conduct the ceremony. Cora watched, furtively, from the wagon seat, her heart beating faster whenever La Rue flashed his roguish eyes upon her. When the actor bought three tickets, for two bits apiece, and insisted on presenting one each to Chris Lentz, Eli Hauser and Cora, in consideration of the ride they had given him, Cora began to tremble with forebodings. She sensed that something unprecedented, and of great import, was about to engulf her. This fear was aggravated when it turned out that she held the lucky number and, while everybody in Trembles cheered, waved and stared at her, admiringly, she found herself with a huge tom turkey in her arms. Her father, Chris, was glad enough to get so many pounds of food for nothing, and accepted Cora's good luck as coming from on high. Eli was sullen and furious, and did not say a word, either during their stay in Trembles or on the way home.

In Trembles, Thanksgiving came and went, and all was merry. But in the foothills of Fox Creek a most disturbing incident took place, and threw the formerly homogeneous colony into confusion and perplexity. For when Cora, preparing the family dinner to which many neighbors were invited, started cleaning the big turkey's crop, she found in it six matched and wondrous stones, the like of which neither she nor any of the Mennonites had seen before. No one doubted that they were precious, in terms of values the outside world held dear. The stones were oval in shape, carefully cut and flattened on top and bottom. The color was a deep cornflower blue, as if they had been distilled from the sky itself.

Cora, who had never handled any beautiful objects except wild flowers, was breathless, and afraid, when she looked at them. She trembled, her breath came short, she tried to pray. And her prayers were scrambled up with thoughts and images of the handsome man with the mellifluous voice and admiring, almost worshipful eyes, who had come into her life on the stage road at Fox Creek, had given her a slip of paper which, somehow, in a way she dimly understood, transformed itself into a huge and useful bird that meant, in her father's bleak house, a feast the like of which that house had never known. Now came this visitation, in the form of gems so beautiful they took her breath and her defenses away.

Could it be that an atavistic hunger for beauty and ornament, suppressed through generations, was revived and, like an evil familiar, had materialized to tempt her, wreck all she had known of order and austerity, and make of her, first the victim, and then the instrument of Satan? The sapphires, as she polished them tenderly with her apron, did not appear vile, but like distillations from heaven. What troubled her was the feeling that the gems made her life and surroundings look sordid, as never before.

Of course, Cora called her father from the fields, and Chris consulted with Ivan Twedt, Klaus Lohmiller, Yodder Gingerich, and the other co-religionists and brethren. Little work was accomplished from that moment on until they had arrived at a decision.

Cora knew in her heart what it would be. The clear blue stones, which radiated magic and made her giddy when she even thought about them, were not hers. They had not come down from God to cheer a maiden's timid heart, but belonged to somebody who must be missing them sorely. The tom turkey had been plucked and his feathers carefully sorted, some to be made into dusters, others to stuff feather-beds with. Not being the strictest congregation of the *Amische-Mennonitische* faith, some of the Fox Creek colonists pampered themselves to the extent of sleeping on mattresses. It would be impossible to put the turkey together again, in any shape recognizable to a former owner. And nobody could guess to whom the bird belonged or where he had picked up the gems.

Two of the men, Old Chris, and the pious Klaus Lohmiller, who sometimes was moved to preach six hours without stopping and knew all the hymns, words and tunes, by heart, rode at once into Trembles, with the blue stones wrapped in a worn chamois purse.

"Can you beat it? Them's sapphires, and good ones, at that. They're alike as peas in a pod," Bert said, his face lighting up with delight.

La Rue, who, once he had seen Cora, was galvanized with interest whenever any Mennonite showed up, joined the group, to the discomfort of Chris, who already suspected his daughter of harboring dangerous thoughts on La Rue's account.

"How beautiful they will look, around Miss Cora's neck!" La Rue said.

Klaus Lohmiller eyed him severely and said, in halting

English, mixed with low German, *"Zu der* owner *zurück* they go! *Und schnell!"*

"Let us send for Helen and reason with these dolts. Or the good Hans will do," La Rue said.

Bert, with the chamois sack in his hand, led the way to the butcher shop, where Hans, when he saw the stones, gaped in astonishment. The word had spread through the town, and two dozen men joined the consultation.

The Mennonites were firm and resolute. Herr Lacey, they insisted, must keep the jewels until he could locate the rightful owner.

"And how in heck do they expect me to do that? Them turkeys came from a dozen different farms, scattered over half of Dakota! Tell these scissorbills to give 'em back to that girl. I'll take up a collection to have 'em set," Bert said.

"Put me down for five dollars, at the head of the list," said La Rue, and others agreed to chip in. Always Lela was careful to see that her husband had enough money in his pocket to discharge his social obligations.

It was finally agreed that the story of Cora's finding the matched sapphires in a turkey's crop should be published in all the weeklies of Dawson County and near-by Dakota. If no one put in a plausible claim to them, then Cora would have to accept them.

Not at all satisfied that the unfortunate matter was at an end, Lentz and Lohmiller rode back to the colony without uttering a word to each other, and very few to the horses, en route. Eli Hauser angrily told Cora that some of those evil men in Trembles wanted her to wear the jewels on a gold string around her neck. That there would be no such nonsense Eli made all too clear. Like a modest Amish maiden, Cora bowed her head, and submitted to his dictum. Through sleepless hours at night she reproached herself for sinful

248

thoughts she could not eradicate from her mind. If she grew paler and lost a little weight, it only served to make her eyes larger and more luminous.

Soon she began to have other reasons for self-reproach. She became aware that Eli smelled strongly of manure and sweat. Try as she might, she could not help feeling slight nausea whenever he was near. She dreaded his comings and caught herself praying for his goings. That clearly was sinful. She had to tell her father, and he was very stern and troubled. He told her quite bitterly that her handsome face and figure were not of God but Satan, that they had been a curse to her and a trial to him since she had been born. They would surely prove a heavier curse to Eli, her future husband.

"Perhaps, Father, I would do wrong to marry any man, and bring a curse on him," she said, with an eagerness that betrayed her.

Chris stamped and roared, clenching his fists and calling upon heaven to aid him.

"Shameless girl!" he said, in hoarse German. "You are thinking of that wicked married man, who lives by his poor wife's earnings!"

"You must punish me, Father," Cora said, bowing her head in shame, and acknowledging the fault.

The enormity of that was too much for Chris. He did not strike her, because violence was forbidden by the tenets of their faith. Instead, he allowed her only bread and water, and forbade her to speak to anyone except her fiancé until she could tell him truly that she had wrestled with her evil desires and subdued them. To her horror, after a few days of semi-starvation, she began having dreams of La Rue so terrible and colorful that she dared not tell her father about them, and could bring herself only to refer to them in censored form in her prayers to Almighty God.

249

CHAPTER TWENTY-ONE

"Tomorrow, Maybe, There'll Be Snow"

AS SOON as the Thanksgiving feast was over, and the *animateurs* of the lower valley had recovered from "too much love of living," old-timers, newcomers, solid citizens and bums, alike, spent much of their time speculating as to when winter would set in. There was a lull in the work, excepting building construction, and the clear cool weather made the hours seem shorter. The sky gave no answer to the overwhelming question. In eastern Montana it is usually blank and blue, until about twenty minutes before some unprecedented meteorological atrocity is perpetrated on that hardy ancient land.

The cattle on the range, however, seemed to have secret information. My beloved and ornery little Crocus started growing a hair shirt that was thicker and longer than ever St. Anthony wore. All the steers, cows and calves on the range, between the river and the Canadian border, were following suit. The wind rose in the afternoon, before sunset, and again in the morning, after sun-up. At noon it was calm and warm, and around the Clark Hotel the practical jokers who were to make it hazardous and lively in the time of snow began practicing and experimenting.

Two new families from Iowa, each with a couple of growing boys, moved into cabins south of the Highpockets and Arndt claims in order to get an early start in the spring, and

250

the good weather held so long that they got one hundred acres plowed, between them. So Josefa's school, which had been reduced to three girls by the mishap that had caused Tena Hastey to go back east for a new start, in December enrolled Mark and Elar Kleepsie, twelve and thirteen, respectively, and the two adolescent Sylvester brothers, Elmo and Bryan.

"Thank God for a couple of Democrats," Bert Lacey said, when the Iowa men arrived. Bert wanted plenty of both Republicans and Democrats, so that at least half the town would be satisfied no matter how state and county elections turned out.

Alanson La Rue had begun to take a lively interest in the school, firstly, because Josefa was so aloof and unapproachable that she offered him a challenge worthy of his brass, and, secondly, because he dearly loved to perform.

"The children should be privileged to hear the King's English, as delivered by Garrick and John Drew," he said, and twice each week, in the afternoon, La Rue would dress with special care and read or recite for two hours at a stretch, from Shakespeare, Tennyson, Mark Twain and Joe Miller. Josefa's pupils, who liked better to receive than to give, enjoyed those hours of respite from writing, spelling and arithmetic, and several of the tradesmen and stray cow hands often attended La Rue's performances, hats in hand, standing or squatting circumspectly in the rear of the school room. La Rue thrilled them with "Curfew Shall Not Ring Tonight," "The Corn Song," "The Wreck of the Hesperus," and "The Ancient Mariner." Even the farm boys shivered when he let himself go and recited "Seeing Things at Night" and the touching verses entitled: "I'm a Lunkhead," in which the dunce becomes a hero and shows the solid worth that often finds itself at the foot of the class.

251

A Ghost Town on the Yellowstone

Grant Marsh, after winning reinstatement following the charges brought in the Glendive court and before the county licensing board by the pilot he had tossed into the Yellowstone, tied up the *Expansion* and went to his home in Yankton, North Dakota, to rest until spring. The charge of assault and battery did not trouble the old captain at all, and it never came to trial. A group of friendly Glendive business men took care of that. But Marsh was deeply hurt and indignant because the licensing board revoked his pilot's license for "dishonorable conduct," after he had conquered all the principal rivers of America and had navigated with unequalled skill during more than fifty years. Pressure was brought to bear by all his friends on the group of politicians who had been influenced by the sheriff and Captain Marsh was exonerated and got back his pilot's ticket.

In the late fall, another steamboat, *The Dancing Sal,* made frequent trips from the Missouri to Elm's Ferry, opposite Sidney and Trembles, and brought in load after load of winter supplies. The river froze over, lightly, in mid-December.

Mexican Joe, my all-round musician and the best bronco buster in the region, started buying an elaborate outfit for a visit to his native Mexico. He had put in a few winters in Montana and did not look forward to another.

"Jesus," said Bert Lacey, to me, alarmed, "we can't let talent drift away. The way I look at it, Skeet (that was my local nickname), we got to offer him inducements."

So Bert and I took Mexican Joe aside, told him the band would be a shell of its former self without his artistry, and he was promised the warmest job in town. There was a mountainous woodpile near the corral behind the hotel and the café. Joe was assured that he would not have to callous his hands with an axe, but only would be expected to stoke the stoves and hover near them. With all the grace of his Latin heritage and the dignity of his Indian strain, Joe acquiesced.

Work was still going strong, on the ditch, and I had been told that, as soon as the snow fell, I would be assigned as instrument man on a surveying party that was to trace the course of the Lower Yellowstone and prepare a new map. The previous survey had been made sixty years before, and I think the surveyors never got nearer the valley than St. Paul. In countless instances we had found the stream five miles or more from where it was indicated on their map. The river survey could not be accomplished in the summer or the fall, because of the thick underbrush in the river bed, which was anywhere from one hundred yards to two miles in width. No one could cut vistas through those thickets, on every quarter-section line. Instead, we would have to let the snow cover them, and work on skis, unimpeded.

Every clear day that passed, men would say, "Tomorrow, maybe, there'll be snow." No snow came. There were frosts at night. The migratory birds had flown. Bears were seen or reported less and less frequently. But another sign from nature pointed to a hard winter. In the bad lands and foothills, large gray wolves appeared, in unusual numbers. At night, we could see pairs of luminous relentless eyes across Cedar Coulee from the aspen grove. The bounty was high, and some of the wolves were shot, but not nearly enough.

Undoubtedly Zuleika Donaldson, when she got back to Minnesota, told her father about her misgivings concerning Chet and the work at Donaldson's camp. Due to Fidlio's sabotage and the zeal of the Wobblies, Chet's section of the ditch had gone from bad to worse. When, as the date approached for a final settlement with the sub-contractors, Noel Prentice and B. F. Shoat, and the financial statements from the Glendive bank could no longer be concealed, the elder Donaldson found himself on the verge of bankruptcy, he arrived, without notice, at the Donaldson camp. The show-down was painful for both father and son.

Immediately Wendell Donaldson, the father, relieved Chet of his title and his pay as camp superintendent and put him to work as dirt foreman. Anne had never turned him down, irrevocably, and whatever else happened to Chet, he was determined to follow her back east and marry her that winter.

Wendell Donaldson, in his extremity, consulted my brother Charles, to ask if there were any competent men working for the government without bright prospects in the public service who might be hired to supervise work on the Donaldson contract. Charles' first thought was Frank Crowe, but Crowe had already decided to go into contracting for himself and had teamed up with a trustworthy Czech named Fred Lzicar. Scotty McVeigh, who also had attracted Charles' attention because of his good sense and judgment, had been signed up by Noel Prentice, partly because of his ability and also because Anne had urged her father to hire him. It was ironic that Anne, on whose account Walt Murray and Chet Donaldson were losing what remained of their minds, had set her heart on marrying Scotty, who was equally determined to remain foot-loose. Chet did not fear Scotty's rivalry, because the latter had no money except what he earned each month. Walt was not as much worried as he should have been on Scotty's account because Walt knew that McVeigh was not in love. How any man could fail to love Anne was bewildering to Walt, but it also was reassuring. Anne, Walt believed from experience, would require complete adulation and submission on the part of her husband. In those departments, Walt felt that he, himself, could not be surpassed.

Charles liked and trusted Wendell Donaldson and was anxious to help him. He suggested that Wendell have a talk with Noel Prentice, who had done well and wanted to expand. The elder Donaldson made a deal with Prentice, who offered, in exchange for an equal partnership in the Donaldson concern, to put back into the firm the money Donaldson owed him for the season's work. Prentice, who always had been decent with the meek B. F. Shoat, persuaded Shoat to invest the bulk of his earnings, and accept a note, at a good rate of interest, payable a year later.

When Chet heard that Scotty McVeigh was to have his former job as superintendent, he waited only until the time when Anne was leaving for Minnesota. Then Chet slunk out of the camp, went to Glendive, forged his father's name on a big check, cashed it, and, without Anne's knowledge, got on the same train she was taking eastward. Wendell Donaldson, broken-hearted, was obliged to swear out a warrant for the arrest of his son.

The hated railroad dick, J. Peemiller, and Chet had been as thick as thieves frequently are. Peemiller tipped off Chet that he was to be taken off the train by the authorities in St. Paul. Chet tried by every means to persuade Anne to jump the train with him, allegedly for the purpose of an elopement. When he lost his head and attempted to use force, Anne stabbed him in the shoulder with a hatpin.

So Chet, who in the summer had swaggered around and shot whom he pleased, found himself, a fugitive from justice, disowned, rejected as a suitor and painfully wounded, in a strange town. From then on, during ten years or so, he subsisted by gambling and appealing to Zuleika, who would not see him but shared her allowance, secretly, with him, to shield her father from more grief in case Chet should again be caught stealing.

In the army, beginning with his service in the "punitive" expedition into Mexico, whose inhabitants he loathed and killed with relish, Chet made good, and attained the rank of majo. by the time his country got into World War I. While with the A.E.F. in France, Chet won several decorations for bravery and, on returning, was forgiven by his father, on the latter's death bed, inherited his share of the Donaldson fortune, and went back to contracting, but always in cities, where he could count on co-operation from the politicians and their engineers.

Walt Murray, for a while, fared worse than Chet. He wrote Anne impassioned letters, twenty pages long, every day, and sometimes twice a day. Her replies were noncommittal, and became more and more infrequent. One day before the ditch work closed down, Walt happened to be in Donaldson's camp when the stage drove in and the mail was distributed. Scotty McVeigh, then Donaldson's superintendent, was busy on the ditch, but Walt caught sight of a large sheaf of fat letters, addressed to Scotty, in Anne's precise and dainty handwriting. While Walt had been deluging Anne with love letters, she had been spending most of her time writing passionately to Scotty, who never had said that he loved her.

Walt, never having too much stamina, blew up like a kite. He quit his job, went to Trembles, and hung around Bert's bar until his money and credit were gone and Bert had to ask him to leave.

There was only one place Walt could take refuge, where no amount of drink or despair could bring him to talk about Anne. Stella, warm-hearted as always, let him stay at the Little Casino a while and when he got completely out of hand, and began stamping on nonexistent centipedes, she overpowered him, locked him in a room, bound him in a makeshift strait jacket, tapered him off, fed him, and hired a livery rig to take him to Mondak, where a job in a store was open to him, thanks to her influence.

In a letter from Scotty McVeigh that I received several

years later, in 1910, I think, he informed me that Stella had "cried like a baby" (with joy) when the news spread through the valley that Walt Murray had pulled himself together, made good as a certified public accountant, and had married Anne Prentice at last. No one was happier about the good tidings than Scotty himself, who had had a very close call and still was fancy-free.

When, still later, the income-tax laws put accountants in the upper brackets, Walt hobnobbed with the powerful and rich, Anne blossomed in society, and they lived the fine, un- fettered, gracious life Walt's ability and Anne's beauty so well merited. So war rehabilitated Chet Donaldson, and high taxes set Walt Murray on the top of the world.

Howard Wise was another of my Yellowstone friends with whom I was in intermittent contact during many years of adventure. And Wise had much more difficulty with the kind of heart trouble so prevalent in our Montana equiva- lent of the *Ile* of Cytherea.

Romances, in the valley so highly recommended by the N.P. and Great Northern (whose publicists never mentioned how tricky the barometer of love would prove to be), shot up and flowered profusely, like certain of the cactus plants that lie dormant for months and years, then send a stout stalk heavenward and burst into extravagant bloom. The autumn season always intensified the amatory instincts of the males, and quite a few of the females, who were still far outnumbered.

Wise, on one of his trips to Glendive, attended a picture show at the Opera House, where a newly arrived soprano, named Lulu Lucas, had just been hired to sing "illustrated" songs between pictures. Lulu was a sightly little trouper, with ambitions to sing in opera, or musical comedy, at the very least. She was pert, with soulful eyes, and had come to

Montana because she could make fifty dollars a week more than anyone would pay her to sing in New York. Her salary in Glendive was fifty dollars, weekly. Wise was a delightful companion, a tolerant, sentimental German, well-read, versatile, and possessed of an easy philosophy of life. When he got singed by the love of a woman, however, he was transformed. He became glib and persuasive, tender and dandified. His lusty thirst for whisky served to bring out his attractive qualities and suppress the others, if he had any that were unattractive.

After the show in Glendive, in the course of which Lulu sang "Daddy's Little Tom Boy Girl," "Sunbonnet Sue," and "When It's Moonlight, Mary Darling, by the Old Grape Arbor Shade," Wise induced Howard Roby to take him backstage and introduce him to the "artiste." Wise impressed Lulu with his manners and tact. He invited her to go with him for a bird and bottle at the Nippon Restaurant, where there were private booths curtained with glass beads, grouse could be provided, and any amount of Mumm's Extra Dry.

When Wise was in funds, that is to say, right after he had been paid, there was not a more lavish spender in the valley. He liked to do things up brown. He was respectful to Lulu, and pandered to her healthy appetite and expensive tastes. The little singer began to believe in the principle of Santa Claus. Christmas, then, was less than a month away.

After the first supper, since the champagne seemed to have relieved Lulu's fatigue, Wise ordered a hack and they were driven to the Yellowstone bridge, from which they watched the moonlight on the waters and the buttes and bad lands. He was so circumspect and anxious to win her confidence that he did not lean close enough to touch her elbow. At four A.M. he drove her to her hotel and said "Good night" at the door, most properly.

258

Each night, after Wise got back to Trembles, as soon as the crowd at the hotel began to scatter, he would ride his rangy roan called "Schnitzelbank" to the Newlon engineers' camp and bribe the night operator to let him take over the switchboard for an hour or two. He would call Lulu at the Jordan, and run up bills that reached three figures the first month.

Bert got worried. He forsesaw that, unless something were done, he would lose his hotel clerk. Finally, he authorized Wise to offer Lulu fifty dollars a week, plus room and board, if she would winter in Trembles. Lacey planned to run pictures twice a week in the Opera House, have Lulu sing during intermission at the Saturday night dances, and on other days spend an hour at the school house teaching music to the children. Miss Dotsen did fairly well, but would be willing to step aside in favor of a professional singer.

Lulu was disappointed almost to the point of panic when she first caught sight of Trembles. As fast as the town had progressed, it had not caught up with Wise's powers of description. But she was well received, most particularly by Alanson La Rue, who, as a fellow trouper, regaled Lulu with tales of stage triumphs.

It was touch and go for a while as to whether Lulu would stay. What clinched her decision was a glimpse of the cornflower sapphires, and the story she was told about their having been found by a Mennonite farmer girl whose folks were "crazy" (from Lulu's point of view) and would not let her keep them. Lulu, as hard as she tried to hide her feelings, was fascinated and her mind was addled by those stones. She, more than anyone else in Trembles, had an idea that they were valuable beyond the conservative estimates the local wise men had made. There, in a soiled chamois pouch, lay the equivalent of what Lulu could only hope to gain after years

259

of striving, worrying, humbling herself, fighting rivals to the death, and wheedling influential men. She was no harder or more greedy than other girls with little talent and large ambitions who had to make their way, with pretty faces, shapely bodies, and youth as their principal assets. Already she had had six proposals of marriage, some from well-to-do men, in the valley. Security was not what Lulu wanted, but fame and flattery. Wise, who eyed her like a sick calf, and let all his judgment go numb, was not the answer, in Lulu's mind, unless he really was smart and devoted, and would go quickly to the top, for her sake.

Lulu reasoned thus, and Wise gradually was obliged to adopt a similar pattern of thought. If he loved her, there was nothing he would refuse her. She wanted the sapphires. They belonged to no one in particular. That sloppy and dim-witted jill in the foothills did not count. If Wise was as smooth as he claimed to be, he could get the gems from Bert, or Cora, or anyone who had no bona-fide claim to them. When Lulu lay in her bed, at night, she would dream with her eyes wide open, as if already the sapphires were hers. Everything else she wanted, Lulu assumed, would come to her, once she had those luminous blue stones. She must have them, or her life was a failure, and her hope of abundance and recognition would be withered in her youth. Unless Wise came through, and got the gems for her, she was just one more canary, who could sing a few years in the sticks, fall for the line of some masher one night when she was tired, and wind up in the chorus of a burlesque show that never hit Broadway but was always on the road. Lulu would wake up, exhausted, after being thrilled and depressed, alternately, by her castles and dungeons in the air, which she built between one o'clock in the morning, when she said good night to Wise, and six o'clock, when she fell into a troubled sleep from which almost nothing could arouse her until long after lunch time.

Wise, on his side of the partition that divided their rooms in the Clark Hotel, lay awake long hours trying to figure out how he could perform the quest Lulu had laid out for him.

Paid advertisements and editorial items concerning the sapphires continued appearing in the newspapers of northwestern Dakota and northeastern Montana. No response was received. Whoever owned the gems must have departed the country or died without trace. With each day, Lulu's passion for the jewels got more intense. When it was discovered that some of the turkeys had come from a Dakota farm on the Canadian border, at a point where, since the days of Astor's fur trade, considerable smuggling had been going on, Bert and Wise both saw a possible explanation of the appearance of a fortune in sapphires, matched well enough to figure as museum pieces, with no one coming forward to claim them. Had they been brought into the country by smugglers, naturally the crooks would have to keep mum, or shift their point of operations.

When Lulu sang, in Trembles, I accompanied her on the piano and Wise worked the magic lantern and the colored slides. Like many willful young women who have "voices," Lulu was impatient of the restraint involved in keeping time. She dragged the tunes, got shrill on the high notes she held too long, and thin on the low notes beyond the range of her soprano register. If anything went wrong, she was caustic with me, and only my regard for Wise prevented me from telling her off. I realize now that accompanying Lulu was excellent training, because since then I have found it relatively easy to accompany almost anyone else, and play in all kinds of ensembles without getting lost.

Mexican Joe, having no diplomatic obligations in connection with Lulu, invariably left the hall when she was about to perform, and stood outside, at a safe distance, talking softly to God and the saints, in the presence of horses.

Christmas came, and the approach of the holiday season in eastern Montana usually meant that Dawson County lost a few more inhabitants, for good. A large number of the old-timers believed the country had gone to pot when Montana became a state. That brought upon the ranchers and free-booters a tangle of Federal laws that did not apply to terri-tories, and an avalanche of state laws, mostly framed by men who were incapable of listing their own laundry without gross mistakes. The ranchers along the Lower Yellowstone insisted that the agitation in favor of statehood, successful in 1889, had been motivated by the mine speculators around Butte and Helena in order that Montana mineral deposits and the land above them could legally be sold to foreigners. It seems that one cannot sell a chunk of a "territory" to subjects of a foreign government, but disposing of a state, piecemeal, is permitted.

In the late fall, when there was less work to be done in the fields, camps and corrals, men whose social life centered at Trembles had more time to read the local weekly papers. Items like the following appeared frequently in the *In-dependent,* that glorified the staunch pioneers:

"Earl Thurston, of Burns Creek, and his faithful spouse and daughter, Emily and Ann, sold out his shebang last week and as we go to press the Thurstons are on their way back east to Pennsylvania, whence Earl came to these parts in 1891.

"Earl's many old-time friends are pleased to hear that he retires from stockraising with a handsome competence made in Montana."

Having the same set of facts to start with, the fiery young editor of the *Review,* who had set the past resolutely behind him and wished the fate of Lot's wife on anyone who would look backward, headed his editorial column as follows:

"Mr., Mrs. and Miss Earl Thurston from down the valley pulled out of Montana with a good fat sum to deposit in some eastern bank and live on, if the bank does not fail.

"The glutted profits of mine owners in Montana remains untaxed; the cattle from free-range areas take back to Chicago all of Montana's good grass in the form of prime beef. Then their masters depart with the boodle, in gold and silver, and we see them no more. Montana is being emptied and turned inside out, like a gunnysack.

"But as we say farewell to those who quit, let us dismiss them from our minds, and devote our attention to the new-comers who, even before they get here, look upon eastern Montana as their future home."

When the cowpunchers from Texas, who dreaded Montana winters more than punishment after death for their sins, took a job in town to tide them over the cold months, the *Independent* printed the foregoing comment:

"The genial Hi Newman has jumped from the hurricane deck of a fuzzy-haired cayuse on Fox Creek to at last strike his gait as a counter jumper at Dickman and Burk's where he is temporarily selling sweetly scented and highly variegated confections."

Christmas meant less than nothing to most of the hoboes on the ditch, but they got tired of waiting daily for the snow to fall, called for their time, one by one, and started hiking up the long stage road and out of sight.

"This weather can't last much longer," Old Johnny O'Brien would say. And then another old-timer would remind Johnny that, back in the eighties, one year when all the stock froze to death, the month of December was just like the one we were enjoying.

· Naturally skeptical, and convinced that most of the people can be fooled by themselves nearly all the time, I began to disbelieve in the rigors of Montana storms and cold. Because of the lack of snowfall, our job surveying the Yellowstone and tying its course in with the quarter-section lines could not be started, and for want of a useful occupation, I was back at cost-keeping again. By that time I had learned that reports on government forms can be written more easily without the handicap of rigid facts, so my field work took little of my time. I rode in the foothills and bad lands, lingered in the Trembles saloons, and, with the aid of Lulu Lucas, taught the school children to sing "Columbia, the Gem of the Ocean," "My Country, 'Tis of Thee," and a Salvation Army song in spirited waltz time entitled: "Don't It Beat All How Jesus Loves Me."

In the course of my first season on the Yellowstone I had acted as rodman, chain-man, and instrument man on two different grade parties, as "amanuensis" for Worthington T. Stackpole whenever he was in the valley, and twice, for a few weeks at a stretch, as "cost-keeper." I had taught smart men to read and write, Letty Gregory to play the melodeon very badly, and Mexican Joe to play the piano well. There were few men or women in the lower valley whom I did not know by name, and I had made the acquaintance of skilled workers and hoboes, Wobblies, scissorbills, bosses and roustabouts, Bohunks from a dozen different European lands, and three kinds of Indians: Sioux, Gros-Ventres and Blackfoot.

CHAPTER TWENTY-TWO

"The Moon of Cold-Exploding Trees"

DURING December, I had been sleeping in a tent which Lem Gabel shared with me, just far enough from the cook shack and wooden bunk-houses of the government camp at Newlon so that only the hardiest bedbugs would be likely to walk that distance. Crocus was stabled in the Dotsen barn, two miles east, near the river. I had taught this supposedly wild, man-killing mare, ten years old, to come to meet me, of her own accord, at the western boundary of the Dotsen land, when Josefa turned her loose just before five P.M. Thus, Crocus saved me an extra mile afoot, before I rode her to Trembles or elsewhere for the evening.

The small group of engineers in the Newlon camp rode in a wagon to the Dotsen cabin for breakfast. Josefa had taken on the task of feeding us, mornings, to round out her activities as rancher, housekeeper and schoolteacher. By that time, we had learned to love that stern Norwegian girl, but we were even more awed by her than in the beginning. Her energy was inhuman. When, thirty years later, I learned that her oldest daughter had won a dance marathon without yawning, I assumed that Josefa, herself, was not competing. But I still revered her.

Lem Gabel and I slept very soundly, on those clear cold nights. Lem was naturally a sound sleeper and, because I seldom left Trembles before one o'clock in the morning, I

265

had to crowd a lot of sleep into comparatively few hours. Now and then I would take an evening off from pleasure, go to bed right after supper, and catch up on my sleep for a week. Our tent was of good strong canvas and we had staked it down securely. We had a board floor, an empty box for a washstand, hooks for clothes along the sides, two wooden bunks, and, between them, a Sibley stove. It was then chilly enough so that we had to break the ice in our water pail with a hatchet, but not so severe as to warrant building a fire to dress by, in the morning. Both of us had the habit of leaving our high leather boots in front of our respective bunks and draping our trousers over them, since we had no chair.

The night of January 6, 1908, fell on a Monday, and after a hard week-end, I decided to turn in early. Lem usually studied a while, in the cook shack, but he went to bed that night before ten. He assured me afterward that the sky, at that hour, had been as clear as it had been for weeks, and had contained as many or more stars than usual. We woke up, simultaneously, in confused darkness, for the simple reason that our tent had ripped loose from the rear stakes and was flapping over our heads like a giant shirt tail, leaving us exposed. It took me a minute to realize that the wind was singing, not high and shrill, but mean and low, and that particles of something like shredded mica were stinging my hands and face. The rest of my body was covered. We wore flannel shirts, underwear and socks to bed, as a matter of precaution.

A second later, just as I saw Lem struggling to sit up and swing his legs over the edge of the bunk, I realized that the snow had drifted eight inches deep all over our tent floor, and that our pants and boots were filled with it. We got ourselves together, managed by joint efforts to light a railroad lantern in the gale, dumped the fresh snow from our outer clothes, and put on our trousers and boots. Then we tried to stake down our tent again. It was like catching a torn sail in a tempest at sea. The wind was from the north and continued blowing, spasmodically, so that sometimes the snow was sharp and felt like needles, then for a moment would come in larger flakes, quite soft. It took half an hour to get our tent in shape. The other camp buildings were dark. There was nothing to do but go to bed again, and wait for morning. This we did, after removing our boots and placing them upside down in the shelter of the footboards. We both fell asleep promptly, and a couple of hours later, I awoke. The darkness was gone, but no daylight seemed to have come to take its place. Our front flap had blown loose, and the snow-drift on the tent floor was two feet high. The engineers in the other buildings were stirring and cursing. All of them had said they wished the snow would come, but now that it was with them, they grumbled and complained. Old Knick, again a government crumb boss, was growling merrily. He wanted to see how the young wise men from the east would stand a dose of real Montana weather.

The tune of the wind had changed, to a higher, more querulous pitch, and drove the snow so thick and fast that now it was difficult to see between the buildings. Lem and I joined the others in the wooden bunk-house, and decided to start for the Dotsen ranch for breakfast. We were dressed for the storm. I had put on three pairs of heavy woolen socks, and cloth overshoes in place of leather boots. I wore a sheep-lined leather vest over my flannel shirt, and overalls over my corduroy pants. Because I would have to scribble figures or turn the screws of a transit if we went surveying that day, I wore black silk gloves under heavy buckskin mittens. The snow was coming too hard, driven almost horizontally now, for snow glasses, but I did not forget to put a pair in my shirt pocket, along with a box of safety matches.

None of us realized how quickly a storm could rise to blizzard intensity. Lem, Andy Hays (division engineer from Maine), Reggie Hurdle (later Dawson County surveyor) and I started out, in the direction, so we thought, of the Dotsen cabin. We had a mile to walk, across the flat, before we would strike the wire fence. We had not gone twenty yards from the Newlon shacks before we realized that we could no longer see three feet away from us. Still, we figured that blizzards come from the north, and that, when the sharp snow is stinging one's left cheek, one must be headed east.

We trudged on and on, until, in spite of our condition, we were short of breath. Each step became a struggle. We had to fight to keep from turning our backs to the storm and drifting off our course, too far to the south. When we lost Hurdle, for a minute or two, although he was not five yards away, we decided, as soon as we found him, to keep within touching distance, in double file, and take turns on the windward side.

I was then a little overawed by the force and majesty of the storm, the vast swirling white nothingness that howled like all the fiends descending from the Arctic to conquer our world. But I was more thrilled than apprehensive. After all, it did not seem possible to miss a whole mile of wire fence. It was safer to keep going than to try to turn back to camp. We all knew that. The Newlon camp was not fenced, and offered no sure target.

The first hour was a contest, but a fair one, and bearable. At the end of the second hour, we paused for a council meeting. Most obviously, unless we had been walking in a circle, we had missed the mile of fence. Afterward we learned that, in being so careful not to veer southward, we had gone too far north, into the face of the blizzard.

We considered sitting still, huddled in a group, backs to the wind, and waiting for a lull. That did not make sense, because both Hays and I knew from our New England experience that blizzards and northeasters often last three or four days. It seemed too frightfully silly, not to be able to find an area a mile square, with fences along the four sides, only one mile from our point of departure. We had traveled the same route every morning for weeks. But we were stranded; none of us knew where or for how long. If we kept going until we got too tired, we might go to sleep in the snow and suffocate. In order to converse we had to shout into one another's ears and relay the message all around. There were no slopes by which we could determine the direction in which the river lay.

We decided to keep going, resting ten minutes every half-hour. Unaware that our zeal against drifting with the storm had caused us to overshoot the mark to the north, we continued as before. We were moving in a circle, but since all of us were engineers, of a sort, and knew a few elementary facts about the behavior of men who are lost, we made a bigger circle than lost men usually do and missed the whole Dotsen farm, not only to the north, but to the east as well.

It had been seven o'clock in the morning when we had started out. At noon I, in the lead beside Lem Gabel (we seemed to stand the gaff better than the older men), blundered off a cut bank and went down out of sight. Lem and the others dug me out, but in doing so they all got over the bank and into some underbrush.

We were on the west bank of the Yellowstone, but how far upstream or downstream from any other point we had not the remotest idea. We were tired, if not exhausted, and

269

hungrier than wolves. It was our hunger that drove us on. We could have scooped out a cave with cottonwood sticks, in the face of the steep bank, and sat there, warm and sheltered, for the better part of a week. But we all wanted something to eat. Our thirst we quenched by eating snow.

We struggled up the cut bank again. It gave us no clue about direction, except that we must start out with our backs to it, in order to avoid falling over it again. Now the force of the blizzard struck our right cheeks, for a change. My left one was slightly frozen, over the cheekbone, but not enough to bother about. I held my mittened hand over it for a while and kept going.

At one o'clock in the afternoon, according to our watches, I bumped into what turned out to be a fence post. We had another powwow. Undoubtedly the post we had struck was part of Dotsens' fence, because there was no other for miles around. The question was: in which direction stood the gate that would indicate our way to the cabin? We could see nothing but an angry white blur in continuous movement. We still could not hear one another unless someone shouted directly into our ears.

We tossed a coin. Lem, the strongest of the party, went with Hurdle, the slightest, to the left, feeling his way along the strands of wire, from post to post. Hays and I took the opposite way, according to lot. In less than half an hour we found the gate, and, on our hands and knees, made Dotsens' cabin, where Josefa had been waiting seven hours for us.

Hays and I, while eating oatmeal, country ham, fried eggs, biscuits, muffins, warmed-over macaroni and beans, and drinking mugs of coffee, thought, not without a twinge of malicious amusement, of Hurdle and Lem, who had started the wrong way, and would have to grope along four miles of barbed wire. We figured that, if they made a mile an hour, they would reach the cabin about six o'clock that night, two full hours after pitch dark. Regretfully, Hays and I, refreshed and warm, filled a pack with food, borrowed a bottle of whisky and started around the fence. We met them more than halfway, at five P.M. They drank the whisky, ate the food with gusto, then we all started back, along the fence, and made the cabin again just after eight o'clock. By that time we were ready for another huge meal and more whisky. The question now arose as to what had become of the other four men we had left in the Newlon camp. Had they started out after us, and got lost? Or thought better of it and stayed in camp, where there were unappetizing supplies in the abandoned cook-house?

We bore them all the good will in the world, but none of us could figure out a way to help them. If they wandered around long enough, and used common sense, they would arrive somewhere, some time. In their condition, they could surely keep going a week, if they took turns sleeping. They were Charley Tufts; another inspector, named Lincoln; a sturdy Norwegian engineer, named Nelson; and Old Knick. We felt that it would be uncomplimentary to worry about the ability of any of those men to take care of himself. So we stopped worrying, got drunk, and sang while Josefa played her guitar (exactly, but unmusically) . Later, we went to sleep in the hayloft. We were Josefa's guests until Friday, when the blizzard let up. The snow that had fallen was blown and drifted by an icy wind that sometimes reached a velocity of forty miles an hour.

We all decided that Trembles would be a better place than the government camp in which to get accustomed to the winter. So we loaded Josefa into one of her own pungs, took the strongest and best pair of work horses she had, and started on the three-mile journey. I rode Crocus, in the

lee of the rig. We had picks, ropes and shovels and, before
we got out of sight of the cabin, had to use them freely to
break out the road. When a horse got out of his depth in a
drift, we shoveled him out. In places the chill wind had swept
away the snow until the ground was practically bare. Where
the drifts were piled high, they reached a height of four feet
and sometimes two yards.

By leaving the Dotsen ranch at seven in the morning, we
were able to make Trembles by eleven o'clock, and break
out the stage road in between. Josefa, having been absent four
full days from her school, was uneasy. She was worried about
the rest of the winter, knowing there would be many days
when the trip from ranch to schoolhouse would be impossible.

The moment we got into Trembles, we were hailed by
Hans Sauerbier, Perce Gardner, the natty bar proprietor
from New York City, and little Kurt Mook, the albino druggist and medical student.

"Seen anything of the actor?" they asked, hopefully. By
the "actor," of course, they meant Alanson La Rue.

"No! What about Old Knick, Charley Tufts, Ole Nelson
and Abe Lincoln?" we countered.

"Haven't seen 'em. And the telephone wires are down,"
they said.

We pushed on, and little Helen Weckerling came running
to meet Josefa. Helen looked to Josefa for affection and
guidance, and the fact that she had behaved so well in the
presence of La Rue was a tribute to Josefa's scrupulous advice.
Her eyes were shining, as she said:

"Uncle Alanson's lost."

In the Clark Hotel lobby we found Bert Lacey, Shunk
Cundiff, and Lela. The men were trying their best to be
optimistic and reassuring. The ex-widow was in a state approaching collapse. While La Rue had been with her, she had

not touched alcohol. He kept her too busy supporting him and waiting on him. His disappearance had strained her nerves to the point where she had had to resort to the bottle again. Lulu Lucas, who invariably spent her mornings in bed, came downstairs in flowery negligee and two Indian blankets, to comfort Lela and share the drinks.

More citizens were gathered in the Central Bar: Lam McGlynn, Johnny Highpockets, Howard Wise, Old Buck Mavity, and the scissorbill, Cever Seale, who seldom appeared in public, away from his claim. From Wise I learned what had happened, as far as anyone in Trembles knew then.

On Monday, when the day had been moderate and fair, with weeks of ideal weather behind it, La Rue had sought out Bert Lacey. Wise was embarrassed and mildly indignant about what the actor had said, but ruefully acknowledged that there had been some basis for his statement.

"He told Bert that Lulu had her eye on those sapphires and would get her hands on them, one way or another," Wise said.

"So?" I said, eager to get on with the story.

"So La Rue talked Bert into giving him the sapphires to take up to the Mennonite colony, and hand them back to Cora Lentz. I gave Bert hell, because we already knew that the Lentz girl's old man and the other Christers up there wouldn't let Cora keep them. La Rue hired a saddle horse at the livery barn," Wise said.

"Which saddle horse?" I asked.

"Legs," Wise answered.

"Legs!" I repeated in dismay. Legs was a wonderful old cow horse, a gray, nine years old and wiser than a hawk, but his home range was over near Wibaux, one hundred and fifty miles away. If Legs had got loose, and had drifted, riderless, for days with his back to the storm, he would be nearer

Wibaux than Trembles. On the other hand, if La Rue had
got as far as the Mennonite colony with Legs, and had been
caught by the storm on his way back, Legs was big, strong
and intelligent, and had weathered many blizzards before.
But if La Rue had stayed in the saddle too long, he would
have been frozen there, and Legs would have been carrying
a corpse. La Rue, unfortunately, was little versed in the ways
of winter in the open spaces. Off the boards, bars and bou-
doirs, he was not at his best.

The two men most capable of organizing a search party
were unaccounted for. They were George Knickerbocker and
Charley Tufts. When they rode into town, in the surveyor's
rig from the Newlon camp, on wheels because there were no
runners there, everybody cheered, drinks were set up, and
they were welcomed by Lela, dramatically, in tears. They refreshed themselves, not with whisky, but with beer. One of
the best lessons I learned on the Lower Yellowstone was that
whisky is a treacherous and dangerous cold-weather drink,
if one must go into the open, whereas beer, having a lighter
alcoholic content and a higher food value, warms the stomach
and sustains one for hours, out in the cold, and does not
cause a strong reaction that saps the strength and energy.

Trust Charley Tufts to produce a bright idea, like a rabbit
out of a hat.

"Where, for Christ's sake, is Petekillemquick?" asked
Charley.

The men of Trembles looked crestfallen and ashamed. Of
course, the half-breed was the man of the hour. Pete had
not strayed so far from his Sioux heredity that he could not
follow tracks like a hound, or, in the absence of them, figure
out what a horse like Legs would do in a storm.

Petekillemquick had been asleep for three or four days
and nights, to all intents and purposes. His squaw, Emma

274

Goldman, with the help of Charley and a few more men, got him off his bunk, plied him with soda pop, and aroused his interest as quickly as possible. Pete's wife was nicknamed "Emma Goldman" because she bore a noticeable resemblance, physically, to that intrepid anarchist, who was then much in the public eye.

The half-breed stepped to the door of his shack, squinted out over the expanse of snow that covered the flats and foot-hills, blending with the leaden sky at the invisible horizon, and uttered two words to fit the occasion.

"Heap shit!" he grunted, and made a move to go back to bed again.

Dissuaded forcibly from that, Pete shrugged, took up a tribal blanket and led the way back to the Central Bar. Bert Lacey was a strict observer of the law forbidding selling strong drinks to Indians, but he inferred that, if Pete were successful in finding La Rue, the white half of him might be allowed occasional pints of whisky, to be consumed on Pete's own premises, providing all firearms, hatchets and blunt in-struments were deposited beforehand in Bert's tool shed, and left under lock and key.

We rode out from Trembles toward Fox Creek, two and two. Petekillemquick was paired with Charley Tufts. I rode with Old Knick, not because I had the requisite experience, but because I had the best horse for the task in hand that ever walked, and she would let no one else ride her. Other men followed, to the number of eighteen, that being the number of mounts available. One pair headed for the Simard ranch, to enlist the aid of the Simard boys and the O'Briens. Another rode north to Sidney, to give the alarm there.

Tufts and the Indian started up the bed of Fox Creek, but proceeded slowly, stopping to look for signs which would escape the eyes of anyone but the half-breed. Old Knick and

I plowed ahead, straight for the Mennonite settlement. The distance, as a crow might fly, was about ten miles. We had to make it before dark, or spend the night in the snow. The thermometer, at noon, read twenty below zero. It was falling steadily. With the old pioneer within sight, I felt as safe as if I were in the Boston Public Library.

I had loved little Crocus before, but my regard for her stamina and sense increased by leaps and bounds that day. She cut up a little, to get the kinks out of her spine, the first hour or so, then settled down to business. She bucked the drifts, breaking trail for Knick's horse, who was at least two hands higher and five years younger. When she got stuck, she would look around at me, always with the pale blue eye, as if to say:

"Do something, you chump."

I had a spade, with the handle sawed off short, strapped across the back of my saddle. While I shoveled, the mare would nip at my leather vest or my fur cap, stamp to keep warm, snort, and shake her stubborn head to free her muzzle from icicles. When she got tired and winded, I stopped and fed her oats from my hand.

Old Knick fussed and growled, and squinted at the ravines and hills, muttering to them as if they were to blame for everything. Twilight was approaching, and I did not know exactly where we were. A dull faint streak of red in the west was the only sign of winter sunset.

Knick pointed ahead and to the left.

"Two miles that way," he grunted. "We'll have to sleep with that lousy passel of Hunyackers, if we get that far."

We made it, before the darkness closed in. The first Mennonite cabin, in a little ravine, was that of Klaus Lohmiller. I contrived to make it clear to Klaus that a man from Trembles had started out, the day before the blizzard, bound for

276

the Lentz cabin. Neither the stern, pious Mennonite nor his shy sister, Gusti, knew anything about that. We would have to press on to Lentz's place.

"We'll have to wait till the moon rises," Old Knick said. That would be two hours later. Lohmiller and Gusti thawed out some boiled beans, on the Sibley stove, and gave us bread and coffee. While we were eating, Petekillemquick and Charley Tufts came in. Knick had started a signal fire on the top of a near-by hill, and the Indian had understood what was meant.

The temperature had dropped to thirty below.

Again I saw the silver moonlight of Montana, this time across the pale expanse of snow. We skirted the foothills, because the collective farm was hidden beneath drifts too deep to cross. Gray wolves howled, stray suffering cattle lowed piteously. We caught sight of none of them. When we got to the Lentz cabin, the window was dark, and it took a great deal of pounding to arouse Old Man Lentz. The girl, it seemed, had heard us instantly and was too badly frightened to respond.

Charley Tufts spoke fluent German, and adapted his pure Hanoverian *Deutsch* to the Mennonite's dialect. When he explained our errand to Chris Lentz, the old man's face showed blank bewilderment which turned to sullen suspicion when Cora gasped and fainted.

The girl was much thinner than she had been when I had seen her on the day of the turkey raffle, and had a wild, hunted look in her eyes. As soon as we revived her, her father started questioning her, angrily. In a kind of trance, she went to her bed, screened from the main room of the cabin by means of a shawl, and returned, trembling and demoralized, holding six glowing sapphires in her hand. Chris flew into a rage, and Klaus Lohmiller was so shocked that he forgot the rest of us and started berating her.

Tufts got very angry. He turned on the two men with a torrent of guttural German that brought them up short, stepped between them and the girl, controlled himself, and got her story, as much as she could then bring herself to confess.

Monday afternoon, about two o'clock, Cora had been weaving a grass basket, alone in the cabin. Her father was far distant, mending a fence. La Rue had knocked, then entered before she said a word.

The girl could not tell exactly what happened, but she insisted, again and again, that La Rue had not offered her any injury. All she could say was that, after he went away, she had found the sapphires on the table, and had hidden them, knowing that her father and all the men in the colony would blame her, if they knew she had them, and that she would lose her standing in the community forever and ever. She did not need to say that the stones had cast an evil spell over her, so that she had been powerless to discard them, irrevocably, or to risk their loss. She was utterly helpless.

Lentz broke away from Old Knick, grabbed up the precious stones and was about to throw them in the stove when Tufts snatched them out of his hand. Lohmiller started shouting and braying, and quiet was only restored after Charley had lifted Cora and carried her back to her bed. Then Tufts agreed to take the sapphires back to Bert Lacey again, for the time being. Under angry protest by both Mennonite elders, he assured Cora that they still were hers and that, eventually, she should have them.

The entire scene was weird and unreal, in the bleak log cabin, through the chinks of which the bitter cold penetrated and loose snow sifted. The only light was from a couple of railroad lanterns, as long, scissorslike shadows moved crazily. Through it all, Petekillemquick dozed cross-legged in a corner near the stove. There was a crack, like artillery fire, outside in the cottonwood grove. A tree had "exploded" from the cold.

It was agreed, grudgingly, by Chris Lentz that those of us from Trembles could sleep in his barn until daylight. I was too tired and sleepy to worry any more about Cora Lentz that night. Old Knick aroused me when, at seven in the morning, there was enough light for us to continue our search for La Rue.

In the morning, Cora had a high fever. Her eyes were dull. She was prostrate and listless. She did not complain, but Tufts could see, when she tried to sit up, that her back hurt her terribly. Over the protest of her father and young Eli Hauser, her fiancé, who came as near being belligerent as a good Mennonite permits himself to be, Tufts questioned Cora again, and threatened the whole colony with arrest if they did not take the girl to a hospital at once, or bring in a doctor. They were sullen, resentful, and ominously unresponsive. From their point of view, in the light of their long persecution, we were malicious intruders, and one of our kind had perverted the best example of their womanhood.

Charley found out from Cora that La Rue had not ridden away in the direction of the creek bed, but had veered southward, into the foothills, toward the south branch of Fox Creek. He had left about four o'clock.

"He had eight hours in which to ride, before the storm struck, at midnight," Charley said.

"He'll be in the Jordan bar," Old Knick said.

"The railroad must be blocked with snow, in both directions," said Tufts. "I don't see how he can get out of town."

We all knew it would be ten days before the trans-valley government telephone line would be in repair again.

Old Knick went out and built two signal fires, meaning that all the searchers were to return to Trembles. The wind had died down in the night and had not yet risen.

While we were arguing among ourselves about the probable fate of La Rue, the Mennonites—there were six or seven of them crowded into the Lentz cabin by that time—were raising an ominous hubbub in low German. Eli Hauser had overheard Cora say to Tufts that La Rue had departed at four o'clock in the afternoon. The evening before, she had said that La Rue arrived in the cabin about two o'clock. That left two hours to be accounted for. The last glimpse I caught of Cora that morning, she was propped up in her bed, her face distorted with pain and horror, and the men, young and old, were in a grim half-circle confronting her.

I had a terrible, inescapable feeling that the girl would never know another tranquil hour. And why? Because someone false had shown her something beautiful.

When we got back to town, we found Lela in mild hysterics. The Indian—first man in—had told her that La Rue had ridden to Glendive and was snow-bound. She begged to be driven there in time to head him off, in case he was planning a getaway. Shunk Cundiff and Lam McGlynn, ever faithful, volunteered to drive her to the county seat, if possible. So Lela was bundled up, a bob sled rigged for four horses, provisioned and blessed, and the trio headed south, along the stage road. Little Helen went home with Old Buck Mavity, where his rip-snorting old mother-in-law, Mamie Rhorer, took charge of her. By that time, the child felt like the ball in a game she did not understand.

Tired as he was from his exertions, Charley Tufts borrowed a sleigh, rode up to Highpockets' cabin, and from there drove

280

Edna to Sidney with him, leaving Johnny to cook supper. Charley thought the air would be good for Edna, and she nestled at his side, as if the moments she spent there were recompense for all her toil and privations as a "Monkey Ward wife." Nearly everyone in the valley was aware how close Edna and Charley were, spiritually, but few sly remarks were made about their relationship. That, in itself, set it above the ordinary. Highpockets counted on Tufts' friendship, for himself, and especially for Edna, as his best asset. Johnny felt, in his dumb way, that if things were not just as they were, his marriage would have proved a failure. He felt that Tufts and he, between them, were almost good enough for Edna.

In Sidney, Charley sought out Doc Morrill and told him about Cora's hysterical condition, her wild eyes, fever, and excruciating backache.

"Backache? Backache, did you say?" the doctor asked, alarmed.

"She could hardly move, and I know her father didn't beat her. That's one thing about the Mennonites. Violence is taboo, thank God. I don't know what they'll do to the poor girl, short of beating her, but corporal punishment is out of the question," Charley said.

Doc Morrill already was reaching into his medicine cabinet.

"You better be vaccinated now," Doc said. "You, too, Edna."

"You mean, Cora's got smallpox?" Tufts asked, horrified.

"Sounds mighty like it to me. Take off your coat and roll up your left sleeve," Doc said.

Tufts complied, and when Edna was about to offer her white arm, Charley gently dissuaded her.

"Not where it'll show," he begged. "I want to see you, some time, in a light-blue evening gown."

"Do you, Charley?" she said, her eyes turned up to his. With utter lack of self-consciousness, she raised her skirt and petticoats on the left-hand side.

As soon as they left the doctor's office, she went into a kind of reverie, and on the way back home, in the sleigh, she un-gloved her left hand and let it rest, under the blanket, just above Charley's knee. He nodded and smiled, but twice he nearly overturned the sleigh.

"I love to see your eyes shine thataway," Johnny said, when Edna re-entered the cabin. "You ought to get out oftener from this little ol' shack."

That evening, I saw a crowd gather around the bulletin board in the Clark Hotel. Bert had just pasted up some pages from the old N.P. bulletin, for the information of his customers and friends. The text read as follows:

BLIZZARDS

This unique word is used to describe the fierce polar storms which, at intervals during the winter months, rage through western Minnesota and eastern and middle Dakota. They are caused by what our weather bureau calls "Polar waves," and are very high winds accompanied by blinding snow and very low temperature.

They cause much suffering and frequently death to those exposed to their frightful power. They are the chief reason why stock-raising can never become profitable in that section. These winds blow straight southward from the North Pole, passing over the frozen surface of Hudson's Bay, and extending their effects even so far south as Texas, where they appear as "Northers." Each storm usually lasts from three to five days, and during its continuance it is dangerous to venture long exposure to its effects.

From these storms the valleys of the YELLOWSTONE and MISSOURI are in a great degree protected by the

"The Moon of Cold-Exploding Trees"

Chinook winds, which, blowing from the west against the line of the northern storms, drive them eastward.

No storms comparable to these prevail in the YELLOWSTONE VALLEY. During the winter high winds are uncommon, and snow rarely drifts. The grass is easily got at through the light uncrusted snow. Neither artificial shelter nor hay are needed for the wintering of stock.

"Hell, man," Old Buck Mavity said to Bat Horner, "who ever told you you was a champion? You ain't no liar at all."

CHAPTER TWENTY-THREE

Vaccination Day

◆

THE news that everybody in Trembles would have to be vaccinated the next forenoon spread from one end of the community to the other before the evening was half over. Lulu Lucas received it in her room at the Clark Hotel, which, because of clothes and costumes hung, draped and heaped all around, and the red-hot Sibley stove, looked no bigger than a closet. The blizzard had unnerved her, to the point where only the lure of the sapphires was strong enough to keep her from flight. That smallpox had broken out in the "neighborhood," notwithstanding that the Mennonite colony was ten miles distant, threw Lulu into a fit of hysterics. She was not faking. Lulu was frightened out of her wits. The singer was incapable of anything except screaming, stiffening, gasping, and convulsions. By the time Doc Morrill got to her bedside from Sidney, Lulu had spent her strength and strained her vocal cords beyond their capacity. She could moan, shudder, stare wildly with distended eyes—nothing more. Doc gave her a shot in the arm, and she sank deep into a drugged sleep. Wise, beside himself with solicitude, sat holding her hand, his heart eaten away by fear that she would quit him and the town.

Lulu had been very frank with Wise, in her way. She had told him plainly that she would never marry a hotel clerk in a jerk town. She needed a powerful and influential man.

He had assured her that he could earn plenty of money and advance her career if he put his mind to it. He never had had an incentive before, he said.

"I'm not from Missouri, but New Jersey," Lulu had said. "In Jersey a person has to be shown twice."

Wise had noticed that Lulu had two or three dozen patent medicines, in boxes, phials, and bottles, not only cosmetics, but laxatives, sedatives, and specifics for all the ills that female flesh is heir to. He could sympathize with her feeling that Trembles, from a visual aspect, looked shabby or jerry-built. She had neither the time nor the insight to discover that its people had hearts of gold. Now the threat of smallpox, with only what Lulu called "a hayseed pillshooter" to protect her, and no hospital facilities, was more than a high-strung artiste could be expected to bear. When Lulu awoke, she would think of nothing but getting out of the Yellowstone country by any means at all.

Then Wise remembered that her initial despondency, upon descending from the stage at Trembles, had been overcome by the sight of the sapphires. He left Mexican Joe at Lulu's bedside, to call him if her eyelashes stirred, and sought out Bert Lacey.

Naturally, Bert had had a busy evening, notifying everyone of the vaccination bee scheduled for the morning. But Bert still was anxious not to lose Wise, even after his trying experiences with Lulu, whom nothing seemed to please. Wise borrowed the sapphires in their chamois sack and returned to his vigil. While he had been absent, Mexican Joe had gone through the dresser drawers and inspected the various bottles and pill boxes, but, not knowing which, if any, were poison, regretfully refrained from dropping anything into Lulu's glass of water. He glanced up and nodded at

Wise pityingly and made himself scarce when the latter re-
entered Lulu's room.

Sitting there through the long night hours, Wise's head
buzzed with plans. He was desperate, and by no means devoid
of mental resources. The six matched gems of cornflower
blue he kept before his eyes, holding them this way and that,
so that the light from the kerosene lamp stirred their depths
and surfaces, reviving fond hopes, inciting rash promises.
What were those cool bits of blue, in the vastness of the
Lower Yellowstone? Where had they dropped from? What
fiend had taken the form of that strutting turkey gobbler
whose beady eye had spied them, whose beak had speared
them, and whose crop had stored them away, with worth-
less gravel and plump kernels of corn? Wise could feel their
sorcery undermining and enveloping him.

He had spent all his money at Christmas time; in fact, he
was so far in debt that his pay had no meaning until March.
Bert was good-natured about advancing cash, but Wise was
too much of a gentleman to impose on Bert's generosity. In
the reaches of the night, when nails, contracting from the
wood around them, snapped like pistol shots aimed in futile
bravado at the cold, Wise thought he saw a way out of his
predicament. His thoughtful, careful father, when Howard
had been fifteen years old, had taken out a life-insurance
policy in what, for the Wise family, had then been a handsome sum, four thousand dollars. There were twenty payments to be made, of which Wise's father had made six, and
Howard, taking over at the age of twenty-one, had accounted
for four. Surely a policy like that, half paid up, would be
negotiable, Wise thought. If he could raise enough to buy
the sapphires from the Mennonites and offer them to Lulu,
she would certainly wait in Trembles to give him a chance
to complete the transaction. The question struck him at

once: "How much are sapphires worth?" And also: "How much are these six large matched sapphires worth?" Wise could not even be positive that the stones were sapphires. They were surpassingly beautiful, but so was a chip of window glass when touched by a ray of the sun.

Again Wise called Mexican Joe to Lulu's bedside. She was sleeping sounder than the beauty in the well-known fairy tale. Wise, naturally on the cold-blooded side, bundled himself up until he looked like an ogre. He put on a leather vest, a sheep-lined coat, a woolen scarf and fur hat, mittens with the skin-side inside (like Hiawatha's), two extra pairs of socks, cloth overshoes, and went out into the night. Stars snapped, the hard snow creaked. Wolves watched from across the narrow coulee. A snow-white owl winged overhead. Flitting here and there, in frost-bound Trembles, was no longer to be undertaken lightly, no matter what was at stake.

Charley Tufts and I were seated in Perce Gardner's bar. Two or three evenings a week we gave Perce our patronage, to encourage him to keep up the excellent standard he had started to maintain. Perce dressed as carefully as La Rue had, but in another conception. Perce was the New York sport, *par excellence*. He spoke with a Bowery accent, which he exaggerated because his customers found it droll. He wore checked suits, colored stickpins, a fawn derby, high white collar and white cuffs. Of all Gardner's customers in the smart Westside Saloon, Charley Tufts was the most entranced by Perce's haberdashery and treatment of the King's English, so Perce invariably did his utmost for him.

"Did yuh pipe the canary t'row de jimjams this P.M?" Perce asked.

"The singer had hysterics," I translated, for Charley's benefit. Charley hastily scribbled a few notes, so he would not forget the phrase.

"She was perturbed," Charley said, with his habitual under-statement.

Perce looked at the Professor with one eye, like a macaw.

"I never met a citizen who could play a scene lower than you do, Mr. Tufts," Perce said, admiringly. "I've lamped some smooth ones, too, you bet'cha boots."

Just then Wise came in, looking haggard and eager at the same time, and dressed like Amundsen. The subject was instantly switched.

"Do you know anything about sapphires?" Wise asked Tufts.

"They're decorative, and dear," Charley said.

"How much do they cost?" asked Wise anxiously.

Charley had no idea, but Perce brought out a star-sapphire stickpin for which he had paid three hundred dollars, the year Cresceus took the trotting record of $2.02\frac{1}{4}$ at Columbus, Ohio.

Immediately Wise's expressive face lit up with hope and relief. Three hundred dollars times six made eighteen hundred. Surely he could raise that much on a four-thousand-dollar insurance policy, half paid up. In his innocence, Wise assumed that a sapphire with a star gleaming from its depths would be more valuable than a plain one of cornflower blue. Because Lulu was sleeping so tranquilly, and he had a long vigil ahead of him, Wise consented to sit with us for three or four quick ones. Mexican Joe, he knew, would warn him if Lulu awoke.

While Wise was fortifying himself in the Westside Saloon, with the sapphires in his shirt pocket, Mexican Joe was involved in an adventure of his own. The dark, diminutive, wrinkled cowboy, gazing on Lulu's comely face and the hints of her figure revealed by the contours of the bedclothes, began to mutter. The more he looked at Lulu, the less he liked her, because she was making a fool of one of the nicest men in town. No sooner had Joe got well started with his muttering, in Spanish, which would have sent Lulu into another fit had she heard it, and understood the words, than Lulu began to coo and murmur, too. She spoke softly and indistinctly at first, quite at random, but in the course of her ramblings, she repeated more than once the name of Roger. Mexican Joe's black eyes gleamed maliciously.

"I am your Rogerito. I am with you. See, *hija de puta*, I touch your hand," Joe whispered, cajolingly.

He touched Lulu's hand, then her arm, and she murmured again, like a cat that is being caressed.

"Roger, I've been dreaming," she said.

"Of me," he suggested.

"The cottage."

Joe had heard lots of ballads. *"Con vinas y moonlight,"* he added. "Just us two."

She turned, almost awoke, and Joe lost contact for a while. His eyes now were murky with indignation. *Coñeta!* His friend Wise was being flimflammed and cuckolded.

"Darling! *Querida!*" Joe murmured, making a throaty sound like a wild dove at feeding time.

Her eyelids fluttered, closed again, and she said something indistinct. Then came from her rosy lips what Joe most wanted to hear.

"You used to talk about getting married," Lulu said.

Ah! Joe said to himself. This Roger has the best of her. I honor him.

"You know why I can't," Joe said, dolefully, at the same time wondering which of two or three good reasons was holding Roger back.

Mexican Joe now had a problem more difficult than Wise's. Should he warn his friend, the polite and educated clerk, who knew about everything except livestock and women? Before Joe could decide, Wise returned, looking so happy that the little Mexican could not bring himself to reveal anything unpleasant just then.

Somehow, as Wise thought things over alone, he came to the conclusion that it would not be wise to tell Lulu how he was going to raise the money. In order to make her feel secure, he felt it his duty to build himself up in her mind, to impress her with his sincerity, resourcefulness and acumen. He went over to Bert's bar, got the keys to Lam's barber shop, and took with him to the sick room several back copies of a Minneapolis newspaper. Wise read avidly the financial pages, in order to get an inspiration. The panic was still on, throughout the east, but some smart plungers had made money in the stock market by selling stocks short and commodities long. Wise studied their methods, frantically.

So when Lulu awoke in the morning, before she could recapture the mood of terror that had gripped her the night before, Wise showed her the sapphires, to soften her resistance, and said that he had found a way to raise the money to buy the gems. Lulu was so overjoyed that she forgot about smallpox, threw her fragrant arms around his neck, and, when he kissed the tip of her ear, she turned and offered her lips, deliciously parted.

That was on vaccination day, eventful in the history of Trembles. Believing that Lulu would prove to be his most troublesome patient, Doc Morrill drove straight to the Clark Hotel, with Charley Tufts beside him, and mounted to Lulu's room. When she showed signs of another nervous crisis, Doc slapped her so hard that the blue marks were visible for days.

Worse than that, he did not compliment her on the shape of her leg, when she bared it to the scalpel.

"Doc don't know his own strength," Bat Horner said, when he heard what had happened.

In the schoolhouse, the vaccination orgy started rather badly. Bert and Doc Morrill had decided that if the school-children were inoculated first, the adults in town would be ashamed to show fright or reluctance. Doc, himself, was most anxious for everyone to be immunized. He was not merce-nary, but only good and scared. An epidemic in the country-side, during a Montana winter, reduced Doc's chances of survival to about one-half of one percent. He was sure to get caught in a storm and freeze, unless he disregarded the Hip-pocratic oath, which had as grim a hold on medical men in eastern Montana as in more temperate regions.

With a jangle of bells, Doc Morrill's sleigh drove up to the schoolhouse, which was up to the eaves in snow, from drifts and the heaps beside the paths the boys had shoveled. The interior was neatly swept, the desks were in order, two plaster replicas of classic Grecian friezes adorned the top of the blackboards, and behind Josefa's podium were chromos of Washington, Lincoln, and Teddy Roosevelt. Elsewhere on the walls hung framed Perry pictures, "Landscape with Mill" and "The Spirit of '76."

As the doctor, Charley Tufts and Bert Lacey entered, the latter carrying the ominous black bag, the three girls and four boys rose self-consciously and stood at attention. Josefa blew her icy pitch-pipe and they sang a western children's song about a Montana flower that, just then, was frozen stiff be-neath loads of ice and snow for countless miles around. Some of the lines were for the pupils, others for the teacher. It had an appealing melody, and the words made a haunting kind of sense.

291

A Ghost Town on the Yellowstone

(Chorus)   *Paint brush! Paint brush! Indian paint*
                          brush!
                     Do the Indians paint with you?

(Teacher)   *Children, children, I'm not certain,*
                     But I sometimes think they do.

(All together)   *When an Indian goes to battle,*
                     So we've often heard it said,
                     He takes his little Indian paint brush,
                     Paints his face with streaks of red.

The men beamed proudly, although none of them was an Indian or a father. Josefa smiled, stood before the children, and, as she bared her long strong arm, made a reassuring little speech.

"Girls and boys," she said, "in years gone by, the disease known as smallpox was a terrible plague. Hundreds and thousands were afflicted in the lands from which our fathers came to America. Here, just a few miles down the Missouri, the trappers, Sioux, Yanktons and Crows lost their bravest men and finest women when, in the winter season, smallpox broke out among them.

"But while good people were dying, and those who lived were marked and pitted for life with ugly scars, wise doctors were fighting to save us all, and learned that, by means of vaccination, contagion could be avoided. Perhaps none of you has been vaccinated before. It is nothing. A mere scratch, a touch of the vaccine, and you will be safe. Not only will you be safe, yourselves, but you will make our country safer for others. I shall be the first, to show you how simple and easy it is."

She smiled at the doctor, who, feeling very warmly about

his chosen profession, sterilized his scalpel in the flame of a candle, grasped Josefa's bare arm respectfully, washed a small area with alcohol, dried it with gauze, and deftly made a scratch.

There was a startling instant of unexpected swaying, and Josefa fell senseless to the hard board floor with a thud that jarred the whole structure. The girls and boys stared, giggled nervously, and stood transfixed in their places. Doc and Charley kneeled quickly, covered the teacher's exposed lower limbs with her skirt, and dabbed cool water on her wrists and temples. She revived, sat up, blushed, bit her lip, and rose again. Resolutely she indicated that Doc was to proceed.

"Don't be afraid. That was only a reflex," she said. "It doesn't happen often."

The second time she keeled over, Doc took advantage of her unconsciousness to complete the job before he revived her. Then, a bit uncertainly, he looked at the three girls and four farm boys who still were at attention in their places. Before he had time to ask for volunteers, the two tomboys, the Arndt sisters, made a dash front and center and in unison rolled up their sleeves.

Glowing with pride, Bert Lacey turned to Charley Tufts.

"You see, Professor, what kind of stock we raise in Trembles," he said.

After the schoolchildren had all been vaccinated, and excused from classes for the day, each with a big silver dollar to spend, the official party moved from shop to store, and house to house. Things went well until they got to Buck Mavity's house. Old Buck and his complacent wife were vaccinated with dispatch, but old Mamie Rhorer, deaf as a post, lit out, without her wraps, and started running through the town. In front of Lederer's Eastside Saloon, Joe Jeffries from Three Buttes was mounting his horse. He had been drinking heartily, in preparation for his turn. When he saw Mamie running, with the Doc in close pursuit, he took the rope from the back of his saddle, whirled it over his head and set the loop down neatly around Mamie's scrawny waist, pinning her arms and throwing her into a soft snow bank. While she screeched maledictions and kicked like a heifer, Doc did his work and the bystanders cheered and yelled.

White Stella and the girls of the Little Casino had been told what was coming and were ready, but they had heard that some of the respectable women had chosen to be vaccinated somewhere where the scar would not show.

"Doc," Stella said, "maybe you ought to vaccinate us hookers on top of our heads. That won't hinder our work, not even if the stuff you rub on leaks down into our brains."

Mert Honey, the deputy sheriff from Sidney, rode into town just as the doctor and his aides were headed for Petekillemquick's cabin. Unfortunately, Emma Goldman's brother, an Indian boy about sixteen years old, had arrived on his pony the night before. The lad, called Alkali Jim, had recently been hearing tales from the older Sioux about the tactics of the pale-faces. When the official party rode up, and Pete and Emma started arguing with them, Alkali Jim, unnoticed by the white men, was standing behind his pinto, with a shotgun in his hand. Jim was a boy of direct action. He blazed away at Mert, the sheriff, and peppered him with duck shot, and a few of the stray pellets blew Doc's hat off into the snow.

Jim mounted, bareback, and streaked away. Nobody pursued him, until some cowboys who had heard the shots from the seclusion of Bert's bar saw him heading north, jumped into their saddles, and overtook him four miles down the stage road. He was sullen and defiant. Petekillemquick started to clout him with a length of stove wood, but Charley Tufts restrained him. By that time, it had been ascertained that Mert was not wounded seriously.

"What'll you do with the kid?" Bert Lacey asked, uncomfortably.

Mert frowned and thought it over. "What the hell," he said. "I can't be bothered pinchin' a minor."

"I'm not a miner," Jim said, sullenly. "I'm a hunter."

"Be damn sure you don't hunt no more officers of the law," cautioned Mert, and dropped the matter there. Mert and the others were fond of Pete and Emma, so the young defender of his dwindling race rode back to the reservation and, so Charley Tufts heard later, carved a couple of notches on the coup stick his famous grandfather had left behind on departing for the Happy Hunting Grounds.

After Doc had finished picking duck shot out of Mert, the deputy, who was as thin as a rail, weighed himself on Lucian Gibbs' grain scales to make sure that none of the pellets had been overlooked, following Bat Horner's advice.

The hardest part of the vaccination program was still to be accomplished. When Doc Morrill, Mert (stippled with gauze and court plaster), Charley Tufts and Edna Highpockets rode up the creek to the Mennonite colony, I went with them. Since last I had been there, I had not been able to get the terrified face of Cora Lentz out of my mind. I already knew that Wise, with the best of intentions, was planning to offer the Mennonites eighteen hundred dollars, more money than they had ever seen in one lump before, for the sapphires that had brought such grief and discord into Cora's bleak existence. I could not resign myself to any arrangement that would deprive Cora of the joy of their possession, at any cost whatever.

The men of the colony swarmed straight to the Lentz cabin when they saw us approaching. Their faces were grim and resentful, but they were unarmed and had only their faith and dogged resolution to stand between them and the forces of the law and wicked worldliness.

Charley tried in every way to reassure them. We were their friends and neighbors, he said. The disease Cora had was undoubtedly smallpox. Grudgingly they allowed the doctor to examine her, with her menfolk looking on.

Eventually, one by one, the Mennonites submitted to vaccination, and only young Eli Hauser forgot the restrictions imposed by his creed and fought like a tiger. Charley, Bert and the doctor finally overpowered him, and did what had to be done. When Charley explained that a shack Johnny Highpockets had put up for a tool house had been fumigated and prepared as a pest house, and that Cora would have to be removed there, the men rebelled again. Mert Honey showed his badge, drew his six-shooter, and they had to submit. For them, our action was a sacrilege and outrage. Cora was too sick to care. Finally, Laura Schwanke agreed to risk contagion and go with Cora, to nurse her and guard her. We rode back toward Trembles, escorting the pung on which the sick girl lay, bundled in blankets.

Meanwhile, Johnny Highpockets, in trying to shovel a path to the tool house, found that his back hurt him so badly and that he was so hot and weak all over that he could not lift a shovelful of snow. The tool house, equipped with a stove and bunks, was divided in the middle by a screen. Because Johnny was so worried about the winter work, and Edna was helpless around sick people, Old Knick, who had no fear of disease or anything else, installed himself in the pest house, to act as male nurse, messenger and crumb boss. The last thing Johnny Highpockets did before he was incarcerated was to plead with Charley Tufts to sleep in his shack and take good care of Edna.

296

Vaccination Day

Coincidentally with the town's first epidemic, in the drafty tarboard shack of Cever Seale, the first child was born in Trembles. The given names of every man in town were written on slips of paper, tossed into Perce Gardner's natty derby hat, and the one drawn forth for the infant by little Helen Weckerling, who was blindfolded for the occasion, was Alanson, which had been included scrupulously because the actor was not yet accounted for.

Thus the youngest inhabitant of Trembles was christened Alanson Cever Seale.

"Some class!" Bert Lacey said.

CHAPTER TWENTY-FOUR

"If Thine Eye Offend Thee..."

◆

SINCE the first blizzard, the cold had moved into the valley, immobilizing the flats and bad lands, distorting what already had been misshapen. The snow had crusted over the foothills, converting each cut bank and ravine on the vast range into a death-trap for the cattle. The cows whose calves still followed them and looked to them for protection fought until they foundered, spending the little that remained of their own strength in blind maternal resistance against the sleek gray wolves, light-footed, insensate, cunning, and seemingly innumerable. The calves died first, being smaller and having no winter experience. The steers, wary, confused, almost equally helpless, lunged and sideswiped as long as they could move their scrawny necks. They had no chance fighting phantoms. For if one wolf, or a band of wolves, was stood off, the vise of cold was tightening, overhead, around, and underfoot where dead earth had frozen solid as rock to the depth of a grave. Supplementing the cold was the rack of hunger, that, when its screws are turned too far, defeats its purpose of torture and yields its victim the lassitude preceding starvation.

"None of us is immortal," Charley Tufts would say, if we stumbled on the carcass of a dead cow in a snowdrift, and saw that, before she had died, her tail and flanks had been chewed. He did not fool me an instant, because, as he spoke, and touched the dead cow with his moccasin, his eyes would suddenly grow dull and weary, and later, light up slowly again.

The day after the grand vaccination at Trembles, the surveying party to which I was attached, started for the Headgates, thirty-two miles upriver. Once we had found an authentic section corner, we had succeeded in squaring the crazy and desolate expanse of snow, over flats, buttes and gullies, with the world that was pictured on maps. Our task was to run quarter-section lines east and west from the nearest section line (north and south) to the western edge of the river bank, the western border of the stream bed, across the ice-bound Yellowstone to the eastern edge of the stream bed, and beyond to the edge of the east bank. What introduced a fantastic element of chance into our work was the fact that the only available map was more than sixty years old and ludicrously inaccurate.

In land surveying, one finds continual temptation, over and above that gleaned from school books and personal encounters, to dislike the English. By them, a foot is divided into twelve inches, which in turn are divided into sixteenths. Three feet make a yard, 1.515152 links make a foot, 0.181818 rods make a yard, etc., *ad nauseam*. It must have taken all the ancestors of the Shakespearean fools to evolve such an illogical scheme of measurement, and it is especially maddening for a patriotic young American surveyor to swallow the imbecility of his elected representatives who persist in following the British into chaos, instead of adopting for America the lucid metric system of our allies, the French.

For the first week or so, we made our headquarters at the Headgates camp, where we were received with the cordiality that skunks are tendered at lawn parties, because of the outbreak of smallpox to which we had been exposed. We were given a shack that had formerly been used to store powder and dynamite, built into the side of a cut bank and so far from the camp lulu that all of us ignored it. Chamber pots cost only four bits and, having been used, could be flung out the door and their contents would freeze solid in a matter of minutes and remain so until spring.

Abe Johnson had made the skis we used, and they were good ones; not the kind, with engraved foot rests, coats of arms, banana-oil rubs and poles made from the True Cross, or beds Lafayette had slept in. Ours were plain and serviceable, with simple cowhide straps, and if we broke one, in the course of a day's work, we always had a few extras to fall back on. Abe had also made some serviceable sleds we could drag behind us, with instrument cases, food, beer, and whatever else we needed. We started out at daylight, when the temperature was around forty below zero, and if the wind rose, we checked every minute or two on one another's faces and warned one another if they were frozen. It was all such great fun and good exercise that I could not, at first, admit the lurking danger.

I had the coldest job, that of running the transit. It was fussy work, setting it up, sometimes on two skis placed to form a "V" to accommodate the legs of the tripod. The lens would freeze over in less time than Petekillemquick, our rear chainman, could say what Sioux Indians say when things look bad. I carried a special chamois rag inside my shirt, where it was warm, in order to clear ice from the front end of the telescope. I stamped, slapped my hands, and cursed the chainmen if they were too slow. Religiously I protected my eyes from the glare.

On the second day, our chief of party, a fine fellow from Maine, named Mason, started out with leather-laced boots on. Petekillemquick did everything but dance around the stove and recite incantations to the Great Spirit to dissuade Mason from going out into the cold in stiff boots. Mason grinned in the knowing way I had seen so often in New England, when a man was either dead right or dead wrong.

"I come from Bangor," he said.

Pete shrugged. He had done his best.

That morning, after a record night when the thermometer hit forty-eight below, as if the cold were not enough, the wind kept on blowing, without the customary morning lull. Had I been in charge, I would have said: "Boys, no work today," and reached for the cards. But I was second in command to Mason. So I took more precautions than usual, and waved affectionately at the red-hot Sibley stove as I left the shack. As the air struck me, I felt something pushing me and closing in. Always the wind was shoving, from one side or the other, and the cold became lopsided. Once in a while I would forget myself and breathe too deeply, and feel that steely impact in my throat and lungs, and the reaction that seemed to be tearing the tissues, inside.

Petekillemquick caught his foot and stumbled, falling headlong and cutting his face—two deep gashes—so sharp was the crust of the snow. He, the most sure-footed man for miles around, had been eyeing, disconsolately, Mason's leather shoes.

We had found our section corner the evening before, but the snow had drifted and crusted over the hole we had dug. Near it, lying on their sides, were four dehorned Texas steers, three dead and one dying.

"Crack!" I never saw a man who could shoot so fast with a revolver as Petekillemquick. Another steer's ordeal was finished. I did not like the omen. Too many things were dead, all over the flat. I slapped my arms, wriggled in my loose clothes, stamped my feet, protected by four thick pairs of woolen socks and limp cloth overshoes.

301

Lem Gabel dug. Pete helped. I got the transit out of the box and ready for the setup. Mason stood scribbling in his notebook, his hands in woolen gloves. Pete, again watching Mason ruefully, got his foot in the way of Lem's spade and nearly lost a toe.

I knew then that something was going to happen. All I could do was be extra careful that, whatever it was, it should not happen to me. I had an infinity of springs and summers, two-steps, waltzes, whisky, beer, birds and books, roses and chrysanthemums ahead, if I could stick out that winter. I was not afraid, to the point that it made me quake, but I realized that I had got into something, for once, that was no pushover. Better men than I had succumbed to Montana winters, but none of them could have been more cautious than I.

We started from the section corner. Lem and Pete skied straight and skillfully ahead, with the chain, first one in the lead, then the other, end over end. Mason, with his note-book, and drawing the sled on which was the lunch box, kept pace with them.

"Cold?" he asked me, as I packed the snow hard and danced on it, to keep my blood in circulation.

"Yes," I said.

"Your face is frozen, kid," he said.

"So's yours, as a matter of fact," I answered, a little sharply. Cold works insidiously on one's temper.

We both rubbed soft snow, from under the crust, on our faces.

At lunch time, in a cottonwood thicket with a small clearing near the center, we camped at the level of the treetops, broke off branches, built a roaring fire, and approached it carefully. The heat would melt the soft snow on our vests and overalls, in front; then we would turn our backs to the

302

fire and the front of our clothes would freeze solid while the back thawed out. The slum the Headgates cook had put into a kettle was thawed out until we could chop it up with a hatchet, and thus hasten its melting. Pete, the half-breed, usually very happy just before meals, kept looking at Mason's feet. He pointed at them and grunted.

"Feel something?"

Mason touched one boot to the other and grinned.

"Not a thing," he said, moving back from the fire.

Pete, tired of trying to talk to such an obstinate man, turned to Lem and me.

"White man build big fire, stand way back. Indian build little fire, stand up close." He paused for rhetorical effect, and added: "White man damn fool."

Mason sat down on a sled and started to unlace his boots. I was dismayed to see Pete draw his gun, shaking his head grimly.

"Boot come off, so foot come off, too," Pete said.

Suddenly Mason, who was no fool, caught on that Pete had been right all the time and that he, Mason, had been wrong. Mason looked at me.

"We'd better go, quick," I said.

"Ask Pete what I should do," Mason said. I did. Pete thought gravely. He was sure that Mason should not slip his frozen feet back into the stiff ski straps. He motioned toward the sled.

"Me drag him," Pete said.

Obediently Mason sat down, his feet, still booted, wrapped in gunny sacks. Pete slipped his feet into his ski straps, lit out, and before we could get ready, was out of sight in the dim whiteness. Lem and I packed up the stuff and the instruments and headed back to camp.

"We Yankees are pig-headed," I said.

By the time we got to camp, Pete had cut off part of Mason's shoes, enough to convince him that the feet and ankles could mostly be saved, but that the toes would have to go. Mason, sobered and repentant now, was hauled to Glendive, and was six weeks in the hospital there. He submitted to several amputations. When he came out, he was able to walk, somewhat awkwardly, but never as he had before that unlucky day.

Lem and I lost one hundred and fifty dollars apiece, because the No. 2 Party, working below Tokna, beat us by two quarter-section lines. But the next week, Mason was replaced by Ole Nelson, the stocky Norwegian from the Newlon camp, and we got most of our money back. Coincidentally, we finished our first fourteen miles of river, and leap-frogged the No. 2 gang, so that we could live in Trembles, at the Clark Hotel, for a while, and eat at the Cathay Café.

Smallpox had struck three more victims, one in a coal mine over on Bonne Pierre Creek, across the river; another in the Lzicar Camp, where two roustabouts had been left as watchmen through the winter; and little Helen Weckerling.

When I talked with Mrs. Baron about Helen's case, the woman I so admired, from so respectful a distance, turned away, to hide the hard look that occasionally passed over her face.

"What next will be heaped on that poor child's shoulders?" she asked.

Lela Weckerling was alone, again. Before she and her escorts had reached Glendive, La Rue had taken an eastbound train, leaving a note, attached to Legs' saddle in a livery barn:

"Darling wife," it began. "Art calls. I will return with fame and fortune to lay at your feet. (signed) Alanson."

That left Lam McGlynn in a worse fix than ever. Lela insisted that her husband would keep his word, eventually, and that she must wait. Lam was with her every evening, and she accepted his faithful attentions in a melancholy way, getting more rapt and resolute with each glass of whisky they sipped, side by side.

The little girl, hoping she would never see La Rue again, counseled her mother earnestly against divorce, because as matters stood, they were relatively safe from men again.

Of course, Helen's illness caused the maximum of confusion in the Trembles pest house. She had to be installed in a double bunk, above Cora Lentz. Laura Schwanke, frantic with misgivings, had to sleep in the bunk above Johnny Highpockets, who shook it perilously in his delirium. Old Knick, at forty below zero, with two regulation blankets and no pillow, slept on the floor.

When the news got to the Mennonite colony that their women no longer had the privacy and protection afforded by a cloth drape (one that had been left behind at the Opera House by the company that had played *Quincy Adams Sawyer*), Chris Lentz, Klaus Lohmiller, Eli Hauser (whom I hated pathologically), and Gus Schwanke came storming into town to confront Bert Lacey. Getting little satisfaction from Bert, who had too much on his hands just then to coddle anyone, the Mennonites hurried toward the pest house. Old Knick, whose patience was short at best, seemed to have been hoping for something like that. He met them six paces from the door with a loaded shotgun in his hand, and it was not primed with pellets for game birds, but solid buckshot. Klaus Lohmiller was the only one who could understand Knick's English.

"Herr Schwanke has heard that you're sleeping in the room with his *Frau*," Lohmiller said. "That isn't decent."

"Tell him his damned old woman's no more to me than a

nanny-goat. I wouldn't touch her with a piss-elm pole, if I hadn't seen a woman in ten years," Knick bellowed.

Lohmiller translated painstakingly, and Schwanke's honest face brightened, as if he were receiving a new thought.

"*Also!*" Schwanke said, nodding, his low brow contracted with effort. ". . . *Also, gut.*"

Laura, who was inside, trying to look through the heavily frosted window, could hear none of the dialogue. She appeared at the doorway, a gaunt, patient woman who was risking much and working hard.

"*Grüss Gott, mein armer Mann,*" she called, to Gus.

"*Geht's ziehmlich mit mein Kind?*" Chris asked, anxiously. Laura lowered her head, and murmured, "*Geht's schlimm.*" Inside, Highpockets, in delirium, roared, "Let 'im up, he's all cut." Cora lay in semi-coma, aware that something unusual was happening, but not caring what it might be.

Little Helen, who was having a light case of pox, and a profound experience, called out, cheerily:

"*Ihr durf nicht bös' auf Knick sein. Er ist ein lieber Mann.*"

That reassured the Mennonite men and, sadly, they trudged down the slope, back to their wagon, and rode into the cold and dreary hills again. Meanwhile, Knick was grumbling and muttering to himself, trimming lamp wicks, heating water to wash bedpans, and cursing all hammer-headed Hunyackers pink.

I dropped in to see Charley and Edna, that evening, and found them snug, cozy, and in widely different moods. I had never seen Charley so troubled and uneasy, or Edna so radiant and blissful. There was a screen dividing that cabin too, a discarded back-drop from *Swell-Elegant Jones.* Charley had set up a canvas army cot, as far as possible from Edna's double bed. From the south window, the shabby pest house was visible, whenever the frost melted for a while.

Charley did not want to talk about his own affairs. I was sure of that. So we discussed Wise and the sapphires. Tufts was as fond of Wise as I was.

"Howard's talked with the lawyer, Dobrovnik," Charley told me.

"I know," I said.

"Since the sapphires have been advertised all over the region, and no one has claimed them, they belong to Cora. Since she won't accept them, they revert, most likely, to Bert, who won't keep them, either. Somehow, Wise's got hold of a thousand dollars. He says the gems are worth eighteen hundred. So he's borrowing eight hundred," Charley said.

"And he'll give them to Lulu," I said, disgustedly.

"First, he'll turn over the eighteen hundred dollars to the Mennonites, to buy farm animals. It's a Godsend to them, and I think they'll accept it, as a community asset," said Charley. "That'll make them all feel better toward Cora," he added, to cheer me.

"Can't somebody get the girl away from them?" I asked.

"Too late. She'd be lost, outside the colony," Charley said.

"She's lost now," I said.

Edna sat and listened, agreeing with Charley, sympathizing with me. She was too happy to feel another woman's sadness. She was ashamed of her insensitivity about Cora. There was nothing she could do about it. Nothing touched her but the present. She knew that Charley could not resist her much longer.

Before I left the cabin, Doc Morrill came stamping in from his visit to the pest house. He was in a frightful condition, trembling with fatigue and anger, utterly at his wit's end. Edna rose, pale and shaken.

"Johnny? He's all right?" she asked.

"He'll pull through," Doc said. "It's that God-damn girl."

I sprang up like a jack-in-the-box, stunned and dizzy.

"She isn't dead?" I asked.

"Hell, no. Do you know what she's gone and done? She's ripped the scabs off the sores on her face. After all the pains I've taken, she's disfigured for life."

I was too crushed to react. I wished dimly that Cora was dead, and still beautiful. All the piety in the world, and self-abnegation, was not worth one lovely woman's face, or a single stone of cornflower blue.

Doc was continuing, indignantly.

"There are three or four deep pustules, near her eyes, underneath. They'll draw the lower lids down, when they heal, so the red'll always show. She'll look like a freak in a madhouse," he said. "And the whole damn valley'll blame me."

"Where was Knick?" I asked.

"That Amish woman—the bloody old hag—let her do it. The old bitch says it's right. 'If thine eye offend thee, pluck it out,' she says. I'd like to pluck her out," Doc said. "Knick was so mad he tipped over a lamp, and damn near roasted the whole kit and kaboodle."

I thought of the six matched sapphires. I, too, had become mildly obsessed, and stole a look at them whenever I could. That anyone in human form could believe they were evil, or that Cora was wicked, was beyond my comprehension. I had detested Puritans, zealots and crepehangers always, but never with the loathing I felt then toward the Mennonites. I was glad they had been persecuted, and hoped that they would suffer much more. I tried, from then on, not to look at the pest house or dramatize what took place between those crude and narrow walls—the lamps and stinking bedpans, the fevered cries, the sores and scabs, a sturdy old man, a drab hag, a

308

solemn schoolgirl, and the shapely young body with a hideous mask for a face.

Every time Doc Morrill came to Trembles, in the days that followed, I tried to get him aside, and at last succeeded.

"Is there nothing you can do for Cora?" I asked, so tensely that he looked at me, astonished, then grinned.

"Forget it, kid," he said. "Christ, you don't know how many cases go wrong."

"A face like that belongs to everybody," I said.

"Have another talk with me, six weeks from today," he said. "That's how long men remember women's faces."

CHAPTER TWENTY-FIVE

Ching How

FROM the moment that the first clump of sagebrush had been grubbed from the site of what now was the flourishing town of Trembles, there had been a lot of hard work done. The pair who had worked hardest and most steadily, not less than fifteen hours each day, were the Chinks, Ah Cook and Ah Flunk. Sundays and holidays, for them, meant extra guests, more food to prepare, an avalanche of chores and improvisations. Under stress that lasted through days, sometimes, they would slow down a little before midnight, holding their narrow shoulders in place with stolid effort, and economizing their movements, even those of their jet black eyes. Everyone knew them and spoke to them. No one got close to them. There was co-operation, but no communication.

When the cold clamped down and the blizzard howled over the town, the two Chinese went about their work as before, with everything changed in the fair-weather routine they had established. Bert said they had heard about snow, and seen a little, somewhere, but nothing like a Montana storm. Their thin cotton clothing and heelless slippers were inadequate. Their hands and faces turned blue. Their teeth chattered and their bodies shivered so the clacking and shuddering could be heard and seen at some distance. Bert got together whatever he could that would fit them, and gave them piles of extra blankets. As soon as the road was open as far as Sidney, he took them down to Baron's store and outfitted them for winter. Within ten days they seemed to have adapted themselves, and when a contracting nail would pop like a pistol in the night, one of them would grin at the other and say: "Ching how." I learned that in Cantonese that means: "Good luck."

The stage got through a week after the blizzard spent itself, and made on the average of three trips a week. The first mail bag contained a letter which, from the way they read it, must have been addressed to both. They deciphered the characters eagerly, but without undue excitement, showing no signs of grief, so we all concluded that our Orientals had received no bad news and were content that they had contact with the great outside.

Early in February, after a period of snow flurries and devastating cold, during which I had been up-river on the survey, we saw Ah Cook and Ah Flunk, bundled up to look like twin Esquimaux, leave their kitchen just before stage time and line themselves up on the porch of the hotel. It was the southbound stage from Mondak they were waiting for, and we knew they were not leaving for Glendive, to celebrate the Chinese New Year, until two days later. But all of us felt that since the Chinese preferred to be mysterious in all things from flavoring to philosophy, we should respect their privacy and did not press them with questions.

When Matt drove up, three Chinese, swathed in fur garments and blankets, got out and were greeted with extreme courtesy by Ah Cook and Ah Flunk.

Shunk Cundiff, the husky old blacksmith, and Bat Horner shook their heads in amazement. They had seen the Chinese letter, on gay red paper, with black bird-tracks painted all over it, and for them to realize, suddenly, that by looking at those outlandish marks, their two Chinese friends had been able to deduce that a bevy of their countrymen were arriving from Mondak, opened entirely new vistas in their alert mentalities.

"I give up," Bat said. "I'm a'goin' to quit lyin'. It's no use."

It took several minutes for the Trembles residents to discover that one of the visiting Chinese was a woman, one a middle-aged man, and the third a thin young boy. Bert was doing his utmost to make them feel at home, and tried to find out how many rooms they wanted him to place at their disposal.

"They stay with us," Ah Cook said, indicating the 10 by 12 room with two bunks, one above the other, the Trembles Chinks occupied.

Bert tried to object, but desisted when he was convinced that the Chinese preferred it that way. All five disappeared into the sleeping room off the café kitchen. They had as many as ten bundles with them. A few minutes later, Ah Cook emerged with a bag of lichee nuts in his hand and, smiling, passed them around. Everyone tried them, and some of us liked them. Ah Cook then had a conference with Bert. By means of their common vocabulary in pidgin English, totaling about thirty words, it became understood that the three visiting Chinese were jugglers and acrobats and wanted permission to put on a show at the Opera House the following evening. They offered to pay for the hall, but Bert would have none of that. Word was circulated around the countryside, the stoves were well stoked by Mexican Joe, the band offered its services, and when show-time arrived, at least seventy men, women and children were gathered on the benches nearest the fire, for the cold, which formerly had been bitter, started getting down to grimmer business that afternoon and at twilight (about four-thirty) the main street of Trembles was cluttered with starving cattle from the range, lowing and stumbling, some falling on the doorsteps, others standing in sheltered places and looking at all comers with dull, reproachful eyes. Bert knew it would only prolong their agony, but he could not stand by and see beasts die of hunger in Trembles. He ordered them watered and fed, with care. More came.

The stoves were red and roaring, and within a couple of feet of them, considerable warmth could be felt. Elsewhere in the hall, the audience sat with all their heavy clothes on. Blankets had been hung on both sides of the stage, to stop the drafts, and when those three Chinese, a man, a woman and a boy, in clean thin tights, stepped out and the band hit the chord of "G" major, the frosty breaths of audience and performers mingled with the grotesque lights and shadows. All twelve of the footlights were glimmering, if not ablaze.

Man, woman and boy tied themselves into knots, so that faces were staring wrongside up, legs were where arms should be, small tight buttocks appeared in disconcerting places, and the members of the audience banged their mittens together, to show appreciation and warm their stiffened fingers.

As contortionists, the Chinese performers were competent and conscientious. But when the man bowed, went to the prop room, and emerged with three swords, of varying sizes, they were so cold that they stuck to his hands.

He bowed, murmured an apology, and took them to the nearest stove, to warm them before attempting the swallowing act. Shunk Cundiff got into action. He cleared a space around the largest stove, and the rest of the performance took place in that area. The band was moved to another stove and we played with our backs to the heat.

Before the show was over, there was a harsh, gritty sound and a whine of the murderous north wind. Those who lived at any distance lit out, then and there.

Another blizzard.

The Chinese accepted the situation stoically, and with little apparent emotion, but Bert Lacey was desolate. He had paid his faithful cook and flunky handsome bonuses, given them leave of absence for a full week, engaged a comfortable rig to take them and their guests to Glendive, and he could not resign himself to their unspoken disappointment.

He called his principal aides to a council around the stove in the bar. Bat Horner, Shunk Cundiff, Buck Mavity, Kurt Mook, Perce Gardner, Charley Tufts, and all my musicians were there.

"What the Sam Hill do Chinks do, to celebrate New Year?" Bert asked.

The information he received was very sketchy. None of us knew. But we caught on that Bert was going to find out, somehow, and, blizzard or no blizzard, was going to stage a celebration in Trembles, with the Chinese as guests of honor. We called out Ah Cook and Ah Flunk and when they understood what was afoot, they stood very erect and bowed a half-dozen times. The Occidentals could do no less. They bowed, in response, in a variety of styles, reminiscent of reels and quadrilles.

We listened to a linguistic *tour de force,* at the end of which we knew that during the New Year's feast, in China and Chinatowns, the Chinese ate copiously, every few hours; drank *ng ga far* which could be made promptly from rice; took steam baths; called on their friends; wrapped presents and money in red paper, as gifts to the children; paid their debts; got haircuts; and had a parade led by a huge dragon with a tiger's head. The dragon could be made of red cloth and the acrobats, inside it, could cause it to stand erect, climb balconies, and perform merrily.

That night was spent in extravagant preparations. There

314

was no red cloth, but a large stock of serviceable white cloth.

"Send for Petekillemquick," Charley Tufts said.

A posse fought the blizzard as far as Pete's shack, aroused him, and brought him back. Bert and the rest of us explained that yards and yards of white cloth had got to be dyed red.

"Can do?" asked Ah Flunk.

"Eeeeeeee," said Pete, which is Sioux for "yes."

Pete had some roots cached away in his cabin. He bucked the blizzard again, returned, boiled them in two wash boilers, and the eyes of the Orientals gleamed joyfully when the water turned scarlet. The cloth was dipped; Pete fixed the dye with annis root from the drug store. By that time, a journey to the drug store and back was hazardous in the extreme.

Lela Weckerling, Lulu and Edna Highpockets helped the Chinese sew the dragon together, and the middle-aged man, head of the acrobatic troupe, painted an impressive tiger's face, and dragon's scales and claws. When the crowd at the bar saw the trial performance of the dragon, whoops and cheers competed with the whine and howling of the wind that was blowing sixty miles an hour.

The ensuing days were hilarious. Everybody, except Edna, got happily drunk. Groups staggered from house to house. Lam's barber shop was never closed. Whoever was able, paid his debts, and the creditors spent the money promptly.

Bert decreed that all prosaic business should cease and all shops, except the barber shop and the saloons, close their front doors. School was called off, and the pupils all presented with gifts of money, wrapped in red paper and marked with the Chinese characters meaning "Ching how." Josefa brought her three brothers in from the ranch and relaxed sufficiently to keep up with them, drink for drink, in old Scandinavian style. That was her first and only binge, but she carried it off well and when, by mistake, found that she and Ole Nelson, our chief of party, had gone to sleep in the same bed without seeming to know why or how, she made the best of it, graciously, and soon afterward broke her engagement to Ed Wilson. Josefa and Ole spent a couple of days, at the various bars, trying to explain to one and all and to each other the differences between Swedes and Norwegians. I listened to a great deal of their argument, but like the sage of the Rubaiyat "left by the same door that in I went."

On the third day, someone suggested that the dragon should perform outside the pest house, where the patients all were recovering. Johnny could sit up and take nourishment. Little Helen was almost ready to be released. Cora Lentz, her face horribly pitted and distorted, was thinking, night and day, about returning to her father's house. The storm got worse instead of better. Horses could not face it. Men could barely cross the street. The party started out, struggled and foundered, and, before fifty yards had been traveled, had to give up and return to the café.

There was continual feasting, and drinking, but the Chinese were not permitted to do any work. The cowboys and shopkeepers served them, and they responded with such charm and dignity that enormous strides were made toward human brotherhood. When any of us got so tired we could not stand up, we ducked into one of the bedrooms upstairs and slept until the hubbub aroused us. Then we drank coffee, ate a half-dozen eggs, and started in again. There were card games, dances, music, and the Chinese made gongs out of covers and drums out of tubs and tin cans.

The fireworks was one of the hazardous and unpredictable features. There was black powder and dynamite handy, and some of the cowboys made mines and cannon crackers so powerful that, in one instance, they blew out a half-dozen windows of the Clark Hotel, which had to be boarded up to keep the storm outside. Doc was busy treating scorched hands and powder blisters and headaches. Cartridges were tossed into stoves, and scattered embers far and wide. Petekillem-quick, illustrating how the Sioux of old used to play football, tackled a hot stove, tore it loose from the pipe and had to be roped and hogtied.

Old Hans Sauerbier, who drank beer by the case, sang German songs in the midst of such a din that not a word could be heard; still, he must have heard the songs himself, because he cried unrestrainedly, and opened his mouth to capacity, head upturned like a coyote baying at the moon. Somehow, Bat Horner caught a live coyote that was lurking in town, seeking shelter, and swore for years afterward that the critter had heard Old Hans singing, and had howled in sympathy till he froze himself tight to the ground.

When the feast was over, the three Chinese acrobats took the stage south, after bowing politely at the doorways of all the shops, stores, shacks and houses, along the snow-piled road, from the bare aspen trees to the drug store and return, and saying something significant in Cantonese while the Americans and immigrants called *"Grüss Gott," "Au Revoir," "Adios,"* or "So long." The Chinese troupers had all received nicknames which they recognized and remembered. The young boy, "who could stick his face down where his bum ought to be" and "scratch his ear with his toenail," was called "Slim." His mother, who did more bowing and less talking than any of the other Chinese, and had aroused the usual speculation concerning the anatomy of Oriental females, although no man, however drunk, had molested her, was named by one of the crap shooters "Phoebe" because she was so small. The dignified father, who caused the huge red dragon to do incredible things, such as standing up and leer-

317

ing with his tiger face into second-story windows (the acrobats inside standing on each other's shoulders), was named "John D.," because, from behind, he was built like the oil king and multi-millionaire.

When the sharp snow had stopped blowing, and the wind had gone down for a while, Ah Cook and Ah Flunk went happily back to their kitchen for another year of gruelling toil and devoted service. They looked just the same, talked just the same, dressed just the same, and were, somehow, quite different inside. They had discovered America.

CHAPTER TWENTY-SIX

A Chinook and Quick Freeze

THERE came a day when the last of the patients, Johnny Highpockets, was released from the pest house. Little Helen had returned to the Clark Hotel, to watch over her mother, a fortnight previously. Cora Lentz was taken by Doc Morrill to his own house outside of Sidney for the last days of her convalescence. Doc already had forgiven Laura Schwanke, the gaunt, pious, patient woman, for her negative part in the destruction of the loveliest face ever to be seen in the valley. The Amish woman was so sound and good, at heart, so unassuming and uncomplaining, so thoroughly purged of idleness or unkindness, that Doc—and I, I must confess—began to try to see her point of view, and Cora's, and to admit the possibility that beauty, however divine, may prove unwholesome in certain surroundings and connotations.

I was adolescent, then, but I recall my feelings and reactions all too vividly. Many times I wish that I did not. But the fact that Cora, in making hideous her oval face, so that the red-rimmed eyes at ill-matched angles stared out of a background of pits and pocks, had not attacked her body, left her practically intact, as far as I was concerned. There remained her shoulders, a little like those of Madame Recamier, and her breasts that had a suggestion of the *Maja Desnuda* (well covered), her slim wrists and hands, ears, ankles, knees, thighs. I caught myself daydreaming, as to how one could

319

make it up to a beloved young woman whose face had been marred and, as a consequence, might have concentrated more of love and affection in areas not always exposed.

Little Helen Weckerling was such a deep character that no one could guess what she was thinking about, or be in any doubt of the import of anything she said. She was devious when silent, and direct when she spoke, like one of our finest writers of today, Maritta Wolff. In fact, I never read Maritta or see her without thinking at once of Helen Weckerling. Thus are memories stitched into the fabric of our continuous present, like spontaneous, automatic embroidery. It seemed to me that Lela, Helen's mother, was sailing just a bit off her course that would have kept her in the realm of strict reality. She became more hopeful and serene and positive that La Rue would come back, as if it were a foregone conclusion. While at first she had shown agitation and dismay, she began to believe that she, herself, had made the sacrifice, sending Alanson back to the world of the theatre he had eschewed for her sake, to win his proper place, so they could, later, look back on a life that had been fruitful and abundant. In the same way, the absent Alanson's stature as an "artist" grew in Lela's mind. The world needed him. The theatre had suffered from the loss of him. Where would hams and artists be, without women to ennoble their gifts, or lack of talent, on the sounding board of love, where only pure notes are sustained?

Did it trouble little Helen, to listen to her mother and gravely agree, she who had rebuked and denounced all Lela's husbands and suitors firmly such a little while ago? I think so. I think little Helen realized, before anyone else did, that her handsome mother, still without gray hairs or wrinkles, with a soft, smooth olive skin, and cries and murmurs in her

throat at certain climactic moments, sometimes dimly overheard, was starting to walk an inch or two above the floor,
and might ascend, like Murillo's "Virgin Mother" of the
Perry pictures, to a plane that the world called "goofy" and
so, in her weariest moments, did little Helen.

Lela's problem centered around La Rue's big theatrical
trunk, which contained costumes, small props and programs,
clippings and scripts, and packets of letters tied with faded
ribbons. These Lela had never opened or examined too carefully.

"Alanson is in need of his trunk," Lela said. "I can't
imagine why he doesn't send for it."

To my astonishment, I heard Bert Lacey reply, with a
perfectly straight face, "Aren't most of them costumes old-
fashioned? He'll be needing new ones, in more up-to-date
plays."

Lela looked at him sadly. "How can people here understand that Shakespeare is un-dated?" she said.

"Oh! Shakespeare?" Bert said. "He wouldn't have to send
for Shakespeare costumes. They'd have plenty of those, in any
live town."

"Forgive me," Lela said, contritely. "You, Mr. Lacey, are
one of the understanding ones."

That was about the time of our first Chinook. I had experienced cloudbursts, hail storms, seen lightning roll like a
tumbleweed along a wire fence, endured frost, fought blizzards. Now it was Chinook season. Again I will fall back on
the old N.P. pamphlet.

> "The winter climate of the Yellowstone country is greatly
> tempered and modified by the warm winds which, following
> the great Japan current across the Pacific Ocean, break upon
> our western coast in Oregon and Washington, producing
> there the enormous rains which almost drown that country

in the winter. Having discharged their moisture, these winds blow through the low passes and gaps of the Rocky Mountains, at the head of the Missouri, and are carried on eastward, tempering the winter cold of eastern Montana, until they meet, in Minnesota and Iowa, the fiercely cold winds directly from the Arctic regions.

"The effect of these Chinook winds is so great that the winter ice in the Yellowstone breaks up sometimes weeks before the Missouri."

In mid-February, on my seventeenth birthday, the first effect of the damp Chinook was to cause Johnny Highpockets to have a sharp relapse and go out of his head for a while in high fever.

The snow melted on the range, the water holes filled, the cattle still living, drank, pawed through the limp crust to the grass, and took on another lease of existence. That would have been miraculously good for everyone except surveyors, who had to ski on heavy, sticky snow, and never knew whether wheels or runners would be the more useful on a given day. Having been cold every minute we were out of doors, we now were soaking wet, and after a day's work had to wrap ourselves in two or three blankets and sweat like porpoises on the way back to camp, to avoid bronchitis and pneumonia.

The gods of Montana weather had a joker up their sleeves. On the fourth night of the Chinook, the temperature dropped from thirty-eight above zero to forty-eight below. That is considerably more of a tumble than the stock market took in 1929, twenty-one years later, and had a proportionately devastating effect on the Lower Yellowstone. It sent the percentage of loss on the range from about forty to seventy-five. In terms of Annius Gregory's cattle, that meant that, instead of only 2,000, 3,750 would probably die. At $50 a head, that cold spell cost Annius $87,500 U. S. dollars.

A Chinook and Quick Freeze

We surveyors no longer could use skis, and had to fall back on snowshoes, which we carried across the bare areas. There was still enough snow, glazed with a six-inch coating of ice, for us to surmount the underbrush of the river bed. The Trembles pool, each day, amounted to more than a thousand dollars, so we worked hard and faithfully, for the sake of our pay and our backers.

Now we saw the rejuvenated shaggy steers, the wolf-chewed cows, and the hardiest of the calves, one in a hundred who had been turned loose in the fall, pawing wearily at sheets of ice that were just too strong for them. Whatever range cows think about, it cannot be wholesome and nice, especially when they can see the grass through clear ice, and have to die without tasting it. The ranchers could no longer think in terms of individual cow psychology.

In Trembles, the lucky ones who had strayed there at the outset of the Chinese New Year blizzard, hung around, to the despair of every man who had oats and hay. The hardest-hearted of the citizens let the animals low and starve for a while, but they all broke down in the end and forked out whatever they had, imperiling their own survival in the months to come.

Petekillemquick, who was allergic to certain kinds of work, was phenomenally industrious at others. Not only did he continue to act as rear chainman, and help us win bets and break records, but he skinned most of the dead cattle we came upon, and added to his income by selling the hides at two dollars each, making about ten dollars, thus, a day. When he saw a dead steer, Pete would sling him on a sled, dragging him until the moments came when I was fiddling with the transit, or searching for section corners. Then he would perform his gory task, with such address that the unsightliness of the process lost much of its power to disgust. The only present

323

we ever saw Pete give Emma Goldman, his wife, was a huge buffalo robe he bought near old Fort Buford. Wearing it, Emma looked like Emma Goldman in one of those trick mirrors that accentuate the horizontal, or two bears stuck together.

"How's Cora?" I asked Doc Morrill, who was going through another frightful period because of the prevalence of pneumonia, bronchitis and sore throats.

"She went back up Fox Creek," he said.

"Was she all right?" I asked.

"Toward the last, she seemed calm, almost happy," Doc said. "I can't figure it out. She acted as if she must have come to some decision."

"Resigned, you mean?" I asked, anxiously.

"No. Not exactly. Her eyes were too bright, and she prayed too much," he said.

I heard, soon afterward, from Hans Sauerbier, who had become quite intimate with the irrepressible old Mennonite madman, Dimitri Slaubaugh. There was no joy on his face when he told Hans about Cora. Just after she got back to the colony, at the first Sunday meeting she was able to attend, she rose and asked permission to make a confession. It was granted, and the older Mennonites listened, half-fearfully, at first, in consternation as she progressed.

La Rue had entered the cabin, in which she was alone, at two in the afternoon.

"Er ist ein wunderbarer Mann," she repeated, and interjected again and again, in his defense.

She had felt strange and light in weight, as if an angel had come down, had touched his sleeve, his hand, then his forehead. He had talked to her in a tongue she seemed to understand, had placed his hands on her forehead, then her shoulders, and gently had blown his breath into her mouth.

"Don't get married," he had said, before he departed.

They had been together two hours, and she was lying on her bed when she felt like herself again and the cabin walls had lost their lustrous light. Then she had found the sapphires, and they had spoken, too, but what they said she failed to understand. She had called her father, become confused, and what had happened had flown from her head again, until she was sick with the fever. Then she had seen La Rue again, in white robes, with a scroll in his hand.

Perturbed, the men of the congregation questioned her searchingly, again and again, and insisted that the women ascertain whether or not she was actually unharmed.

Her triumph, when old Laura Schwanke, the only married woman, had testified in her behalf, and confirmed her condition, was complete. But Eli Hauser was in a rage, and insisted that his rights were being violated. She was promised to him. If angels told her not to marry, they should also tell him, and the congregation. He turned on the bewildered Chris Lentz, and demanded that he keep their bargain, unless directly instructed to the contrary from on high.

"The jewels are from the Devil, that man who cast spells is the Devil," Eli insisted.

"Look at my face," Cora begged Eli.

"*Gott sei dank, dein Gesicht ist nun ganz besser von ein Bauers Weib,*" he said, stonily.

It was decided, according to Dimitri, that Cora and Eli should wait, and that if no further revelations occurred, before spring, the wedding should take place.

In the course of the waiting period, and the icy weather following the Chinook, Wise and Lulu, with Helen for an interpreter, went out to the colony and offered the Mennonites eighteen hundred dollars in cash, in return for a signed paper from Cora and her father amounting to a bill of sale of the sapphires. Lulu, when she got a look at Cora's face, said:

"Jeez, darling. What would a face like that do with a sapphire lavaleer?"

Wise returned, a little shamefaced, with the sapphires and his bill of sale. Mexican Joe went around for a couple of days in black depression and rage. He kept his eye on Lulu, wherever she went, and when he saw her concealing a letter she received, at a moment when Wise was occupied elsewhere, he stole into her room, took the letter, and deciphered it. It was signed "Roger."

A week later, Mexican Joe, an hour before it was time for the south-bound stage from Mondak, disappeared down the road. He was wearing two guns, being a good shot with either hand. He hid behind a snowbank, just across the coulee, and soon Lulu, bundled up and very surreptitious, appeared. From the direction of Mondak, a sleigh came into view. Lulu hurried toward it as it drove nearer.

Mexican Joe, from behind the snowbank, drew both his six-shooters deliberately. Then he hesitated, put the guns back, and watched the couple drive away. He said nothing about the incident to Wise, even when the latter was half-crazy with grief and worry, thinking Lulu must have wandered out of town and got lost, or succumbed to the cold.

The sapphires, of course, went out of Trembles and the valley with her.

Six weeks later, on Doc Morrill's and Bert Lacey's advice, Joe told Wise what had happened, mentioned the talk about Roger he had overheard when Lulu was asleep, the letter signed "Roger," and the ways of women, generally, who chanced to be the wrong kind.

Late that night, Wise, pale but smiling wanly, stood up at Bert's bar, called all those assembled to attention, asked

Bert for credit, casually, and ordered drinks for the house.

"To the biggest sucker on the Lower Yellowstone," he said, and the others grinned, nodded companionably, and drained their glasses.

Then he had to borrow some more money and make a trip back to Wisconsin, to face his "old man" and tell him the insurance policy was gone, and promise, on the family Bible, to take out another before he fell in love again. As far as I know, Howard kept his word. At least, when I met him later, in the Mormon part of Idaho, he had another policy for four thousand dollars, and two or three payments made, and was going pleasantly daffy about the sister of the wife of a Mormon missionary at whose house he roomed and boarded. He confided in me then that in Duluth, where he knew a reliable jeweler, he had priced a sapphire not quite as large as the ones Lulu had acquired. Before telling me the price, he took another stiff drink, quickly, and forced himself to smile.

"For one sapphire?" I asked, dumfounded.

He nodded, and grinned, sheepishly, then added, "Six matched ones are more expensive, in proportion."

The value of the one, the Duluth expert had estimated at $5,000. Lulu's loot added up to at least $50,000.

"Well," Wise said, tolerantly, "Lulu was a girl who knew what she wanted, and got it at an early age. More power to her."

"Lucky break for you," I said.

He nodded in agreement, and sighed. "You'll admit she had—something," he said, judicially. "But you must meet Eleanora. She's a saint."

"Another type," I said, absently.

"By the way. Whatever happened to that Amish girl?" he asked, then, seeing the quick change of expression on my face, considered that the words had not been spoken, and went on to another subject.

While the Chinook winds were alternating with freezing spells, and the range cattle and their owners were being spared the very worst the country could produce in the way of winter climate, Johnny Highpockets got out of the pest house. He was the last to go, and Old Knick stuck with him to the end. Then it was Knick's turn to be the town problem. The old Indian-fighter accepted the role and played it with distinction.

But first of all, there was a conference. The unofficial "government" of Trembles met and acted. Bert Lacey, Doc Morrill, Charley Tufts and Old Knick took a last look at the miserable little shack which had stored such concentrated suffering and confusion. Probably, of all the "hospitals" of the known world, it had been, unavoidably, the most stench-ridden, stuffy, drafty, crowded and unsanitary. There was nothing decorative about it. No one, in viewing it, was stirred with delicate or noble sentiments. It had cost about two hundred dollars to build as a tool house, counting labor and materials. The four men looked at each other, understandingly. Old Knick got a lantern from inside, dumped the kerosene over the floor boards, and tossed in a match. From wherever they sat or stood, the inhabitants of Trembles watched it go up in smoke, leaving a dark charred patch on the white slope. Within a half-hour, this had been covered by the drifting snow.

Knick lit out for the Central bar, thought better of entering when he got to the threshold, and restrained himself long enough to go to the Clark Hotel washroom, take off his clothes, wash and fumigate himself with sulphur, duck into a near-by bedroom to put on a new outfit like the one Ah Flunk was destroying by fire. Then Knick set out on the binge of his long, active lifetime, and all hearts and hands went with him, from bar to bar. Naturally, he eventually got to the Little Casino, where he kept the place and its inmates roaring and soaking up champagne for six nights and days.

Mexican Joe shook his head in puzzled admiration, looked at me, and said, reverently:

"How is it possible for folks to get so drunk, and no one gets killed?"

"Anything's possible in Montana, *maestro*," I answered.

He grinned and looked embarrassed, as he always did when I gave him his proper title.

"*Maestro* prune-face, five feet high," he said, ruefully, glancing at his wrinkled, weather-browned face in the mirror. "Still, *señorito*, many tall women have loved me."

He said this not at all boastfully, but as if he were speaking in his own defense.

I had learned a few words of French from my first fiddler and a few Spanish phrases from Mexican Joe. One of the things that interested me most about the latter language was that the word *señorito* is, at once, the most insulting and contemptuous conceivable, or the most affectionate and intimate. When Joe called La Rue *El gran señorito*, he implied that the actor was a traitor, a pervert, a pimp and a fraud, all rolled into one. Applying it to me, he meant "my well-born, kind, loyal, educated, accomplished young friend and teacher."

The first evening Johnny Highpockets got home from the pest house, a strange conference took place in his cabin. Charley, his face gray, and Edna, her eyes glowing and her breath a little short, owned up to Johnny what most husbands dread mortally to be told. Johnny, honest farmer and true friend, reacted, not in the conventional way, but with obvious relief.

"Shucks, Professor," he said. "I know I haven't been no good to Edna."

"If I could have a room by myself?" Edna said, timidly, not sure how Johnny would take it.

"We'll build one, right away," Johnny said, brightening. "Then I won't feel like such a gosh-blamed fool, every night, and you'll rest better, maybe."

Johnny shook his head and sighed as if a big load had been lifted from his mind.

"What folks don't know, won't hurt 'em," he said, patting Edna on the arm and smiling at Charley. Then his face grew grave, and he asked, quite tremulously:

"We can stay married just the same, can't we? There's no harm in that."

"Of course we can, Johnny," Edna said, and Charley nodded in agreement.

As soon as the weather got milder, Johnny, Charley and Bat Horner started building a one-room annex to the cabin.

"I guess Edna's expectin' one of them blessed events," Bat said, and no one thought it strange.

CHAPTER TWENTY-SEVEN

The Rites of a Wanderer's Spring

SPRING came twice that year, once in mid-March and again after a freak blizzard that hit the country on the eighth of May, and crossed up the ranchers, farmers, contractors and all hands. According to Bat Horner, he saw dozens of the range cows sitting on their haunches and rubbing their creased foreheads with a front hoof, trying to think the thing through. I am sure they gave it up, eventually, as a bad job.

The first sign of a change of season was a letter I received from Worthington T. Stackpole, the consulting engineer. On the same day, our jolly waitress at the Clark Hotel hummed joyously as she served us that evening, and brought two courses of soup that seemed identical. We all ate the second plate of St. Germain Ah Cook (split pea soup with ham-bone) to the accompaniment of Annie's deep blushes and giggles. I treated my own letter as confidential and did not give her away.

At Headgates, where I was to meet Mr. Stackpole on his way down the valley, I kicked an old stump and some wood ticks peeped out. A quick thaw hit the country like a warm wet sponge and at mid-day the cracking of river ice sounded like the Battle of Gettysburg. Snow vanished in patches; the damp areas spread. The surveying party went out one morning, not on skis but in the wagon, to check up on a doubtful section corner. There was little prospect that our lunch would freeze, so we took along a few cans of fruit, to supplement the rougher rations. The team Lem drove that day consisted of two roan geldings named Peanuts and Jack. We hitched them to one of the hind wheels of the wagon and strayed a couple of miles away with our instruments, rods and chains.

A local bear, emerging famished from his hibernation, must have smelled the food. Anyway, when we got back at noontime, the rig was tipped over, the horses were gone, leaving only a frayed end of their halter ropes, and the lunch had been eaten. The bear had bitten or clawed into the cans and regaled himself with freestone peaches and their sweetened juice. We walked through mud, snow and slush, ten miles back to camp, and saw that the ice-bound river was freeing itself, in places. Soon the Yellowstone was humming and whispering sibilantly with slush ice and ill-assorted fragments bearing snags, logs and all kinds of debris.

The diversion dam, which was threatening an outbreak of war between the Army and the Interior Department, then consisted of double rows of matched piles that extended three-quarters across the river bed. In a few hours, the tops were under water. By the time Mr. Stackpole got there, an incredible junk heap of ice and flotsam had begun to raise itself behind the unfinished structure. We watched it grow. A feeble attempt was made to break up the floe with dynamite, and this resulted fatally. One of the foremen, who had come in to open the contractors' camp for the season, got out some sticks of dynamite and, finding some of them were frozen, built a wood fire in the open. Somehow, a few sticks caught fire. Normally, this would not have caused the nitroglycerin to explode, but the foreman, in trying to salvage some of the explosives, must have kicked one or dropped one. He was blown to bits, the good sticks were set off by the concussions, and the fire was scattered fifty yards or more.

Two days later, with Stackpole and the rest of us looking on, the engorgement of ice and debris, piled up to a height of forty feet behind the dam, pressed too hard against the piles. A few gave way, the floe began to crack and shift, and, with the accompaniment of Herculean sound effects and enormous crystalline mass movement, the work of two years was smashed, shattered, and went drifting downstream in the slush ice.

Mr. Stackpole's personal and professional problem was gravely complicated by the mishap. The War Department engineers, on hearing that the obstruction to navigation had been removed by an act of God, redoubled their efforts to prevent the Interior Department from rebuilding the dam without locks. The contractor refused to build another dam at his own expense. The Reclamation Service engineers held that the contractor was liable for the damage, confiscated his plant and equipment, bankrupted his bondsmen, and started reconstruction on their own.

The U. S. Engineers' office in Missouri reported to the chief of the Army engineers, who in turn reported to the Secretary of War. The Montana politicians started petitioning Congress, in behalf of Yellowstone navigation. The Secretary of the Interior consulted the Director of the Reclamation Service, who turned the heat on Mr. Stackpole.

During two or three ensuing years, the new structure, without locks, was built while Congressmen and Senators debated, the War Department and Montana politicians stormed, and the Secretary of the Interior stood pat. Eventually, the dam was finished, part of the Yellowstone waters were diverted, and navigation on the historic and turbulent stream was cut off at the Headgates, leaving Glendive without water transportation and the Northern Pacific without competition.

The snow had left the flats and mesas, lingering only in shaded ravines in the bad lands and foothills. Mosquitoes hatched by the quadrillions near the confluence. Butterflies and less colorful insects came out of hibernation, in all stages from the egg, through the larva, caterpillar, and cocoon. The sun was warm and gay. Conditions underfoot were variable, but daily more bearable. We shed our heavy clothing, got out our leather boots as the snakes reappeared in fresh, gleaming skins with mysterious patterns. The males sought out the females, and vice versa.

First came the butterflies called "Painted Lilies," to refute the idea that flowers need not be gilded. They were soft light brown, with darker spots and markings, and light touches in the sepia, perfectly matched, wing to wing, antenna to antenna, and for each some particular plant was tinged with green, budded, and burst into early bloom, shy at first, then, as the sun grew dominant, extravagant and incredible.

Spring is the season when the prairie shows all the colors, welling up through the drabness. We smelled the sage again, the blue-top grass was bluish-green and the red-top grass was pink. Birds checked in from the south, along the river and the underbrush, on the mesas, and all through the awakening hills. What were left of the cattle grazed indolently. The ranchers started the spring roundup.

Some of the most sightly plants were poisonous, and the Indians and a few of the ranchers knew it. Others were deadly, and almost no one suspected it. Large numbers and great varieties were friendly and beneficent. Between the time of ice floes and the scorching summer heat was the season for the flora to disport themselves and the fauna to gambol, mate and return.

The Rites of a Wanderer's Spring

By night, beneath the stars, owls winged noiselessly, and moths, the crepuscular beauties which, for the most part, are born to blush unseen—the rose- and dove-colored titans, the peacock spotted cecropiae, the tiny juanitas, the pandorae, with garnet and ruby shades, the vague green lucidus, the tiger striped bodies, matched flying jewels. No matter what one sees, there remains the infinity of sights beyond, to paraphrase Joyce: "the myriads of God-possibled visions we nightly impossibilize."

Hawks soared by day, the red-tails, the rough-legs, the swift prairie falcons. Mergansers fished in the flood waters and pools. Herons stood on one leg and stared straight ahead. The kingfishers dipped, and brought up crawfish, while early fishermen angled for trout, catfish and shiners. Crows cawed and baffled their enemies. Magpies multiplied their mischief, in pairs. The fool meadow larks were cheery again. The curlews were cautious, more wary than before because they were older.

Lupines, larkspur, Indian paint brushes, water hemlock, loco weed, tumbleweed, buttercups, crocuses (mostly deadly poison), worts and cockleburs, anemones, wild artichokes, wild strawberries. No one could have thought there were so many.

And in the vast and varied natural setting, those humans who had wintered in the country, and had got away with it, breathed deeply of the spring, and relaxed. In a few short weeks, our memories had played their merciful tricks again, and cold was an abstract, remote condition; snow thoughts caused no blindness; frost, in restrospect, contained no threat to life and limb.

The bums came back, riding into Glendive on the rods or in freight cars. They were tempted by the contractors' agents, and came down the valley, singly, in pairs, occasionally in squads. Some were Wobblies, most of them un-class-conscious. The Americans called themselves "white men," the foreigners were "Bohunks," as before. Contractors' camps were active again, and had not had time enough to reach a stage of in-sanitation commensurate with summer heat.

Farmers were plowing deep furrows, not knowing what colossal disaster they were helping to prepare. The stage ran daily, and the weekly papers circulated faster. The wild roses bloomed on scheduled time.

The May blizzard was in the nature of a cosmic joke, in the worst of taste. It lasted, in full fury, three days, subsided, and was soon forgotten, most thoroughly and particularly by the men and beasts who got caught unaware and froze to death.

The first brown-spotted butterflies were joined by the milkweed butterflies, the gaudy swallowtails, and the danc-ing Dianas, the females of which wear on their wings the richest blue in nature, not enough to be ostentatious, not too little to be noticed. Years later, in Paris, I saw a half-dozen of them mounted and framed in the apartment of Paul Poiret, who clothed the most glamorous women on earth and spent the money giving evening parties that dimmed the tales of the Arabian Nights.

Green, always a fleeting color in eastern Montana, was less assertive, as the last of the migratory birds returned, and trainloads of new scissorbills came in, from both ends of the valley. The umbrella plant and velvet-leaf sunflower, and ox-eye daisies appeared, tentatively at first, then glowed for a while. The sage, with hues refreshed by hibernation, like snake skins, began to dim for the summer. All along the canal, slip scrapers were being dragged around elliptical or-bits, and the four-horse fresnoes eased their way down steep side hills. Derricks gestured aloft, with buckets dangling, and into clay and sandstone the steam shovels rooted, like the prehistoric animals who previously had ruled the land.

In a June number of the *Glendive Independent* I read that a marriage license had been issued to Miss Cora Lentz and Mr. Eli Hauser, of the *Amische-Mennonitische* colony on Fox Creek. I assumed that no angels from on high had descended to protect the girl who, from the neck down, would stir jealousy in the hearts of famous beauties inured to being on display. In effect, I was struck dumb, in my heart, with chill fear that at last Cora Lentz was defeated.

The day I read the item, Mr. Stackpole, who had a magnificent sense of timing, asked me if I would accompany him to American Falls, Idaho, for a few weeks, to look over another stretch of desperate scenery (with none of the color and majesty of the Lower Yellowstone) that the Government soon might try to irrigate, this time from the waters of the meandering Snake. My heart sang, for so many insects, birds and bums were on the move that it seemed to me that spring was moving-time for me. I gave Crocus to Josefa, and, although she never would let a woman ride her, she submitted to a single harness and Josefa drove her up and down the valley, to and from school, during several seasons afterward. The last look the pinto gave me, out of that baleful blue eye, was hard for me to interpret, so hard that I see it, when I close my eyelids, today.

Naturally, having no definite plans, I did not tell all my friends in Trembles that I would never see them again. Actually, I met quite a few of them in later years. But before I had finished work at Rupert, Idaho, with Mr. Stackpole, I decided to go east that fall, as far as Orono, Maine, for a dose of book-learning. As I rode out of the lower valley, toward Glendive, I saluted passers-by, in Newlon, Tokna, La Mesa, Donaldson's camp (now humming busily with Scotty Mc-

Veigh as superintendent), Burns Creek, and said dozens of farewells in Glendive, from one end to the other.

In the early twenties, I read in the *Boston Globe*, with a twinge of respect and regret, of the death of Jack (or Jacqueline) Little, who was mentioned as a famous "dancing woman" of the west. I never read about anybody else who hailed "from Glendive."

When I left Trembles, in so far as anyone can "leave" a place that has seeped all through his consciousness, Mexican Joe took over the band, and was thoroughly competent. Memory is not visual or intellectual, exclusively. One can recall music and laughter, feel the moisture of tears or of rain, hear children whisper, coyotes howl, and stroke the furry thickness of a pinto's winter coat. Fear not the Big Wind that tries to blow such indestructibles away.

L'Envoi

"It has taken the white man a long time to learn what his predecessors (in Montana) took for granted: you can fit your economy to nature but you can't fit nature to your economy."
John Kinsey Howard, in *Montana: High, Wide and Handsome.*

THE tyrannosaurus and other dinosaurs perished in the Yellowstone valley. So did the buffalo, the Rees, the Sioux, the trappers, quite a few members of the U. S. Cavalry, ranchers, steers, cowhands and, finally, dry farmers. The high end of the river (Colter's Hell, or Yellowstone Park) is a natural Mecca for the tourists of the world.

What happened, at the "wrong" end of the valley?

The W. P. A. Guidebook of Montana devotes about four lines to the lower valley, mentioning that there is a county courthouse in Sidney (now capital of Richland County) and a beet-sugar refinery. The former is an eyesore. Mr. Howard's own end-paper map of his state designates my obscure little territory between Glendive and Mondak as "Sioux County."

As a matter of fact, Sidney and two or three small settlements outlying, and under the government ditch, are all that remain today of the inhabitants and the progress of 1907–1908 of which I have written.

For a few years, rain was plentiful. So the farmers felt no

need of irrigation and the project settled slowly. Then there was a false war prosperity, and as the range played out and the cattle business shrunk to token proportions, the price of grain and beef soared.

After that, there were years of utter drouth, and the land parched like a toad caught in the sun.

Following the drouth, in the course of a period of rain, the Hessian wheat fly selected my battered area of Montana as its world headquarters and devoured grass and crops.

As if that were not enough, the wind began to blow, and forgot to stop, and the topsoil that had nourished the grass and had been plowed nine inches deep (on advice of Jim Hill's fancy men) blew away. The settlers gave up, most of them. Sidney, under the irrigation project, now has a population of 2,500, about the number that used to attend its Fourth of July celebration. Newlon is completely gone, and so, I regret to say, is Trembles.

The last I heard of Bert Lacey, he was king-fish in a booming Nevada town that is devoted to mining, dude ranching, and gambling. He had made seven sizeable fortunes and only gone broke six times, so just then he was sitting on the world. Glendive is dry, except for those who take out licenses and measure out their debauches in coffee spoons. Better had it blown to smithereens, and spared its lusty past the ignominy of its respectable present. Williston, near Mondak, has retained some distinction. At least there is a good Scandinavian restaurant in town, which is more than can be said for ninety-eight in a hundred American communities.

Some of the men who were young when I was in the Yellowstone country are now "old-timers" and talk of the old days. The majority of those men, women and children I knew are scattered over the United States and are spreading what they learned in eastern Montana as a significant contribution to our civilization.

"Nothing is lost that's wrought with tears," or smiles. Work is not lost, fun lasts even longer. Fun is our modern Phoenix, a fabulous bird that rises from its own ashes. Grief and frustration form the dark under-side.

It cannot be said too often that the reason our American forefathers and western pioneers (to say nothing of our soldiers in all the wars) were able to accomplish so much is because they were gay and abandoned whenever possible, and formed the protective habit of covering their justifiable fears with a jest, and meeting life or death, success or temporary failure, with a glint of mirth, defiant, in their eyes.

.

www.ingramcontent.com/pod-product-compliance
Lightning Source LLC
Chambersburg PA
CBHW032234010726
47494CB00002B/490